THE GOSSIP AND THE GRUMP

PIPPA GRANT

Editing by Jessica Snyder
Proofreading by Emily Laughridge & Jodi Duggan
Cover Design by Qamber Designs

This book is dedicated to Schrodinger's Boob. You know what you did.

This book is also dedicated to anyone struggling with life throwing you a curve ball when you're already at the very end of your rope. I hope Sabrina, Grey, and Jitter give you a few hours of escape.

Greyson Cartwright, aka a guy who should've picked a different bar…

IT WOULD'VE BEEN nice if today could've told me it didn't intend to go as planned.

Rude, today. Very rude.

But not as rude as the woman currently sitting next to me.

Correction.

Pretending to sit next to me while _actually_ attempting to crawl into my lap and take my kombucha.

"Ooh, is that the lime mojito flavor?" she asks, poking at a glass in my sample flight. The outdoor beach bar is lit mostly with tiki torches and the music is drowning out the sound of the ocean waves. But it's not drowning out the woman. "They ran out before I got any. Is it good?"

Should've picked a different seat.

In a different bar.

Considering how much of a failure every bit of today has been, I didn't even need to come to this state.

My phone buzzes on the bar. I lift it, see that both my sister and my former business partner are sending me walls of texts, grimace, and flip the device back over without reading it.

Much.

The main points are hard to miss.

Selfish asshole.

You agreed to this.

If you were really over it, you'd send her a birthday gift.

Quit being a dick and get the lights turned back on.

Both of them mad at me for vastly different things.

Both of them telling stories vastly different from the truth in order to—oddly enough— try to get back on my good side.

I should change my number. Maybe my name too. And if I don't quit gripping this glass so hard, I'll have to change my shirt as well.

I make myself put it down as I realize how badly my hand is shaking.

"Can you think of anything sadder than leaving Hawaii without trying lime mojito kombucha?" The woman leans even closer, her hair brushing my arm.

I landed in Hawaii four hours late because of a maintenance issue with the plane. Then I was assigned a rental car with a flat tire and waited an extra hour before the company could find another car. And once I arrived at the resort where I was supposed to attend—okay, *wreck*—a wedding, everything was crickets.

The whole reason I flew across the Pacific was canceled. No destination wedding. No reception. No chance to watch Chandler Sullivan's face when I announced to his family, friends, and new bride that he was a failure who had to sell his family's Colorado mountain café to me because of online gambling problems.

A jilting, apparently. At a resort with so few staff, I gave up on finding someone to check me in and found a different hotel a few miles up the road.

And while Chandler Sullivan deserves every shit thing that's ever happened to him, I'm irritated that I didn't get to play a part.

Not that I'm normally a dick. Current circumstances happen to be extenuating.

I enjoy the hell out of justice being served, and the opportunity presented itself at the exact moment when I needed something to land on the right side of karma but couldn't get justice anywhere else.

And now I'm debating if I want to finish my flight with this woman next to me, or if I want to give up on trying to figure out the mystery flavor in this lemon ginger kombucha and find a better place to attempt to enjoy my limited time in Hawaii.

Plenty of places to choose from.

Can't beat paradise, even if I didn't get to enjoy my long-coming revenge.

Yet.

I still own Chandler Sullivan's café. Signed the papers this morning before boarding the flight that was supposed to get me here just in time to destroy his life the same way he once destroyed mine.

Not the *exact* same.

But close enough.

And I still get to watch everyone in his hometown

3

realize what he's done and what will ultimately happen to his family's business.

Just not at his wedding.

"Not that I'm asking you to share." The woman giggles a high-pitched giggle that threatens to split my eardrums while she tries to lean even closer. "That would be too much, wouldn't it? Or would it? Wow. Your hands are *really* big. Look at your thumb. That's...a really big thumb."

I suck in a breath through my nose, twist on my stool to block her with my body, and pretend I *can* hear the ocean surf over the sound of this woman's chatter and the '80s music playing on the bar's speaker system.

"*Really* big thumb," the woman repeats.

I take another swig of my lemon ginger kombucha and close my eyes while I swirl it around my mouth.

What *is* that aftertaste?

It's different. Reminds me of the holidays, but *fir tree* isn't right, and also doesn't make any sense.

I love a good puzzle, especially after a long day of not much going right.

"Are your...feet...as big?" the woman next to me asks.

And this kombucha is a mystery I won't be solving.

Today's a wash.

I start to move, leaving most of my flight still intact in front of me, when a whirlwind arrives on my other side. "Hi, honey," a short redhead says. To me. "Sorry I'm late. Parking the car took *forever*. Did you order dinner yet?"

Is she—is she talking to me?

She subtly moves her green eyes to the woman on the other side of me, then adds an equally subtle eye roll.

"Honey?" she repeats.

4

My brain kicks in, and so does my mouth right as my phone vibrates on the bar again. "No."

"Silly. You're so good at ordering for me. You didn't have to wait. I know you were starving after..." She winks.

It's a massive, exaggerated wink that's so unexpected and legitimately goofy that it startles a small laugh out of me.

That hasn't happened in weeks. Months?

Laughing at a stranger is uncomfortable enough that I almost reach for my phone to see what half-truth message my sister or my former business partner has sent now.

Instead, I make myself nod at the woman. "I was hungrier than a whale," I agree.

"And so mellow you forgot to save me a seat." She laughs and pats my hand like touching me is the most natural thing in the world, her fingertips soft and light as a butterfly's wings, then pulls away before I can process that she invaded my personal space.

A wave of goosebumps spreads up my wrist and forearm.

Do I know her?

I don't know her. I'm positive I don't know her.

Not that it's likely I'd run into someone I know at a random bar in Hawaii. To the best of my knowledge, Chandler was the only person I anticipated seeing here that I would've known before.

Any of his old friends from college would not have been friends of mine.

And this curvy redhead in a shimmery green halter top, flowery skirt, and high-heeled ankle boots wasn't one of his friends in college. I'm positive I've never seen her before.

She has an air.

A *sparkle* that almost reminds me of my grandmother.

I'd recognize that sparkle if I'd seen this woman before.

"Excuse me," she says to the kombucha flirt who's been falling all over me. "Do you mind moving down a seat so I can sit with my husband?"

It should be the most ball-shriveling statement a woman could make.

Especially given the subject of one of the conversations still making my phone vibrate on the bar.

Instead, I realize I'm subconsciously leaning toward *her* the same way the kombucha flirt has been leaning into *me*.

The unwelcome space-invading, kombucha-thieving woman stutters out an awkward response while the redhead circles behind me, trailing those butterfly-wing fingers lightly up my arm, over my shoulders, and down my other arm, setting my skin on fire under my Hawaiian shirt. "Thank you so much! You're the best."

I barely register that the kombucha flirt is retreating far, *far* down the bar.

All of my attention is on the redhead.

It's curly.

Her hair, I mean.

It's a mass of curly copper frizzing all over her head.

She's so short, even in the heeled boots, that she has to boost herself into the newly vacant bar stool. And now that sparkle is fading as she gives me a pained smile. "Apologies for invading your bubble. You looked like you needed a save, and I need to do about five thousand more good deeds today. I'll pretend to talk to you for a few more minutes and then be on my way. You can ignore me."

"Stay." The word falls out of my mouth while my guard goes up.

If there's one thing marital counseling taught me and that recent business developments reinforced, it's that I'm historically terrible at recognizing when I'm being manipulated.

So I'm studying this woman closely while her smile goes from pained to *I have sunk to the most miserable depths of hell and will never get out*.

"Oh, *honey*," she says, rapidly shaking her head, "you do *not* want my stink on you."

Yep.

I'm officially intrigued.

Still massively on guard—can't help it—but intrigued. "You murder someone?"

She grimaces. "Only their reputation."

"And how—"

"Get you something?" the bartender interrupts.

The redhead flashes a smile at him. "Water, please. And his drinks are on me."

Before I can utter a word, she passes a credit card across the bar.

I have umpteen messages from my sister making my phone vibrate endlessly because I failed to contribute to or RSVP for the massive birthday bash she's throwing for my ex-wife in Antigua next month.

My parents regularly request that I lend—and I do mean *lend* without *repayment*—them money because *you owe us after the top-notch education we gave you at boarding school all of those years. You know that's why our part of the family trust fund ran dry.*

My business partner just took five years' worth of my research and sold it to his buddy's start-up company because *you don't need the money, Grey. Do somebody a favor for once.*

For once.

For once.

Fuck that.

So someone else picking up my tab purely for the purpose of doing a good deed for someone else?

This is refreshing.

And paranoia-making.

Is she playing me? Does *she* know who *I* am?

Seems unlikely.

None of my siblings or their children were quick or smart enough to become celebrities for being rich, and the trust fund from the old Cartwright apple farm empire dried up before any of them thought to try it. We're obscure in the world of old rich families. Plus, we're not actually rich anymore.

Not as a family.

As for me personally, the only people who care who I am and where I made my own small fortune are in apiology or the food packaging industry. Which is exactly how I like it.

"No arguing," the redhead says when she catches me watching her while the bartender runs her card. "I have too many more good deeds to do today."

Kombucha forgotten. I like this mystery better.

Dangerous spot, to like the mystery of a woman. The

last time, it ended with a hellacious divorce that most of my family still hasn't forgiven me for.

"How's a woman like you come to dabble in ruining reputations?" I ask.

She squeezes her eyes shut. "You don't want that story."

"Seems like something a *wife* would share." Not that mine ever did. I found out what she'd been doing online *after* our separation.

The redhead laughs, but it's a sad laugh.

Did I imagine the sparkle?

"I really thought that woman would demand to see our rings," she says.

"I'm allergic to anything on my fingers, and yours is being upgraded."

"Quick work making a cover story. But the minute you say *allergic to anything on my fingers*, every woman in a ten-state radius will know you're allergic to *commitment*."

"We're in Hawaii. No state radii."

"It extends beyond the ocean and wraps back around the other side of the world. Also, did you just say *radii*? That's adorable. Mathematician?"

"Sure. Let's go with that."

"It's a deal, Mr. Mathematician."

"Excellent. And your industry is…?"

"Reputation ruination. We've covered this."

"Unique profession, reputation ruination. Is it your side job, or is that your nine-to-five? Is it a work-from-home thing? Or do you have an office? I know a person or two who could use those services." I add a smile even though I'm dead serious. If my new life mission is to be the superhero *Super Vengeance Man*, I could use a sidekick who can ruin the reputations of people who deserve it.

She sigh-groans. "Look, you seem like a nice person—"

"Ah, and here comes the blow-off." I'm actually smiling out of instinct instead of forcing it now. Feels good.

"This isn't about you," the redhead says. "It's about me using gossip improperly."

"Go on."

"No."

"Look, I can take a no. This isn't me not taking a no. This is me observing that you look sad and you're still sitting here. You did me a favor. Seem like a good wing woman. Just saying, if you need to get something off your chest, I'm here."

"Nothing good ever comes of gossiping."

I lift my brows.

And she sigh-groans again. "That's such a lie. *Lots* of good comes from gossiping. Do you know how many of my friends I saved from not just *bad* relationships, but potentially *dangerous* relationships because of gossip? How many people I've saved from getting into the wrong job? The number of family reunions that weren't even mine that I saved with a well-placed *you should consider bringing something else because potato salad is your fiancé's aunt's thing and if you tread on that, she'll leave her dogs to his sister instead of him and you know how much he loves Fluffy and Sparky?* When you know everything there is to know about your community, you can use your knowledge for good. You don't have to just use it for evil."

"Saving someone from being disinherited over potato salad seems like a good use of gossip."

"I'm off gossip."

"Those poor dogs. I hope they're happy with second-rate parents." Huh. I'm being *funny*.

She chances a look at me, a hint of an actual smile twisting her curvy lips and a little sparkle coming back into her green eyes.

Confirmed.

I *am* being funny.

"What's your name?" I ask her.

She shakes her head.

"I'll go first. Hi. I'm Duke. Lovely to meet you."

"You're *Duke*."

"Don't I look like a Duke?"

She bursts out laughing, which does a funny thing in my chest area that I actively ignore no matter how much I want to like it. "No."

I fake a gasp of horror. "You gossip *and* mock my name?"

"It's just so ironic, since my name is Duchess."

It's my turn to laugh.

Actually laugh.

Who am I, and what's happening to me?

She props an elbow on the bar and settles her head in her hand, watching me while she swings one leg. "Are *you* a gossip?"

"I'm a hermit-in-training."

She gestures around the open-air bar. "Clearly, that's working out well for you."

"This is me being the bigger person and *not* burdening you with gossip about *my* life."

She studies me as though she's trying to decide which of those statements I'm serious about.

Both.

I might've given her a fake name, but I would absolutely be a hermit, and I had no intention of being the bigger person at any point today, so it's quite remarkable, really.

"You didn't need a save, did you?" She drops her head in her hands and groans. "I can't even do good deeds right today."

"No, no, I did. And lucky me, my savior is fascinating."

The bartender returns with her credit card and a glass of water. She glances back at the kombucha flirt while she tucks her card away before I can get a glimpse of the name on it, clearly trying to decide if her good deed is done or not.

"You like fried calamari?" I ask her.

"No," she says, "but thank you."

"Shrimp cocktail? Poke? Sashimi? She's still watching us, by the way."

Apparently one laugh is all I'm getting. Her smile has ghosted her once again. "You're entirely too good for me tonight. Please. Drink your drinks. I'm not here. Thank you, stranger in a bar who's being far kinder than I deserve—"

"I'm *Duke*," I interrupt. "We're not strangers anymore."

She has incredibly expressive eyes.

They're emeralds in a sea green bay simultaneously telling me she knows I'm lying about my name, that if I was *Duke* I'd pull out my driver's license and prove it, and also that exchanging even fake names is too much of a relationship for her.

"Truly, you don't want anything to do with me," she insists again.

"I'm failing to understand what someone who saves dogs from awful futures and relationships from splitting over potato salad could have done that's so terrible that you have to decline the best of what Hawaii has to offer in appetizers."

Her gaze wavers. "Do you have siblings?"

I grimace, then grab my phone—which is still vibrating with text messages—and shut the damn thing off before shoving it in my pocket.

"Siblings of your *heart* then?" she presses, obviously not missing what's going on with my phone. "Someone you love so much that you'd do anything for them?"

Zen springs to mind immediately. My brother's eldest child doesn't fit the family mold. Mimi, my grandmother, is such a close second that she might not have been second at all.

How a woman as fascinating and kind as Mimi birthed such an ungrateful and unpleasant man as my father is beyond me.

I tend to blame my grandfather.

And I used to include Vince, my business partner, as my family, but he launched himself firmly into the *former* friend category when he lied to me about what I was signing. He's single-handedly responsible for sending me into my villain era and no longer deserves my time.

"Thought so," Duchess says softly. "Have you ever hurt them so badly you weren't sure they'd forgive you, or that you could forgive yourself, because you forgot the rules?"

Dangerous question. "Is there a person on Earth who doesn't have regrets?"

"I just—I don't want to know what I know anymore. I want it all gone. Permanently erased from my brain."

"You know where they keep the bodies?" I stage-whisper.

"No. But I know where they water down the drinks and who's running the fake ID scam for seniors who want an *elderly discount* before they honestly qualify and why you should never, ever, ever get a muffin from the bake sale at Winter Fest."

"Why shouldn't you get a muffin?"

"Because Mrs. Pineapple beats the batter too much and thinks lavender doesn't make them taste like chewy soap." She claps a hand over her mouth, but keeps talking. "I have to go. I really, really do."

"Mrs. Pineapple?"

"Thank you for that being all that you'll remember of what I just said. Is your admirer gone yet?"

"Nope. Still watching us. Probably really curious why we haven't gotten any food yet. We should be starving after our afternoon activities. You'll have to sit here and actually have dinner with me."

If her lips weren't trying to tip up despite the grief in her eyes, I'd leave her alone.

But she did me a solid.

I'm intrigued, and I feel like I owe her.

"Or we could get out of here," I say.

Her gaze shifts to the flight of kombucha still in front of me.

"Doing good deeds is a much better partner activity." I rise off my stool and offer her my hand. "And we'll look like horny honeymooners, and my admirer will fully get the hint. Whereas I'll be completely and totally at her

14

mercy if she thinks we're having a fight. You basically have to come with me. At least until she can't see us anymore. Wouldn't it be horrible if we happened to do one of your five million good deeds *together* along the way?"

Her eyes almost light up with amusement. Almost, but not quite. "You are *trouble*."

"Not generally. This has to be you." While she's clearly struggling, I'm smiling broadly.

Odd sensation. My cheeks will probably hurt tomorrow.

But there's nothing in the world I want more right now than to see where a night of doing *good deeds* with a woman who's having a bad day and trying to do better will take me.

She looks at my hand, then tilts her head to look up at me. Despite how far she's craning her neck, she hits me with straight-on eye contact with those fascinating green eyes that makes goosebumps break out on my skin again.

Spontaneity and I are distant acquaintances. We get along fine on the rare instance when we're thrown together—see also, I wasn't planning on buying a mountain café, but the opportunity presented itself with the *best* of timing—but neither of us go out of our way to see each other.

Nothing else about today has gone as planned.

I'm leaning into the unexpected and salvaging what I can.

Considering I intend to ruin Chandler Sullivan's life the minute I set foot in his hometown, it wouldn't be bad for me to do a few good deeds myself.

No matter how much he deserves it.

"The last time I took someone with me for a string of

good deeds, four chickens terrorized the grocery store for a full weekend and the town council asked me to refrain from participating in Random Acts of Kindness Day ever again," Duchess says.

I don't even know her real name, and I am all-in on spending the rest of my time in Hawaii with this woman. "I've officially been warned. And I've had a shitty day that should be balanced with good karma as well. Would it count as a good deed if you took me out on your string of good deeds so that I can have fun and improve the world too?"

She hesitates for another long breath.

But then she slips off the stool, going back to being even shorter, and she takes my hand.

Electricity jolts through my entire body.

I don't know who she is. I don't know why she's having a bad day. I don't know how much I'll regret this tomorrow.

"Punishment comes in all forms," she mutters to herself.

Oh, yes.

This will be a night to remember.

2

Grey

I'M EMBARKING on a mission of evil for the first time in my life—I prefer _justice_, but I'm well aware it'll be called _evil_, so I'll own it—and the world is testing me. Making me face the fact that karma is real.

How, you ask?

By presenting me with the woman that I would, in this moment, abandon all of my plans for to move wherever she lives and to do good deeds with her day in and day out.

I know this is temporary. It's infatuation with a gorgeous distraction. It's a consolation prize for my day going sideways after finally having something _right_ within reach. It's _fun_.

But I don't care.

This is the first time I've felt content to just _be_ with anyone who isn't Zen or Mimi in ages. I want to be near her, to listen to her talk about people I don't know, and to watch her do what she's doing right now.

Which is bending over, her curvy ass in the air, her skirt riding up almost enough for me to see the very bottom of that ass, while she refills a dog's water bowl outside a closed-up shop down the beach from where we met a few hours ago.

The moon reflects off the ocean while the surf rolls to shore. It crashes over lava rocks among the sand just beyond a half wall on the other side of the walkway where we've paused. Everything smells like coconut and flowers and salt.

And I'm not bunching my shoulders or grinding my teeth or curling my hands into fists.

I'm simply *here*. And *happy*.

"There you go, you sweet thing," she croons to the mutt, who wags his tail and attacks the water bowl. "Who's a good puppers? Who's such a good puppers?"

I want to be her good puppers.

I want the rest of the world to not exist, and for me to be her *good puppers*.

This is a sign that I need to head back to my hotel room and appreciate this for what it's been and quit thinking it could be anything more.

Instead, I stick my hands in my pockets and rock back on my feet while I try to get my cock under control. Touching my phone helps.

I should chuck the thing in the ocean, but I don't litter. Especially with electronics in the ocean. "Are you the resident dog lady who feeds all of the strays back home?"

"No, but I can tell you that Mr. Trix's dogs should *not* be at the dog park the same time as Mrs. Pebbles's dogs.

They each think it's the other's fault, but I can guarantee you that Mr. Trix's dog is the problem."

Every time she uses cereal as code names for people she knows, I wonder if she knows who I am.

But the next minute, she's calling people Ms. or Mr. Sports Team or Little Coffee Style and talking about property boundary wars and power struggles between shop owners in a business owners association and who plays drums while the baby next door is trying to sleep, and I'm back to being utterly charmed.

"Do you have a dog?" I ask.

"We're not talking about me."

"You're much more interesting than Mr. Trix."

She straightens, looks around, and for the first time since we left the kombucha bar four hours ago, instead of charging off to the next task so fast on her chunky boots that I have to hustle to keep up with her, she makes it maybe ten steps continuing in the direction we were headed—which is very close to my hotel—before she stops.

I watch, entranced, while she turns in a slow circle. She looks up at the moon, then sighs and sinks to sit on the concrete half wall separating the row of shops from the beach beyond.

I angle around and sit next to her, my leg nearly touching hers. "Run out of ideas?"

She shakes her head, still gazing at the moon. "Ran out of people."

Oh.

Oh.

I've been so focused on Duchess—I *will* get her real

name before the night is over—that I didn't realize no one else was around.

Huh.

Come to think of it, the last four good deeds she's done have been for animals. Three stray cats, and now this dog.

I squeeze her thigh. "Stay here. I'll go knock on doors and wake people up so we can do good deeds for them."

"That is *not* how good deeds work."

I love the moon tonight.

It's bright enough that I can see her chiding smile.

"Maybe we need to redefine how good deeds are done."

The sigh that comes out of her is so deep, she must've dragged it from beneath the ocean floor.

I want to pull her into my lap and kiss her until the only sounds she's making are happy sounds. *Ecstatic* sounds.

Since we left the bar, she's serenaded a couple who were fighting until they couldn't remember why they were mad anymore, chased down a guy who dropped his wallet, and honest to god, not making this up, saved a toddler from walking into a street in front of a car.

Together, we've stealthily bought dinner and drinks for a lot of people.

Me more than her, though I made sure she was distracted before I pulled out my own credit card and added to what she'd asked the bartender or waitstaff to do.

And all the while, we've both been hiding our credit cards and receipts so neither of us can see the other's real name.

But that look is back.

The *I am a terrible person who will never do enough good to make up for the harm I've caused* look.

"C'mon." I make a *hand it over* gesture. "Out with it. Let this one go too."

"Let what one go?"

"Whatever has you sighing like that. Spill it and forget it."

"Spilling it to you won't repair the relationship I murdered today."

"You've been out here avoiding that relationship all night."

"Stop being *smart*. You're with me because you're cute and funny, not because you're smart."

Did I just sprout feathers and preen like a damn peacock?

Why, yes. Yes, I did. She sees me as something more than a brain without feelings. She thinks I'm *funny*.

"Maybe I have layers," I tell her. "Maybe I can *also* be smart."

"Hate to break it to you, my friend, but if you were smart, you wouldn't have left that bar with me."

She doesn't believe I'm smart.

This is even better than her buying my drinks.

"Most people wouldn't be smiling quite so big at being told they're not smart," she says dryly.

"It's just nice to have a woman want me for my body instead of my brains."

She cracks up.

Actually cracks up with a full belly laugh that morphs into a bent-over, side-clutching, full-out hyena guffaw at my expense.

"You don't think my body's hot?" I wiggle my brows,

even though I don't think she can see me with the way she's swiping at her eyes.

I haven't felt this light in *years*.

"You're very hot," she assures me between giggles.

"Clearly that's where all of my good genes went. I won't remember a word you say about whatever's bothering you. Too much of an airhead."

"I take it back. You're smart, Mr. Mathematician. You were *kind* to leave the bar with me."

"Psh. I'm an asshole."

She's sparkling again. Eyes lit up, lips spread in a wide smile. "Well, I deserve to only have assholes in my life, so I'm glad to hear it."

I nudge her, mostly looking for any excuse to touch her the way she touched me in the bar. "Spill. What'd you do that's so awful?"

Bye-bye sparkle.

My fault.

But it's for the greater good. She'll sparkle again once she has it off her chest, I'm positive.

But first, I get another heavy sigh. "I'm here with friends."

"Lovely people, I'm sure, if they're your friends."

I am currently living for the way her lips tip up when she fights smiles after I say something devastatingly charming or amusing.

I am also currently living for the way she gives my arm a playful shove.

"You're trouble," she says.

"Rarely, but I'd like to be more."

She winces.

I wait.

"I let one of my very best friends in the entire universe sleep with a guy even though I knew he murdered kittens," she says quietly. "And she fell for him, and when one of my other friends told her about the kittens, she was more devastated than I thought she'd be, for very good reason, and it's my fault she's not living the life of her dreams right now."

"Because she would've been happy if she *didn't* know he murdered kittens?"

"Yes."

Not the answer I expected.

"People have layers," she adds quietly. "I thought…the rest of his personality…would compensate for the kitten-killing."

"Just so we're clear, he didn't actually murder kittens, right?"

"Same magnitude." She winces again. "Kind of."

"If someone else told her the information she needed to have, then why was it your responsibility and not theirs in the first place?"

"Because *this is what I do*. I listen. I study. I read between the lines. I know things *before* other people know them. And I knew this one a long time before the person who told her. I grew up in a—a hair salon, learning from the best of the best how to be the good kind of gossip. And then I choose to share or not share based on the theory that I know how to parse out if sharing or not sharing will cause the greater harm. I chose wrong. She thought we were coming here for…the next step… in their relationship, and instead, our entire friend group is splintered. And they're not just *friends*. They're *family*. At least, they are to me."

I stifle an instinctive response of *family sucks*. I have Zen and I have Mimi and I know family can be great.

But when I think of my siblings and my parents and the rest of my nieces and nephews, *family sucks*.

When I think about my business partner and newly former best friend, *family sucks*.

But this woman—Duchess—has family that she loves enough to feel bad for hurting, no matter how good her intentions.

Her hair lifts in the breeze, and it's instinctive to tuck it back behind her ear for her.

Soft. So soft. And deliciously curly.

I want to sink my hands in it and twirl it around my fingers and grip it while I kiss her.

She sucks in a breath but doesn't pull away. If anything, she leans closer. "You shouldn't be nice to me. I hurt people who are nice to me."

"We all do."

"Not like this."

"You're being very hard on yourself for someone who went out of her way to do nice things for dozens of people and animals tonight."

"That's not enough to make up for what I did."

There's so much more to her story, and I want to hear it. I want to hear *all* of it. "If it helps, I'm a disaster myself. Helping me is a bigger burden than you could ever imagine."

Her lips tip up again. "You are *not*."

"Oh, I am. I think *I'm* your biggest good deed tonight."

"You *want* to be my biggest good deed tonight."

"Guilty. But I had a shitty day. Wouldn't I be a good good deed?"

"My high school English teacher would have a field day with that sentence."

"See? I'm trouble. I need good deeds done to me."

She laughs again.

And then she shrieks and leaps to her feet, swatting at her hair and spinning in a circle. "Get it off *get it off!*"

Behind us, a cat yowls and takes off into the night.

"What—" I start, vaulting to my feet as well.

"Get it off!"

"Get what off?"

She's dancing in a circle, shaking her fingers through her hair. "Bug! Lizard! *Lizard bug in my hair*!"

"Hold still. Let me see."

"I can't hold still! Creepy crawlies. *Creepy crawlies!*"

I grab her by the shoulders on her next circle around. "Duchess. Let me see."

"It was—wait. *Wait.* Was that a cat? Was that a *freaking cat* playing with my hair?" She quits fighting and looks up at me, her hands dropping away. "Tell me that was a cat playing with my hair."

I comb my fingers through her hair, enjoying this more than I should. "Can't find any big bugs. Small ones either. Or lizards."

"Oh god." She clenches my shirt while I keep combing through her hair. "I thought a cockroach was crawling in my hair. Or one of those geckos."

"Nope. You haven't been *that* bad."

"I have."

"You haven't."

She grips my shirt tighter.

And then she seems to realize what she's doing.

How close we're standing.

Shit.

If I can feel her belly against my half-mast cock, she can tell I'm turned on too.

Her breath quickens.

So does mine.

"I do *not* deserve your kindness," she whispers.

"Call it my selfishness. You fascinate me. And you're hot as fuck."

She doesn't smile.

Instead, she simply gazes up at me in the moonlight while the waves roll to shore just beyond us.

And then she arches her belly into my hard-on.

Fuck, that feels good.

And when she slides her hands up my chest, to my neck, holding eye contact the whole time, rocking her belly against my cock again?

I swallow hard, but it's not enough to keep the primitive desire from making my voice husky. "My hotel's right around the corner."

"Can you make me forget today happened?"

"Duchess, it would be my absolute pleasure."

3

Sabrina Sullivan, aka a woman who can't stop piling on the regrets

I AM GOING TO HELL.

Or maybe I'm already in hell.

Either way, the reward for ruining my best friend's Hawaiian destination wedding should not have been the hottest one-night stand of my life.

Yet here we are, with me sneaking around a man's hotel room, wallowing in guilt and trying to find my clothes in the dark without waking him up so I can go pay for my sins.

My *sin*.

Just one.

But it's the only one that matters.

I probably shouldn't have told Duke that I let my BFF sleep with a guy who murdered kittens.

But it was preferable to the truth.

You know that video rapidly going viral on social media of that hot mess of a wedding this afternoon where the bride stopped everything right before the vows to confront the groom about letting her adult entertainment star brother go to jail for something the groom did a decade ago? I was the maid of honor. Might've seen me in that video too. And I could've prevented the very worst moment of Emma's life if I'd told her about the jail thing years ago, but I didn't, because I forgot the first rule of gossip, which is that sometimes, there's no right answer to sharing a secret, only the less-wrong answer.

He'll figure it out eventually. Pretty sure you can't log on to the internet right now without seeing Emma's wedding video.

Duke will likely think Chandler murders kittens.

That, I don't care about.

What I do care about?

Emma will probably never talk to me again.

And I don't blame her.

There's no amount of *she knew who Chandler was and she chose to love him and wanted to marry him anyway* that can make me feel better.

I should've told her.

He might be my cousin, and until yesterday when he unexpectedly sold it, he was technically my boss at our family's café—which is *one more thing* I need to process emotionally and deal with when I get home—but Emma is my sister in my heart, and I shouldn't have assumed she knew what he did to her brother, especially when I was nearly certain she also didn't know he was having money problems.

We don't have secrets, she always told us.

She didn't keep secrets.

But he did.

And I knew it.

Oh, good. There's my bra. Still can't find my panties, but at least I have my bra. I shove it in my pocket and crawl closer to the bed, feeling for both my underwear and my second boot.

It *has* to be here.

Unless Duke hid it and is planning on keeping it because he has some kind of Cinderella fetish.

Or unless he's holding it for ransom to make sure I don't spill any of *his* secrets.

Not that he seems to have any beyond the fact that he has a Latin phrase scrolled along his broad ribs, had a bad day yesterday for reasons he didn't disclose, and didn't want to give me his real name.

And if I wasn't suspicious Duke wasn't his real name, the fact that I called him that and he looked around like he was expecting to see someone else instead of answering me after we left the bar, and then the way his cheeks went pink when he caught himself and stumbled through replying was all the proof I needed.

Definitely not a secret though?

He's hot. His dark hair is thick and unexpectedly soft. When he grins, his blue eyes crinkle at the edges, there's the barest hint of a dimple that pops out in his left cheek, and the whole world stops spinning. When he watches you, you feel like he wants to know everything there is to know about you. He's effortlessly charming with an irresistible sense of humor.

And most important of all for someone like me who has zero interest, *ever*, in pursuing long-term relationships but loves to enjoy a short-term fling here and there, the woman at the bar was right.

He has very long thumbs.

And everything you'd assume that goes with long thumbs.

Bonus?

He doesn't take his equipment for granted, and he doesn't let its size do all the work.

Java have mercy.

I did not deserve what that man did to my body last night, and I'll be feeling it for *days*.

"Ah, you're doing the sneak-out-before-he-wakes-up thing," he murmurs from the edge of the bed entirely too close to my ear.

I shriek and fall back on my ass.

Dammit.

I was breathing too loud.

"No, no. I was going for ice." I am such a liar.

Until yesterday, I was merely a gossip. But for the past ten hours or so, anytime I've looked at Duke, the only thing I can do is stretch the truth.

The thing about studying humankind and their relationships and weaknesses and vulnerabilities your entire life, about learning every secret you can learn and realizing the implications of those secrets, is that you learn when to divulge things and when to keep your truth close to the vest.

I need to leave this room.

I need him to not follow me.

And that's for both of our sakes.

I don't think he'd stalk me all the way to the airport and board my plane with me, but I do think he's *this close* to wearing me down and getting my phone number, and I need to leave before I break and give in.

Of all the things I thought I'd find last night, a *friend* was not one of them.

"I can get ice," he says. "Come back to bed."

"I'm already half dressed. Call it my first good deed of today."

"If my time-telling skills are correct, you already did me two good deeds since midnight."

Heat courses through my body and makes my cheeks flush. "I enjoyed those good deeds more than you did, so they don't count."

"Doubt it."

"Completely positive."

"How about we each take one then, and we've both done a good deed for the day."

This is exactly the problem.

He's fascinating and charismatic mixed with the slightest hint of awkward that makes him so *real*, and the combination makes him a million times more tempting than he should be. I can think of four people back home I'd introduce him to if they didn't care that I'd slept with him first.

Except for the first time in *years*, the idea of introducing a guy that I had a short fling with to a friend actually makes me ragey.

I need to go.

This hot Hawaiian one-night stand with a nice guy after a bad day is screwing with my emotions. "Deal," I say, rather than arguing as I keep scrounging for my boot.

"You're not ghosting me, are you?" he says.

"I'm *getting ice*." I'm ghosting him. But the longer I

search for my boot, the more likely he is to figure that out. I can go barefoot to the ice machine near the elevator. "If you want to get up though, you should run a bath. My life won't be complete if I don't see what you can do in that bathtub before I go home."

And once again, the reward for *becoming a liar* should not have been the best sex of my life.

Guilt gathers so hot and heavy around me, it's a wonder it doesn't take physical shape and beat me with my missing boot.

"Go home?" I see the outline of his head lift in the dim light of the moon peeking in from around the curtains. "You go home today?"

"Yep." *Finally.* Something that's the truth.

"To Jawbone?"

"Yes." Oops. Lies again. "Jawbone."

So original, Sabrina. Why didn't I tell him I was from *Springfield*? There are Springfields in practically every state. But there's only one Snaggletooth Creek, or one Tooth, as we locals tend to call it, and the Tooth isn't big.

Jawbone was the first thing that popped into my brain.

"Where you've completely forgotten that your Aunt Applebee and your Uncle Five Guys are secretly having an open marriage because they can't stand each other or their dear child Little McDonald?"

I wince.

Regretful Sabrina is *talkative Sabrina.*

I don't live with regrets often, which is my only excuse for not realizing once I started *downloading all of my gossip* on him, I wouldn't stop.

He knows about stolen mail. He knows about

awkward blind dates. He knows about secret babies. He knows about family feuds.

He might not have the right names and a few details may have been changed here and there, but he knows.

The man laughed so hard when I told him about the long-standing disagreement between the Dodgers and the Seahawks over oil rights—actually a feud between the Harpers and the Bryants about a creek on a property line —that I told him more.

And more.

And more.

All to hear him laugh and assure me that he'd store my gossip safely so I didn't have to.

I wish telling him truly had left me without the memories too.

"Where's the ice bucket?" I ask him. Have to make this believable.

"Tea stand, maybe?"

Tea stand. I'd call it the coffee stand. And why does calling it the tea stand make him even more adorable?

"Right. Got it."

"I can't believe I'm saying this, but I wish I could be ice enough for you so you'd come right back to bed."

See?

He's *so funny*. Who says stuff like that? "I'll just be a minute."

"I could give you an orgasm in a minute if you want to come back to bed before you get that ice."

My overworked vagina clenches.

She believes him.

"I'm high-maintenance. I demand a bathtub orgasm next. After ice."

And now my vagina has declared me the enemy.

Rightfully so.

She knows I'm lying.

After last night, the word *orgasm* should be what makes me say fuck it all and dive back into bed with him. Skip the plane ride home. Ignore the ugly reality waiting for me with Emma being mad and the café being sold and my entire future completely uncertain.

Who wouldn't want to have another several hours of holy orgasms instead?

But it's not the orgasms that have me desperately wanting to strip off the clothes that I don't think I put on straight to climb back into bed with him.

It's the simple kindness in his small gesture of patting the bed. "Let me get the ice."

I don't deserve that kindness.

Not when I know my best friend is hurting and it's my fault.

I *deserve* that Chandler sold the family café, which is where I've always planned to spend my entire life. I *deserve* to worry that everything will change and I'll never be able to talk the new owner into selling it back to me. I *deserve* to know I couldn't afford it even if I *could* convince whoever it is to sell it to me.

I *deserve* for Emma to hate me forever.

I swallow another nauseous wave of guilt that I staved off overnight but is back in full force and even bigger this morning. "*Stay*. I'm getting the ice."

"I have longer legs. I can do it faster."

"Would you *please* let me have this?"

"If you give me your phone number."

"You don't want my phone number."

34

"But I do."

"You're hungover and not thinking straight."

"I'm stone-cold sober, *and* a morning person, and you fascinate me."

Why?

Why?

If I were anywhere else, and my entire world hadn't just imploded because of secrets and gossip, I would be crawling back into bed with this man and playing a game of *I'll give you my number one digit at a time after you earn it with sexual favors*. Then we'd go to breakfast, I'd invite him home to walk my dog with me, and we'd see where this goes.

Which, for the record, is *not* normal for me.

I'm a casual hook-up type of woman. Spend your youth learning how to listen in and get the gossip, you hear things you don't want to know.

And then you start to see things you don't want to see.

Sometimes, before you know better, because you're *nine years old*, you're right in the thick of making relationships implode. And you don't know it until you find yourself getting hustled back to the café kitchen where Grandma calls your mom to come get you before someone hurts you for repeating things you were never supposed to hear in the first place.

And you get a little older, still hearing the same things, but keeping them to yourself now. And you hear enough to realize that truly solid relationships with mutual love, respect, and appreciation are rare, and the pursuit of such a relationship ends with heartbreak more times than not.

Add in that I know the full and complete truth about

my paternal lineage, and just how badly my mom and grandma were hurt by men, and I'm *nope*-ing right out.

Yes, Grandma ultimately got to spend her life with the very best of the best of men in my grandfather. And yes, my mom has no regrets about how her life turned out.

But the degree of hurt that they both suffered to get to *satisfied* rather than *ecstatic* with their lives?

No way. I'm flat-out uninterested in relationships.

Even Emma, who was my favorite example of someone who could love another person through all of their flaws, ultimately couldn't have that one-in-a-million love story.

So *wanting* to leave my phone number with this man?

Thinking that if we were home, we'd spend more than one night together?

Wanting him to *meet my dog*?

I am not in my right emotions. Or my normal intellect.

This room smells like sex and more sex, except it actually smells like guilt and regrets.

"I'm only coming back if you promise that your fascination stays in this room," I tell him.

"You know you have me at your complete mercy to promise you anything you want right now?"

My entire body lights up like the lake back home on Valentine's Day when we illuminate it for a midnight couples skate.

He did naughty, naughty, delicious, *please, yes, again* things to me in the name of being completely at my mercy all night long.

Not that I haven't also been completely at his mercy.

"I'm going to get ice," I tell him.

"Start the bath on your way out the door, and I'll join you there."

"You should talk to someone about your taste in women."

He chuckles. "I like you. And I don't like people easily, so you must be worth it."

"Do I need to not come back? I'm serious. This stays in this room."

"You tipped my bartender two hundred dollars on a thirty-dollar bill and didn't think I noticed. You covertly took pictures of a couple getting engaged on the beach when they didn't think anyone was watching and made their night even better for giving them that souvenir. And you rescued a stuffed octopus from a mongoose for a kid that some people would say was too old to have a stuffed octopus and still too young to have been up that late. I recognize special when I see special."

I need to go. Get back to the resort where Emma's wedding was supposed to happen yesterday. See if she'll talk to me and let me do something to help make this better. Check in with Laney, my other best friend, whose heart is *also* currently broken because I didn't tell her what I should've about Emma's brother, whom she is *so* crushing on, soon enough.

I *want* to find my mom and have her hug me and promise me that she still loves me.

I know she will. I know she does.

I probably need to find her and tell her I'm okay more than I need to hear that she still loves me, because I don't want her to worry.

And then I want to fly home to my dog. And I need to make sure my grandpa is okay. He couldn't make it to the wedding after coming down with a pretty bad cold, but I know someone back home will have filled him in on the entire disaster.

After that, I want to go live in a cabin in the woods where I'll hunt and fish for food, completely forget every morsel of gossip I've ever acquired, and never, ever, ever hurt anyone I love ever again.

"I'm not special," I force out. "I'm a disaster."

"Whatever it is, we can fix it, Duchess," Duke says.

He sounds so much like Laney—whose last words to me last night before I tucked her very, very drunk ass into bed were *we can't fix any of this, Sabrina*—and yes, I mean I tucked her in at like eight in the evening, and yes, I left someone I trust to watch her while I went back out—that tears actually threaten my eyeballs once more.

And I don't cry.

I don't freaking cry.

"Ice first," I force out. "The world's problems later. Be right back."

"Counting the minutes, Duchess."

I grab the ice bucket off the tea stand, limp out of the room in only one boot and no panties, and then I do one more thing that makes me feel like the world's worst human being.

I take the stairs, drop the ice bucket at the front desk, and ghost the nicest man I've met in years.

4

Nine days later…

Sabrina

THERE'S a black Mercedes sedan parked in my normal spot behind my family's mountain café when I pull up at an ungodly early hour for my second Monday at work after Emma's wedding disaster.

Do you know what this means?

This means that the happy, reality-denying bubble I've been choosing to live in since I came home from Hawaii is about to pop.

No matter how much everything *looks* the same—the piles of late January snow around the parking lot, Mr. Durbin's beat-up old VW van parked next to the dumpster, the string of fairy lights glowing in the morning darkness on the balcony of the apartment over the art gallery next door to Bean & Nugget—nothing is the same.

Not when I know that black Mercedes means the café's new owner has finally shown up to do whatever he intends to do with the one place that defines home and family to me more than anything else.

My gut clenches.

In the back seat, Jitter, my one-year-old Saint Bernard puppy, whines and strains against his doggy car seat.

He's been doing that a lot since I got home from Hawaii.

Maybe I haven't been as successful at denying my new reality and how much anxiety it's giving me as I'd like to think.

"It's okay," I tell him.

He whines again.

"Yep. You're right." I take a swig of coffee out of my travel mug and look back at him again. "Today will likely suck, but we'll get through it the same way we've gotten through everything else. And maybe it won't be that bad. Maybe we'll walk in there and the new boss-guy will tell us we're doing a fantastic job. Maybe he'll be so impressed with the books here that he'll tell us he's going back to San Diego and leaving everything in my capable hands."

Not that I know anything about the café's new owner.

I'm off gossip.

I just happened to notice that his assistant's email signature line indicated a San Diego address.

It's not gossip if it's in a signature line.

Jitter *harrumphs* like he's calling me out on my plans to keep pretending everything is fine when it definitely is not.

"Don't start," I tell him. "If I wasn't living in my own little happy bubble, there's no telling if I would've remembered to feed you."

Happy might be a stretch for my bubble, but the lies I've told myself have at least kept me functional.

No, Emma won't hate you forever for not telling her that Chandler set Theo up to spend time in jail for a crime Chandler committed, and yes, she'll talk to you again whenever she gets home from her solo honeymoon.

No, Chandler didn't really sell the café to some stranger who knows nothing about Snaggletooth Creek and what Bean & Nugget means to both you and the town.

No, you didn't spill every last secret you know to the kindest, sexiest, funniest stranger on the planet, and you don't spend any time at all wondering if he hates you for the way you ghosted him.

I should not be dwelling on that last one.

I shouldn't have thought it *once* in the past nine days. Never mind thinking it once *hourly* for the past nine days.

In the grand scheme of life problems, what happened to *Duke* after I left Hawaii isn't my concern. I'm not the dwelling-on-a-man-I-slept-with-once kind of gal.

And I left a note with the hotel staff to tell him I was alive when I asked them to take ice up to the room.

Jitter snorts again like he knows where my brain went.

Or possibly I need to let him out of the car so he can do his business and shake it all out one last time before we head inside to meet the new boss.

I'd been hoping to get in and start the coffee before *Mr. Greyson Cartwright*, the new owner of my family's café, arrived for his first actual day in town and on the job, but even before five a.m., he's beat me.

Not good.

For so many reasons.

After a week of regular communication from his personal assistant with instructions to keep the café running as usual *for now*, I had convinced myself that the new boss would forever be a distant presence. That I'd keep running the café the way I have since I got home from college. That I could pretend it was still in my family, and I could sign us up for a booth at the spring festival, for sponsoring the rodeo when it comes to town this summer, and for participating as a crew in the fun run this fall, and know that we wouldn't be backing out because the new boss didn't like it.

"Think positive, Sabrina," I mutter to myself while I climb out of the car and into the cold morning, clutching my coffee tumbler as if it's my lifeline. I let Jitter out of the back seat and walk with him to the edge of the parking lot, where he does his business like a good puppy while I finish caffeinating myself. Then I turn my back while he does the one thing I wasn't fully prepared for when I decided I wanted a Saint Bernard.

He gives his massive, furry, still-not-fully-grown-even-at-a-hundred-pounds body a shake that makes his jowls flop and sends drool flying in all directions.

"Good boy," I say. "Shake it all out. *Good boy*."

We have an agreement.

He shakes it all out before we go into the café.

If he shakes it all out *inside* the café, he doesn't get to come back.

"Best behavior today, okay, Jitter?" I tell him.

He'll go to doggy daycare soon, but before the café

opens, while I get everything prepped for opening, he hangs out in his doggy house in the kitchen with me.

This is *normal*.

I was told to do *normal*.

Jitter and I head for the building, and for a split second, I see my grandma sitting in a folding chair just to the left of the concrete pad. I can still picture her leaning back against the brown wood shingles, wiping her forehead with a white rag, recovering from the heat of the kitchen after pulling the last batch of her famous scones out of the oven and telling young Sabrina stories about the trouble her brother and Grandpa used to get up to back in their own youth.

Or offering advice on how to handle Theo, Emma's brother, when he was picking on Emma and Laney and me.

Or explaining to me—patiently, and without judgment —that some things aren't supposed to be said out loud, and I'd have to learn the difference between things that needed to be shared and things that needed to be kept quiet.

God, I miss her.

I wish I'd thought to ask her while she was still alive what I should've done when I found out ten years ago that Chandler was the one who'd damaged the statue of Ol' Snaggletooth at City Hall.

Not Theo, who ultimately spent time in jail for that crime.

Would she have told me that if Theo wasn't willing to tell his sister what really happened, then it was none of my business?

Or would she have told me that Theo was so hellbent

on living up—or down—to his reputation at the time, even if it meant self-destruction, that I was the only person who *could* tell Emma the truth when she started dating Chandler again after college?

I know why I didn't ask Grandma the questions.

I didn't want to tell her that her golden grandson who was their pride and joy after leaving to attend college at Grandpa's alma mater had actually done something pretty shitty.

Jitter whines and pushes against me, making me take a step back to steady my balance.

"Sorry, pup. Hard day."

And it's barely five in the morning.

I shake my head as we reach the door, where I have no idea what to expect inside.

Chandler's parents might have bought out the rest of the family to take full ownership of Bean & Nugget while I was in high school, and they might've retired and signed the café over to Chandler when Grandma passed away a few years ago, but ever since I came home after college and demanded a job in the family business, I've been in charge here.

Not because I'm bossy and have to be in charge.

More because I just know how to get things done, and it was always easier for the rest of them to let me do the hard work that I loved and took on as a tribute to the café that built me.

I'm about to find out how much longer that will last.

"You ready for this?" I ask Jitter.

He leans against me again and pants up at me, and since he's not a small dog, and I *am* a woman of shorter stature, his nose lifts almost to my boob.

Jitter's ready.

I need to be too.

Can't find out what's behind door number one of my future if I don't *face it*, so I balance everything to shove my key in the lock, twist the knob, let Jitter in first, and follow him with a forced-cheery, "Hello? Anyone here?"

My pulse is racing. Dread makes my shoulders feel like they weigh ten thousand pounds each. The lights are on when they shouldn't be, which means I am definitely not alone here. The kitchen smells like coffee beans and croissants and bacon though, just like it should. The stainless steel sink is gleaming, the prep table is clear, the racks are ready, and the floor is mopped, exactly the way I find the kitchen every morning.

Nothing new on the old metal desk where Grandpa used to do the schedule by hand. Nothing new on the bulletin board over the desk where my and all of my cousins' artwork used to be hung beside the employment policies posters and weekly schedule and slips of paper where former crews would request time off.

The powdered cheese from Chandler's ridiculous *we should sell flavored popcorn in the afternoons* era still sitting on top of the large white fridge that should be replaced with a built-in, but hasn't been because Chandler was a cheap-ass.

The only thing different is the black leather jacket hanging from the coat rack above Jitter's doggy house in a little stone nook in the kitchen.

And that's enough to turn the coffee in my stomach into a rock.

A tall person with short-cropped, straight blond hair, coffee-brown eyes, a slender face, overly freckled white skin, an eyebrow ring, and a black blazer over a black turtleneck over black jeans immediately swings into the doorway from the counter area as I head toward the front of the café. "Sabrina Sullivan. I'd recognize your hair anywhere."

I smile a smile that I have to work past nerves to reach as I cross the kitchen to offer a handshake. "You must be Zen."

"Excellent guess. The boss—*oh, puppy.*"

Zen's email signature line lists they / them pronouns, a marketing degree from UC Berkeley with a graduation date of almost two years ago, and *also* the last name Cartwright.

Just like the new boss, whom they referred to as *Mr. Cartwright* in every email.

Father? Brother? Lover?

I don't know.

And I'm torn between wanting to know *everything* and knowing that the less I know, the better.

I am *off gossip.*

But I am all in with doing everything in my power to be Zen's new favorite person.

Fighting won't get me what I want.

Especially fighting before I have a chance to get off on the right foot with the new boss.

"This is Jitter," I say. "He'll go to doggy daycare soon, but it's not open yet."

Zen shoves their hands in their pockets like they have to or else they'll drop to their knees and fling themself at my dog, who's straining on his leash and wagging his tail like he's spotted his next best friend.

And I draw a full, relieved breath.

Zen loves my dog, even if they don't want me to know they love my dog.

I like them.

They have good taste. We'll get along fabulously once they warm up to me as much as they've already warmed up to Jitter.

"I'm sure the health department will appreciate that," Zen says with a stiffness that's in direct contrast to the moon-eyes they're making at my puppers. "The boss is waiting for you by the fireplace."

That's an ominous statement. Almost as bad as Emma's *you knew my brother went to jail for Chandler and you didn't tell me?* right before she fled her wedding and became the world's most famous runaway bride.

Happy feelings all gone.

Dammit.

"Did I do something?" I ask in a hushed tone. "You said to carry on as normal. This is normal. Jitter's with me here often, and the customers love him, and—"

"Aww, you are da *cutessssst*," is the only response I get as Jitter nuzzles his body against Zen's tall, lanky form and tries to push them over. "Who's gonna need a lint brush? Yes, who's gonna need a lint brush today?"

Definitely not the dog.

At least Zen doesn't seem upset about it.

"I sincerely hope you don't talk to customers that way," a chill-inducing deep voice says from the front.

"Of course I will," Zen tosses back over their shoulder. "People *love* to be talked at like they're dogs. Oh, excuse me. *No, sir, I would never.* Ms. Sullivan, this way, please. And as for you, you adorable abominable monster of fluff, you can stay right here and help me find the schedule."

"Jitter's more likely to eat the schedule than read it if you don't keep a firm hand on him," I say quickly while I tug my dog toward his normal spot in the doggy house that Laney bought him for Christmas when he outgrew his old kennel. "But he's excellent at sniffing out when it's time to clean the mophead. And he knows to stay in his spot over here."

"Do you eat mopheads?" Zen says to Jitter. "I'll bet you eat them, you beautiful thing."

I secure Jitter with his doggy door shut. He wags his tail so it audibly thumps against the walls inside and gives Zen puppy dog eyes over the half door like he *knows* they'll be his friend if he could just get to them. And then I slip out of my coat and hang it on the rack in the alcove by the fridge next to the black jacket that I'm assuming is Zen's, since it matches the rest of their outfit.

My grandpa bought this building almost seventy years ago, but it's been around since the late eighteen-hundreds, and it truly was built into the rock wall at the edge of Main Street. So this alcove is framed on one side with actual boulders.

We have a lot of character in our building here.

We.

The anxiety gnawing at my insides has grown jaws bigger than Jitter's.

I need to make *such* a good first impression.

"Are you gonna help me make Mr. Grumpy Pants his morning tea?" Zen says to Jitter. "Yes? Yes, you are? Ohh, who's such a good puppy-wuppy?"

I am officially jealous of my dog. Bet he gets a delicious breakfast while I'm sweating in front of the new boss.

Logically, I know there's no reason for me to be nervous.

I'm a good manager. My crew loves me. My customers love the crew. My customers love me. I keep us involved in the community, and in return, the community supports us. We turn a profit every month, which I know can't be said for the two other locations Chandler expanded into over the past few years and that I expect the new owner will have to deal with sooner or later.

But I'm quaking as I step into the dining room. I'm quaking so hard, I actually leave my coffee on the checkout counter for fear it won't settle well, which is a fear I've had maybe three other times total in my entire life.

When I say I lived in this dining room while I was growing up, I mean it.

Until I was old enough to walk to my grandparents' house after school, this was where I was if I wasn't in school or at home with Mom. I colored on the walls under the booth closest to the register. I've sat at the tables in the picture window or at the stools along the bar and listened in on countless conversations while I pretended I was daydreaming or stared at the lake down below town. I helped Grandma convince Grandpa to replace all of the taxidermy animal heads with local artwork—no disrespect to Emma's dad, who stuffed them all—and when Grandma passed away, I took over her job of picking the artists that we'd feature on the wood plank walls, which are currently lit up while the rest of the lights in the dining room are off.

I've changed dozens of lightbulbs and cleaned thousands of spiderwebs off the low-hanging metal dome light fixtures around the dining room. I've rewritten the chalk menu boards on the wall behind the bar quarterly like clockwork since I was fourteen. I convinced Grandpa to add the picnic-style tables that now take up half the dining room, and until the Great Chimney Incident That We Don't Talk About right before I graduated high school, I'd refill the wood in the massive stone fireplace in the center of the room all winter long.

Now, it's a gas fireplace, the flickering glow casting a dancing light across the easy chairs on this side of the stone structure.

They're Grandpa's preferred seats now whenever he comes into the café, but this morning, there's someone else occupying one.

My new boss's haircut strikes me as odd before I realize he's wearing a beanie and I'm seeing the curled tips of his hair beneath the cuff. I notice his hands next. They're large, and he's rubbing them together near the fire as he leans his elbows on his knees. I can't fully see his profile, as he's turned away from me.

"Sit," he says gruffly to me as I approach, making me nearly certain he's watching me approach in the reflection of the dark windows.

This doesn't feel like it's shaping up to be a happy conversation.

Or maybe that's lingering anxiety over everything that's changed.

I brace myself, sit in the open easy chair, and reach deep for the Sabrina Sullivan charm that's propelled me through every day of my life working here at Bean & Nugget.

I say *charm*.

Some people say *bullheaded, take-charge attitude*.

It's a mix of both. And honestly, the past week, I've been completely faking all of the happy, *everything's fine* things.

"Good morning, Mr. Cartwright. I'm Sabrina, the manager here. Welcome to Snaggletooth Creek, and thank you for what you've done for Bean & Nugget. I hope the wind didn't make your travels too difficult yesterday."

"You want to discuss my travels?" my new boss repeats to me, like I've just asked if he tried the new colon cleanser that at least seven customers were talking about yesterday.

A tiny alarm pings in the back of my brain in the space that's reserved for *you are missing a very important clue in this discussion*.

"Oh, are you from nearby? I assumed you—never mind. Apologies. I'll quit making assumptions." I googled this man, but I hate the internet.

Hate it.

It never works right for me, and I don't want to spy on people from behind a screen. I want to talk to them face-to-face. Find out their story. Who they are. What matters to them. Feel it for myself.

When I googled *Greyson Cartwright*, the first page of results included a blog about succulents, a recipe for cornbread, and random facts about ocean tides, because that's how my search engine works.

I might've been born in the internet generation, but the internet isn't having me.

When I added *person* at the end of my search for my new boss, I got a list of high school athletes, musicians, and pages and pages of Facebook profiles that I didn't want to comb through, none of which looked anything like this bearded, stiff, apparently cold man in the shadows.

I can't tell how old he is. What color his eyes are. If he's passing judgment because of me already doing something wrong, or if there would be some clue about something making him uncomfortable that I'd notice if I could see him in the light.

Zen leans between us with a steaming mug of what is definitely Earl Grey tea. My nose doesn't lie. "Drink, Uncle Grey. There are eggs in the fridge. I'll make you an omelet."

Uncle Grey. I'm off gossip, but I *need* to know their relationship, so this is good.

"Not hungry," he says.

"Okay, grumpy pants. Did you see this pup—*oh*. Oh. Well. You're seeing him now, aren't you?"

"*Jitter*." I lunge for my dog, who's currently attempting to climb into my new boss's lap instead of staying in the kitchen where I left him locked up. Because Zen let him out? Or because he pulled a Houdini? Not that it matters. The point is, he's not a lap dog, but he's still trying to climb into the boss's seat. "*Down*. He's a puppy. I mean, he's not a puppy, but he still has a lot of puppy in him and some growing to do. Doggy daycare opens soon, and I—"

I cut myself off with a grunt before the words *I was hoping you were a dog person and Jitter would break the ice* come out of my mouth.

It clearly worked with Zen.

Jitter pants happily at me as he settles on his haunches in front of the fire.

"Down," I tell him.

He flops to the floor with an enthusiasm that you can

sometimes feel in the floorboards, rolls over so he's lying across Mr. Cartwright's feet, and shows us his belly and his manhood.

"He doesn't do that with customers," I stammer. "He goes to doggy daycare—"

"So you've said," Mr. Cartwright interrupts.

Something inside my brain hiccups like I'm having déjà vu.

And not because I keep repeating *doggy daycare*.

There's something about Mr. Cartwright that feels familiar and wrong.

I swallow the *he's going through a phase where if I'd left him at home, he'd have eaten my dirty laundry* excuse that my new boss does *not* want to hear, and instead, dive back into the script I've rehearsed in my head ten thousand times since I found out my cousin sold our family café. "Mr. Cartwright, can I ask why you bought Bean & Nugget? My family is grateful for the problems you've solved for my cousin, but we were surprised since we'd never heard of you before."

He doesn't answer me right away.

Instead, he stares at me like I'm the world's largest idiot, which I can see more and more clearly as the lights in the dining room come up.

And as my eyes register what my brain's been trying to tell me, heat starts at my nape and travels up and over my scalp, down my forehead and nose, and leaves me sweating in my cheeks while my jaw unhinges itself.

Yay, playtime! my vagina cheers.

She's a little primitive. Definitely not picking up on the vibes he's throwing down. She's only remembering what he did in that bed. And against that wall. And in that bathroom.

"*Duke*?" I choke out.

Oh, no.

Oh, no no no no no.

My brain tries to tell me what's going on here while simultaneously telling me that this isn't possible.

It's *him*.

His hands.

Large hands.

Long fingers.

The voice.

The déjà vu.

I know him.

I know him.

But unlike the man I knew briefly in Hawaii, this man has no warmth.

Not like he had in Hawaii.

And his eyes—he stares at me with flat, unamused blue eyes and a grumpy scowl lingering on his lips. No dimple. No fun. Not even the slightest hint at that occasional *awkward*.

I try to shut my mouth and I can't.

My Hawaiian one-night stand is sitting in the chair where my new boss is supposed to be.

"How do you know about Duke?" Zen asks somewhere behind me.

Wait.

Wait. "Oh my god, you're not Duke. You're his twin! Are you the good twin? You can't be the good twin. He was the good twin. He didn't tell me he had a twin. But how—why—"

Zen chokes on air.

Duke—or not Duke?—narrows his eyes at me. "Stop talking."

"You're...not...Duke's twin."

"Not unless he's twins with a—" Zen starts, but cuts themself off when Mr. Cartwright sends a blistering glare their way.

"Fine, fine, I'll go make your breakfast," they say, and they slip into the kitchen.

"What are you *doing* here?" I blurt, even knowing that if I were Zen, I'd be absolutely listening in to all of this from just out of sight in the kitchen. I should watch what I say.

"I'm investigating my new café." Duke—*Greyson*—or Grey?—hunches forward, elbows on his knees, hands dangling between them, while Jitter attempts to roll up his legs.

I should tell my dog to go back to the kitchen, but my tongue isn't working right.

And then the full impact of what's going on here hits me.

My hot Hawaiian one-night stand is my new boss.

Whom I ghosted.

Hardcore.

I am so fucked.

"Am I fired?" I whisper as a giant black hole opens in my chest and sucks at my hammering heart and my topsy-turvy stomach.

His eyes flick toward me, still flat, still unamused.

"And how would that look?" he says sardonically.

Oh, god.

It would look like he fired a woman he slept with for his first official action as the new boss.

I should quit.

But those three little words make me want to throw up. Cold sweat trickles between my shoulder blades. My heart cramps. And heat gathers behind my eyeballs.

I don't cry.

I know the theory that it's okay to cry, but *I don't do it*. It's not in my nature to let people see me upset.

I've seen too many people put their guard down and get hurt worse by letting someone in when they're vulnerable. Overall, I think people are good. We're all doing our best.

But that doesn't mean it's safe to just cry in front of anyone.

"I wouldn't hold it against you," I force out. "But you should know I was born here. My mom's water broke and she delivered me in the kitchen because I came so fast, there wasn't time to get us to the hospital. I've basically lived in this café my entire life, and it means the absolute world to me. I'm a good employee. I swear."

"I'm sure you get ice very well."

I wince. The world is spinning with the *wrongness* of all of this. Why was he in Hawaii? How is he here now? How did Chandler know him? How was he so kind and funny and *sexy* in Hawaii while he's so—so—so *cranky* here?

Yep.

There's spinning.

Spinning in the room, spinning in my head, and no amount of gripping the armrests and pressing my feet into the floor can stop it.

Jitter flops his head while he stays splayed on his back,

looking between me and Mr. Cartwright—*Duke*—like this is a casual tennis match instead of something making my head pound and my stomach sink and my pulse skitter erratically.

"I didn't think—" I start, but he cuts me off.

"That I'd worry when you didn't come back?"

"I left a note."

"With the staff member you sent in thirty minutes later who got a full-frontal view and an inappropriate proposition when I thought you were finally back and pretending to be housekeeping?" he deadpans.

Oh, fuck me. "I *had to leave*. And I thought you'd follow me."

"Yes, ghosting instead of saying *I have to go and I need you to not be a creeper* is quite the good deed."

"*You were not supposed to be my new boss.*" This is not the argument I should be making, but *I left a note*.

"And you weren't supposed to be Chandler Sullivan's cousin."

There's a chill in his voice when he says Chandler's name that I need to pay attention to, but that's for later. "*I was going viral.* As a minor secondary character, but *I was still going viral*. I can't believe you didn't know who I was."

"I bought your family's café. How do I know you didn't know who *I* was?"

Jitter whimpers.

I want to whimper too, but everything is backward and upside down and all of the dread I've been ignoring and suppressing for the past nine days is roaring back like a boulder falling off a cliff on a trajectory to steamroll my life. "If I'd known Chandler was in talks to sell the café, I would've found a way to buy it myself."

He stares at me.

I stare back, and if he thinks he can win a staring contest with me, he can think again.

"This isn't exactly a hair salon, is it, though?" he says.

And that boulder steamrolling my life turns to ice.

I think he just called me a liar and reminded me that I told him all of the secrets about everyone I knew in one breath.

This isn't the man I slept with in Hawaii who's lingered in my thoughts way more often than I'm comfortable with any man lingering.

He's far more terrifying.

And I am absolutely fucked.

5

Grey

Iт's remarkable how quickly your opinion of someone can change.

In Hawaii, it was thirty minutes from thinking I'd found someone worth knowing better to realizing she'd ghosted me—lesson learned, *again*—and only a few hours after that when I discovered my *Duchess* had been a bridesmaid in Chandler Sullivan's wedding. Once I turned my phone back on to a message from Zen—*isn't this the dude whose café you just bought?*—and I saw that viral video, everything changed.

I went from exhilaration to worry to irritation to *fuck me*.

All over a short redheaded bombshell whose presence I felt the minute she pulled into the parking lot this morning, and whose ass I can't tear my eyes away from when she beats a retreat to take her massive dog to *doggie daycare*.

Worse, though, is recognizing that part of me is sagging in relief at putting eyeballs on her myself to verify she's still in one piece, that she didn't drown in the ocean or fall down an elevator shaft or get in a fight with the wrong mongoose after she left my hotel.

I've spent more hours having emotional whiplash over this woman than I spent in her presence in Hawaii. And I sincerely dislike that I still care when her connection to Chandler Sullivan puts her in spot number one on my *sus list*.

Did she know who I was when she picked me up in the bar?

I don't know, but I know I'm the lucky bastard who now gets to live with constant reminders of her unless I can find a legit reason to get rid of her that won't make me look like the asshole who fucked her and then fired her.

Zen sets a plate of eggs on the low table next to my chair, then drops into the seat Sabrina vacated with an uttered excuse of *I'll get Jitter to doggy daycare and be back for my shift.*

They prop their feet up on the small hearth around the central stone fireplace in the dining room and give me a look that means I have some explaining to do. "I expected Sabrina Sullivan to be fabulous after her emails and what I found out about her from the town's socials, plus there was how much your good friend Charlie—"

"*Chandler.*"

"—Your good friend Douche Canoe clearly didn't like her based on how he treated her in that video, but I had no idea she'd be *that* fabulous. How awesome is that dog? Oh, and by the way, the next time you *sleep with an employee*, maybe a heads-up beyond *we made passing acquaintance in Hawaii* would be appropriate? This changes everything."

"I highly suggest you don't repeat a word of that out loud ever again."

"*Uncle Grey.* You haven't dated *anyone* since Felicia-who-makes-me-wish-I-could-have-amnesia. A one-night stand is something to celebrate, even if it's with Chazarella's cousin. And you didn't even tell me."

I lift the tea and hold the warm mug in my hands, grateful for the heat. It's chilly here. Zen insists it's almost seventy degrees in the building, but I'm still cold. Fingers. Toes. My nose too, so I take an extra moment to sniff the fragrant Earl Grey scent in all of its steaming glory before taking another sip. "I was a target."

Was I?

Did she know who I was?

I don't know. I have no idea what Chandler told her or what she found out on her own by listening in to everything around her.

But I know I've been stabbed in the back enough times in my life that it's safer to assume she targeted me.

Even if logic tells me that if I'd been a target, she wouldn't have ghosted me the way she did. Unless she was counting on me to be so thrilled to see her again that I'd forget how much I worried over how she left.

But that seemed like genuine shock to find me here this morning. Was it genuine, or did she have a lot of time to practice?

Trying to think like a vengeance mastermind makes my

head hurt. And considering how much I love a good puzzle, that's saying something.

Zen makes a low, displeased noise. "Word of advice from someone who's been misjudged because of assumptions their whole life—don't treat her like Charisma two-point-oh."

"*Chandler,*" I correct instead of letting myself feel the guilt that comes with Zen's reminder. If Sabrina had been anyone other than Chandler Sullivan's cousin and my new employee, I would've been thrilled to see her this morning.

"Do we like him enough to call him by his real name? You squeezed a china tea cup so hard you crushed it with your bare hand when you got his first email asking for money."

"Would you prefer I call you Zsa Zsa?" I toss back.

"*Uncle Grey*. I would be *honored* that you'd think I was that fabulous."

I blow a slow breath out my nose, sending steam flowing around my nostrils since my tea mug is still so close. "Sabrina Sullivan told me herself that she's a gossip, and she's also a liar. Don't tell her anything you don't want repeated."

"She's a liar?"

"She told me she worked in a beauty salon in Jawbone, Virginia, and that she was a horrible person for screwing up her best friend's tropical vacation by not telling her she was sleeping with a kitten murderer."

Zen screws up their face, and then bursts out laughing.

"So glad you're amused," I say dryly. "You realize it's a lot easier to fire you than it is to fire her?"

"Look, Uncle Grey, I'm not saying she'll be my best

friend, but you can't blame a girl for fudging details when she's prominently featured in the internet's most viral video since Baby Shark. You look at how this location's running, especially compared to the two other locations Chipmunk bought, and it's clear she's a good manager. Someone who's this integrated into a community will make or break a business. If I were you, I'd give her the benefit of the doubt and make sure she wants to keep working here after the renovation and relaunch. Or at least make sure she doesn't sabotage us."

"You just like her dog."

"Don't be an ass. If that dog had belonged to anyone else, you'd be sharing your eggs with it right now."

They're not wrong. And that's annoying too.

Perfect woman in Hawaii.

Fluffy, furry, drooly doggy here.

And *I don't trust her*. Mostly because I *want* to and I know better.

I mutter something incoherent into my tea mug.

"You decide yet if this new job direction is a forever thing or a *just until you realize you're not built to be this kind of asshole* thing?" they ask.

"No."

They shrug and rise. "Cool. For what it's worth, I like it so far. But we haven't met many people yet, so I might change my mind. *Eat*. And drink. I love you, but I'm not interested in dragging your ass back to the emergency room if you make bad choices."

Point taken.

Blacking out and waking up in the back of an ambulance—after realizing what Vince's betrayal meant to my lab and my future in bee research had sent my body into a full-on stress meltdown—wasn't my favorite moment either.

Would've preferred to enter my villain era more like the Incredible Hulk, but apparently instead, I get blood pressure issues in my early thirties.

Yay.

I dutifully dig into the eggs. Zen retreats back to the kitchen, and when I take my plate back to the sink, they're giggling with glee over a hidden cubbyhole behind a small door under the desk that's full of what seems to be stacks of fliers for events from many, many years ago.

Hard not to smile at that glee.

Being Super Vengeance Man will have its problems, but watching Zen enjoy themselves like this is priceless.

They dig into testing the coffee machines while I head back to spread out on a table and bury myself in researching everything I need to know about converting a café into a kombucha brewery and bar.

When I told them I was considering buying a mountain café to destroy it for personal satisfaction, they smirked, asked the address, and did some digging. Three days later, they presented me with a full marketing plan for changing the café into something that would likely thrive here.

No competition in this niche market. The demographics fit, especially with the tourism that comes in due to nearby ski resorts. And Zen's watched me make my own kombucha at home for years.

They knew what they were doing with giving me something good to try on top of getting revenge.

And now here we are.

And all is well—including meeting the normal

morning crew who show up around five-thirty—until Sabrina returns.

She doesn't say anything to me when she gets back to start her shift, but there's a new stubborn sheen in her eyes while she ties on her apron that I recognize all too well.

I've seen it on myself often enough when I've encountered test results in my research lab that didn't make sense, but that I was determined to figure out.

And *I like it*.

And I don't like that I like it.

When Zen calls me to the kitchen to look at water leaking out from the fridge, Sabrina reports she called the local repairman already, but he's demanding prepayment for the fix since Chandler apparently has some outstanding bills and the café's reputation has taken a hit.

She also leaps in, poker-faced, to introduce me to the food truck driver and the coffee supply rep, along with the health department inspector who's in not for an inspection, but a cup of coffee.

And every time she introduces me to someone, she says something nice about me.

He saved the café.

He's so dedicated, he was here even before me this morning.

He's very good at math, so I know we're in good hands.

I recognize this.

This is *good deed Monday*.

And that pisses me off too.

She doesn't get to use me as her good deeds anymore.

Not when she's on my sus list.

"Where's Sabrina?" someone asks at the counter mid-morning while I'm tapping my foot at a side table and rubbing my hands together to keep them warm, impatiently waiting for a late contractor who's supposed to be here to talk about the renovations I want done in both the dining room and the kitchen.

My shoulders bunch at her name.

I wish the answer was *she quit and is packing to move to Siberia*, but alas, it is not.

"She gave herself kitchen duty," Willa, the normal kitchen duty person on the crew, whispers in a hushed voice. Willa's a round-cheeked, brown-skinned, middle-aged lady with cat pins all over her Bean & Nugget apron and blue streaks in her brown hair.

She hugged me for saving the café from being turned over to the IRS when she introduced herself.

I pretended I didn't buy Chandler Sullivan's family business so that I can watch him watch me destroy it piece by piece in the process of building something even better in its place.

Not that he's stopped by this morning.

Nor have I invited him.

Wouldn't break my heart to not see the bastard until the new signage is put in, even if I'm paranoid about when he might randomly drop in and catch me unprepared.

"Again?" the customer asks.

"Again," Willa confirms.

"Poor thing. I saw her grandpa this morning, and he just looked so *sad*. I hope the new—"

Willa clears her throat. "Did you want a cinnamon latte today? Since Sabrina's in the kitchen? Not every day you get a Sabrina Cinnamon Special."

I need to focus on what I'm doing and quit listening in on this conversation, but as I'm turning my attention back to my research on kombucha brewery suppliers, something tickles my nose.

Something sweet.

Hot.

Fresh.

Is that lemon? Do I smell lemon?

My mouth waters.

Profusely.

Like I need to surreptitiously wipe away the drool threatening to slip out of my mouth.

I glance around the dining room. The moms and their little ones at the picnic table across the way don't notice. The older couple at one of the three tables in the picture window are staring out at the snowcapped mountains, or maybe at the lake below the town that you can see clearly from this side of the café. The dude wearing headphones and staring at his computer in front of the fire is smirking.

But none of them are sitting up and sniffing like the whole entire dining room smells like freaking *heaven*.

Except Zen, who's at the other end of the counter, watching everything.

I can't see their nose quivering, but I'd bet it is.

"Is she making Elsie's lemon scones?" the customer asks reverently.

So it's not just me and Zen.

Someone else smells it too.

Also, who's Elsie?

"Oh. Yes. That too," Willa confirms.

"I want the Sabrina Cinnamon Special and one of Elsie's scones."

"You got it, Ms. Isabella."

"Sabrina!" the customer at the counter shrieks.

I look back.

Can't help it. *Everyone* looks up at that.

And there she is, Duchess Sabrina with the absolute *audacity* to be bright and cheery and gorgeous as she pauses on her way past the doorway in the kitchen, a silver tray held aloft in one oven-mitted hand.

She looks like she belongs here.

Was born here.

Grew up here.

Is comfortable here.

This is her happy place, and I can't help wondering how much of the grief in her eyes in Hawaii was from knowing that it wasn't hers anymore.

I shake my head.

Not my problem.

What I'm doing with this café has nothing to do with her, and she doesn't get to be in the soft spots of my heart anymore.

"Hey, Isabella," she says cheerfully. "Be just a minute on your latte, okay?"

"Oh my god, you poor thing, how *are* you?" the customer, Isabella apparently, replies.

My shoulders bunch higher. I grunt, turn back around, and distract myself with a sip of my tea, which is cold now.

The chill makes a shiver slink through my body, but the tea itself?

Still delicious.

Dammit.

Everything I've had here this morning has been good, and Zen's made a point to tell me that they haven't used any of my tea stash that we travel with.

That *all* of this is what they sell here at Bean & Nugget.

"I'm doing great," Sabrina calls back.

"How's Emma?"

"Still solo honeymooning."

"When I think about all of the things Chandler did... Did you know he once double-charged me for breakfast, and I thought it was just that I forgot to pay the first time, but he was actually a shithead who double-charged all of us sometimes?"

"That's awful. I'm so sorry. You should mention that to the new boss and see if he'll give you a coupon for a free meal. He's over at the corner table by the windows. Be right out with your drink. I need to set these down."

Off gossip.

Sure, she is.

I snort softly to myself.

Concentrate. Kombucha. Equipment. Suppliers. Contractors. Change.

Ignore the scent of heaven coming from the kitchen.

Ignore the little violin playing a sad song deep in my gut with lyrics to match, suggesting that Chandler betrayed her as much as Vince betrayed me.

"Excuse me, are you the new owner?" Isabella asks.

Can't ignore that.

I look up and nod.

She's maybe thirty or thirty-five, an average white lady with brown hair and eyes, in a puffy vest over a long-sleeve shirt, hiking pants, and boots.

And that nod is all the permission she needs, apparently, to crush me in a hug with my cheek smushed to her breast.

"Oh my god, *thank you*. I don't know if you know how

69

much this place means to all of us here in the Tooth, but we would've just *died* if it went away. This is such an institution here, and to think Chandler would've let the government auction it off to pay for the taxes…"

"My pleasure," I choke out.

I should be doing my work in the kitchen, but *Sabrina*'s there, and I thought I could be left in peace out here in the dining room.

Wrong.

Zen makes a noise somewhere behind me that says they're completely and totally amused but trying hard to stifle a laugh.

"Do you see that view?" Isabella says, still cradling my head to her bosom with one arm while she sweeps the other out to indicate the snowcapped mountains and blue sky above us and the frozen lake in the valley below us. "This is the most coveted real estate in all of Snaggletooth Creek, and it could've gone to someone *awful*. We're so grateful you've kept the café running for us."

For now.

Zen's idea.

Keep the café running to profit off of it while we wait for all the pieces to fall into place for the renovations. Integrate ourselves in the community so they'll want to support us.

Zen's fucking brilliant.

"Isabella, not everyone likes to be touched," Sabrina calls.

One more good deed for her today.

Isabella leaps back. "I'm just so happy, I forgot myself. But he's cute too. Are you single, Grey?"

"He's very single," Zen supplies.

I glare at them while they pretend to be counting mugs on a tray behind the counter.

"But not currently interested in dating, thank you," I say.

"Oh, I wasn't asking for me. I was asking for everyone else in town." Isabella winks. "You're going to be *very* popular here for saving Bean & Nugget."

"How popular?" Zen asks.

"We don't get a lot of single fresh blood in town. Not permanently, anyway." Isabella looks over at them. "And who are you? I missed your name, but you're clearly new too."

Zen freezes.

"This is Zen," I supply. "They're my personal assistant, and you should feel free to go to them if you have any concerns."

"I'm a nepo-hire, so I don't actually have to be good at my job," Zen says.

If I were drinking, I would've just choked on my tea.

Zen being a sass-hole? Yes. All the time.

Zen being a sass-hole in front of a room of strangers?

Never.

Not out of respect for me and want for us to look like we have a respectful boss-assistant relationship.

More because they have an inherent distrust of the world in general. You don't get the *real* Zen, any part of *this* Zen, until you've earned it.

Which means either this place is magic, or they're just pissed enough at me to let down their guard in the name of shoving me under the bus.

No matter how much they're excited about a

kombucha bar, they're not a fan of me trying on this new role as Super Vengeance Man.

Considering how well they know me, they probably have a point, but it's not a point I'm willing to concede yet.

"Coffee and scone are ready, Iz," Sabrina calls.

"*So* good to meet you," Isabella says. She looks for a second like she wants to hug me again, but instead pats me on the shoulder. And then she pauses to shake Zen's hand and thank them too.

While Isabella gathers her order, Zen slinks around the counter and down the row of tables to sit opposite me.

"Is that the twentieth person who's treated you like a savior today, or did I lose track?" they ask.

I eye them.

They shrug. "Not judging what you're doing here. Just wondering if you're up for it."

That sweet lemon smell is lingering, making my mouth water again. Sabrina strolls past the open kitchen door, which I don't see so much as I *feel*. And Willa steps up next to our table. "We noticed you're out of tea. Here. Sabrina made you another. This one's hot. And I thought you might want to try one of Elsie's scones."

My eye twitches.

"Who's Elsie?" Zen asks.

"Sabrina's grandma. Our favorite Mrs. Sullivan, rest her soul."

The guy on the laptop slides us a look, and I realize why he's familiar.

He was in the video too.

One of the groomsmen.

That makes him one of Chandler Sullivan's cousins as well. Also grandson to Mrs. Sullivan.

72

And the fact that Willa doesn't point *that* out makes me suspicious all over again.

Is he spying on me?

Zen pulls their knees up to their chest in the chair and watches me without blinking while Willa strides back to the kitchen. "You're in trouble, Uncle Grey. I don't think you can do what we want to do and not make people upset. I didn't count on that."

They're not wrong.

Worse, though?

They reach into their pocket and slide my phone across the table to me. "Can't help but wonder what she'd think of this place. Bet she'd love it. We all know how much she loves a good lemon muffin."

I look down at a preview of a text from Mimi.

When I swipe it open, I get a full-screen view of her life-weathered face grimacing over a bowl of something gray and lumpy, accompanied by a message.

Enjoying my oatmeal like a good girl. I know you're tired of everyone asking you for things, but if you could invent a way for sugar and fat and donuts to be good for an old lady's cholesterol level, I promise I'll live forever and tell you you're handsome every day.

Zen's right.

She'd love the atmosphere in this place.

But as far as she knows, I'm still nursing my wounds from having all of my research sold out from underneath me in San Diego and the contract I accidentally signed barring me from doing further research in apiology unless it's for Vince's buddy's company.

She has no idea I'm in a little mountain town righting the only wrong I can fix right now. And she won't either.

73

Not until I've made it better and I can look her in the eye and tell her I did this for any reason other than to destroy someone.

Just because vengeance is necessary doesn't mean it's not ugly.

I'm keeping Mimi out of it.

6

Sabrina

I SPEND HALF my day wanting to breathe into a paper bag. The mad dash that I made to see Laney between dropping Jitter at doggy daycare and reporting back for work helped. As did the fact that Theo gave me multiple paper bags so I *could* breathe into them.

Laney's opinion on what I need to do, while right, is sitting heavy.

When my shift is over, there's no small part of me that wants to go find a blanket fort and camp there forever with my dog, no matter how much I love people. Eight hours of forced proximity with Greyson Cartwright and his massive size taking up every square inch of Bean & Nugget and his growing beard making him look like he belongs in the Tooth and his *you betrayed me* wounded blue eyes have done me in.

I cannot believe he's my new boss, and I would very

much like to wake up from this nightmare and discover that it's still early January. That I told Emma about Chandler letting Theo take the fall for the damage to the statue of Ol' Snaggletooth that winter after we all graduated high school, that she called off the wedding before it happened. And then that I'd gone to the bank to get a loan and enlisted the help of everyone in my life to convince Chandler to sell Bean & Nugget to me.

But since this isn't just a nightmare, I reach deep for some *I can do this*, go get my dog, peek in on my grandpa at his retirement community, and pretend everything's fine while somehow finding things to talk about with everyone that don't make me feel like I'm only asking about what's up to refill my gossip well, which is most definitely emptier than it would be if I'd spent the day working the dining room instead of the kitchen.

"How's the new owner?" Grandpa asks me as he studies the chessboard in the brightly lit community center in the middle of his retirement home complex.

I wince. Grumpy? Stone-cold? Vengeful? Yes, I did, in fact, get an email from a friend in construction who got a request for a quote to gut and re-imagine the entire interior of the building right as I pulled up at the senior center. "I'm saving my opinion for later."

"That's not like you," his friend, Pearl, says. She's in her seventies and retired from being the secretary to the mayor for fifty years, so she knows as much as I do about town.

I hitch a shoulder up. "Everyone else in town loves him so far."

Pearl squints at me like she can ferret out that I slept with him in Hawaii, he's pissed at me for ghosting him, and I noticed today that every time anyone said Chandler's name, Grey would clench his fist and get this *look* on his face.

I actively ignore the squint and stare at the chessboard. Not really my game, but I can kind of tell that Grandpa's losing.

"It's hard to see Bean & Nugget in someone else's hands," I acknowledge. "I'm not exactly impartial here."

"Should've come to me for money," Grandpa says while he moves one of his pieces.

"I didn't know until too late."

"*He* should've come to me for money."

He being Chandler.

And while I adore my grandfather—he's the last of the really good men in the world, I swear he is—I don't intend to insult my cousin in front of him.

"Is the new guy cute?" Pearl asks as she carefully selects a piece and moves it, knocking one of Grandpa's pieces off the board.

Grandpa grunts while my entire body has an *oh my god, yes*, reaction to the question.

"What does that have to do with anything?" Grandpa asks.

"Sabrina's single. If he's cute—"

"You didn't ask if he was single."

"Oh, honey, if he's not, that's solvable."

I force a laugh I don't feel. "Miss Pearl, I am *not* seducing a man to get the family café back. Sorry, Grandpa. I have my lines."

"This is war, Sabrina," Pearl replies. "You need to use all of your feminine wiles on him."

Grandpa grunts again and takes his turn.

"What are you doing?" Pearl says to him. "Are you trying to throw this game? If you didn't want to play, you should've just said so."

"If you wanted to play this game, you'd quit talking about my granddaughter's *wiles*."

Pearl looks at me.

I hold up my hands in surrender. "Okay. Okay. I'm clearly a distraction. I'm going. But here. I snuck some lemon scones out of the kitchen today."

There's nothing guaranteed to make this entire room of senior citizens move faster than the promise of my grandma's scones. Jitter, who was happily panting on his back while getting all of the love from three different friends at once, whimpers, flops to his belly, and slinks behind a pink flower-patterned couch to get out of the way of the mad rush of senior citizens.

Poor puppy's tired after a good day at doggy daycare.

"You pay for these?" Grandpa asks.

"Getting fired for stealing on the new boss's first day wasn't in my plans, so yes. I paid for them."

One more old man grunt.

The only other time I've seen him grumpy was when Grandma died.

He's hurting. Bean & Nugget was a part of his family too. He *built* it, and he lived long enough to see Chandler squander it.

Wonder if he heard too that the new owner is planning to completely change everything.

I hope not. But I know it's a legitimate possibility. My friend told me he knew he wasn't the only contractor in town who was contacted about getting a quote.

Other people will be talking about this soon enough.

I kiss Grandpa on his puffy white hair and squeeze his shoulder gently. "Don't give up on me, okay? I won't let anything happen to Bean & Nugget, even if it's not ours anymore."

"We have faith in you, Sabrina," Pearl says.

I'm talking big talk, and I don't know if there's enough faith in the world for me to pull this off.

I know I need to apologize to Duke—to *Grey*, as he asked everyone else to call him today. I know I need to get on his good side. And I know I need to use every tool at my disposal to stop him from ruining Bean & Nugget.

So after visiting Grandpa, Jitter and I head to the grown-up version of the clubhouse that Laney, Emma, and I hung out in all the time after Theo dubbed us the *ugly heiresses* in grade school.

Silver Horn isn't a treehouse in my grandparents' backyard though.

It's—actually, I can't tell you what it is.

Or how I get into it.

All you need to know is that I'm camped out at a bar that Grey won't be able to find, and I'm surrounded by friends.

I need help.

It's a hard thing to ask for, but I do. I need help.

"Can you get the scoop from Chandler on *anything* with Greyson Cartwright?" I ask Jack, one of my triplet cousins. We're sitting on curved suede benches beneath a painting of Snaggletooth Creek's original gold mine. It's hung on a brick wall with red velvet curtains on either side of it that follow the curve of the benches around to give our seating area a modicum of privacy.

We *do* get a little swanky in certain places in the Tooth.

79

But they still let me bring my dog inside—again, provided he shakes it all out before coming in—which is why Jitter is panting happily on my feet and against my leg, gazing at my cousins with absolute adoration while they both work on their laptop computers, doing research on my new boss their way.

Jack winces and rubs his chest right over the dice printed on his black T-shirt. "You know how Chandler didn't tell Emma that the Ol' Snaggletooth statue was his fault and not Theo's?"

My eyelid twitches. "Gosh, no, doesn't ring a bell."

Decker delivers me the *don't be an ass* look to end all *don't be an ass* looks. "We're starting to realize our dear cousin is fucking batshit. Or at least an egomaniac. Even if he'd tell us anything about how he set up this sale so quietly with a dude he supposedly knows from somewhere, I wouldn't trust it. *That guy and I were best friends?* Doubt it. *He owed me a favor?* Don't believe it. *He reached out to me and wanted to buy a shop in the mountains and the timing was good?* Nope, nope, and nope."

"Cosigned," Jack says.

He, Lucky, and Decker are genetically identical. All white-skinned, brown-haired, and blue-eyed, though their styles are so different that it's easy to tell them apart. Jack, the engineer, has short-cropped hair and is always in jeans and geeky gamer T-shirts. Decker's a novelist who wouldn't be caught dead in jeans *or* short hair. He's totally the scruffy mountain dude perpetually in hiking pants, performance fabric T-shirts—long- or short-sleeved depending on the weather—and puffer vests. Lucky's not with us tonight. He's a nurse and has less flexibility than his brothers, who both work from home.

Or from Bean & Nugget, as Decker did today so he could spy on the new boss too.

Not that Grey seemed to realize who Decker was, even though the triplets had an appearance in that viral video too. And the fact that Willa and Cedar, my weekday morning crew, didn't tell Grey who Decker was either speaks volumes to how much they're leery of the new ownership too, no matter the smiles and gratitude they expressed.

The triplets also might be Laney's half-brothers, which I didn't tell you, because I'm only *back* on gossip for a very specific reason and this is not it. However, they're obsessed and it'll come up eventually.

Probably within moments, considering the door just opened and Theo's carrying Laney inside.

Not something any of us would've seen coming three weeks ago, let me tell you.

Theo's been in hiding most of the past week after getting exposed in Emma's viral wedding video as being the biggest solo creator on a very popular adult entertainment website. Yes, *that* kind of adult entertainment website. He never showed his face in his videos, so it was a big deal when people figured out who he was, what he looked like from the neck up and with clothes on, and where he was from.

Since Emma left for her solo honeymoon and the rest of us got home, he's retired from his profession largely because of Laney. She broke her leg skiing last week, and when he found out she was hurt, he finally got over himself, apologized for being an ass to her in Hawaii, and begged her to be his girlfriend.

She didn't ask him to quit his naked side hustle.

He insisted on doing it himself.

And if Emma were here, she'd be absolutely loving everything about this. At least, pre-Hawaii Emma would've been.

I don't know how she'll feel now.

Laney and Theo making up and falling in love after years of animosity is the only thing I currently believe in wholeheartedly. And yes, I'm saying that as someone who doesn't believe in relationships.

Laney does.

I won't take that from her, because if anyone can find a way to be happy and work through the problems, these two can.

I know they still have secrets from each other, but not malicious secrets. More like *I forgot to tell you I was the one who started the rumor that you didn't wear underwear in high school*, which will not come as a surprise to Laney at all when Theo confesses.

Nor will it bother her.

She knows who Theo was and how much he's made right since high school. And I know all the dirt there is to know about Theo, even if I don't want to remember it anymore, and I have no concerns for them.

None.

They're one of the few couples that I honestly expect to make it.

They both know relationships take work and are willing to do it.

And tonight, when she's perfectly capable of using her crutches to compensate for the leg in the cast, he's carrying her in here instead. The one thing Theo's not short on is energy. Next up is utter and complete loyalty and dedication to the people he loves. Followed very closely by *basically lives to test boundaries.*

Put it all together with him secretly being in love with Laney nearly his whole life, and that makes a recipe for Theo being the best boyfriend on the entire planet right now.

Swoon.

Also, *fuck you, Greyson Cartwright, for being nothing like the man you were in Hawaii who would've understood why I had to go.*

Even though I should be thanking him.

If he were the man he'd been in Hawaii, beans only know if I could've resisted him.

If he were the man he'd been in Hawaii, he would've walked into my café and asked how we could work together to make it even better instead of being Mr. Grumpy Pants Secretly Plotting To Change Everything all day.

Jitter scrambles to his feet and wags his tail, then presses his body against me and whines softly as Theo approaches with Laney. I scratch his neck while I hold his collar. "Sit, boy. Theo will love on you in a minute."

Jack and Decker both rise on either side of me. "Here, Laney, take my seat," Jack says while he snaps his laptop shut.

"Mine's better," Decker says while he tucks his laptop under his arm. "More room to prop your leg up."

"You get a chance to take a DNA test yet?" Jack adds.

Called it.

And now I'm realizing I have one more regret.

In Hawaii, I told *Duke* that the high school English teacher, Ms. Crackerjack, had an affair with one of the parents of one of her students, Mr. Arbys, that resulted in quintuplets.

He'll probably figure out the whole truth on that story pretty quickly, though maybe not that Laney's father is the man we suspect of having an affair with my uncle's wife. The triplets' dad definitely isn't their biological dad, but we have yet to nail down for one hundred percent sure if Mr. Kingston is.

And I definitely need to stop in to see my neighbor down the street.

The new twenty-three-year-old high school English teacher that Grey will suspect has quintuplets if he bothers to think about all of the gossip I told him at all.

"Let a woman get settled before you pester her about who your father is." Theo sets Laney down in an empty barrel chair across from us, then pulls the entire low table closer to her and helps her prop her cast on it. "Mai tai?" he asks her.

She tips her head back and laughs. "*No.*"

"Save that for home," Decker agrees. "None of us want to see her lose her clothes again. No offense, Laney. It's just like…seeing your cousin naked."

Laney's average height, with brown hair, blue eyes, a tan still on her white skin after our week in Hawaii for the wedding that wasn't, and the cutest butt on the planet. Her wardrobe is entirely functional business casual, but today, she's in a super baggy pair of Theo's sweatpants to accommodate her cast, with a bright blue-and-green patterned blouse that would be appropriate on a video conference call. Her future involves taking over the online custom photo gift empire that her parents built as we were growing up, and she's going to rock it when they retire and hand over the reins.

She brings the best surprises since she can have anything custom-made.

"You okay?" she asks me after Theo leaves for the bar to get her a glass of wine, leaving Jitter brokenhearted at having to wait even longer for love from Theo. My dog has favorites in town. "You're very...still."

"I'm processing."

"Hear anything new?"

Hear? Yes. But more—*pick up on*?

Greyson Cartwright has a tea obsession. Between the beanie and the way he kept gravitating toward the fireplace and rubbing his hands together, he doesn't like the cold. He has at least one *someone* he's avoiding talking to, if I was reading the signs right once I figured out Zen was holding on to his phone for him.

Plus, there was the way his phone wouldn't stop buzzing in Hawaii until he shut it off. I don't think this is a new avoidance.

And more than once, I caught him watching me in the reflection of one of the windows or glancing back at the kitchen with utter misery etched on his face. Like he didn't *want* to be the grouchy asshole that he was being, and like he wanted to be back in Hawaii too.

But that might've been me projecting.

What would today have been like if he'd understood why I had to leave the way I did in Hawaii?

I swallow and meet Laney's gaze. "He's getting bids to renovate Bean & Nugget entirely."

"How entirely?"

I know I need to say it, but I can hardly bring myself

to force the words out. I run my hands through Jitter's fur to make it more palatable. "He wants to convert it into a kombucha brewery with a completely redone menu, add mead if he can get a liquor license, rename it *The Hive*, and keep a wall of board games for regular gamer nights."

Jack makes a noise.

I know that noise.

That's a noise of *he's building my idea of heaven*.

Decker reaches around me and shoves him. "Shut up."

"No, I get it." I sigh. "It would sound interesting if he was doing it to *another building*." I'd go there and destroy the triplets in a round of Settlers of Catan every once in a while if we had a gaming hangout in town. Instead, I have to do it in the privacy of one of our houses.

Boring.

"And I think he's planning on putting beehives on the roof and I heard his assistant say something to him about finding a place that can make the fiberglass bee that he wants to mount on the building," I add.

"Isn't Chandler deathly afraid of bees?" Laney asks.

"Yes."

"Does your new boss know this?"

"*I don't know*. But I got the impression he doesn't like Chandler."

"*Fuck*, that's funny," Decker mutters. "I hate this guy. I'm not supposed to think he's funny if he's a dick to our family and the café. How did you pick up on all of this and I didn't today?"

"You didn't get the same emails I got."

"What else do you know about him?" Laney asks me.

"Not enough. I'm working on cracking Zen, his

86

assistant, but I don't think they trust people easily. It'll take me some time."

"I'm googling," Decker says.

"*I'm* googling," Jack adds.

Decker's on a MacBook. Jack's on a PC laptop. Do *not* get them started on who *computers* better.

"We got you, Sabrina," Decker says. "By the time we're done here, we'll know everything from his social security number to his favorite brand of socks."

He wears socks with pandas on them.

At least, he did today, and *fuck you again, Greyson Cartwright, for making me swoon over your ridiculously cute socks.*

The worst part about having *Duke* in my everyday life now?

I get it. I totally understand why he's mad at me, and there's nothing I can—or will—do about it. I'll apologize, and I'll be a good employee so long as Bean & Nugget exists, but that's all he gets from me.

Theo strolls back over from the bar and hands Laney a glass of red wine, then hands me a fresh coffee in an old Bean & Nugget mug, one with the original logo before Chandler started changing things, and my eyes get hot at the simple gesture of kindness.

Both that Theo would get me a coffee without me asking, and that Silver Horn keeps old Bean & Nugget mugs on hand.

"Where's my coffee?" Decker asks.

Theo's tall like Emma, though she's a freckled pasty white blonde while his complexion is two shades less pasty and his hair falls on the light brown side. He's significantly more muscular these days after bulking up for his side gig, and the man is always hot. Temperature-wise, I mean. Hence showing up here tonight in jeans and a T-shirt that shows off the ink all over his arms. No coat for Theo, even in fifteen-degree weather. He smirks and shakes his head. "First you want coffee, then you'll want a private show. I know how this works."

Jack whips his head up. "Dude. Keep your clothes on."

"No, no, I think he should take them off," Laney says.

"Are you *kidding* me?" Jack yelps as he points to his computer screen. Jitter yelps too, then dives and tries to hide under the curved couch I'm sitting on. Unfortunately, there's like an inch of space under the couch, and Jitter, who's a foot tall even when he's lying flat on the ground, can't make it work. He looks at Jack, who's still making outraged noises, then up at me with his massive puppy dog eyes that silently ask if he can climb into my lap.

"Go sit on Theo so he doesn't take his clothes off and horrify Jack," I tell him.

"Love you too, Sabrina," Theo says while Jitter scurries around the table and climbs up on his lap.

"I'm not worried Theo's getting naked," Jack says to me. "Look. *Look.*" He spins his computer around so we can see a picture of Grey in a suit in some business article. "The guy invented those self-sealing cereal bags and he basically makes bank every year just for licensing out his patent. I fucking *love* those things. Why? *Why?* Why does it have to be *him?*"

"No," Decker says. "*No.* Shit. Have we been quietly funding his rise to world domination this whole time by loving Lucky Charms?"

"Two-faced asshat," Jack mutters.

Decker scowls. "I hate him extra for making me love him without even knowing it before he betrayed me."

"*Oh my god*, are you two serious?" Laney says. "*Him inventing a better cereal bag is not personal.* It's also not something we can use against him unless they're bad for the environment or cause weird diseases or something."

Jack sighs. "Nope. They're ecologically and environmentally friendly too."

Theo pinches his lips together and buries his head in Jitter's fur like he's afraid they'll hear him laughing at them. And considering Jitter is massive, it doesn't take much for Theo to hide behind him.

"It could be personal that he's converting Bean & Nugget into a bee heaven though," she says. "That feels personal."

"It does," I agree. "How well does he know Chandler? And what about his family? *Ugh*, I hate this. I want to go *talk* to his family. Not ask a stupid computer to tell me the news. Computers have no nuance. But it'll take me a while to get on Zen's good side. They're hardcore private. It's a vibe."

"I gotcha, Sabrina," Decker says. "Smartest of the bunch right here, four steps ahead of these doofuses. Guess who started undergrad at Carnegie Mellon?"

I sit straighter. "When?"

"Looks like his junior year corresponded to Chandler's freshman year."

Chandler was a legacy admission at Carnegie Mellon. Special treatment because Grandpa went there too. That's likely how he would know Grey, considering Chandler's never lived anywhere except here and college, and there's no indication Grey's ever been a mountain person.

"What do you mean, *started* undergrad?" I ask.

"You wanna do this googling yourself, Sabrina?" Jack asks. "Here. I'll show you how to use a keyboard."

"She sucks at Google," Laney says. "Like, she'll google *when does the sun rise?* and she'll get answers about astrological anomalies. It's a fascinating superpower. Haven't you ever noticed?"

"Oh, shit, that's all the time?" Decker whips his phone out.

Yes, it's all the time. And I'm fine with that, because I prefer—*preferred*, in my gossiping days, which are numbered—to hear news from *people*. Not machines. "If you write my internet failures in your character quirk notebook, I swear on my newly reclaimed powers of gossip that you will regret it," I tell Decker.

He eyes me.

I give him the raised brows of *don't test me on this*, even though I would absolutely not spill any secrets that I'm trying to forget I know about him.

"*Fine*," he grunts. "But the next time I have writer's block, I'm remembering you wouldn't help me."

"If using someone's terrible googling powers is what you need to get over writer's block, you need a new profession."

Jack snickers. Theo keeps his face buried in my dog's side while he rubs Jitter's fur.

And I thrust my fingers into my hair. "Sorry. That was rude," I mutter.

"No, I think that was spot-on," Jack interjects.

Theo's phone audibly dings, and Laney and I look at him.

It dings again as he's pulling it out of his pocket.

My heart takes flight and hovers in my throat.

Laney leans closer to him, peeking as he glances at the readout.

"Are his texts that fascinating?" Jack asks.

"It could be Emma, dumbass," Decker mutters.

"But she's on her honeymoon through the end of the week, isn't she?"

"Her *runaway-moon*."

"Oh, look at you, finding your writer words."

"Off, Jitterbug," Theo says, lifting up from the chair and shoving his phone in his pocket.

Everything inside me freezes like I've been dipped in dry ice at the expression on his face. My pulse rockets and makes my fingers and toes tingle. "Emma?" I ask.

He ignores both me and my dog, who's pushing against him like he can shove Theo back into the chair and climb back into his lap.

"Bring my crutches?" Laney says.

He kisses her on the head. "Yep. Who do you want to take you home?"

"I've got her," I say.

"Sabrina's got me," she agrees.

Theo eyes me.

I toss my hands up. "I'm not going to drop her and break her other leg. *Go*."

"What just happened?" Jack says to Decker while Jitter slinks around the table to settle his head in my lap and whine.

"Emma's coming home?" Decker guesses.

Theo doesn't answer.

He doesn't have to.

There are very, very few reasons he'd leave Laney

alone in public and dependent on anyone else to get a ride home.

If there was something wrong with his dad, he'd say so.

The fact that he's saying *nothing* means it's Emma and she asked him not to.

And the fact that Theo wants Laney to get another ride home means that Emma doesn't just want a phone call with her big brother. It nearly certainly means he's headed to Denver to get her from the airport.

Theo kisses Laney once more, then salutes the rest of us and heads for the door without filling in any blanks that I'm not filling in for myself.

"Do *not* read anything into this," Laney orders me.

"She doesn't want to see us?" I whisper.

"*Do not* read anything into this."

Translation: I saw the text, she doesn't want to see us, and we need to give her space to fill in the answers whenever she's ready.

While Laney was the one who let it slip to Emma that Theo had taken the fall for Chandler with jail time a decade ago, she didn't know until basically the minute she relayed the information to Emma shortly before the wedding was supposed to happen.

I, meanwhile, was the one who's known it for practically a decade.

"*Theo* should've told her since Chandler didn't," Laney says softly, like she's reading my mind, which she probably is. We've known each other for a long, long time. "And he'll be the first person to tell you so."

"Gotta agree," Decker says.

"Thirded," Jack chimes in. "And fourthing for Lucky.

THE GOSSIP AND THE GRUMP

He'd be on Team *Theo Fucked Up Second Most After Chandler*. And all of us say that as dudes who love the guy. But mostly, I think we need to remember that Chandler can be a charming asshole when he wants to be, and Emma wouldn't have believed any of us."

I hear them. I hear their words. But—"It's hard for my heart to agree when she's hurting and I could've prevented it."

"You're a font of information about our community, but you aren't psychic," Laney says. "Cut yourself some slack. And have faith in her. We've been through too much for this to break us apart."

"Have we?"

All Emma's wanted since she was little was to get married and have a massive family.

And now, after waiting for Chandler to walk down the aisle with her for seven years, she's alone.

No husband. No kids. No white picket fence with the dog in the yard and the cat inside.

It's not my dream, but it was hers. If I'd told her, would she have found a different dream man and be living her dream life now?

"*Stop it*," Laney says. "Let's get back to solving the problems we can solve and waiting until we know if everything else even *is* a problem, okay?"

Jitter whines and puts a paw on my knee.

I bump my forehead with his. Cute massive dog.

"Okay," I agree, even though my heart isn't in it. "Solvable problems first. What else does anyone have on Greyson Cartwright?"

7

Grey

It's cold and dark when Zen and I finally leave the café and head to the townhouse we're renting for the next few weeks. I'm hungry, tired, and in need of three solid days without people around.

Did *not* think through my stamina for peopling with strangers when I made the decision to buy and destroy Chandler Sullivan's café.

And having Sabrina there until mid-afternoon didn't help anything either. I could use an extra four days to process her reaction to me being her new boss.

I'm still irritated that she ghosted me in Hawaii. And knowing she's related to Chandler has made me wary. So did her absolutely chipper attitude all day long.

I pieced together enough of what she told me in Hawaii with what I saw of the viral video to assume her desire to do good deeds that night had everything to do with her bride-friend's wedding imploding. I also completely believe she was blindsided by Chandler selling me the café.

But no matter how nice she was today, I still don't trust her. Not when she made it abundantly clear that night that she deals in people's secrets.

"Do you want your phone back, or do you want the highlights?" Zen asks as I pull out of the Bean & Nugget parking lot, taking my thoughts in a direction that probably isn't any better.

Other than when I took off for Hawaii, intent on ruining Chandler Sullivan's wedding day, they've been holding my phone more or less since the news broke among our family that I walked away from my own research and development lab.

How soon will you sell it? is the primary question I've gotten.

Not *are you coming home?*

Not *I heard about what Vince did. Are you okay?*

Not even *guess it's a good thing you can afford to start over.*

It's just *how soon will you sell it?* as if selling a lab is worth anything once the primary research is off the table as an asset in the sale.

I know what they want to know.

How much more money does Felicia's lawyer need to demand you send her now that you're disposing of another asset that you owned while you were married to her?

And I know why they want to know.

Because we are on Team Felicia and think you're an asshole for divorcing her so we want to see her get every dime she can from you so you know what a mistake you made.

"How bad was it today?" I ask.

"Twenty-three texts from Aunt Camille about FroYo Fucklebutt's birthday party, three from the piece of shit formerly known as your BFF who wants you to sign more papers so he can get utilities restored to the lab, a call from your attorney reiterating that you will *not* be signing more papers for that shit under any circumstance, and three calls from the real estate agent you picked to sell the other two Bean & Nugget locations. She thinks one location will go quickly and the other will be a pain in the ass."

I grimace in the dark. Chandler's desire to run a café empire in the mountains wasn't his downfall, but that's what he told people. And the fact that the original Snaggletooth Creek location is doing well is almost insult on top of injury.

Speaks highly of Sabrina's management skills and everything she said today about how much she loves her family's café.

The light off my phone glows in the dark beside me under Zen's management while I follow the car's GPS instructions out of downtown. "You also missed a call from Mimi."

I sit straighter in the driver's seat. "Mimi texted *and* called?"

"Yep."

"Is she okay?"

"Other than being worried about you for going nearly radio silent on her, yes. She wasn't satisfied with your response to her text."

I wince.

"I told her you were a secret-keeping butthead who

didn't deserve her concerns or to hear her voice today," Zen says with full sassitude.

They did not, or I'd be talking to Mimi right now and we both know it. "How'd she sound?"

"Tired."

"More tired or less tired?"

"The same tired."

Mimi weathered my grandfather dying just fine, but unexpectedly losing her twin sister a few months ago was a blow. It's been hard to watch. And yes, I know *a ninety-something-year-old woman should be expected to die at some point*, but my aunt was in good health. Active and fun and spry for being in her nineties.

"Do I need to fly back to see her?" I *hate* going home to Connecticut. I'd rather gnaw off my own foot. But for Mimi, I would.

"You need to not be within three hundred miles of Aunt Camille until after Ficklerella's birthday party. Or possibly ever again."

"Do I need to fly you back to see her?"

"And leave you solo with the vultures here? No. Only *one woman* asked if you were single today. You know what that means?"

"I'm unattractive and moody?"

"They're talking about you behind your back."

"Don't care."

"Yes, you do. Your shoulders just hunched up to your ears."

"It's the cold." It truly is stupidly cold here. I wasn't prepared for that, even if I told myself I was.

"Or *maybe* it's that they were so very, very, very nice to both of us today, and now you're grumpy because you don't know if they're only being nice to your face, or if they're actually good people that we can trust to help make your vengeance dream turn into something beautiful."

I slide a glance at them in the dark.

"Yes, yes, I'm the tornado calling you a thunderstorm," they say. "But I'm not wrong."

They are indeed not wrong. "Sabrina Sullivan runs this town. She could've told them all to manipulate us so we don't change a thing."

"Before or after you slept with her?"

"*I don't know.*"

"Makes you want to light the whole place up with dynamite, doesn't it?"

In response, I blow out a slow breath that coats the windshield in a light sheen of fog. "It makes me glad there's wine and a puzzle waiting at the townhouse."

"I'd tell you to call Mimi, but it's past her bedtime. Also, I don't think you'll call her until you can look her straight in the eye and tell her you bought this place because it was a long-standing dream to be a mountain-kombucha-bar man and not that you bought it because you want to destroy a man's life and needed something to actually turn it into."

"She'd understand." I am absolutely not calling her until I decide what I want to do with the rest of my life now that it's shown me, *again*, that research into how to save the bees might be my first true love, but it's not what I'm supposed to do.

As for what I'll do if I discover this kombucha bar isn't the path for me, I'll sell it.

After it's no longer recognizable as the café Chandler

grew up with. "I found a place to get a new SCOBY so we can start brewing kombucha samples."

"Are you picking it up or am I?"

"I'll get it tomorrow."

We pull into the parking lot of the little townhouse neighborhood, and Zen steers me to the correct row of parking garages across the street from the line of brown, two-story townhouses where our unit is located.

"Do you remember the code for the door?" I ask them after we've parked and pulled out the rest of our luggage that we didn't bring in with us when we arrived late last night. They let us in, and I haven't looked at the reservation.

"Does a duck wear shoes?"

"Can you *get* the code for the door again please?"

They flash me a grin in the dimly lit parking area. "Ducks totally wear shoes. Grab my bag too. I'll go get the door."

I fling Zen's backpack over my shoulder and grab a rolling suitcase with each hand. They're already across the street from the parking garage to the front door of the townhouse. And I'm moving as swiftly as I can to follow.

It's fucking cold out here. Hope the heater's set above seventy.

Should've sent them to bring in the rest of our bags hours ago.

I'm nearly to the sidewalk in front of our unit when a laugh at the next door over catches my ear.

"You're so silly, puppy," a little girl says while a massive dog licks her face.

"Jitter, be nice," a very familiar female voice says some-where on the other side of the dog.

And even though I know that dog, and I know that voice, my chest tightens in undeniable desire.

Not for Sabrina, I tell myself.

But for the life she has.

The dog. The little girl shrieking with laughter. The lights glowing inside the house.

Home and family the way you see it in the movies.

I scowl to myself, put my head down, take three more steps, and everything goes topsy-turvy.

Ice.

I hit ice.

I hit ice, and my feet slip from under me. The bag on my shoulder drops, throwing me more off-balance. I grip the two suitcases, but both are on wheels, and both go in opposite directions, which leaves me landing hard on one hip and an elbow at the snow-covered curb.

"*Uncle Grey,*" Zen says.

There's a woof, two more shrieks, and then I'm drowning in fur while the dog reaches me first and lies down so close to me that he's practically on top of me.

He whimpers.

And then Zen's there on one side, Sabrina on the other.

"Are you okay?" Zen asks. "Where does it hurt? Did you break anything? Can you move?"

Cold seeps through my coat. Cold and wet seep through my suit pants. The dog whines and puts his face in mine.

"Jitter, come," Sabrina says quietly. "Give him breathing space."

"It's your ass, isn't it?" Zen says. "You broke your ass."

"I did not break my ass," I grit out.

101

Jitter whines again and moves his head to rest on my chest while I try to push myself up.

Ice water is already penetrating my gloves.

"So you're the mystery first tenants next door," Sabrina says to Zen. "I probably shouldn't be surprised, should I?"

Zen looks at her. Then at me. Then back to her. "Oh, this is gonna be fun."

"Has anyone told you yet that the walls are paper-thin?"

"Ew. Thanks for the warning. Glad you worked him out of your system in Hawaii."

"*Zen,*" I snap.

The dog whines again and shoves his face closer to my chin. His head is bigger than mine. His jowls are flopping on my chest and leaving drool on my coat. And his breath smells like the best doggy breath in the world, and yes, I fucking miss my dog so much I'd live in doggy breath.

I push his head away.

"*Jitter,*" Sabrina says. "Who's a good boy who wants a steak dinner?"

I was wrong.

Jitter wasn't whining before.

This is a whine. A sad, mournful, *I love steak dinners but I can't move* kind of deep, thick, long whine.

"Aww, he knows you're a dog person." Zen holds a hand out to me. "Can you move? Or do we need to call for help?"

"I can move."

"You're acting like you're eighty-six instead of thirty-something."

"That young?" Sabrina says to them. "And how old are you?"

"Do *not* answer that." I pull myself up to my full height.

The dog presses against my legs and almost takes me down again, but Sabrina grabs my arm and steadies me.

Lightning streaks up my arm and hits a bulls-eye in my chest, and I'm back in Hawaii, strolling down a dark sidewalk toward my hotel, with her grabbing my arm and pulling me out of the way of a bicyclist hurtling down the path like I didn't have over a foot and at least eighty pounds on her.

One more good deed? I'd asked her.

She'd licked her finger and made a tally mark in the air, and I'd gone hard as a diamond.

Having her touch me again?

Nearly the same reaction.

Fucking hell.

I still like her. I understand why she ghosted me. I *respect* what she's doing here.

This woman has the power to hurt me, and she's already demonstrated she will without hesitation under the right circumstances.

I jerk back, keeping my balance out of sheer determination to not mortify myself again.

"You're gonna want boots with better tread," she tells me as if we're normal acquaintances and not two people who slept together under questionable circumstances. "We get plowed last in our little circle, and since we face north on top of that, we tend to be the iciest around here."

Do not think about plowing her. Do not think about plowing her. Think about ice. Icy, cold, nasty ice.

"Find a new rental," I tell Zen.

"I got your suitcase, mister!" The little girl who was

sitting on Sabrina's step dashes over the icy parking area like it's nothing, dragging my suitcase behind her. The other one is lying on its side next to the dog.

"That was super nice of you, Aspen," Sabrina says.

"I know," the girl replies.

Zen snickers.

Sabrina smiles at her. "We should get you home. You ready?"

"Can Jitter come?"

"That's my plan. Go get him a treat and call for him."

The young girl dashes off to Sabrina's porch.

"And I should get you inside," Zen says to me. "Can you walk? Does it hurt?"

"I'm fine." I'll be bruised, but I'm fine.

My ego's more at stake here.

I bend and grab Zen's backpack while Sabrina and her dog hover.

"Thank you," I say crisply. "You can go."

She doesn't break eye contact. "If I'd known who you were in Hawaii, I would've told you who I was. I just want you to know that. The café isn't a game to me. It's my life."

God, she's pretty.

How the hell does she have the right to be that pretty? And why the fuck can't I quit noticing?

"And I'm sorry I lied when I said I was coming back," she adds. "I don't know what your relationship is with Chandler, but mine's pretty shitty. I just didn't know *how* shitty until that day. Family and friends are everything to me, and I'd just lost two of mine. I was in a bad place. I won't—I won't lie to you again."

"But you'll gossip?"

"Bean & Nugget is my *life*. It's my *home*. Name your price and I'll buy it back."

"Not for sale."

She swallows as she stares up at me. "Please don't ruin it," she whispers.

I don't have a fast answer.

She hovers, waiting, just long enough for me to know she knows I'm not that quick on my feet.

The worst part, though?

The worst part is when she blinks rapidly like she's on the verge of tears.

It makes me want to wrap my arms around her and hold her tight and protect her from the bad things in the world, the same way I wanted to when we were in Hawaii.

Except I'm the bad. I'm the bad in her life right now.

"I can help you with anything else you want here," she says. "But please don't ruin my home."

She turns away, reiterating her offer of a steak dinner to Jitter with her voice almost normal, and I stand there.

Just stand there.

I should go inside.

Shower in scalding hot water.

Eat. Put on seven layers of clothes and get warm.

Instead, I stand there and watch Sabrina stroll away, the swing in her hips subtle enough that I only notice because I can't take my eyes off her ass.

The dog whines one last time, licks my gloved hand, and then trots after her while the little girl on the porch calls his name and holds up a dog treat.

"Aspen?" a woman calls from around the corner.

"I've got her, Marley," Sabrina calls back. "She wanted to say hi to Jitter."

Zen's watching me with the front door propped open. They've already gathered the luggage and shoved it inside while I was busy staring at a woman I shouldn't want and will not have. "She's already figured out you're changing things?"

"She's a gossip."

"And you like her."

I don't answer.

They're right.

I still like her. Despite not trusting her, despite planning on doing exactly what she doesn't want me to do, despite not *wanting* to like her, I do.

Zen sighs. "Uncle Grey, you ever consider that vengeance doesn't suit you?"

I've disliked that word more with every passing minute, and not just for the knot that's been growing in my stomach all day. Could I open a kombucha bar somewhere else?

Yep.

But it wouldn't hurt Chandler Sullivan if I did that, now would it? "Or maybe being *Super Vengeance Man* isn't supposed to be easy."

They crack up. "Inside with you. Time for a shower, clean clothes, and food. And then I'll show you the super cool puzzle I got you with *my* credit card last month."

A new puzzle should make me happy. I've given up contemplating new fields of research that might interest me and let my mind engage in puzzles instead since I found out what Vince did, and so far, it's working.

Tonight though?

Tonight, Zen might be right.

I might not be cut out for vengeance.

Should be a good thing, right? Means I'm not like my family.

Just this once, I wanted to be the badass asshole getting justice.

But as I cast one last glance at Sabrina's front door, all I can think is that this isn't nearly as straightforward and easy as it should be.

8

Sabrina

I ARRIVE fifteen minutes before my eight a.m. shift is scheduled to begin at Bean & Nugget and use the spare time to sit in the backseat of my car with Jitter and check my text messages while I finish the travel mug of coffee I brought along.

Nothing from Emma. For once, I don't know what to say to start a conversation.

If she'd broken up with anyone else, under any other circumstances, I would've camped out at her house with wine and chocolate and sourdough from the bakery at the other end of Main Street. Laney would've been there with a custom dartboard printed with Emma's new ex's face.

Instead, I'm staring at a text from Laney telling me that Emma's back and camping out at Theo's old place on their dad's property just outside of town, and that she's requested that she not have company.

Any company.

Or that anyone else is told where she is.

Laney adds that it's because she's feeling super vulnerable after being the subject of a massive viral video at such a horrible time, but naturally, paranoia, guilt, and anxiety make me wonder if that's all it is.

And how much she might blame me for the video having to happen at all.

I'd still bring wine and chocolates and bread, even if she wanted to yell at me and cry, if it meant we could work it out.

I move on to the next text message thread. I need something else to concentrate on if I'm going to successfully get through today. The Mercedes isn't in the parking lot, but that means virtually nothing considering I watched Zen take it out solo last evening after we had all retreated to our respective townhomes.

Decker apparently hasn't slept since we all left Silver Horn early last evening. I have a string of texts from him at various intervals all night indicating he was diving deep into everything he could find on Greyson Cartwright.

Decker probably does have writer's block if that's what he was doing all night.

Poor guy. I should send him some Writer's Tears whiskey.

But his brothers have likely beat me to it.

During his all-nighter, he dug up some new information.

Like that Grey's divorced, and it was ugly.

Accusations of cheating on both sides. Arguments over who broke which part of the prenup. A whole series of videos his ex-wife posted on social media about how to love a man who ignores you regularly. Grey's sister going public, taking her sister-in-law's side and calling him cold and uncaring.

Grey's public defense going radio silent after that.

Cold and uncaring sticks with me.

That doesn't jive with the man I met in Hawaii.

The man I met in Hawaii was funny and kind and all-in with doing good deeds with me.

And then there was an utterly killer text in the string of texts from Decker. *Look at this dog. He had a dog. It's fucking adorable. And his ex got it in the divorce. I'd be a cranky-ass bastard too if someone took this dog from me.*

I clicked the last link to Instagram and instantly wished I hadn't.

It's a picture of Grey in sweatpants, jogging on a path with the most adorable chocolate lab, his tongue hanging out crooked, his legs all akimbo while he ran too, looking like a total goofball who would be so easy to love.

The dog, I mean.

Grey just looks *hot*.

The fucking *nerve*. I prefer men that I've slept with who are now unexpectedly my boss—which has *never* happened and I hope will never happen again—aren't hot when I'm remembering that they were kind and funny and generous while I'm simultaneously being told there is a *story* behind his divorce.

But the biggest kicker?

The dog's name.

Duke.

He told me his name was his dog's name.

And now my heart is melting a little more.

My phone lights up with a text as I'm staring at the picture.

Final thing, Decker says. *Turns out Grandpa was at Carnegie Mellon the same time as both of GC's grandparents. Guess Chandler and GC were both legacy admissions. Wonder if they knew that? And now I'm off to boycott all cereal and crackers that use the magic self-sealing bags. And to nap so I can write some words later.*

I wish him luck and thank him for the info, then check the messages from Lucky.

Didn't expect much, and that's what I get. It's just three GIFs of people falling asleep along with a message that he'd ask around his friend circle to see if anyone's up on the gossip once he's had enough rest to fully process the information he's getting, and also that he's pissed we went to Silver Horn without him.

And now I'm done with my text messages, and I have exactly one minute and thirty seconds to walk through the back door.

Time to get to it.

"C'mon, Jitter," I say. "Let's go shake it out and get inside."

Yes, he should go to doggy daycare.

Yes, I'm shamelessly using him to continue winning over Zen and Grey.

No, I won't apologize for it. Not when my family's café is on the line.

My pup whines with excitement while we get out of the car, shakes himself off, does his business, and gets it all done in time for me to get to work right on time, down to the second.

I'm bracing myself as I go in through the back entrance,

prepared for whatever today might throw at me, when I spot Zen where I'm half expecting their uncle to be standing.

If Zen's here and the car is not, I assume Mr. Mood Swing is also absent.

"Morning," they say, sliding a glance at Jitter. "Can you work the counter today?"

"I'd love to, but I can't," I chirp happily while I steer Jitter to his house, and honestly, I'm annoying myself here. I hate being fake happy. "I have this gossip problem that I'm trying to give up to make me a better employee, and if I work up front, people will tell me things, and then I'll repeat them, and it'll cause the equivalent of an international crisis here in the Tooth. But I have a little *welcome to Snaggletooth Creek* present for the boss-man. He around?"

There's a long, suspicious pause before an even longer, more suspicious, "No."

"It's actually from Jitter. He feels terrible for being too forward about making friends and drooling all over Mr. Cartwright's coat last night. Can I leave this on the desk for him?" I hold up a small stuffed pillow with Jitter's face on it—*thank you, Laney*—that I've attached a dry-cleaning gift certificate to with a red bow.

And I thought their first suspicious pause was long.

Rightfully so.

We both know it wasn't my or Jitter's fault that the man tumbled head over teacups in the parking lot last night. We probably both know this is a bribe attempt to get back on his good side too. And we both know I either had to pull some massive strings to get a present this perfect put together overnight, or that I randomly keep apology gifts on hand.

It's the latter. Though sometimes it's just a good deed gift.

Either way, I suspect Zen's thinking this isn't a very good gift at all, considering the man lost his dog to his ex-wife.

I'd be pretty upset if someone took Jitter from me at the end of a relationship, and I don't know if I'd want reminders that other people have their adorable pets still.

"Sure," Zen finally says, shooting another look at my dog that I interpret to mean *I can't wait until she's not watching so I can love all over you because you're adorable and perfect*.

I smile so hard my cheeks *and* my eyeballs hurt. "Fantastic. Thank you! Are you a breakfast person? Anything you'd like me to whip up for you today?"

They squint at me, but instead of questioning me, they shake their head, politely decline food, and go back out front where I can hear Cedar and Willa helping customers.

Such a weird spot to be in.

I know Grey wants to destroy this place. I suspect something happened between him and Chandler, but Zen doesn't trust me enough yet for me to tease details out of them, and Grey was so poker-faced last night when I half apologized for ghosting him in Hawaii that I don't think he'd tell me what he wants and why either.

And yes, it was only a half apology on purpose.

I wanted to see how he'd react and take it the rest of the way from there.

On the off chance he'd consider selling Bean & Nugget back to me—not that I can afford it on my own, but I have a massive community behind me and faith in myself—I need to not do anything to jeopardize my chances.

Anything *more*.

No more sleeping with him. No more flirting with him. No more hurting him. No more ghosting him.

Hence the present from Jitter.

And my continued cheerfulness.

The morning drags forever.

And ever.

And ever.

Zen checks on me occasionally, always with a look of *I want to trust you because you have a cool dog but I don't like people who hurt my uncle*.

Willa and Cedar whisper questions when they walk by about why I'm still being a stubborn ass and insisting on hiding from people in the kitchen.

"This is where I fit best right now," I tell them.

I got questions at Silver Horn last night too, and the only answer I'd give anyone was *come in to Bean & Nugget tomorrow. Don't give up on us just because we have new management. It's still great*.

No one will be able to tell Grey that I'm sabotaging him.

No one will be able to tell him I don't want this place to succeed.

But also, hopefully no one tells him about Silver Horn, because now that *we're sharing a wall* off-hours, I *need* the speakeasy to stay a secret.

I *need* the place I can go when I need to let my guard down. And with Laney and Theo in the throes of young love and Emma possibly never talking to me again, it's the best I've got when it's too late to bother Grandpa or my mom.

I'm scouring the grill controls with a toothbrush when I feel a presence behind me. Instead of turning, I start singing along with the radio.

"You are *not* that happy to be scrubbing a grill," Zen says.

"I love this place. I'll do anything to make it shine."

"Even though it's not yours anymore?"

"It hasn't been mine since my mom sold her share to Chandler's parents. So this isn't much different than it was a month ago."

There's silence, and I don't know if Zen's deciding if they want to ask more questions, and if so, which one first, or if Zen's deciding to walk away.

Did Grey assume that Chandler sold the café on behalf of the whole family and split the proceeds with us? Does Zen think the same?

I angle a glance at the silver back above the grill.

Zen's blurry reflection is still there.

They want the tea.

"Mom wanted me to go to college," I say. "We were in that spot where her regular profits from the café— moderate as they were, considering they were split three ways—on top of her income as a stylist pushed us into a tax bracket that got lower financial aid, but if she sold her part to her brother, I'd leave school with fewer loans. So she sold her third of Bean & Nugget to her brother."

"What did you major in?"

"Communication."

They make a noise that's clearly a stifled laugh.

"I know," I say. "Already mastered that. I should've

116

been like one of my other cousins and studied engineering or nursing."

"Why'd you hook up with Uncle Grey in Hawaii knowing you were just going to ghost him the next morning?"

Hello, direct questions. I pause in my scrubbing to turn and look them straight on. "I didn't head out that night with the intention of hooking up with anyone. All I wanted to do was make up for some of the bad that I did to one of my best friends by spreading some kindness in the world. He was supposed to be a random stranger I saved from an awkward situation at a bar, and instead, he was funny and charming and impossible to resist when he insisted on helping me do a few more good deeds."

They don't look like they believe me. Whether because *funny and charming and impossible to resist* doesn't fit their view of Grey or because they don't want to believe me is anyone's guess.

"I ghosted him because I was a supporting character in the viral video of the day, and he either hadn't seen it or he didn't recognize me or he was kind enough to pretend he hadn't. I thought he deserved way better than someone like me who was a complete and total disaster, but he was just so *nice* about wanting to know me better. I thought I was doing him a kindness in making a clean break. I left a note so he wouldn't worry."

They're studying me like they've sworn a blood oath of loyalty to the man who's apparently way more grumpy than he let on when we were in Hawaii and don't want to consider that I'm not the bad guy.

"And in case he left this part out," I add softly, "he gave me his dog's name as his own first."

They visibly startle. "Did he actually tell you about Duke?"

"No. Everyone in town is super curious who he is, and someone sent me a picture of him and the dog off his Instagram."

Now I'm getting the eyeball of *so it's true. You're the town gossip.* "Someone sent you a picture. You didn't go digging yourself."

"I'm off gossip."

"I hear you *are* the gossip."

"Small town. I'm not the only one."

"But you're the best?"

"*Was.* I'm recovering. Unless there's a critical reason in my life that I need to not be."

They are definitely suspicious.

As they should be.

"I am so curious why you haven't really pushed harder to find out why Uncle Grey would bail out Chippy from his internet gambling addiction," they say. "That seems like it would be a critical piece of information in your life."

I blink.

Blink again.

And then I burst out laughing instead of taking the opening. "*Chippy*?"

They shrug. "Whatever his name is. I also saw his wedding disaster video. I'm on Team Emma, obviously, because who wouldn't be? Word around town is you are too. Even though you're related to him."

"Can't choose your blood. He hurt us all in nearly unforgivable ways. He doesn't qualify as my family anymore."

They shudder like they get it, freeze, and then their

expression goes blank as the page I imagine Decker's staring at right now if he's up yet.

Note to self: Zen has family issues too.

According to a random note from the rest of Decker's research, Grey's maybe two or three years older than I am, so no more than thirty-two.

Zen's somewhere in their early to mid-twenties.

We're speculating that Grey's siblings are probably much older, or else *Uncle Grey* is a found family term.

Zen shoves away from the prep table. "When you're done with the grill, the fridge could use a serious tooth-brush scrub too."

"On it, mini-boss."

"I'm a foot taller than you."

"Eight inches, max, but you're still shorter than the mega-boss."

They suck one cheek into their mouth and head up front with their lips wobbling.

I silently high-five myself.

Zen doesn't trust me.

Yet.

But I amuse them. And I gave them gossip and asked for nothing in return.

People think gossip is all about being a blabbermouth.

To me, it's about listening. Observing. Reading between the lines. Digging deeper.

And waiting.

You don't get the best story in the first round.

You get it when you have all of the pieces. Zen's starting to give me pieces.

Whether they know it or not.

9

Grey

I AM NOT HIDING from Sabrina Sullivan—and all of my complicated feelings about her—when I send Zen in to Bean & Nugget solo on Tuesday morning.

It's a responsible business owner thing to get the ball rolling on selling the two other locations that I haven't seen yet. Plus, I'm taking advantage of the heated seats in the Mercedes to soothe the ache in my hip from last night's tumble. Today is about taking care of myself and giving myself some stress relief.

Even if I'm carrying my phone today.

Damn thing is *still* pinging off the hook.

Muting the conversations only goes so far when I can still see them every time I open my phone to text Zen about something.

But overall I'm being productive with starting the process of dismantling every bit of Chandler Sullivan's footprints. I start at Elk Knee, a town about five miles away as the crow flies but which takes me forty-five minutes to reach on the winding mountain roads that are lined with snow, sometimes slick, and apparently misleading, since I take the wrong turn at least three times.

When I finally locate the small shop, it's not open despite the posted hours indicating it should be. I can't reach the manager on the phone, and the neighboring business owner reports he hasn't seen any staff here in three days.

It's in line with Zen's report that they haven't had any contact with the staff here over email or phone in a few days either.

"Never made any sense that Bean & Nugget opened a shop here," the neighbor tells me. "We have two other coffee places that were already popular. Even more popular to argue over which one's better. Weren't gonna pick an outside café to get our coffee when which one of the original two you went to defines your personality here."

It's an easily confirmed story, and I leave town with the trunk of the Mercedes loaded with paper goods and non-perishable food that can be used in Snaggletooth Creek. I've already hired a real estate agent to get the building up on the market, so there's not much else left to do.

My next stop is a quaint little town called Tiara Falls, where Bean & Nugget Café is open but nearly empty of customers.

Despite the dearth of paying patrons, there are five employees hanging out in the kitchen. All five leap into action cleaning or doing inventory or prepping food for the lunch rush they insist is coming, though the books that

I've seen indicate it won't be enough to justify five employees running it.

I get the impression Chandler was in love with the idea of *having* a café empire in the mountains, but not in love with *doing the work* of running an empire.

Including market research.

"Is the other café in town that popular?" I ask the acting manager in Tiara Falls.

"It fits the theme," is the answer I get.

I don't immediately understand, but when I leave town, it starts to make sense.

Everything is fairy-tale themed. Including *Beanstalk*.

The *very* busy roastery on the next block that also serves light breakfast and lunch fare in line with what Bean & Nugget offers.

I've given half a thought to converting one of these locations to coworking space, but I don't need the extra income and the thought of being an office space landlord doesn't excite me.

Not the way changing Chandler's hometown location and putting a massive bee on the side of the building excites me.

He killed my research bees.

Intentionally.

And—shocker—set me up to take the fall for it.

So now he'll see a bee sitting on his family's building for the rest of his natural life.

I take my time enjoying the snowcapped mountain views on my way back to Snaggletooth Creek, stopping to get that SCOBY on the way. If it weren't so damned cold and slippery here—and also where Chandler Sullivan lives, even if he hasn't shown his face at the café yet—this would be a beautiful place to call home.

I could even see myself learning to ski. Or skate. Or snowshoe.

Which is definitely me in a warm, toasty, heated car talking, and not *actual* me. My fingers aren't tingling in the car. My toes aren't frozen. Not the way they were yesterday just being in the café.

When I pull into the Snaggletooth Creek Bean & Nugget parking lot after a quick stop home to get a batch of kombucha going, Sabrina's SUV is here, which gives me a hiccup in the heart area.

She hasn't quit.

Not actually a surprise, but it's still the first thought in my head.

Am I afraid she'll quit?

Or am I hoping she'll quit?

I don't know.

I just know she's in my head and I wish she could've been someone who didn't love this café so much. Because I could still be someone who likes her if she didn't want the exact opposite of what I'm here to do.

I'm contemplating how if I were in her shoes, the last thing I'd do would be to keep working for me as I pull open the kitchen door—where the first thing I see is Jitter.

He's sleeping in his massive house near the desk, front legs crossed and jowls twitching in his sleep.

The next thing I see is Sabrina herself.

She's at the sink, her back to me as I make my way through the kitchen, curvy hips shaking in her tight, dark jeans, the apron strings tied around her waist swaying, her curly red hair bouncing in time with her head bopping along to the pop music coming out of the café's speakers. She steps onto a stepstool and reaches to put a massive silver bowl up on the wire rack above with hands enclosed in bright yellow rubber kitchen gloves.

And she reaches.

And reaches.

Still shaking her hips.

Still bopping her head.

Her black T-shirt lifts to reveal creamy white skin above her waistband, and yes, my dick instantly notices.

What I wouldn't give to have never seen this woman naked.

Because it's all I can think of every time I look at her round, perfect ass.

Why couldn't she have been one of the worker bees here? Or better yet, the artist next door or a dental assistant up the street?

Someone I could ask out to dinner without worrying that she was only going with me because I own the café she always thought would stay in her family.

She's as far up on her tiptoes as she can go, and she still can't reach the upper rack to put the bowl away.

I head across the kitchen to help, and I'm nearly there when she jumps.

From the stepstool.

My entire world freezes while she's airborne.

"What the hell do you think you're doing?" I snap before I can stop myself.

She shrieks, stumbles on the landing, and the stepstool slides out from beneath her.

She shrieks again as her feet slide too.

The dog leaps to his feet, making an *aroo?* like he's confused but also ready to wake up and take on the world.

I practically fly the rest of the distance to her as her body sways and her arms flail.

She's teetering and falling.

She's falling because she was *jumping on a stepstool.*

I know how this ends, and I see it all happening in slow motion.

This ends with her banging her head on the sink, passing out, and crashing to the ground unconscious. Hurt.

Broken.

Bleeding.

Dying.

The dog charges through his doggy door with a yelp-bark.

I bump my sore hip against the prep table, almost trip over the dog, and lunge for her, grabbing her by the arm as she catches herself on the stainless steel sink with her free hand, spins so her back is to the sink, and recovers.

Without the actual need of my help.

Naturally.

Because she's some kind of beloved freak who can somehow defy even gravity, and *it's goddamn adorable.*

The next time Zen tells me I'm in a mood, I can tell you why.

It's because Sabrina Sullivan has seeped into my every waking thought and she's a terrible idea.

"Wow. Well." She straightens, then seems to realize how close I am as she slowly lifts her head to peer all the way up at me. "That wasn't how I saw my early afternoon going, exactly, but would you look at that landing? Apparently my mom thinking I was short enough to be a gymnast when I was little still has some benefits with dexterity and balance. But maybe don't startle people when they're standing on stepstools next time, boss-man? Yeah? Great. Good talk. Sit, Jitter. Mama's fine."

Zen, Willa, and Cedar all stare at us from the doorway to the dining room.

I'm still standing too close. I'm still gripping her arm.

I'm so close, when she breathes, her chest brushes my abdomen.

I need to step back.

But I don't want to.

I don't want to let go. Not when my brain is still full of images of her sprawled on the floor bleeding out from a head wound and adrenaline is sending my heart into over-drive and putting me at risk of getting my blood pressure into that zone that my doctor told me to avoid.

And especially not when I'm touching her skin with my bare hand, and she's radiating warmth and her breath is coming more rapidly and her eyes are going dark, and I know she feels this too.

I don't want to be attracted to this woman. I don't want to feel sympathy toward her. I don't want to fantasize about the noises she makes when I'm buried up to my balls inside of her and I don't want to remember how good it felt to make her laugh when she was so sad in Hawaii, or how many times I've thought of her since I left the islands.

I don't.

But I can't let go.

It feels too damn good to hold on to her no matter how much I logically know this is a bad, bad idea.

"Back, boss-man," she says. "Like I told my dog, I'm fine."

She delivers it with a smile, but there's a bite in her narrowing gaze.

I drop her arm like it's on fire and step back, nearly tripping over the dog again.

Zen's amused, which I only know because I know them well enough to spot the subtle smirk barely tipping up their mouth on one side as they stand in the doorway watching me.

The two other crew members watching us look mildly horrified.

"*Sabrina*," Willa says. "You should've asked for help."

Sabrina turns a grin on her as if she's completely immune to being near me.

She probably is.

This is a *me* problem.

"Wasn't much time between falling and catching myself," Sabrina says.

"*To put the higher dishes away*," the woman chides.

"You shouldn't be on kitchen duty at all," Cedar says. He's a tall, slender, younger man in a different Bean & Nugget apron, and I don't miss the not-so-subtle side-eye aimed at me.

Like he thinks I'm the one who's keeping her in here.

"I like kitchen duty," she tells him. "Reminds me of when I was little and Grandma was running this place. *Jitter. Sit.*"

The dog leans sideways against me. He's so big, his body rests against me mid-thigh, and he has no hesitation in pressing me away from Sabrina while he grins a happy doggy grin at me.

Being this near to a dog again is opening other old wounds.

I'm just off-balance enough now that being around another dog fucking *hurts* today.

This dog?

He belongs to Sabrina, and therefore, he's as off-limits as she is.

Self-preservation says he has to be.

It's not safe to like people who've already let you down, and it's even less safe to like people who have made it clear they want the opposite of what you do.

"The dog has to go," I tell Sabrina. "We can't have it in the kitchen."

It. That might be too far even for *Super Vengeance Man.*

But Sabrina doesn't blink at my attitude or my order. "Great! You can tell Shirlene when she gets here. She's the health inspector, by the way. You met her briefly yesterday, but you met so many people, I don't know if you remember which one she was. She asked me to bring him in today because she misses him since she moved in with her boyfriend. You're living in her old townhouse. First guest, actually, since she converted it into a vacation rental. I don't think she mentioned that part."

I'm momentarily speechless.

But only momentarily. "Don't you all have work to do?"

Willa eyes me.

Cedar eyes me.

Zen mouths something that looks like *they know.*

Know what?

That Sabrina and I slept together? That I can't convince myself to not like her? That I adore her damn dog?

While I'm still puzzling that out, all three of them head back to the dining room.

"Get your dog off me," I tell Sabrina.

She grins.

She grins.

And it has that damn *sparkle* to it. "Sorry. He licked you. That means you're his now. It's the rules. If you don't like it, I believe the mayor's coming in for a late lunch with Shirlene. You can see if she can get that rule wiped off the city books."

"I don't belong to people who lick me."

She blinks at me.

Just once, but she does.

And it's enough to take me back to my hotel in Hawaii where she did so much more than just *lick* me.

It's damn cold in here, and I'm sweating.

"Go *sit*," I tell the dog.

He stares at me forlornly for a beat too long, but then he ambles back across the kitchen to collapse dramatically to the floor inside his doggy house.

I look down at my fur-covered pants and stifle a sigh. Then I look up and find Sabrina righting the stepstool.

"What are you doing?"

"My job," she answers cheerfully as she climbs onto the damn thing and reaches to put another large stainless steel bowl on the high rack.

"Stop."

"Gotta get done."

I stroll back to her side, take the bowl, and put it up high myself. "Ask for help with the high shelves."

"I won't sue you if I hurt myself while I'm doing something stupid."

"And you were going to be right back." *Fuck*. I did it again.

I brought up Hawaii again.

"Would you have still spent that whole evening with me if you'd known who I was?" she asks.

"Irrelevant. You're not who I thought you were."

"People are complicated. I can be who you thought I was that night and also be who I am today. Just like you can be the guy who was randomly in Hawaii on Emma's wedding day after buying Chandler's café, which prompts a *lot* of questions, by the way, and also be the funny, kind, supportive person who helped a stranger having a bad day out of the goodness of his own heart."

"Digging for gossip?"

She hands me another bowl to put up high. "I was born exactly in that spot where you're standing. Jitter's doghouse? That little nook used to have a table where I'd do my homework while my grandma kept an eye on me when my mom was working. And she *does* work at a salon down the street. That dent in the wall next to the stove? My cousin Lucky's head print. He and Chandler were fighting over who got the last blueberry muffin and Chandler shoved him into the wall. Grandpa took blueberry muffins off the menu to punish them both, and Grandma never made another batch for either one of them. She *did*, however, make them for me and Emma and Laney whenever we'd sweet-talk her into them, which we generally only did when one of us had had a bad day."

I almost smile despite myself, because Mimi would've done the same.

Also, I love the idea of Chandler Sullivan being punished.

But I don't smile, because Sabrina hasn't earned my smiles again.

She points to the desk before going back to the dishes. "There are marks on the wall under the bulletin board where Grandpa tracked my mom and uncles' heights while they were growing up. My uncles had a mashed potato fight once fifteen years or so ago and there are probably still spuds behind the stove. I can tell you why those six floor tiles by the back door are different, why we don't have a more efficient coffee roaster, and who'd come back to work here and take this place to the next level with both our food and our coffee game now that Chandler's not involved anymore, but I'm off gossip. However, I'm not off doing whatever it takes to save my family's café. So if there's something you want to tell me about why your face twitches like that every time someone says *Chandler*, now would be a good time. I can help you. We can help each other. But only if you trust me."

Heat creeps up my neck again, but this time for an entirely different reason.

Trust her.

I trust exactly two people. Zen and Mimi.

I'm not putting my hard-won *Super Vengeance Man* suit in Sabrina's hands.

Not when she ghosted me. Not when she shares genes with Chandler Sullivan. And not when I'm rapidly picking up on the clues that she'll do anything she can to save this café.

"Maybe it's always been a dream of mine to run a kombucha bar in the mountains," I say.

"Big change from running your own research lab."

The heat gets hotter. "Doing a little googling?"

"No, I'm awful at it. I have friends that work computers much better than I do and who have made it their current life mission to help me." She hands me another bowl, this one soaking wet.

I grab the towel she was using. "Find anything else interesting?"

"I'm sorry about your dog."

My shoulders hit the ceiling tiles. "Off-limits."

"*Everyone* in town is looking you up. You get one chance to tell your story before they fill in the details."

"And how many details are you filling in for them?"

She pulls her soapy hands out of the water and looks me dead in the eye. "Only what they need to know."

"What *you* need them to know."

"Same thing."

"Like that I know about Mr. Shredded Wheat and his two girlfriends?"

She doesn't blink at that either.

Because she's that good?

Or because she lied about the gossip in Hawaii?

"I'm not threatening you," she says quietly. "I'm explaining to you how this town works. I can help you or I can stand in your way. Happy to do either. But I need to know what you *want* if you want my help."

For a split second, I'm back in Hawaii. Carefree. Light. Hustling to keep up with the whirlwind that was my temporary Duchess as she tried to make the world a better place.

I want that.

I *crave* that.

But it's not why I'm here.

"You left," I grit out.

133

She looks up at me for a moment longer, then nods slowly. "Got it. Good luck to you then."

That sounds ominous.

Worse, though?

It does nothing to cure the overwhelming curiosity about how different the next few weeks would be if I just kissed her.

Right here.

Right now.

"Sabrina?" Willa sticks her head into the kitchen. "Shirlene's here."

Sabrina smiles. "Jitter and I will be right out."

Moment over.

She's gone.

And I think I just lost her.

Again.

10

Sabrina

AFTER WORK, Jitter and I take a hike, visit Grandpa for a few minutes, and then head back downtown to meet Laney and a few other friends at House of Curry for a low-key engagement party for one of the owner's grandsons. The restaurant is on the next block down from Bean & Nugget, but it feels seven thousand worlds away.

Nani Parvati's restaurant isn't in danger of being taken over by someone who wants to gut the Tooth's favorite Indian restaurant. Her kids and grandkids are all ready to keep running it into eternity. Unlike Chandler, whose favorite part of his job was driving around to the various locations and telling people what they were doing wrong, Nani Parvati's family is always in the kitchen or working the dining room, laughing and joking and teasing each other in the best way.

Jitter shakes it all out outside, and then we join the party.

The restaurant's about two-thirds full and still open to the public, so it feels like half the community is wandering through tonight.

I get asked a few dozen times how the new Bean & Nugget owner is.

I smile and report things are great at every opportunity. Whatever Grey's issues with Chandler, they're separate from my own desire to make sure my cousin doesn't get to think he's hurting me too.

Is that petty? Or is it self-protective?

I don't even know these days.

Laney's parked at a table in the corner of the red-walled building, and Jitter and I finally make our way to her. Devi, the owner of the gallery next to Bean & Nugget and one of Nani Parvati's grandkids who isn't going into the family business, is sitting with her.

"How's the new boss?" Devi asks me when I slide into the booth next to her. She's in overalls that are speckled with all colors of paint, as are her brown cheeks and her thick black hair that's tied up in a messy bun.

"Grumpy," I reply cheerfully.

Laney makes a *what's wrong with you?* face, and I realize I'm doing it here too.

I'm faking the cheerful.

Necessary outside of this booth.

Inside the booth, probably not so much.

"Grumpy and hot?" Devi prompts.

Ugh. Unfortunately.

The look on his face when I almost fell while doing dishes—that intense focus—was exactly the same as it was our night in Hawaii. And then the way he watched me while he helped me finish the dishes—someone pass me an ice bath.

I can tell you why he made me feel good.

It was because the minute that hotel door closed behind us, the world ceased to exist, and Duke—*Grey*—made me feel like I *was* the entire world.

I'm not surprised he's a researcher or that he'd hold a patent for something amazing. He's intense when he focuses. That likely serves him well in the lab.

Laney hides a smile behind a bite of veggie korma.

I clear my throat. "I think he's overwhelmed at the change in climate from the West Coast and the pace that things move in small mountain towns."

Devi's brown eyes light up. "Ooh, right, he came from California, didn't he?"

"That's what I hear."

Both women eye me.

Laney with *are you seriously pretending you're still off gossip?*, Devi with *is that all you've heard?*

"How's your leg?" I ask Laney, even though I *want* to ask her how Emma's doing, which I won't do unless we're completely alone.

I've been smiling through all of the questions I've gotten about her the past week and a half too. *Runaway-mooning* has turned into my standard answer.

Laney pulls a face. "Annoying. Don't tell Theo I said that though, or he'll make it his new mission to make me more comfortable."

"And that's a bad thing?" Devi asks.

Laney shakes her head. "It's a good thing. But I think he's itching to go snowboarding or to do *anything* other than sit still in his house for one more day, and he won't if he thinks I can't survive eight hours without him."

"He's surviving this party without you."

"I asked him to fix me lasagna for lunch tomorrow, and he took off for the market over in Elk's Knee since he says they have the freshest ingredients for the homemade sauce it needs, and he needs to start it before they open tomorrow."

Laney hates lasagna.

Which means Theo's probably actually doing something with or for Emma.

My heart squeezes. I want to be helping too, but for the first time in my life, *I don't know how.*

"You two are so cute." Devi turns to me. "Almost as cute as a petite redhead being caught in the arms of her devastatingly handsome and stupidly tall new boss in her café's kitchen."

"I'm off gossip," I tell Devi. "If you want the scoop, you'll have to go back to whoever told you that."

Devi laughs.

Laney sighs.

Jitter rolls his eyes.

Okay, he doesn't. He puts his head in Laney's lap and gives her puppy dog eyes like he can't stand it when anyone is less than happy, and her sigh says she's less than happy, and he wants to know what he can do to make it better.

"Is this no-gossip thing because of the wedding?" Devi asks me.

"Yep," Laney replies for me. "I'm against this plan, for the record. Especially since Bean & Nugget's new owner—"

138

"Is planning to convert it into a kombucha brewery?" Devi finishes for her. "I heard he's calling it a *kombrewchery*, which is a dumb word. So I agree. Sabrina needs to use all of everything she has to make sure Bean & Nugget stays Bean & Nugget."

"Who told you?" I ask.

"Frannie. Her mailman's niece's boyfriend is one of the three local contractors that were asked for quotes."

I almost groan.

"Is that wrong?" Devi asks.

"No, that's correct." *I will not howl in frustration. I will not howl in frustration.* "It's just—" I cut myself off and shake my head. "I feel a little out of my league to do whatever I need to do to change his mind," I finally say.

"You are *never* out of your league," Devi says.

"I am now."

Laney eyes me.

I give her a slight shrug and hope she interprets it as *if he were the same guy he'd been in Hawaii, I'd have a chance.*

There are moments when I feel like he's the same, quietly watching me and taking me all in. And then the next minute, he's closed off and guarded.

No heart-stopping, crinkly blue-eyed smiles. No pushing to know more about me. No insisting he's a truly terrible person at heart while he pauses to pick up a piece of trash or tell someone he loves her shirt.

"You ever talk to Chandler?" I ask Devi.

Her brown eyes sparkle in amusement. "So you're *not* totally off gossip."

"I haven't seen him since the wedding. I haven't even heard anyone's seen him since the wedding, and I'm frankly pretty happy about that. Just wondering if—*when* I should brace myself for a confrontation. Since the Bean & Nugget situation is his fault."

"I'm on gossip," Laney says to Devi. "You can tell me everything. Have you talked to him? I want to know how he set up this sale so quietly and how he knows this—*ah!*"

Jitter clamors to his feet under the table and bumps her leg.

"*Jitter,*" I say softly. "Down, boy."

He ignores me and strains on his leash.

At the same time, I realize a slight hush has fallen over the restaurant.

And then there's the tickle between my shoulder blades filling in the rest of the blanks before I spot the tall figure towering over everyone else.

Grey's here.

He's paused just inside the doorway, looking around at the clumps of people gathered between the tables like this is a private party.

"It's the new café owner," goes through the dining room in a lightning-fast whisper.

"Holy *hotness,*" Devi breathes as she turns to look.

"He is—wow," Laney adds, twisting as much as she can with her leg still sticking out on a spare chair to get a better view herself.

"*Personality,*" I remind her.

She smirks. "Okay, Ms. Good Deeds."

"Mr. Greyson," Nani Parvati calls. "You come in. Come have dinner. Meet my grandson and granddaughter-in-law-to-be. Have dinner."

"Nani, you said 'have dinner' twice," Devi's brother says.

"It's the most important."

Everyone laughs.

Everyone except Grey.

He's in jeans and a button-down oxford under his thick wool coat, wearing gloves and his beanie and that beard that he's growing out, and he's more deer-in-the-headlights than I've seen him since I rescued him in Hawaii.

"Dammit," I mutter while the locals descend on him.

"What's he doing here?" Devi whispers. "You have food at Bean & Nugget."

"He came from San Diego," Laney whispers back. "He's probably used to more options for dinner than soup, sandwiches, and pastries."

"Or maybe someone invited him," I say.

"Or he's casing Nani's joint to take it over next," Devi says.

I don't think owning an entire town is his style.

But I do think he'll be as popular with the single crowd here in the Tooth as Jitter is nearly everywhere we go.

Locals are already converging on him. Probably asking the same questions they asked me, but they get to go right to the source.

A few people glance at me like they want to see if I'm reacting at all to Grey's presence.

I pretend I don't notice.

But I do get a little nervous when I realize Kayla Swoosy's talking to him.

She's a retired Olympic trampolinist. Yes, it's a thing. Yes, she did it. But the more important part here?

"What's that look?" Laney asks me. "Why are you making that face?"

"You know how I'm off gossip?" I whisper.

"I know how you keep saying that."

"I...told my new boss...some details about people around town that aren't entirely accurate when I...told him...that I was giving up gossip because I didn't want to know certain things about certain people anymore."

It's not every day that I manage to surprise multiple people around me, but I have clearly done it now.

"You told him gossip about us?" Devi whispers.

"*I changed details.*"

"Names? Situations? What?" Laney asks.

"It depended on what came to me first. But I used code names instead of actual names. And I changed details about who did what. Sometimes better than others. Like, I implied I'm related to an Olympic curling champion whose parents are swingers. And that there was once a huge war in town between the ice cream shop owner and the local spa owner over the spa owner's duck regularly pooping in the ice cream shop owner's yard. That sort of thing."

"*Nani Parvati* and Mr. Monroe had an argument over a taxidermy donkey, which is the closest thing I can even begin to think of to match that second one," Devi says with a glance at Grey and Kayla. "And Kayla's an Olympic medalist, but her mom is single. And you're not related. Or have any relatives who would be—*oh my god.*" She slams her hands on the table, making both Laney's plate of food and Jitter jump. But she lowers her voice and leans in as she whispers, "*Are Chandler's parents swingers?*"

"No, but they have an open marriage," I whisper back when I'm sure no one else is listening.

"*Does Emma know?*"

I jerk straight, scaring Jitter, who dives under the table,

bumps his head, and almost makes Laney's drink spill for shaking the surface.

"*Is she talking to Chandler?*" I demand.

"Abso-fucking-lutely fucking not," Laney replies firmly while she straightens her meal back in front of her.

Devi and I both stare at her. Laney's not one to drop multiple fuck-bombs in a single two-word sentence.

She goes a little pink in the cheeks. "Theo's exact answer when I asked him the same question."

"Because he doesn't want her to, or because he knows for himself that she's not?" Devi asks.

"Both," Laney answers.

"She's home?" Devi presses. "I didn't think anyone had heard from her."

"She was scheduled to get home this weekend," is Laney's cagey response. "Theo's been demanding proof-of-life updates. He's also spent some time at her house this week, clearing out all of Chandler's stuff to take to Fiona Bell's house."

That takes a second to register, and when it does, I get my first real laugh in a week.

Fiona runs an online recycled art store with a specialty in jewelry made from reclaimed junk. She's also Snaggle-tooth Creek's most prominent Wiccan practitioner.

It's a good interest combination.

She cleanses the auras of anything she recycles before she sells it. Everything on her site is guaranteed curse-free.

Ah, fuck.

I told Grey about Fiona and her war with her neighbor.

To the best of his knowledge, I was talking about a water rights war between Ms. Sharpie and Mr. Leprechaun.

143

It's actually about a greenhouse straddling a property line and whether or not she was growing poison ivy for use in spells on him.

And *him* is one of the triplets who gets super mad when I talk about it, so I never say which triplet.

I love the triplets too much to divulge any more than that.

"So they're definitely *over*-over?" Devi asks.

Laney nods while she pushes Jitter out from under the table. "That is the one thing that's crystal clear in the whole situation." She looks at me. "Will your new boss figure out who you were talking about, or do we need to do damage control?"

"I think he's writing me off as a liar, and I changed a *lot* of details, so we're probably good. But it might not be a bad idea for a few more people to tell him some incorrect gossip so he quits worrying about what I might've told him."

Devi squints at me. "There's something you're not saying."

"It's—"

"Addison Hunter at three o'clock," Laney says quickly.

Devi and I both whip our heads around.

Shit.

She's right.

Addison's here.

Addison's here, and she's angling up to Grey like she has every intention of asking him to head back to her place.

Over my cold, dead, gossip-loving body.

"Jitter, you win," I tell him. "Let's go see your new BFF."

"Aww, Jitter likes him?" Devi says.

"Jitter likes everyone."

Except Addison.

I have forbidden him from liking Addison.

And I tell myself Addison is the only reason I'm rising from my seat to cross the room with my dog and rescue Grey.

Again.

If he wanted to talk to Devi, or Laney, or Kayla, or *whoever*, I don't care.

But Addison?

No.

No.

The minute I lift my head to plot my path across the restaurant, he makes eye contact with me as if I'm the only person in the room.

Once again, my breath catches in my throat.

Exactly the way it did when he flew to my side to keep me from falling after he startled me in the kitchen earlier, which I am actively not thinking about.

Not thinking about the fear in his eyes.

Not thinking about the way his breath was coming too fast.

Not thinking about the strong grip of his long fingers wrapped around my forearm.

Not thinking about the conflicted emotions that danced across his face when he realized he was giving himself away.

He cares.

But the fact that he clearly doesn't want to and keeps bringing up how I left him in Hawaii is a major red flag, waving in the wind, broadcasting *I have trust issues and I'm ridiculously attracted to you still and pissed about it.*

And what do I do with red flags?

I have one-night stands with them.

That's my dirty little secret. It's in my DNA to go for the guys that I know aren't relationship material.

Until Hawaii, but that was safe because I was never supposed to see him again.

He stares at me a beat too long before turning back to Addison and whatever she's saying as she crowds him too close for my comfort. I say a quiet thanks to the cappuccino gods that it takes me about ten seconds to reach his side.

"Hey, you made it," I say as I let Jitter stick his nose in Grey's crotch and stand too close to him, craning my neck as I look up. "I didn't see you come in. Have you gotten a plate yet?"

Those blue eyes focus in on me with a mixture of distrust and intrigue. "I made it," he repeats slowly.

I smile.

And wink.

His guard goes up so fast, it's a wonder everyone on the whole block can't feel the aftershocks.

"I see you've met Addison," I say. "She posted Emma's wedding video online."

"*Oh my god*, Sabrina," Addison yelps.

"She did," someone behind me mutters. "I saw it on her TikTok first."

"Have you ever made a mistake, Grey?" the slimy little backstabbing asshole says to him.

I touch his elbow and lean into him. "Oh, you can *bet* he has."

She looks down at my hand.

He looks down at my hand.

At least three people around us suck in a collective breath.

Why, yes. Yes, I have just used body language to communicate that he is *mine*, and they can all *back the fuck up*.

It's mostly for Addison's benefit.

On a scale of one to ten, she can suck mud out of a straw every time she's thirsty for the rest of her life for all I care.

"I have definitely made mistakes in my life," Grey says slowly, "but I don't think I've ever stabbed a friend in the back for a few minutes of fame."

"Isn't he sweet?" I say to Devi's brother, who's leaning in with his new fiancée, listening closely to all of us.

"I'd go with smart," Isabella murmurs behind us.

"That too," I toss over my shoulder with a smile.

Grey leans just out of my reach to bend and simultaneously scratch Jitter behind his big, floppy brown ears while pushing him out of his crotch.

Addison looks at me, then at Grey, then back to me. You can *see* the wheels turning.

The extrapolations.

The calculations.

The excitement at what she's sniffing out as news. *Can I be the first one to tell the entire town that Sabrina's dating her boss?*

"You do *not* want to do that," I say softly, still smiling. "Not to *me*."

Jitter pushes against Grey's legs while the man himself watches me have a stare-down with the woman who became my mortal enemy when she uploaded Emma's wedding video all over social media.

She shouldn't even be here.

She works in Denver.

And—as off gossip as I am—I would've heard if she'd lost her job or had decided to move home.

Also, being off gossip doesn't mean I wouldn't drop every secret I know about Addison to get her to back the fuck off and mind her own damn business.

She goes a teensy bit pale. "I heard Emma's home."

"Have you also heard Theo has about a dozen get-out-of-jail-free cards from the sheriff?" I ask.

She fully blanches now.

I still don't blink. "Grey, you haven't eaten yet. Come on. Let's get you some dinner."

"Nice to meet you," he says to Addison, and I feel like we're back in Hawaii.

Playing off each other. Not hating each other. Not trying to sniff out an angle.

The suspicion is still there, but that could be my imagination.

Or my conscience.

"Off gossip, hmm?" he murmurs to me as I tug Jitter along to make a path for us through the crowd and up to the counter.

"Don't test me when it comes to the people and things I love."

"I didn't need a save."

"You would've preferred to *not* know who she was and what she did?"

He doesn't answer.

148

We reach the counter, and Nani Parvati eyeballs me. "You don't date."

"Correct."

"You look very cozy."

"Whatever he wants, put it on my bill, please."

Grey makes a noise. "I'm paying for my own dinner."

"And whatever he orders," I add, ignoring him, "can you double the naan and add in dessert?"

"Anything you want, Sabrina."

"I do *not* need extra anything, and I'm paying for my own dinner," Grey repeats.

"Nonsense." Nani Parvati snorts delicately. "Your money is no good here. You saved Bean & Nugget. You get dinner from me or from Sabrina, but you don't pay for yourself."

His beard moves like his jaw's ticking beneath it.

Jitter wags his tail harder and keeps staring at Grey like the man hung the moon.

Traitor.

"I'm not another of your good deeds," Grey mutters to me.

"Sorry, boss-man. Looks like you are. If you don't pick what you want, Nani Parvati and I will surprise you."

"We will surprise you anyway," she agrees. "Go sit. I will get you dinner."

"I don't—" Grey starts, but that's as far as he gets before someone knocks into him from behind.

Which would be fine, except it makes him stumble, and however he stumbles makes Jitter yelp, and when Jitter yelps, he shoves Grey sideways.

Right into Marley, my neighbor with the adorable little girl, Aspen.

Who's carrying a plate loaded with butter chicken.

Which smushes all over Grey's button-down and his coat.

I try to make a noise, but nothing will come out.

Jitter whimpers and huddles against my legs.

"Oh, I am *so sorry*," Marley starts, but she barely gets it out before a piece of naan goes whizzing past her ear.

"Hey!" someone yelps.

"Who threw that?" Nani Parvati yells.

No one answers.

But someone shrieks near where Laney and Devi are sitting, and when I look back, Laney is very poorly stifling the most *impish* grin I've ever seen on her face, and Devi's staring slack-jawed.

"Someone threw food on me!" Addison cries.

"Food fight!" someone who sounds *remarkably* like Lucky calls.

And then it's game over.

Nani Parvati's eyes go wide. She opens her mouth, dodges left as a samosa sails straight at her, and retreats to the kitchen.

I'm alternating between gaping at Laney—*she started a food fight*—and shoving napkins at Grey. "I'm so sorry," I babble along with Marley, both of us ducking and dodging flying food in a way that Grey can't.

He's massive.

Tallest guy in the room.

Widest guy in the room.

Even when he's trying not to be a target, he's getting creamed with tandoori chicken and biryani and chana masala. Vindaloo and korma.

"We usually just eat it," Marley says while we both

desperately try to wipe off the increasing number of food stains all over him.

Jitter lunges for an overturned bowl of kheer.

Grey's blocking his head with his arms. "Is this because I'm changing the café?" he asks.

"Every once in a while, we get out of control," Marley says. "Theo's usually involved."

"*Theo's not here*," someone snaps.

"But his girlfriend is," I whisper.

Marley and I make eye contact.

We both slide a look at Laney.

She's coated in something green, and she's laughing her ever-loving ass off.

"*Cover your cast*," Devi shrieks.

"Dammit," I whisper.

"*Hey*," a booming voice calls from the doorway. "Break it *the fuck* up."

The food stops flying.

Theo strides in the door, glaring at everyone. "If my girlfriend's cast has to be reset, I will pay *every single fucking one of you* back with cat shit in your mailboxes. And worse."

Marley fans herself.

She's not the only one.

"Is that the porn star?" Grey mutters to me while he wipes cucumber sauce out of his hair.

"*Naked motivational knitter*," I reply. Jitter's still trying to eat, and I'm still trying to separate him from his dessert.

"Zen's coming themself next time they want curry."

I try to repress a snort of laughter, and I fail.

Miserably.

"I am so sorry," Marley says again, but she's only half paying attention.

The rest of her is watching Theo lift Laney out of the booth where she's mostly escaped the food fight unscathed.

If he hasn't figured out she did this to herself, he will soon enough.

And they'll probably both laugh their heads off all night long about it.

Which shouldn't be what makes my eyes hot with tears again, but it is.

I want that.

I want someone to laugh with and wreak havoc with and someone to tell all of my secrets to.

I just don't *believe* in it. No matter how much I started wishing I did after Hawaii.

"Is your car coated in dog fur?" Grey asks.

I clear my throat and blink quickly while I stare at Jitter. "Of course."

"Good. It can get covered with food too. You're giving me a ride home."

That sounds like a threat.

And macchiatos help me, I am here for it.

11

Grey

Sabrina doesn't argue about taking me home.

But she does make me squeeze into the back seat with Jitter, who drools all over me and tries to eat dinner off of my clothes while my knees are pressed against the passenger seat in front of me on the short drive.

Although now that I'm in the car with her, I wonder if she's actually taking me home, or if she's planning on pulling some mountain woman driving move and tossing me out of the car and over a cliff.

"Are you always so blunt?" I ask her as we leave downtown.

Why not?

She *did* come to my rescue again.

She doesn't ask what I mean. "When I have to be."

"Was that Ms. Cheerios?"

She makes eye contact with me in her rearview mirror.

Her SUV is one of the smaller models and I'm scrunched in back here.

Especially with the dog taking up two-thirds of the back seat.

I smell like an Indian buffet, and I should be looking forward to getting out of here and showering. And since the townhouse neighborhood is so close, it'll be maybe a three-minute drive.

I get a shower *soon*.

Instead, I want her to tell me what *Addison*'s code name was.

Was she Ms. Cheerios who ruined the pompom competition in high school? Or Mr. Arby who was the talk of the town after the car wash went wrong?

I know she switched genders and fudged details, and since I met Kayla the trampolinist in the past half hour and figured out that her parents are *not* running an illegal craps table in the basement of a local art gallery—she said her mom runs the local grocery store and volunteers at a pet shelter—I'm realizing just how much of a puzzle Sabrina gave me.

I'm *intrigued*.

About all of them.

I want to figure this out.

I want to figure it out almost more than I want to see the look on Chandler Sullivan's face after I put a giant-ass bee on the building that built him.

"No," Sabrina finally says.

"The woman who made the wedding go viral isn't Ms. Cheerios?"

"Correct."

"Who is she?"

"I didn't tell you anything about her."

"Why not?"

"Because I was too hurt and mad at her when we met to find a different story for what happened, and I didn't want to talk about her."

I don't know if I believe her or not. The story rings true, but that doesn't mean it's not another puzzle. "What else do you know about her?"

"Nothing."

"Because you forgot?"

"Yep. I'm off gossip."

"You just made sure I knew I was talking to the second-biggest villain in town. Are you sure you're off gossip?"

"It's my new life mission to get everyone off of gossip. Best way to do that is to make sure other people who gossip know the consequences of their actions."

She doesn't ask who I think is the biggest villain in town.

But I'm watching her in the rearview mirror.

I know that little phrase landed. I'm nearly certain she's curious what I meant and has her own suspicions.

"You saved me from walking into a trap and potentially telling all of my deepest, darkest secrets to someone who'd spill them on the internet," I say. "This feels like using your powers for good."

She slams on the brakes, and I realize we're here.

Back in the little neighborhood.

"Here you go," she says. "Front door service. Thank you for flying Jitter Airlines. Be sure to watch your head as you depart."

"Was any of it the truth?"

She meets my gaze again, and she doesn't have to answer me.

I can see it in the *who do you think you are to get all of my truth?* in her bright green eyes. "That's for me to know and people who trust me to find out. Now, get out before I take back the gift card Jitter gave you and use it for having my car dry-cleaned instead."

"I didn't want to be your good deed for the day again."

"I don't want you to be my good deeds again either. So stop needing me, please."

She doesn't mean it.

Not *rudely*, anyway.

Meanwhile, I completely mean that I didn't *want* to be her good deed, but I'm not actually sorry that I was.

I wouldn't have told Addison what's-her-face any of my secrets, but that doesn't mean I wouldn't have felt like a fool if I found out later that she was the original poster of the viral wedding video.

Would've felt a little too much like being back with the rest of my family.

I scratch the dog behind the ears. "Later, Jitter."

Sabrina shoots me another look.

This one is more complicated.

I think it says *I know you like my dog, and I know why, but I'm not going to tell you how I know why so you'll wonder if I really know or not.*

Zen asked if I was cut out for vengeance.

Not so sure today.

So instead of pondering it, I let myself into the townhouse next door to Sabrina's.

It's small and simple, but cozy. Comfortable tan leather

sofa with brightly colored throw pillows facing a stone fireplace with as large of a television as will fit over it. Mountain sunset print over a low wooden bookshelf stocked with a healthy selection of reading material on the lone full white wall in the living room, with a fake plant and a colorful swatch of fabric on the angled wall along the staircase.

I like it more than I thought I would. It feels like a place you could have a kid and a dog and where you love your neighbors.

I'm getting out of the shower when Zen gets home. They drove the Mercedes back here from the café after I let them know about the food fight. Which they had already heard about through the local gossip chain.

"Did you eat, or did you just wear it?" they ask when I descend the stairs in wet hair, sweatpants, and a hoodie.

"Just wore it."

"And then you took a ride from *Sabrina*." They sing her name like we're ten-year-olds on a playground.

"Didn't want to get the Mercedes dirty."

"Or you like her."

"No." Yes. No. Maybe.

I would like her if she worked somewhere else and if I were in a place where I could like people.

Where I could like *women*.

Which I don't see happening again in my lifetime for anything more than short-term flings.

Exactly like we had in Hawaii.

And where she gave me the biggest puzzle of my life, which has me more intrigued than it should.

I wish she'd truly been from Jawbone, Virginia.

Zen watches me like they know my internal debate with myself. "You should like her."

"Because you like her dog?"

"No, because she's like you."

"What does that mean?"

"That despite having some shitty family, she's a good person."

"She's winning you over."

They throw up their hands in exasperation. "If you hadn't slept with her in Hawaii, would you still think she was the bad guy?"

"Yes." No. I don't think she's the bad guy.

I *want* to believe she's the bad guy so that I can sleep at night, face her at work, and keep focused on what I need to do to convert the café that's currently lining *my* pockets with a decent profit for a café without the guilt that's starting to creep into my gut.

Zen's glaring.

That doesn't happen often.

"*Uncle Grey.* You're being ridiculous. Is Chachi an asshole? Yes. But Sabrina's keeping that café running, everyone here loves her even if they whisper to not get on her bad side, which I wish people would say about me, by the way, and I really don't think she has any ulterior motive beyond keeping what's been normal for as long as she can. And the people here *love* the café. She's not doing it for the money. She's doing it for her family and her friends and her community. What about that says *bad guy*?"

None of it.

Absolutely none of it.

"*Ask her for help*. Do this with her instead of in spite of her," Zen says.

"Where's my puzzle from yesterday?"

"*Ugh*. I'm going to the movie theater. They're showing *When Harry Met Sally*. But you stay. I don't want you to come with me."

"You know your obsession with Nora Ephron movies is the reason I can't trust your judgment about people, right?"

I get a double middle finger.

Probably deserve it.

Honestly, I kinda enjoy it.

"Can you at least light a fire before you go?" Yes, I'm pushing my luck here.

But it's fun.

I miss fun.

And I'm finding fun here.

I'll apologize to Zen for being a cranky prick tomorrow.

Probably.

Depends on how long they rant and rave at me.

Not that either of us can generally stay mad at the other for long.

"Here's an idea," they say. "*Ask her out. Talk to her*. Go bang her again. Talk to her some more. And then tell me you don't respect the hell out of the fact that she loves the café that Choochoo Sullivan hasn't once even *driven past* since you bought it off of him."

"*Choochoo*?"

"Way to miss the point, Uncle Grey. I'm out." They stalk back to the door, keys jangling in their pocket. A blast of cold air makes every part of me shrivel as Zen yanks it wide open.

And then makes a stifled *urp!*

"Oh, hello dear. So sorry to startle you," a woman says in a very proper British accent. "I'm Bitsy. Live just down the way there. Are you the new owner of Bean & Nugget?"

I run a hand through my damp hair and step behind Zen. "Hello. I'm Grey. I bought the café."

A slender Black woman with the barest hint of gray in her short hair is standing on my porch. Her dark gaze lifts to meet mine, and a broad smile crosses her features. "Ah, so *you* are the mysterious Mr. Cartwright I've been hearing so much about. Lovely to meet you, Grey. As I told your friend, I'm Bitsy."

Manners take over, and I hold out a hand. "Hello, Bitsy. This is Zen."

Bitsy's beam glows brighter while she shakes hands with both of us. "Welcome to Snaggletooth Creek. My children love the café. *Love* it. They spend more time there than they do with me. Coffee lovers, the lot of them. Not a bit of respect for tea. Not like you, I hear. I blame my husband." She thrusts a colorful cloth bag at me. "I heard about what happened at House of Curry. I thought you might appreciate a home-cooked meal after your hasty exit, and I just happened to have extras. It's not quite chicken vindaloo and chana masala, but here's a pot roast, macaroni and cheese, roasted vegetables, and a sticky toffee pudding for your sweet tooth."

I stare at her, momentarily unsure how to respond.

She has this as *extras*?

"*Bitsy*. This is too much," Zen says.

"Psh. It's nothing for the people who kept our favorite café from ruination. Grey, do stop by soon for a proper cup of tea. I'm on the next block, the red door with the sassy welcome mat. You'll know it when you see it. But now, go. Eat. While it's hot." She winks. "And before someone throws it at you. Very nice to meet you both."

"Thank you, Bitsy," Zen calls, but the older woman is already retreating down the short walkway in her long coat and boots.

Zen shuts the door, and the scent of roasted meat and cheese immediately hits the air.

My mouth waters.

Zen wipes their own mouth and takes the food to the kitchen, which has black appliances and white cabinets behind a half wall topped with a plain Formica counter-top, with a powder room and a laundry-slash-mudroom beyond it. The batch of kombucha that I started this after-noon is in a glass jar covered with cheesecloth on the counter. Need to start another batch with the rest of my SCOBY at Bean & Nugget tomorrow.

"That was unexpected," Zen says. "You think this tastes as good as it smells? Go. Sit. I'll find plates. I'm still mad at you, but I have forty-five minutes before I have to leave. You should buy cafés in small towns more often. Oh, look at this. Heh. Bitsy's husband owns the tavern by City Hall. Her note says to tell the staff who you are, and they'll take care of us anytime we come in. Including getting you *proper tea*."

"Is this a trap to convince me to not do anything to the café?"

They dig into the bag and come up with to-go boxes.

"Don't care. I'm all about the ruination of Chickpea Face, but I don't dislike this place."

"What if we were vegetarian?"

Zen digs into the drawers for silverware. "*Uncle Grey.* Everyone heard you tell Sabrina to put extra bacon on your sandwich after you got back today. Sit. Eat. Pretend to be happy. And warm. Even if I'm still frustrated with you thinking you can actually live with yourself under that *Super Revenge Man* cape."

"*Super Vengeance Man.* Get it right."

"Bad idea, worse idea. Same thing. You're not built for it."

I open my mouth, but instead of words coming out, warm roasted meat goes in, courtesy of my nibling.

My taste buds explode in joy.

Is this what those traditional Sunday dinners that normal families have taste like?

I've had food all over the world. I *like* food all over the world.

But there's something extra about this dinner.

We skip the plates and dive straight into the feast on the raised counter between the kitchen and the living room.

The macaroni and cheese makes me forget about the puzzles of Sabrina.

The vegetables make me forget it's cold outside.

The sticky toffee pudding makes me forget I'm here on a vengeance mission.

"I am totally making BFFs with Bitsy," Zen says with a contented sigh as they eyeball the leftovers that will feed us for at least one more meal. "Do you think she needs an extra kid? Or grandkid? I volunteer as tribute."

"Do you?" I ask.

They make a face at me. "I do in my head where it all goes the way I want it to. You do the dishes and put the food away. I'm stuffed. Do you think Bitsy needs a kidney? I'd give her one of my kidneys for that meal."

Between the food and my body warming up inside the cozy townhouse, I'm mellow enough to laugh at that.

They take off, and after I straighten and clean the kitchen, I head upstairs.

I need to distract my brain, and I have a puzzle up there.

The bedroom is as comfortable as the first floor. Queen-size bed. Rustic wood frame. Matching dresser. Plastic potted plant in the corner. A window looking out into the darkness, but which has an amazing view of snowcapped mountain peaks during the day. Poster print of a waterfall on the white wall that separates my rental from Sabrina's townhouse.

I stare at that wall entirely too long.

Maybe a puzzle wasn't the best thing to do in here.

Now I'm wondering what her relationship with Chandler is like.

If it's just as messed up as my relationship with my siblings.

If she'd get it if I told her why I have to do this.

Why I wanted so badly to see her sparkle and smile in the car while she was driving me home when I was coated in food and should've been irritated.

While ignoring all of my messages means that the barrage of texts have slowed down, I'm still sitting on one more note from my sister that I thought was *normal* until Zen crashed into my life seven years ago.

Uncle Grey, it's not okay for Aunt Camille to accuse you of not caring at all about her feelings just because you don't want to renew your membership to a country club that you never go to and never felt like you fit in at. When does she think about your feelings?

I don't need my sister to care about my feelings.

I need her—and the rest of them—to let me live my life on my own terms without constantly accusing me of trying to make them all miserable.

I don't care if they're happy or if they're miserable. I care that they do what they need to do to get themselves however they want to be all by themselves.

My phone dings as I'm reaching for it to shut it off, and there go my shoulders again.

It's Vince.

Bastard sent a photo of the lab I built with my first big paycheck, the place that I felt most at home, most free to be myself, and wants to know if I'm honestly going to let it fall into ruination when we all know that if I came back, I'd solve a few more problems for the bees and the world.

That spikes my blood pressure enough that I have to breathe through thick dots overtaking my vision for a few minutes before I quit shaking enough to shut my phone off and take it downstairs to let it charge overnight in the kitchen.

That.

That's why I'm here.

Because all of the people in my life think I'm a robot who doesn't care about anything, when the truth is, I care too much about everything.

Vince is right.

I should be in *my lab* right now. Where *I* own all of my

164

own research, where I'm free to work on any project I want and where I read that contract that he put in front of me instead of simply signing it on blind trust.

Instead, I'm on a mission to right the first of many, many wrongs, and everything about me righting a wrong feels wrong.

All because of what's on the other side of my bedroom wall.

I'm full.

I'm showered.

Teeth brushed.

Warm in sweatpants and a hoodie and wool socks.

Complex wooden puzzle of a jungle cat on the small desk in front of me.

Good light.

All of my basic needs taken care of.

And I can't get out of my own head.

A door closes on Sabrina's side of the wall. There's soft humming. I recognize the tune. Something catchy. A pop song that I've heard a million times at the café the past two days. Waverly Sweet sings it, I think.

It gets closer to the wall.

Closer.

Closer.

And then there's something worse.

A low buzzing noise.

Buzzing, but not bees.

Steady, louder, then softer, then louder again.

Like she's moving around something that's vibrating.

Every last ounce of me loses all focus on anything but the sound.

Sabrina Sullivan is mere feet away from me—separated

by a wall, but *mere feet* from me—and she's using a vibrator.

My cock goes hard so fast I feel like someone punched me in the gut, but in the good way.

And that's before I hear the low, soft, grunt-like that noise she made in the back of her throat when I was pounding into her while we were together in Hawaii.

I break out in a cold sweat, and my dick gets impossibly harder.

She's doing this on purpose, I tell myself. *She knows the walls are thin. This is psychological warfare and we are not engaging there too tonight.*

My cock doesn't get the message. It floods my brain with images of Sabrina, naked, thighs spread, pleasuring herself with a vibrator.

Is it a vibrating dildo? One of those fancy toys that'll hit her clit and penetrate her at the same time? Or a simple bullet thing?

Fuck fuck fuck fuck fuck.

Cold sweat?

No.

Full-on chills racing across my entire body while my cock leaks pre-cum and my balls tighten even harder.

I try to stare at the brightly colored puzzle pieces on the desk, but they all blur together.

I can't see straight.

Not with that vibration coming through the walls.

It gets higher pitched, then lower pitched, then higher pitched.

Like she's moving it to the exact right spot to—

I shove up off the chair, banging my thigh on the

underside of the desk, and stifle a yelp. If I can hear *her fucking vibrator*, she can hear me.

Need to get out of here.

Desperately need to get away from this noise.

I head into the bathroom, which *does not help*.

I can still hear her.

I can still hear her making soft noises, and I can still hear her vibrator going, and my dick is getting harder by the minute *which should be fucking impossible*.

Nope.

Not doing this.

Not letting my body control what goes on here.

The vibration amps up, and she whimpers.

Fuck me.

I lunge for the shower and turn it on cold.

Wrong move.

Wrong, *wrong* move.

One, I hate the cold.

Two, I'm moving too fast, and one of my fun new light-headed spells decides to make a reappearance.

And three, I'm still fully dressed.

So now I'm sitting on the floor of the shower, cold water raining down on me and soaking my clothes, pressure easing in my head as the dizziness recedes, but my cock is still hard as iron.

I slam the water off and reach for a towel as Sabrina moans a soft, short moan.

And then I hear something else.

Water.

Spitting.

"God, that feels good," Sabrina says on the other side

of the wall. "Is there anything better than a clean mouth? Your turn for tooth brushies, Jitterbug."

Fuck.

Me.

Just fuck me.

I have a problem.

And it's getting bigger by the day.

12

Sabrina

GREY DISAPPEARS for most of the rest of the week, which is a good thing. The intensity in his expression when he was poking for information about Addison and making it *very* clear that he remembers every word I told him in Hawaii has me off-balance. And the two-gallon jar brewing a batch of kombucha on the desk is an ever-present reminder that he's changing things.

Zen says he's off doing responsible business owner things. The managers from the other two locations seem to think I want to know everything he's doing, so I'm getting regular communication from both that confirms Zen's story.

In Elk Knee, it's simple. The crew had already quit and found new jobs, and the manager is doing the barest obligatory duties to help get the building for sale while working his new job too.

In Tiara Falls though, apparently Grey's been working to help the soon-to-be-displaced crew there all find new jobs, and he's providing severance packages for them until they do.

That's a little above and beyond if you ask me.

Which you didn't.

And it makes me like-dislike him a little more.

He does *so many* good things, but here?

Why does he have to change *my* building?

I can help him find another building in town if he wants to run a kombucha brewery. But the one time I casually mentioned it to Zen, they snorted, muttered *good luck with that*, and climbed up on a stepstool to tinker around the piles of things on top of the fridge and *take inventory of all of this powdered cheese*.

"What happened with Grey and Chandler?" I finally ask Zen just before my shift is over on Thursday.

They're warming up by the day, but I get the blank-faced, *you don't get that answer from me* look. "Who says something happened?"

"My gut."

"Same gut that led to your friend's wedding disaster?"

"Low blow, Zen. Low blow."

They shrug and go about their business.

I spend the rest of the day texting with Laney about how much more time Emma needs to herself before I get to check in on her. I tried sending Emma a text directly, but I couldn't make myself type the words and hit send.

If I don't message her, if I pretend she's still on her runaway-moon and that I'm giving her space, if I tell myself she'll ping me when she's ready to talk, I can almost convince myself that this new normal will be okay.

Jitter and I visit Mom at the salon, and she hugs me and tells me everything will work out.

We go visit Grandpa and he shakes his head and says change is the only inevitable thing in life.

So I spend Thursday night with all three of the triplets at Silver Horn, getting just tipsy enough that one of them drives me home.

And Friday morning, I wake up hungover and antsy and still processing the new gossip I got from the triplets before the martinis took over.

Worse?

It's only like 4 in the morning.

But I want coffee. And to *do something*.

Keeping myself in the kitchen and away from people all week at work has been seriously draining. *I miss the gossip*. I miss the community. I miss feeling like I'm in the middle of everything.

But I don't trust myself to not misuse information, and I *was* rudely blunt to Addison the other day.

This is not me at my best.

I *deserve* to feel like shit this morning.

My car is still downtown, so I pour myself an extra-large tumbler of black coffee, bundle up, and head out with Jitter to walk to work with flurries swirling all around us.

Yep.

Snowing today.

Café should be slow.

Empty, even.

Good day for starting to face the inevitable, which is that I'm going to have to clear out my stuff from the only job I've ever had and the only place I've ever wanted to work.

But when Jitter and I arrive, the lights are on.

And the kitchen isn't empty.

For the first time since the food fight, I'm face-to-face and alone with Greyson Cartwright.

My Duke in tarnished armor.

He looks just as surprised to see me as I am to see him, but I have the advantage of my nearly-empty coffee tumbler, so I fake taking a drink as I pass him at the prep table to hang my coat up. "Morning, boss-man. You're in early. Didn't see your car out there."

When he doesn't answer, I look over my shoulder at him.

He's staring.

Not at my ass.

But at my head.

My head? My hair?

I brush a hand through it, feeling cold moisture mixed with the texture of my curls. "Do I have something—"

"Snow," he says shortly, and then he ducks his head and goes back to the prep table.

My heart does a slow crawl through my stomach and down to my thighs.

Building plans. Design plans.

All of the changes he wants to make to Bean & Nugget.

Can't hide anymore.

This is *it*.

This is what he wants to do to my home.

I swallow thickly and move to stand next to him, looking down at the large sheets. Jack would geek out over the technical aspects, but I'm looking for a broad overview.

And I get it.

There's a front-view illustration of the building, and I can see the rock outcropping at the back corner, and the edge of what's clearly the art gallery next door, but where our old-fashioned *Bean & Nugget* block typeface sign over the picture windows should be, the signage is in a cursive font, spelling out *The Hive*, with a gigantic bumblebee hung at the corner of the building.

I point to the picture windows, which aren't windows, but aren't *not* windows. "What's that?"

He pauses before he answers, and I can feel the weight of his gaze shifting to me. "Plexiglass beehives."

"Chandler hates bees."

"Does he?"

I open my mouth, then close it again.

Grey knows.

There's no way on Earth he *doesn't* know Chandler hates bees. And that's not almost thirty years of studying human interactions telling me Grey knows Chandler hates bees.

That sarcastic, biting *Does he?* clearly says that this is not new information.

"We were maybe twelve or thirteen when he found a tree in a local park that was swimming with bees. He decided he wanted honey, so he started banging on it, and the next thing we knew, he was *covered* with them. Stung probably a dozen times. No anaphylactic reaction or anything. Not allergic. Just stung a lot. One of the stings got infected and he had to go on antibiotics that he *did* have an adverse reaction to."

Grey grunts.

If I were the type of person to read into a grunt, I'd think that grunt said *so he's always been an asshole*.

Grey loves bees.

It's not just his magic beeswax-biodegradable-plastic self-sealing cereal bags. The triplets told me last night that Grey used his first profits off of his patent to start building his own research lab with a tight friend from college. He has a solid reputation as a certified bee genius in certain circles. Works with universities and government organizations sometimes. And suddenly in early December, with no warning, he sold all of his research to a completely unknown company and signed off on an agreement to not do bee research for anyone but them for the next ten years.

Decker found a small corner of the internet where the bee-obsessed hang out, and he said there's speculation that it was a sabotage job.

That Grey and his former business/research partner haven't spoken other than through their lawyers ever since.

I tend to believe you only get a third of the story off the internet. And I know I'm missing pieces of the story.

But the man I met in Hawaii? The man who wanted to do good in the world despite indicating that he, too, was having a bad day? The man who made me feel like I was worthy of basic human affection on what was one of the worst nights of my life?

The man who was a friend when I needed one the most?

I want to believe he's still inside this zipped-up man who only makes noncommittal grunts when I say Chandler's name.

"Why were you in Hawaii?" I ask him.

Those blue eyes shift until he's looking at me straight on. "To crash a wedding and destroy a man's reputation."

I swallow.

Hard.

"What did he do to you?" I whisper.

His eyes flick away.

"I'll believe you, whatever you say. And I know it was bad. I know it *had* to have been bad." I point to the picture of *The Hive*. "This is—this is next-level perfection. He's a selfish ass. He *deserves* this. But there are so many people who will be collateral damage if you do this here."

He still doesn't look at me, and that's when I notice the bags under his eyes and the droop in his shoulders. The dishes at the sink that suggest someone ate here already this morning. The slight scent of bacon lingering in the air.

He hasn't slept.

That's why I haven't seen him.

If he's needed to be here, he's come at night.

When I'm not here.

"Please—" I start.

"I hear Mr. Twizzlers and his *body shop* business could move to a different spot in town if Ms. Red Robin spilled all the dirt she has on him."

I gasp.

I actually *gasp*.

Mr. Twizzlers was my code name for Kurtis, our local chiropractor, and yes, I said he had a body shop business on Main Street.

Fine.

That one was probably easy.

But Ms. Red Robin was my code name for myself. The

175

only time I used it was when I told him about the time I hid all of the flyers for the annual rodeo because I was mad that Addison was going to be crowned Rodeo Princess. And I changed *all* of those details. Something about an art festival and the Crochet King.

"Zen found all of the rodeo posters in a cubby under the desk," Grey adds like he's reading my mind. "I looked it up. Your friend Addison was crowned Rodeo Princess the same year as the flyers. You said you didn't tell me anything about her, but this paints a picture that suggests she's *Ms. Taco Bell* who might or might not have used blackmail to be crowned *Ms. Crochet King* at an art festival."

"Oh, god," I squeak. I'm not hungover anymore, but I wish I was. "That's—that's—"

"Genius?"

"*Diabolical.*"

One corner of his mouth lifts, and god help me, I want to kiss it.

I want to climb him, wrap my arms and legs around him, and kiss that corner of his mouth.

He can expose me.

He can tell *everyone* what he's figured out, and he can probably put more pieces of gossip together.

And I want to kiss him for it.

"You can make the chiropractor move and re-open your café there," he says quietly. "Then we both get what we want."

He doesn't promise to keep all of my secrets as his own.

He also doesn't offer up anything else he might've figured out and pieced together.

He's dangerous. And he definitely hates Chandler.

"Are you blackmailing me?" I ask. "Buying my compliance with your knowledge?"

He meets my gaze again, and this time, there's zero mistaking what I'm reading in there.

It's worse than blackmail.

Worse than tearing apart my café.

Worse than his anger and irritation with me.

It's *forgiveness*.

I blink and try to make myself believe it's something else, but I can't.

Not when he opens his stupid sexy mouth again. "I'm not mad at you."

Fuck. "You should be."

"I get it. I would've ghosted me too."

"I was an asshole."

"You were brutally honest until the very end, and you did what you thought you needed to do to protect both of us."

"Stop making excuses for me." *Keep making excuses for me.*

His gaze doesn't waver, but something shifts in his eyes.

Recognition.

Like he gets why I want him to be mad at me. Like he understands that it's easier to keep people at arms' length and only let them so far in.

Laney and Emma? My mom? Grandpa?

They're *in*.

Emma not talking to me is horrific. I'm hiding from facing it, but it is. It's bad on a *losing my grandma* level, and it reminds me of every relationship I've ever seen go south.

Which is a *lot* of relationships.

I'm feeling that thing with Emma that I've shielded myself from, and having Grey forgive me right now almost makes me feel like Emma's forgiven me.

Like I'm still worthy of being someone's friend.

Or more.

Like it could be okay, even knowing the pain that's come from my friendship with Emma being up in the air.

"Who told you that you have to be perfect?" All of his intense focus is trained on me, his eyes flicking over my face like he's taking stock of how every teeny tiny muscle is reacting to the question.

"Me," I whisper. "Perfect is—"

"Safest."

"*Yes.*" I blink and pull back. "No. *No.* Laney's the perfect one. The safe one. I'm the gossip. I don't have to do anything right. I just have to know—"

"How to *use* it all right," he finishes for me.

Nailing it.

Again.

He shifts, and I realize he's been moving this whole time without me noticing it.

And now he has me trapped between his two long, solid arms, my back to the prep table, him leaning into my bubble, and *oh my latte, this.*

"My parents blamed me for *existing* for my entire life," he says quietly, no hiding, no blinking, no hesitation. "I was the accident. The highest-maintenance. The one who wasn't supposed to disrupt their lives. So I made myself as

178

THE GOSSIP AND THE GRUMP

small as I could be. But fuck that. We get to exist. We get to make mistakes. We get to be wrong. Even when we know we're being wrong. We're *human*. And right now, I want to make another very big mistake with you."

13

Grey

BAD IDEA.

Bad, bad idea.

I should not want to kiss Sabrina right now. I shouldn't be trapping her against the table. I shouldn't be telling her any damn thing at all about my life.

But it's so damn good to see her. To *feel* her. To breathe in the coffee-and-soap scent of her and watch her bright eyes study me while her lids lower and her breathing comes faster and she darts that quick pink tongue out to lick her lower lip.

"Mistakes hurt," she breathes.

"You don't date."

"You don't miss much."

"I don't date."

"You're doing very bad math." She clearly knows where my brain is going.

"Math is my expertise," I tell her.

Her fingers curl into my shirt right at my breastbone. Both hands, clutching the buttons on my shirt for dear life. "Do you have any idea how much I could hate you? How much I *should* hate you?"

"I'm good with you hating me."

Her lips unexpectedly curve up. "*Stop being funny.*"

"I wasn't joking."

"You're a disaster."

"Welcome to the club, Duchess."

She whimpers, and that's the last thing I hear before she tugs my shirt and leans forward, planting those lips on mine, plump and hot and hungry.

"Don't—call me—that," she breathes against my mouth.

"Want you—hate me," I breathe back.

She's nipping and licking and sucking and I'm not in a cold silver-and-white kitchen in a snowy mountain town.

I'm surrounded by heat and humidity while waves roll to shore, my hands roaming over the soft cotton of her T-shirt down to the curve of her hips under her thick pants.

"Can't do this," she says.

"Why not?"

"Fuck me, I don't know."

Her tongue plunges into my mouth.

My cock is hard as iron. I can't touch her enough. Feel her enough. *Remember* her enough.

Fuck, Hawaii was good.

When she was just a random woman having a tough night, and all of my primitive *take care of her* neurons fired and I felt good about myself and my own worth as a human being for what felt like the first time in forever.

182

I want to feel that again.

She's not a safe choice. I know she hates what I'm doing here.

But she understands.

And she's still kissing me.

Maybe I'm still the moron who doesn't know she's using sex to manipulate me.

If I am, I don't care. I'm not changing my mind about what I'm doing merely because she's boosting herself onto the table and wrapping her legs around my hips and arching her pussy against my aching dick.

"Oh, fuck, no," she suddenly gasps.

"What? *What?*"

"Walked in—Emma—here—move. *Move.*"

Is she saying—nope.

Don't care.

I lift her, cradling her ass in my hands while she moans and threads her fingers through my hair and kisses me like I'm the missing piece to her puzzle. And in four steps, I'm shoving her against the back door while I kiss her back like she's the missing puzzle to my lone piece.

She squeezes her legs tighter.

I knead my fingers into her strong ass muscles, pressing my erection against her center through our clothes while she moans in my mouth.

I'm not this guy.

Lust doesn't make me lose my mind.

But I want her naked.

I want her naked and I want to take her against this door and make her eyes light up with that sparkle she had in Hawaii again, and then I want to tell her all of my secrets so I don't have to carry them alone either.

I am so fucked.

This is not how this trip is supposed to go.

"Oh, god, Grey," she pants, and my name on her lips makes me even harder. "There. *There—no.* Nope. Grandpa —my eyes—move. *Move."*

"Are you fucking kidding me?"

"My eyes. But your cock." She flexes her hips and whimpers.

So do I.

Can't lie here.

"I want your cock," she whispers.

"Parking lot."

"Cousin."

I recoil.

"Other cousin. Triplet. Your hair is so soft. How is your hair so soft?" She strokes me behind my ears, then around to my jaw, her fingers skimming my short beard until she's somehow managed to draw me in to kiss her again.

"Dining room?" I murmur between kisses.

"Windows."

Shit. "The dog house?"

"Fridge. Against the fridge."

Done.

I spin again and almost slam her into the prep table when she shifts, rocking her pelvis against my over-achieving dick and sending me spiraling toward a head rush.

Shit.

Shit fuck shit fuck not now.

I blink, breathe deep, and will it to pass.

"Grey?" Sabrina whispers.

184

"You're too fucking hot," I force out, and as the words leave me, so do the impending dots in my vision.

"That's why we can't do it on the stove," she says.

Know the last time I laughed while I was kissing a woman who was unbuttoning my shirt as I carried her across a kitchen to shove her against a fridge?

Never.

But I'm in.

Maybe it's lack of sleep.

Maybe it's lack of regular sex in the past two years.

Maybe it's the constant visions of her pleasuring herself with a vibrator on the other side of my bedroom wall every time I accidentally hear her brushing her teeth.

Maybe it's reminders of Hawaii.

Maybe it's that *I like her*.

She finishes with my buttons while still kissing me and shoves my shirt off my shoulders, then roams cool hands over my chest. "It's so wrong that you're this hot," she breathes against my collarbone.

And then she bites it.

My dick strains harder. A tiny gasp slips from her mouth, and she rocks her hips against me once more.

I tug her shirt.

She reaches between us and pops the button on my pants, then dips her hand inside and brushes the tip of my dick.

I whimper.

Cannot help myself. "More."

She rocks against my shaft and swirls her thumb around my head again.

My eyes cross.

My head falls to her shoulder.

I breathe in coffee and snow and warmth, her hair tickling my cheek, and thrust into her touch. "Why—you?"

"Life's a bitch," she replies.

And then she lurches away with a shriek.

No more Sabrina in my arms.

No more Sabrina's thumb on my raging erection.

No more Sabrina's legs wrapped around my hips.

Just Sabrina gripping my shirt while the whole damn refrigerator rolls backward.

"What—" I start, lunging for her.

The fridge stops with a distinct *crunch* of cracking plaster or drywall.

She stops.

I smush against her.

The fridge rolls again.

And then something bashes me in the head, powder exploding in my vision.

I suck in a breath and choke on—*cheese*?

Is that *cheese*?

Bad cheese.

"Oh, *fu*—" Sabrina starts, and then she coughs.

And coughs.

I suck in another breath, and I come up choking too. "What—" I start again, but I can't finish.

An orange cloud is eating us.

It has swallowed us whole, and it is devouring us, choking both of us.

"Drop roll," I croak. "*Drop roll.*"

"Not smoke," she gasps between coughing fits. "Outside."

"What?"

"*Cheese.*"

"I do *not* want to know what I just walked into," Zen says from somewhere beyond the orange haze.

Oh fuck.

Oh *fuck fuck fuck*.

"Fridge wall!" Sabrina shrieks, and then she doubles over coughing again.

I shove my dick back in my pants. "Mainte—"

Can't get it out.

Can't say *call maintenance*, because I'm choking again.

It's up my nose.

It's in my eyeballs.

It's all over my fingers.

"Is that powdered cheese? Like on cheese puffs?" Zen asks.

I can't see them.

My eyes are watering too hard, and if I keep coughing like this, I'm going to send myself into the bad kind of head rush.

"Maybe take the kinky shit to Sabrina's house next time?" Zen says.

Their hand clamps on my arm and tugs, and a moment later, I get a face full of cold, snowy air.

Sabrina's hacking up a lung next to me.

Zen got us both.

"One of you two rapscallions wanna explain what the hell I just walked into?" my twenty-three-year-old nibling demands like they're the adult and we're toddlers. "And exactly who thought orange powdered cheese belonged *anywhere* inside Bean & Nugget? Tell me you don't use that shit when you're cooking."

"Chandler—obsession—leftover," Sabrina croaks out.

187

Her frog voice is the sexiest fucking thing I've ever heard.

I clearly have a problem.

"Don't—" I start, belatedly catching on to what Zen's snicker means.

"So the Cheese Turd strikes again," they say. "Uncle Grey, mark that down. He has one name now."

"Make you—lattes—life—call him—to his face," Sabrina rasps.

"If the Cheese Turd has the audacity to show his face in this place, I'mma call him a lot worse. Sabrina, give me your keys. I'm taking Uncle Grey home, and then I'll be back with a couple gas masks. Mine's for fashion. Yours is for cleaning up your mess. Not that either one of you can clean up the hot mess that's yourselves."

"Why my car?"

"It's the *Uncle Grey is coated in food* car. Keys. C'mon. He'll buy you a new one if I wreck it."

"You drive in snow?" her voice is clearing.

Zen doesn't answer.

I pry open my eyeballs, half expecting everything to be orange, but it's not.

It's a blurry white.

Snow.

"I...made it here...fine," Zen says.

Ah, hell.

"Back inside," Sabrina says. "You two aren't going anywhere for a few hours."

"You two aren't allowed in the same room as long as I'm here."

I don't call them on telling me to bang her just the other night.

No point.

We all know the rules.

Just don't do it where I have to see it.

14

Sabrina

THE IDEA of being stuck in the café with Grey and Zen while I'm coated in orange cheese is too much to handle, so I break down and give Grey a ride back to the townhouse.

He doesn't say much.

I don't say much.

But when I pull up in front of his door—again—he looks me square in the eye and doesn't even try to get out of the car. "Tell me another puzzle."

"What?"

"Tell me another puzzle. About the people here."

"No."

He shrugs. "Suit yourself. I'll pick one on my own from what I remember in Hawaii."

"That's not—" I start, but my words leave me when he flashes me a grin.

Grey. *Duke.*

Flashing me the most impish grin I've ever seen in my life.

He swings the door open and pulls himself out of my car, then trots up to his own doorstep without looking back.

I think I lost that round.

Actually, I know I did.

And for that smile?

Worth it.

I. Am. In. So. Much. Trouble.

I take a fast shower before heading back to the café solo, where I get funny looks all day long.

Or possibly I don't get funny looks and I'm imagining it all since I don't know if Zen is the type to spread rumors about the cheese incident.

And it's *obvious* to *everyone* that there was a powdered cheese incident in the kitchen.

That takes a lot of clean-up.

Saturday, the roads are clear, but Grey's not at the café.

And finally, it's Sunday.

I have an entire day to myself, and I can't hide from the other thing I've been hiding from all week.

It's time to work up the courage to go see Emma.

Slowly.

I've started a text to her probably every other waking hour since Theo left Silver Horn to pick her up at the airport on Monday, but I haven't found the right words, nor do I want to do this over text.

Laney reports she hasn't seen Emma either, but Theo has nearly daily and says she looks sad. I've fielded questions from more friends and neighbors about if she's back yet, telling everyone I haven't seen her—which is the truth —but the entire *town* knows she's due back this weekend.

And not because she does half the town's taxes as our most popular accountant.

It's more about the viral video and the reporters who were hanging out here for a week or so after the wedding hoping for more juice for their stories.

But today, I'm doing it.

I'm going to see her.

Probably.

After I swing by Laney's and see if she wants to go with me, and if Theo thinks this is a good idea.

I'm packing my car in case Laney's up for crashing Emma's temporary digs with me when Grey walks out of his door.

I freeze and eye him.

Dammit, he looks like a box of chocolates that you know only has the kinds you like in it, even though you know you're allergic to one of them, but you can't help wanting to roulette the whole box anyway.

After a prolonged moment of both of us deer-in-the-headlightsing, he breaks eye contact and glances at the back end of my SUV.

His eyebrows furrow.

No doubt silently questioning why I need a massive box containing two blow-up human-size hamster balls in addition to my snowshoes, dog supplies, and winter safety kit.

Yes, there's a story behind the hamster balls.

No, he's not getting it.

I have places to be that don't involve the kind of trampoline jumping that my heart is doing right now.

Wait.

Seeing Emma probably *will* involve my heart on a trampoline, but there won't be any sexual tension mixed in with it.

And speaking of, I am all in for pretending Friday never happened. "Hey, Grey! How awesome to see you on my day off. Here you are. Here I am. Running into each other since you moved in next door... Jitter! Did you see who's here?"

Grey's eyes light up, and I feel like an asshole.

Jitter doesn't come running, because he's already hanging out with my mom for the day.

She loves taking him for walks around the lake on nice days, and thirty degrees with clear skies and no wind absolutely counts as a nice day. She meets a lot of new people that way.

And he loves her because she feeds him good food and lets him get up on her bed for Sunday afternoon naps. Mom's approaching seventy in a couple years—she had me later—but she's still strong and spry and can handle him.

I snap my fingers. "Dammit. Forgot. He's not here. Habit. Have a nice day."

"What's with the perky attitude?"

"I'm not being perky." I smile. Brightly. "I'm just being my normal, happy, cheerful self."

And *clearly* annoying the ever-loving crap out of him.

Which is good.

He needs to not like me.

I need to not like him.

Get along? Fine.

Us having a repeat of Friday morning?

No.

And not just because I sneezed orange snot again this morning.

"I figured out who Mr. Snuffleupagus is," he says.

"That was a gimme, and there's nothing you can say that would embarrass him." I shut my tailgate, then finger-wave at him. "Toodles! See you tomorrow!"

He doesn't stop me or talk me out of my clothes, though he does smirk-smile in a way that makes my vagina clench, and I decide it's in my best interest to not even consider if he has regrets about Friday or if he wants to try to talk me out of my clothes again.

Preferably in a location without leftover containers of powdered cheese from Chandler's idiotic *we'll add cheddar popcorn to the menu* idea.

No.

No.

There is no wishing Grey will talk me out of my clothes again. I am *not* being rewarded with more orgasms.

And yes, I *did* almost come just by dry-humping him.

Which I am *done thinking about.*

Officially.

For real.

The drive to Laney's house is easy and her roads *and* sidewalks are clear after Friday's snow.

I make myself imagine this neighborhood snowed in to distract myself.

But when I spot Emma's car in her driveway, I almost want to head back to my house, knock on the wall that I share with Grey, and see if maybe we can hide in a blanket fort together.

Not because I don't want to see Emma.

More because I'm afraid she'll tell me she still doesn't want to see me, and it's easier to contemplate Grey rejecting me than it is to contemplate Emma rejecting me.

"You've got this," I tell my reflection in the mirror. *"You've got this."*

We've been friends forever.

I know she knows I didn't mean to hurt her.

Well, I *hope* she knows.

And the other thing that *everyone* has been telling me lately is that *she knew who Chandler was*. It wasn't my job to tell her every bad thing he ever did.

My phone dings, and I glance at the readout.

It's Laney.

I see you sitting in my driveway. COME INSIDE NOW. I'd send Theo out to drag you in, but he's preoccupied with getting his ass handed to him.

When I don't move right away, my phone dings again.

I'll call my mother to come get you if you don't come inside, and you know she'll be here before you can back out of the driveway since she's still upset that I broke my leg.

I almost smile.

And then I brace myself and head inside.

And immediately wish I hadn't.

"What in the world were you thinking?" Emma shrieks somewhere deeper in the house.

My gut clenches, but Laney's stifling a smile as she waves me to join her. She's propping her leg cast up on the couch with two of her kittens on her lap, and she's stroking both of them.

"Is Em okay?" I whisper while I sink onto the couch, almost sitting on a third kitten that was hiding under a throw pillow. "Is *Theo* okay? Wait. Back up. How are you? How's your leg? Do you need anything?"

"I'm good, thank you, and Emma's working on his taxes," Laney whispers back.

She's almost gleeful.

I give her the *why the hell is that funny?* eyebrows while I shrug out of my coat and rescue kitten number three, who's quaking a little. Probably because of the yelling.

Which is not like Emma *at all*.

"He said you already know, so I'm not gossiping to you when I tell you he threw all of his money into that screw-the-hedge-fund-managers thing off Reddit last year and made a hella ton more with it. But he didn't tell Emma, and she's freaking out about him underpaying estimated taxes."

"This isn't about Chandler and jail?" I whisper.

She shakes her head. "It is not."

"Is she still mad at me? At any of us?"

The thing I love about Laney is that she can fix anything. If there's a problem in a four-mile radius, Laney will sniff it out and solve it before most people are aware it even exists. Second-most, I love that she doesn't blow smoke up my ass, even if she sometimes will paint the truth in the prettiest light she can.

But when she purses her lips and has to think about it, I hate that I love those two things about her.

"I don't think she's mad at any of us, necessarily," she finally says, "but I do think she has a lot of feelings to work through still. And who can blame her? She spent seven years waiting for him to marry her, and then the whole thing not only fell apart at the last minute, but the *entire world* saw it. Nice job the other night on calling

Addison out for being such an asshole and posting the video, by the way."

"She's on my permanent shit list."

"Did your boss appreciate it more or less than he enjoyed getting cheesed with you?"

"*Ugh.* What did you hear?"

"Sabrina. You *claimed* him at House of Curry. People are speculating you've done *way* more than dusting yourselves in powdered cheese."

"Devi saw, didn't she?"

"Devi saw, and she swears I'm the only person she told."

I squeeze my eyes shut. "Can we get back to Emma? Did she enjoy her trip at least?"

"I don't know. She hasn't said much about it. Even to Theo."

"Are you two okay?"

Laney was the one who ultimately spilled the tea to Emma about who was driving the go-kart that damaged the statue of Ol' Snaggletooth, the miner, and that Theo ultimately went to jail for about ten years ago. It was a short stay, but it was hard on the whole family to watch him go through it.

And when Laney purses her lips again, I start to breathe.

"I don't know if she's okay with anyone right now. Including herself. It's like seeing rain come from the sunshine."

"*You have to tell me these things,*" Emma shrieks in the other room.

Theo says something quietly enough in response that I can't understand him.

"Of course I can fix it, you big doof, but you're going to have to give the IRS way more money than you would've *if you'd told me*. Do you like throwing money away? Wait. Stop. Do *not* answer that."

I gulp.

Laney winces.

None of us are worried about Theo's finances. The biggest reason Emma's wedding implosion video went viral was because it simultaneously outed Theo as Grippa-Peen.com's most popular adult entertainment star, who'd previously only appeared on-screen faceless with his penis out while spouting inspirational messages and knitting hearts.

As for wasting money—he footed the bill for Emma's wedding, since Chandler asked him to pay for it, and of course Theo didn't hesitate, even if the two of them have never gotten along well.

Laney's hinted he upgraded everything about her solo honeymoon as well, though I haven't asked if that was before or after it turned into a solo vacation.

This Emma?

The screeching, angry, apparently sad Emma?

That's the exact opposite of who Emma normally is.

And I still feel a crushing guilt for not telling her the secrets I knew about Chandler.

Laney squeezes my hand. "Any progress on getting your new boss to reconsider all of the changes? And I swear I won't add any snarky comments about the helpfulness of powdered cheese."

I grimace. "No. And the worst part is that *I get it*."

"But you're still organizing meals to his house and

asking people to come have their baby showers and report card celebrations at the café."

"Guilty." I am one hundred percent on a mission to make sure Grey has it shoved in his face just how much the whole town loves the café and how much we love each other.

"Did Yolanda really tell him about the time you got busted up on Marmot Cliff after you'd had seven shots of espresso in an hour?"

"Yes, and she also told him you refused to join us because you were studying for a trigonometry test on a Saturday night," I tease.

"I have so many more food fights to start."

In true Laney fashion, after starting the food fight at House of Curry this week, she paid for a professional crew to clean it top to bottom the day after the party. She also paid for all of the food that was lost.

When she added the tip, Nani Parvati invited her to come back and start food fights every week.

I love this town. And my friends.

I just wish I didn't feel so weird around Emma right now.

She's always been the first person to tell me it's okay when I've fucked up, the first person to tell Laney to be patient with herself when Laney was stressing with her own brand of parental-inspired perfectionism, and the first person to worry she'd unintentionally hurt someone's feelings when she was trying to compliment them.

I should've realized Em's stress over the wedding wasn't normal.

She asked Laney to *babysit Theo* in Hawaii for the week leading up to the wedding.

That's not like Emma.

It turned out well for Laney and Theo, but it's still not like Emma.

"You didn't answer Decker's text about the college yearbook photo he found with your grandpa and Grey's grandparents hanging out together," Laney says.

I squeeze my eyes shut. *That* is something I've been trying to forget since Decker delivered the yearbook to my doorstep after work last night.

And for the record, I didn't tell Laney that I didn't answer the text.

Decker must have.

"Nothing about what I want to do with that information feels right," I tell her.

She lifts her brows and waits, like she knows I mean it doesn't feel right since I still want to sleep with Grey.

How screwed up is it to want to fuck around with the guy who's actively making plans to destroy the place that built you?

When I don't answer her questioning look right away, she grabs a plate of chocolate chip cookies from the end table next to her and offers it to me over the kittens.

"I'm still mad at you," Emma says somewhere nearby.

I jump.

Laney jumps.

I don't see Emma, but she's definitely closer.

"I wonder if he tried that line about being fine with it if the government uses his extra taxes to fix up more roads on her," Laney whispers.

"That's a good one."

"He was totally ready for her to be mad. He was debating something about paying the salary of the IRS agent who'd audit him too, but decided he didn't want to push her blood pressure that far."

We're both still staring at the hallway that leads to Laney's home office.

My heart is suddenly clawing its way up my throat, and it's sharper than the kitten claws kneading into my thigh.

And there she is.

My tall, slender, blonde friend with the adorable pixie nose whose normally bright, happy brown eyes are dull and sad.

She has a computer bag slung over her shoulder, and Theo's right behind her, his hand on her shoulder like he's squeezing a silent *I'm here if you need me.*

"My other clients better not be as high-maintenance as you," she grumbles, and then she freezes as her gaze lands on me.

My stomach threatens to toss every last cup of coffee I drank this morning. I finagle the kitten, tugging on it gently to try to untangle its claw from my clothes, prepared to rush across the room and strangle Emma in a hug, but make myself move slowly as I give a small finger wave. Both for the kitten's sake and Emma's sake. "Hey, Em. Welcome home."

Her eyebrows furrow, and her lips wobble briefly, and then she fakes a smile.

I'm the reigning queen of fake smiles this week, but she threatens to take my crown with that forced happiness.

And it feels like my heart is pulling my throat with it as it thuds to the floor.

"Oh, don't get up," she says, pulling her computer and

a stack of files to her chest like a shield. "Let the kitty stay put. Sorry. I have to run. Behind on work."

"Right. Sure. Of course. Tax season. I know. But if you want to do our normal Razzle Dazzle film fest for a break—"

I cut myself off as she pulls a face I rarely see on her.

Even Laney seems startled by Emma's outright horrified grimace.

"Thanks," Emma says quickly, so many emotions that aren't her normal joy flashing over her features, "but I don't know if I'll have time. I—I have to go."

"Em—" Theo starts.

She cuts him off with a quick hug. *"Don't hide your money from me again.* Talk to you later."

She waves quickly at Laney and me, then dashes out the door.

My eyes get hot, but I will the sting away and look at Laney.

"She's not mad," Theo says.

He's such a liar.

"She *looks* mad, and she's *acting* mad," I say.

"I can't remember ever seeing her like that," Laney agrees. She's deflated too.

Theo shakes his head. "Never had a broken heart like this before either. Give her time. She'll be back."

"Did it hurt when she yelled at you?" Laney asks him.

He grins, but he doesn't answer. A grey kitten pokes its head out of the kitchen like it's making sure the coast is clear, and when Laney clucks her tongue, that kitten and two more dash out to join us. Theo scoops up two of them and deposits them in Laney's lap with the first two, kisses her on the top of the head, and eyes me like he's considering kicking me off of her couch.

Yes. Yes, they have an army of kittens that they saved in Hawaii.

No, they collectively cannot get more adorable.

I loop my arm through hers and lay my head on her shoulder while the kitten in my lap finally disentangles himself from my pants and climbs over to join his siblings in Laney's lap.

"Mine," I tell Theo. "You get her later."

The kittens meow like they're offended that I'd claim their human mama. Theo rolls his eyes and heads to the kitchen.

The man sits still about as well as these kittens do.

They're adorable, even with their super-sharp claws.

And way tinier than my overgrown puppy.

"So, Bean & Nugget," Laney says, clearly trying to distract me from what just happened with Emma.

"It's hopeless. It's all hopeless."

"Everything's hopeless with that attitude," Theo calls.

"Don't *naked-motivational-knitter-advice* me," I call back. "I'm not one of your adoring fans."

"Anymore."

"Stop, both of you," Laney orders. "Theo, more cookies, please. Sabrina, more positive attitude, please. You have a plan. I can *smell* it."

"That's the kitty litter," Theo says.

Her lips wobble in amusement.

A month ago, she would've chewed him out for the joke.

Today, she's laughing.

And I utterly *love* that for her.

She deserves all of the laughs. All of the love. All of the happiness.

Meanwhile, I'm just a drag.

"Can you tell me that I should do the thing I'm thinking about doing, even if it's a terrible idea?" I say while I reach for one of those cookies on the plate on her other side.

"Would you have hesitated three weeks ago?"

"No."

"Then do it."

"Will you hate me?"

"Not a chance."

"Even if you should?"

"*Sabrina.*"

"The night I met Grey in Hawaii, I was on a mission to do good deeds everywhere I could to balance out my karma."

"That's a thing you do?" Laney interrupts.

I huff out a sigh. "I do *plenty* of good."

"I know, but not usually in the name of karma. It's usually just because it's the right thing to do and you can't help yourself when it comes to doing the right thing for the Tooth."

"Fair enough. But I *needed* to do it for karma that night."

She nods. "Okay. I get that."

"What I'm thinking of doing is basically the opposite of that and really pushes some boundaries beyond what any normal, rational person should ever do."

That might be extreme.

But I don't actually think it is.

Laney flexes her brows at me. "So this is the nuclear option?"

Basically. And I feel like an ass for considering it when I don't think Grey's a *bad guy*. I don't know what Chandler did to him, but I know it was *something*. There has to be another way to make it right besides destroying Bean & Nugget. "The only other idea I have involves blackmailing Kurtis into letting me have his Main Street storefront for opening my own coffee shop, and I really don't want to piss off the only chiropractor in town." And yes, that was Grey's idea, and I know it's not a bad idea.

It's just not a *good* idea.

Bean & Nugget has my family's blood, sweat, and tears built into it.

And it truly is the best real estate downtown.

Laney blinks slowly. "You have blackmail material on Kurtis?"

"No."

I say it so fast and vehemently, Theo pops his head out of the kitchen and eyeballs me.

Laney winces.

"Is that *no* related to you getting off gossip after you told your boss all of the Tooth's gossip?" Theo asks.

"I told him," Laney whispers.

"As you should've," I reply. "Don't keep secrets from each other on my behalf. Also, sorry, Theo, I'm positive he knows that you're Mr. Snuffleupagus and that you strip at a nightclub in Denver three nights a week."

"Mr. Snuffleupagus." Theo grins. "Guy has a long... trunk. I like it."

"It wasn't an intentional flattery," I assure him. "I

thought he wouldn't put it together since Snuffy's so fluffy and you wax your chest."

Laney laughs so hard, she almost falls off the couch, which earns me more of a glare from Theo than accusing him of waxing his chest would ever provoke on its own.

"There anyone who needs a warning about what he might know?" he asks.

Like it's that easy. "*I changed details.*"

Theo shakes his head. "I don't underestimate people who make a fuckton of money while saving a little part of the world. Means they're smart."

"Aww, just like you," Laney says to him with a smile.

These two.

They're sickeningly adorable.

I steal one more cookie and shove to my feet. "I made this mess. I'll clean it up. I don't need you getting your hands dirty too. I just need to decide if I can change his mind on my own, or if I need to take it a step further."

"What's a step further?" Laney asks.

"It's better for you if you don't know."

"*Sabrina.*"

I squeeze her shoulder. "Thank you for the pep talk. I don't want to get more of my bad mood all over you two, or chase Emma off again if she comes back—"

"You didn't chase her off," Theo says. "She's way behind on work."

"The intellectual part of my brain acknowledges your viewpoint, but my emotions are still out of whack. Be good to Laney. Call me if Chandler makes problems for Em. Jitter and I could use an outlet for all of our pent-up energy."

"Where are you going?" Laney asks.

"Overdue for a haircut."

"You got your hair cut three days before you flew to Hawaii."

"The curls got lopsided."

Laney presses her fingers into her eye sockets.

"Now that you mention it, it's totally obvious. This side, right?" Theo waves his hand near his shoulder on his left side.

And I almost check to see if he's right before I remember I never take Theo seriously. "Yes. That side."

"Call me if you need *any* help," Laney repeats.

I won't.

I don't even know if my plan will work or if it's the right thing to do.

Making out with Grey Friday morning definitely wasn't the right thing, as the cheese reminded me.

Showing him what Bean & Nugget does for the community isn't working fast enough.

But if even *Laney* doesn't have a better idea…then I think I have to do it.

No matter the consequences.

Not like I can make this worse, right?

15

Grey

I LEAVE the café in Zen's hands on Sunday after getting a lecture from them about catching up on sleep and lowering my stress levels. And also after they threaten to steal the car to run away deeper into the mountains to find an attractive ski instructor who likes spending half the year on the beach to live out their days with.

They need a break from me.

Another one.

But they still send me updates about locals asking when we'll shut down for construction and if Elsie's scones will stay on the menu afterward and when they can bring by dinner for us.

I know what's happening.

Zen's rapidly deciding this place is living up to their expectations on top of thinking I'm an idiot for trying to be *Super Vengeance Man*.

They're a lot like who I used to be.

Find someone who accepts you for who you are, and you'll do anything for them.

I grunt softly to myself over my puzzle.

Fine.

Fine.

I'd still do anything for someone who accepts me as I am. I just don't believe anyone who says they can.

Not when the *other* conversation blowing up my phone is a group chat where my brothers have joined in on wanting to know why I won't help with Felicia's birthday.

A woman only turns thirty once. And she's such a good mom to Duke. You should quit holding a grudge and help with the party.

The relative silence on that front was nice while it lasted.

Zen's right about one thing for certain.

I should change my phone number.

I manage to nap some—all-nighters are not the joy they once were, but I liked the quiet of the café after hours—and finally immerse myself in a wooden puzzle of a lion while contemplating the logistical issues I anticipate for applying for a liquor license in town.

I'm engrossed enough that I almost don't notice the sounds of my next-door neighbor returning.

Almost.

Jitter doesn't bark much. He's a good puppy. And while the walls are thin, other than Sabrina's nightly toothbrush routine that I try to avoid, I only hear the soft noises of phone conversations or the TV on without being able to hear distinct words.

Not that she's home much.

She's as much a social butterfly as I am a hermit-in-training.

She doesn't turn on the television now though.

No, that's an entirely different sound coming through the wall, and it's one that makes my heart freeze.

Crying.

I stare at the stairwell on the wall separating my living room from what I assume is Sabrina's living room.

"Oh, my sweet girl," an unfamiliar woman says. "Oh, honey. Come here. It'll be okay."

"She's so mad at me, Mom. She practically ran away as soon as she saw me."

Jitter whines.

My gut twists and I angle closer to the wall.

"She's working through a lot of things right now," Sabrina's mom says.

"She used to work through them *with me*. Both of us. Laney and me."

"Is she talking to Laney?"

"I don't know. She's talking to Theo. So she's at least *seeing* Laney. And Laney told her what Chandler did. I didn't. I should've told her."

"Sabrina—"

"*I should have told her*. And I didn't. And now she hates me."

That's not just my gut twisting.

It's my heart.

I shouldn't listen to this. It's not my business. Not my place.

But she's *hurting*.

I know that hurt. The sting of rejection. Of regret. Of helplessness.

And I want to hug her.

I want to hug her and soothe her and find a way to take away the pain, even knowing how dangerous she could be if she decides to use everything she learns against me to get me to leave this place without the satisfaction of seeing Chandler's reaction to me destroying what was once his.

"She's basically the most non-famous famous person in the world right now, and not for a flattering reason," her mom says. "Give her time. She has a lot on her plate."

"I've never not known what to say to her before. I've never not known what to say to *anyone* before."

"You've *both* had a lot of hard change lately. Don't expect yourself to be the same person you were two weeks ago either."

"I'm fine."

"*Sabrina.*"

"I am. I deserve this, so I'll take my punishment."

Shame and regret twist my heart region.

I'm punishing her.

She's the accidental bystander in my quest for justice.

I'm hurting her.

"*You do not deserve punishment,*" her mom says. "Your heart was in the right place, and you did what you thought was right."

"I just wish—I just wish I could go back and make Emma not hate me."

"She doesn't hate you."

"I hate myself. If I'd said something *ten years ago*, she'd be happily married, living the life of her dreams with someone who didn't go from a decent guy with potential to a complete asshole."

I take exception to the idea that Chandler Sullivan was

ever a *decent guy*. And more than once this week, I've wondered what a woman that everyone seems to adore ever saw in him.

"Or Emma would be married to someone who's terrible with kids and in an even worse situation now," her mom says. "You can't second-guess the past, and you have to believe good things are coming."

The dog whines again. Actually, I'm not sure he's stopped whining.

Jitter's hurting because Sabrina's hurting, and I'm hurting because they're both hurting.

The worst part?

It would be so easy to despise her as much as I despise Chandler.

She has everything I've ever wanted.

Friends. Family with *one* black sheep instead of a whole crumbling mansion full of them. Community. Home. A mission and purpose that she's never had to question and never had taken from her.

Until now. Until me.

I could hate her for making me second-guess everything I thought I stood for.

"I'm second-guessing *everything* I thought I stood for," Sabrina says.

I jolt and stare at the wall.

Did I—did I make that up?

Did she just say *exactly* what I was thinking?

Their voices fade.

I angle closer to the wall, straining to hear while a familiar sick feeling churns in my stomach.

Shame.

I am the assholiest of all assholes.

I'm hurting her.

And I know it.

And I *can't stop*.

The world isn't balanced.

My world isn't balanced.

It wasn't until maybe four years ago, while I was still married to Felicia, that I consciously realized my siblings and parents were nearly through their trust funds. That when they manipulated me into using my ever-growing bank account, it wasn't old habits to blame and shame me for being an accidental inconvenience in their lives. They needed the cash I was raking in from my patent to save face in front of their friends.

Having Zen show up on my doorstep asking for a place to live without judgment was the biggest wake-up call of my life.

Second-biggest was falling in love with Felicia only to realize when Zen moved back from college that my wife was playing me more than my family ever had, wanting me to be someone else. *Dress like this. Remodel your lab's lobby like that. Someone needs to talk to Zen about that outfit. And about getting a real job. Your assistant? Seriously? You know how this looks, right?*

Because looks were everything.

But not to Zen.

Zen taught me family.

Uncle Grey, you ever think about how rude it is for our parents to remind us of all of the basic needs of ours that they met when we were kids, despite us not asking to be born to them? I would've picked one of those reality TV families over this one, and I hate reality TV. And being on it. I assume, anyway.

Uncle Grey, what do you do when your siblings treat you like you're an inconvenience despite the fact that you go out of your way to send birthday cards every year and ask about their friends and their dreams and their lives in a way they never ask about yours?

Uncle Grey, you really shouldn't let them take advantage of you like that. You know the only reason they wanted you to marry Felicia was because her father promised Aunt Camille an introduction to his royal relatives, right?

Uncle Grey, this is who I am, and Felicia won't change me, no matter how much she tries.

They *see* things that I always accepted, and they challenge the way they're treated. They challenge the way *I'm* treated.

They challenge the meaning of *family*.

And I thought I understood, but understanding and taking a leap to trust people again are two completely different things.

Can I?

Can I risk letting someone destroy me all over again in the name of doing *good* instead of *justice*?

I might not be from a small town, but I know how gossip works.

I know Sabrina could turn the town against me with a single sentence. Probably no more than three well-thought-out words.

And instead, I have a fridge stocked with food courtesy of new neighbors or local restaurants, all of whom gave me discounts. We've received welcome gifts from other neighbors and shop owners, including six bottles of wine, two loaves of homemade bread, dozens of cookies and cupcakes, bags of vegetables, and a jar of local honey that has me intrigued but unable to track down the source just yet.

We've barely been here a week, and they're taking care of us despite us doing nothing to deserve it.

I press my ear to the wall, straining to hear more of the conversation between Sabrina and her mother, but all I detect is silence.

Are they in the kitchen?

Is she making more coffee?

She hasn't been more than three feet from a coffee cup or mug anytime I've seen her this week. She seems to live off the stuff, which shouldn't be charming, but it is.

She *lives* what she says she loves.

But I don't hear coffee maker sounds either.

Does she know I can hear her?

Are they talking about the café and my plans for it?

I deserve this, so I'll take my punishment.

The number of times I thought that to myself when I was growing up...

I can't do this.

I can't get vengeance if it means hurting innocent bystanders.

It's not about my attraction to her.

It's about doing what's right. What's *fully* right.

If I can figure out what *right* is.

16

Sabrina

Normally on any given Sunday evening, Jitter and I would head out early to Silver Horn or the pub by City Hall and our statue dedicated to Ol' Snaggletooth, our town's proverbial original gold miner, and hang out with friends until it's late enough that I know I'll have regrets Monday morning.

But today's been a hard day, and all I want to do is watch an old Razzle Dazzle film with a cup of coffee in hand and my dog acting like a pillow while I work up the nerve to follow through with the plan that my gut tells me is the key to getting my café back.

Unfortunately, nerves and coffee mean I sit still about as well as Theo, so I eventually shut off the movie that I can recite word for word and grab my coat and Jitter's leash.

We need to go for a walk.

It doesn't matter that Grandma took him for forty-three walks earlier, he's still game. We head in the opposite direction of the dog park. It's too dark to let Jitter off his leash, and even though he's a solid deterrent to some of the larger mountain predators, I don't want him running off and chasing deer or elk.

No one's out and about. No neighbors to stop and casually chat with. I try calling an old college friend, and my call rolls straight to voicemail.

With the sun down, it's cold. Like, breathe in and your nose hairs stick together cold. So Jitter and I cut the walk short.

We're walking past the townhouse next to mine which currently houses someone I'd very much like to quit thinking about when the door opens, and there he is.

Six feet, four inches of lean bulk encased in blue jeans and boots under a thick wool coat—clean now, courtesy of my dry cleaning gift card, I hear—a gray wool scarf, and a black beanie. His beard is getting impossibly thicker, and he's tugging on a black glove as he exits his townhouse, but he suddenly pauses and grips the doorframe.

Jitter barks and lunges for him.

I grab the leash tight. "*Sit*, Jitter," I order, but the dog won't listen.

He pulls harder to get to Grey.

The odd part, though?

Grey doesn't react to us at all.

He stands there, gripping the doorframe, his eyes distant, breathing deeply like he's in a trance, lit only by the porch light.

Jitter drags me all the way over to him, and no amount of bracing myself or tugging back works to stop my dog.

He's *determined.*

Worse, he's whining.

"*Jitter,*" I repeat.

He whines louder and nudges the boss-man's free hand, which is curled into a fist.

"Grey?" I say hesitantly.

He sucks in one more breath and blows it out while Jitter lies down at his feet. "What?" he says.

"Are you all right?"

"Fine."

"You don't *look* fine."

"I'm *fine.*"

He doesn't sound fine either.

Not even close.

My pulse kicks into high gear.

Something's wrong.

He blinks twice, looks at me under the yellow glow of the porch light, goes ruddy in the cheeks, and turns like he's planning on barricading himself inside and canceling the rest of his plans for the day.

Unfortunately for him, Jitter's a big dog and still completely in the way, so Grey catches himself again in the doorway.

"Jitter likes you," I say while I tug on the leash.

"Poor judge of character," Grey mutters.

Oh, yes.

Something is *very* wrong.

Jitter whines at Grey's feet again.

Grey grimaces, corrects his step, and climbs over Jitter, who whines again, to get back into his house.

"Hey. Are you sure you're okay?" I ask as I finally manage to get my dog to his feet and out of the doorway.

This time, I don't get an answer.

This time, he tries to shut the door in my face.

This is *not* the same man who was massaging my ass while he dry-humped me against half the kitchen the other day.

And lucky—or unlucky—for him, I'm not in any position to let him shut me out right now.

Not when he's being so weird.

"Jitter, Grey has steak!" I say.

And yes, that has *exactly* the impact you'd think it would.

Jitter leaps on the door, shoves it open, and drags me inside.

Grey stumbles backward and grabs the handrail to the stairs like he's afraid he'll lose his balance if he doesn't. "What are you doing?"

"My cousin Lucky's a nurse. He'd kick my ass if I left you alone right now."

"I'm *fine*."

I don't argue.

Instead, I dial Bean & Nugget. And of course, no one answers, because it's after five on a Sunday.

No one's at the café.

Which means I have no choice but to dial Zen's personal number. The car wasn't out front, so I assume they're out somewhere with it.

"What are you *doing*?" Grey repeats.

He doesn't advance on me. Doesn't stare at me like he wants to take my clothes off. Doesn't stare at me like he wants to stab me with a rusty spoon either.

He just looks off-kilter, and *I don't like it*.

Zen answers on the sixth ring. "Sabrina Sullivan. This

is a surprise. If you're planning to ruin Uncle Grey's life and quit, can you do me a favor and write him a super-long resignation letter? Like, twenty pages or something. Anything to stall you from making this decision."

Do they know what I'm planning?

Are they acting like they like me so that I don't do it?

Or have I finally gotten close enough to Zen's inner circle to get the full force of the sass they usually aim at Grey?

Who's playing games now, dammit? "Your uncle just had an out-of-body experience in his doorway, and he says he's fine but he's clearly not, and I think he's either mad at me or doesn't trust me since everyone in town seems to think we're sleeping together and that's my fault, so please come check on him so I can quit worrying about him."

"I'm *fine*," Grey snaps.

"Oh, that's his stubborn ass voice," Zen replies cheerfully.

"It's charming. Can you please come home and check on him?"

"Probably just got lightheaded."

"Does that happen often?"

"I'm standing *right here*," Grey says.

"And you're using your stubborn ass voice," I snap back. "Also, my dog is freaking out, which means someone else needs to check on you."

"Wow. This is fascinating," Zen says. "I'll text him a picture of penis latte art, and if he doesn't flip me off in response, make him lie down and put his feet up."

I almost choke on my tongue. *Make him lie down and put his feet up?* Are they pranking me, or is something legit wrong here? "Oh my god."

"I know. Penis latte art is extreme, but I like to remind him life could be worse."

"The other thing."

"Oh. That. He won't die."

"Oh my god."

"Still standing right here." Grey presses his palms into his eyes, clearly standing on his own just fine, but Zen isn't making me feel any better.

Nor is Jitter.

My dog is still laying across Grey's feet, whining and pressing his body to Grey's legs while the man himself leans against the wall under the stairs.

"For real, he's only had one trip in an ambulance, and his stress levels are much lower here compared to then, even if he's making things worse on himself with this *Super Villain Man* plan."

"I swear to caramel macchiatos, if you're fucking with me right now—"

Grey moves, and I cut myself off to point him toward the couch. *"Lay down."*

"I'm *fine,*" he says.

"He's grumpy again. Like, worse grumpy. Is that a good or a bad sign?" I ask Zen.

"He has a minor circulation issue that may or may not clear itself up if he can reduce his stress levels, so he should probably not be grumpy. Did you do something?"

"Are you helping or hurting with the stress levels?"

"Helping. Duh. You? What did you do to stress him out? Did you pull out the powdered cheese again?"

Am I having blood pressure issues now too? I do believe I am. "I walked my dog."

"Aww, Jitter's such a good dog. Hey, has he checked his phone? I texted him."

"Check your phone," I tell Grey when I realize Zen didn't mean Jitter needed to check *his* phone.

Grey looks at the dog, then at me, and he sighs as he sinks to the floor. "My phone stresses me out."

"He needs to change his number, but he won't listen to me no matter how many penis latte art pictures I send him," Zen says. "Oh, yes, there it is. He's flipped off my latte art in text. He's fine. Go about your day with a clear conscience, and thank you for your good deed."

"My—"

The line clicks dead.

"—pleasure," I finish.

Minor circulation issue? Super Villain Man?

"You can go," he says stiffly, not looking at me.

Jitter lifts his head and licks Grey's face.

His whole face.

The whole damn thing.

Instead of grimacing and shoving him away though, Grey half smiles and rubs Jitter behind the ears. "Knock it off, pup. I'm fine."

Still not looking at me.

I sink to the carpet and cross my legs, watching him. "So, Super Villain Man?"

He sighs and swipes his face. "You're fired."

"You're gonna have to put more *oomph* behind that for me to believe it."

"Fine. You're not fired. But please go home."

"With or without my dog?"

"Leave him here."

My heart melts into a puddle of sappy, gooey, warm

puddles of lovey-dovey crap that I absolutely do not have the bandwidth for.

I pull my knees to my chest and loop my arms around them, watching him not watch me while he loves on my dog, who's attempting to climb in the man's lap again. "I won't tell anyone."

Those hooded blue eyes lift and meet my gaze head-on, and my stomach drops like I'm on the best of the best roller coaster. "You have a code."

"I have to, or I can't live with myself."

His focus on me doesn't waver, and my arms break out in goosebumps.

So intense.

And I like it.

I like *him*.

Despite every reason I shouldn't, despite all of my own misgivings about liking *anyone*, I like him.

He feels like a friend.

A complicated friend, but *a friend*.

"My best friend and business partner shoved a paper in front of me and told me it was a purchase authorization for a new piece of lab equipment I'd mentioned wanting to acquire," he says. "It was the authorization to sell off a research project I'd put six years of my life into and a commitment to send the next ten years' worth of my research directly to a start-up that he'd bought into. I have a code too. It's simple. *Don't fucking lie to make money off of someone else.* And I've added *read all of the fine print.* And *don't trust people.*"

It takes everything I have to not launch myself over my dog and hug him.

The thing I've learned about people is that they're never all good or all bad.

Chandler?

He's on my permanent shit list because he betrayed me, but *I get it*. His parents have had issues since the dawn of their relationship, and they continuously one-upped each other in gifts and experiences to him instead of being a family unit, giving him an inflated sense of self-worth constantly battling with an inflated sense of guilt. They fucked him up, but it's on him if he ever wants to be the kind of person who deserves my time again.

Emma?

She has given people the benefit of the doubt her entire life, and she's been taken advantage of. Laney and I have fended off the worst of what we could whenever we'd see someone taking advantage of her sweet nature, but we—*I*—failed her at her own wedding.

Laney?

Rule-following angel of a woman who's taken to starting food fights.

We're all complicated.

Grey?

People have hurt him. I don't know all of it, but I've seen enough in this world to recognize how much it probably took for him to tell me his side of this part of his story.

I don't take his trust for granted, and I won't break it, no matter how much I don't *want* his trust.

And that's my biggest issue with my attraction to Grey.

We're both complicated. We're both afraid. And I think we *get* each other in a way I never thought another human being could get me.

"I didn't mean to lie to you in Hawaii," I whisper.

He shakes his head. "Doesn't matter."

"It does to me."

"We weren't supposed to be *here*."

"But we are."

God, that gaze.

He looks at me, and I feel like I'm the center of his universe.

That's how he looked at me in Hawaii too.

For one amazing night, I was his entire focus.

For one amazing night, I thought he was everything I could've ever wanted and nothing I deserved.

But now he's here.

And I don't want to leave.

I want to know more.

Not because I have to know everything, but because I want to know *him*.

I want to see the man I met in Hawaii again. I want *that* Grey back. The funny, self-deprecating, *smiling* Grey who wanted to do good with me.

"You keep doing good deeds for me," he says.

"You keep making it easy."

"I'm behind on my good-deed meter."

"I imagine being *Super Villain Man* probably interferes with that."

"It's *Super Vengeance Man*."

"Justice, huh?"

"I heard you crying earlier."

I freeze.

Hard freeze.

Only Mom was supposed to hear that.

His gaze still doesn't waver. "I will fucking destroy him."

Café au lait, take me away.

I believe him.

And *I want to see it.*

"But does it have to be at the expense of my café?" I whisper.

When it comes to staring contests, I can win them in my sleep. But holding Grey's gaze right now is the hardest thing in the world.

He's wavering. I can *feel* it.

I don't even know what Chandler did to him, but whatever it was, it was bad enough that this man who insisted on doing good deeds with me and *to me* for one incredibly, earth-shattering night is only wavering.

Not breaking.

The steely determination to destroy my cousin is undeniable.

It's sexy as hell.

The door swings open and Zen strolls inside. "Haven't stopped breathing? Damn. I wanted your comic book collection."

Grey still doesn't break eye contact. He's managed to pet Jitter to the point that my dog has melted into his lap, and he's still watching me.

"There has to be another way," I say to him.

"Find it."

Fuck.

Just *fuck.*

I don't actually know what Chandler cares about.

A month ago, I would've said *Emma*, but since Hawaii,

I don't think he *cared* so much as he thought it meant he *won*. He got to marry the prom queen.

She's not his anymore.

Losing Emma isn't enough punishment or we wouldn't be here.

So I need to figure out what would give Grey satisfaction.

And *I don't know*.

And what does that say about me? And my relationship with my best friends, when I can't even tell you what the man *she was about to marry* cares most about in the entire world?

"I'll give you two weeks," he adds.

"What's going on here?" Zen asks. "I can't believe I'm about to say this, but I think I preferred the cheese incident."

"Deal," I reply to Grey.

Two weeks, I can work with.

One way or another.

17

Grey

THE WORLD IS UPSIDE DOWN. Right is wrong. Left is right. Sweet is sour. Sabrina Sullivan is my new obsession.

She's filling the space in my brain that's usually reserved for research projects in a way that no woman has since I met Felicia.

And look how that turned out.

But I still can't stop thinking about Sabrina.

It's mid-morning on Monday. Not even a full twenty-four hours after I heard her crying and then she invaded my townhouse to make sure I was okay when I had one of my annoying dizzy spells. I'm actively working on convincing myself that she's not in the kitchen—and there-fore not hiding from the places where she could find what would be a better plan for me to finally get justice on an old wound—when I notice a complete and total hush has fallen over the café.

It's not just a hush.

There's a weird vibe too.

I don't like it.

Reminds me of the hush and the vibe that came whenever I'd do something relatively normal for a kid—like the time I broke my mother's favorite vase when trying to fill it with water for the dandelions I'd picked in the yard—and my siblings, who were so much older and therefore less likely to make messes or break things, were waiting for the blow-up that would come.

Both from the broken vase, and from the nerve that I had as a kid to pick weeds as presents when weeds would piss her off too.

I'm hunched over a puzzle in the corner booth, not actually seeing the pieces in front of me thanks to my brain being stuck on the Sabrina channel. As I'm shifting my gaze to covertly figure out what's going on, someone drops onto the cushioned bench across from me, making the entire booth shake like Jitter's flopped down on the table.

"Greyson Cartwright. I thought you'd be an absent owner."

Chandler Sullivan.

Asshole in the flesh.

Sitting there smirking at me with his bulgy brown eyes and annoyingly fresh haircut and preppy button-down under some name-brand coat, his white skin tan like he stayed in Hawaii for an extra couple weeks after his disaster of a wedding.

My pulse launches itself into outer space. A hazy dark sheen clouds my vision. My mouth goes dry.

I consciously remind myself that he has no power here.

He can't hurt me the way he did in college.

I'm still smart to stay on guard, but the man won't hurt me. Or anyone else in this café. *Super Vengeance Man* doesn't take shit from people like him.

I blink twice, clearing the haze out of my vision, and lounge back in my seat, taking a quick sweep of the room to verify that everyone in here is, in fact, staring.

That it's not my imagination.

Sabrina's cousin—one of the triplets—isn't here like he has been frequently this past week, but Bitsy is. She said hi a while ago. I think. I've been very focused on not being focused enough for this puzzle, but a hi from Bitsy feels familiar.

Three women I recognize but can't name are at one of the tables by the window overlooking the iced-over lake and snow-capped mountains. A group of retired men who apparently come in after their morning ski run once a week are at the picnic-style table closest to me.

All of them are staring at us.

Probably ready to pass judgment on me depending on how I react to Chandler.

He picks up one of my puzzle pieces and holds it up to the light. "What the fuck is this?"

Don't flinch. Don't flinch. Don't flinch. "A puzzle piece. When you put them all together in the right order, they make a pretty picture."

Bitsy chokes on her tea.

Chandler doesn't seem to realize I've just insulted him. He's still smirking while he examines the puzzle piece. "Willa! Willa, get me a cappuccino," he calls.

Willa eyes us both from behind the counter. Zen

appears in the doorway to the kitchen, and the scent of lemon scones hits my nose.

"Aw, fuck, bring me three of Gram-gram's scones too," he says.

Willa looks at me, then back at him. "You pay first when you're a customer here."

He freezes.

But only for a second before he aims a grin at her then turns it on me. "You're gonna make me pay for food and drink here now? I thought we were friends."

Does anyone else think that grin is smarmy, or is it just me?

Probably not just me.

"Why's he gonna give food away to his friends when you never did?" one of the older guys says.

"You know who this guy is, Jimmy?" Chandler fires back. "He's so loaded, he makes you look broke. He can afford a drink and a snack for an old friend."

My shoulders hitch. "Classy, Sullivan. Very classy."

"Not like Sabrina isn't telling them all the dirt on you anyway." He leans forward, putting his elbows on top of my puzzle. "She giving you shit? She thinks she runs the place."

"No."

"Oh, fuck, dude—did you fire her?"

Is that panic?

Is he afraid of Sabrina? Afraid *for* Sabrina? Worried about the café?

I might've only been here a week, but I know why this place runs so smoothly.

It's her.

"Not yet," I reply. "Do you think I should?"

That's panic.

That's sheer panic.

He glances back at the counter. Zen's still watching from the doorway. Willa's straightening the remaining pastries in the bakery case.

Sabrina's not in sight.

The scent of lemon scones is getting stronger though. She's back there. She's baking.

I didn't understand at first why she didn't bake them early in the morning, but I'm catching on. Word spreads that they're fresh out of the oven, and we get an influx of customers for the lunch rush.

Chandler looks back at me, and *fuck*.

This would be easier if he wasn't visibly gulping and that wasn't undeniable concern clouding his expression. "This place would die without her."

"So?"

He blanches.

The fucker *blanches*.

Worse?

I think I actually feel sorry for him.

Super Vengeance Man wouldn't.

But I have a conscience, no matter how much I wish I didn't when it comes to this blight of humanity.

"My grandpa would fucking kill me," he says.

That, I feel less bad about. Dude lost this café all on his own. "He know about your gambling problem?"

Chandler slaps his mouth shut and turns a glare on me. He's still holding my puzzle piece, and his elbows have pushed apart half the pieces I already had in order. "If nobody's told you yet, you can't believe the gossip that comes out of *some* people's mouths."

233

It's not gossip.

It's in the report from the private investigator I hired to find out why Chandler was selling his café.

Should've asked for a full report on his hobbies and interests and collections too, but all I wanted was to know why he was selling and how much financial trouble he was in.

"People here gossip?" I say.

He freezes again.

I know that look.

He's piecing out a mental puzzle. *He knows about my gambling problem but doesn't think people here talk.*

Zen stops next to my table and slides a cup of tea and a scone in front of me. "Eat. Drink. Be merry."

Chandler looks up at them and squints, and in less than the span of a single heartbeat, I prepare to end his time on this earth.

If he says a single bad word about Zen, asks a single question wrong, or so much as moves a single *eyelash* in a direction I don't like, I will *end him*.

My fists curl.

My heart fires furiously.

And his phone rings—*loudly*—before whatever he's thinking can come out of his mouth. He grabs it, still holding my puzzle piece with his other hand, still squinting at Zen, and answers. "Yeah, man. What's up?"

Bitsy rolls her eyes.

"Always thought he did that because he was running three cafés and had a lot going on, but now we know he's just a dick," Jimmy mutters.

"What he did to Emma wasn't your first clue?" one of the other men says.

234

Chandler flinches, then palms my puzzle piece and rises from the booth. "Yeah. Sounds good. I'm on my way." He heads toward the door. "No, just dropped by to see if I could help the new guy at my old café. Dude's in over his head. Got new weirdos working here. Gonna be asking for help soon enough."

Weirdos.

When I want to charge out of the booth and tackle him, my vision clouds again while my head goes light. I pinch my lips together and breathe through my nose.

Fuck.

I grab the edge of the table and breathe.

And breathe.

And breathe.

Pushing down the lightheadedness with sheer willpower. Grounding myself.

My vision clears as Chandler reaches the door. He pauses, looks down at a wooden statue of a bear that guards it, and rubs the damn thing's head before shoving out into the winter morning.

All while I sit here barely able to do much more than breathe.

And that's before I realize my scone is gone and he has it in his hand.

The fucker *took my scone.*

Know what's worse than having an asshole think he got the better of you?

Agreeing with him.

"Did he take your puzzle piece along with your treat?" Bitsy asks me as the door shuts behind him.

My nod is jerky.

She *tsks*.

I feel a heavy weight drilling into the back of my head.

Sabrina's watching me grim-faced from the kitchen.

Zen's beside her, even more grim-faced.

Both of them watching me like they want to know what I'll do next.

Answer's pretty simple.

I will fucking destroy everything he loves. But apparently not while I'm face to face with the bastard.

Sabrina looks at the door.

At the carved wooden bear.

Then back at me.

She saw too.

She knows this café means something to him.

She ducks her head and retreats back to the kitchen.

Jimmy, one of the older guys, looks at Zen. "He gives you any trouble, you let me know."

Zen blinks once, then also retreats to the kitchen.

Jimmy looks at me and nods.

I nod back.

The very worst thing about being here? About what I want to do here?

I'm starting to like it.

For me. For Zen.

For the fucking *café*.

But I can build something better. I can, and I will, and I'll do it with bees all over the place so that the Cheese Turd never dares set foot in here again.

For *all* of our sakes.

18

Sabrina

WORK IS AWFUL.

I hate it, and I hate hating work. Even on the hardest days when things break and customers are cranky and food trucks don't come in on time and I burn myself with coffee or a hot pan, I generally love my job and still wouldn't trade it for the world.

But since Chandler finally showed his face this morning, nothing's the same.

Grey's moody and quiet through finishing his puzzle.

When he's done, he leaves it on the table with one piece missing in the middle.

Zen barely says a word. Willa murmurs to me that Chandler needs to eat a bag of dicks. Cedar kicks me out of the kitchen, and he's so furious that I don't argue, even though it means I fake my way through being cheerful while running the counter with Willa during the lunch rush.

At least two dozen people ask me if I'm okay. I lie and put on a perky face and say that I'm great.

More ask me if I've heard from Emma.

My shift takes forever to end, and when it does, I pick up Jitter and the two of us head to one of my favorite summer spots for those rare moments when I want to be alone.

I crunch over the short path from the two-car parking lot to the gazebo that overlooks both downtown and the lake and train station, and then I have to clear snow off of the picnic table inside to get a place to sit.

Good sign that no one else has been here. Also a good sign that everyone else will stay away.

Jitter's in heaven. He can lay in snow forever.

I know I won't make it more than half an hour—not when it's this cold and I'm sitting still—but I need to recenter myself.

When I hear a car on the road behind me, my shoulders twitch. When it stops and a door shuts, I get ready to pretend I'm already freezing and bolt.

Except Jitter beats me to it, and the only thing he's doing is woofing once in absolute glee and darting off to greet his new favorite person.

"Go away," I say.

Grey ignores me, carefully navigating the trail I cut with my snowshoes and still sinking into the path halfway up his calves while Jitter hovers near him. When he reaches the gazebo, he lifts a Bean & Nugget coffee tumbler. "Peace offering."

"Are you giving up on turning my café inside out?"

He sighs and sets the tumbler on the picnic table bench between us.

I smell vanilla and cinnamon.

That's low.

That's *very* low.

"We could build something better together," he says without looking at me.

"You realize how insulting that sounds to someone who's incredibly proud of how hard she's worked to make it what it is today?"

"Didn't mean it that way."

I know what this is. This is him trying to find common ground. It *is* a peace offering.

And I'm grateful.

But it still hurts. Bean & Nugget might not be perfect, but it's where I belong. With coffee and Grandma's scone recipe and the history and the community and everything we can keep doing in the future.

"I'm sorry Chandler took your puzzle piece. And your scone."

"Not your fault. And I got another scone. You might've been there."

This sucks. It just does.

"What are you even doing here?" I ask.

"Café got a call from a concerned citizen who said you were headed this way and shouldn't be alone."

I slide a look at him.

"Zen took the call. Couldn't even begin to tell you what they sounded like."

The coffee aroma is teasing me.

I'm usually a straight black coffee person. Dessert

coffee—anything all doctored up—is reserved for special occasions and bad days.

Today is definitely a bad day.

So I give in to temptation and pick up the mug, sniff it —*definitely* cinnamon and vanilla—and I sip, and I get *everything*.

This is good.

Better than good.

It's sweet and creamy and just the right spicy. A little piece of joy in a dark, dreary, ugly day when the sun still had the nerve to shine.

Dammit. "Can we pretend we're in Hawaii and you're Duke again for just five minutes?"

His blue eyes make a slow perusal of the landscape around us, then settle back on me with more warmth than I'm expecting.

My thighs clench. And not because it's cold.

More because all he had to do was look away, and then look back, and I swear he's everything he was in Hawaii.

He inclines his head while Jitter keeps wagging his tail and pushing his head into Grey's hand. "As the lady wishes."

I sip my latte again, then I point to the far end of Main Street. "See the big log cabin?"

"City Hall?"

"It was a general store that sold mining supplies and food back in the eighteen hundreds. When the gold rush dried up here, they built around it. If you get a tour, Vicki will point out the original walls. They're around the county clerk's office now. So anyone who wants to get married has to get their license in our original general store."

He slides me a look like he wants to ask if I'm talking about marriage for any particular reason, but all that comes out of his mouth is, "Fascinating."

"The statue of Ol' Snaggletooth in front of City Hall was put up in the 1980's. Legend has it that he was the first man to find gold here in the Tooth, but if you go on the tour at the mine, there—" I point in the opposite direction, to the old wooden building rising out of the mountainside above the lake "—they'll tell you that we have the largest mine to never actually find any gold, and that Snaggletooth was likely a scam artist. But he gets credit for the railroad coming through here."

"What was his real name?"

"You'll have to take a tour of both the mine and the railroad depot by the lake to find out all of the different people who are suspected to have been Snaggletooth himself. And some people will tell you that the real Snaggletooth was a shop owner in town who had a tooth with the same snaggle shape as the creek if you look at it from the top of Bobcat Peak behind us."

"So you come by having nicknames for everyone here naturally."

"Exactly."

"Ms. Donut came in yesterday, didn't she?"

I pause. What did I—*oh*. And who—*oh* again.

I try to hide my heating face behind a casual sip of coffee, but I don't think he's buying my attempt at a noncommittal *hmm*.

He grins, and *dammit*, he's still adorable when he grins.

"Stop talking about that," I order. "You're Duke. You've never been here. I'm giving you the grand tour."

He leans back, draping his arm across the tabletop

behind us in one of *those* moves. "Apologies. Please continue."

As if I can just *continue* when I'm wondering if he likes me as much as I don't want to like him. "That building? The A-frame on Main Street just two blocks down from City Hall? That's the salon where my mom has worked my entire life. The building next to it, the one with the blue roof, is an ice cream shop where I had my first kiss. The building on the other side, the brown one, is a gift shop that once caused the biggest drama the Tooth has seen in years by selling taxidermy chipmunks that weren't ethically and humanely sourced."

He frowns. "The GrippaPeen guy's dad is a taxidermist."

"Yep. The gift shop didn't take them off sale, but ownership changed within a year, and the new people did."

"That sounds like it could be a warning to your new boss about behaving himself."

My ass is getting cold. Jitter's keeping Grey warm instead of me. And mention of my *new boss* makes my face have a reaction that I can't suppress. "Speaking of, have I told you that my cousin is a complete and total thunder-twat who sold my family's café to a guy who can be the world's biggest prick but I *get it*. I understand a lot of his issues and I don't blame him for how he feels."

Grey ducks his head and sucks in a heavy breath.

I mean it though.

I don't blame him. I *haven't* blamed him. But if I'm talking to Duke, then I'm going to talk to *Duke*. Not Grey. "I have to find a solution to a problem of saving my café while letting my new boss get the peace he deserves in the next twelve days or else I'm facing the very real possibility that I'll lose something that means the world to me. And the best person to help me find the right solution for justice is angry with me right now, and even if she wasn't, I will *never* say that platycuntapus's name to her. She deserves time to mourn and recover and find her new normal. Not questions about how to make him pay for what he did."

Jitter whines and sets his head on Grey's knee. Such a good dog.

I don't even have to look at the man to know he's struggling with this too. My dog's telling me.

And the fact that my dog hates it when Grey's upset hurts too.

The only other person Jitter loves this much is Theo, which I've never quite understood, but I think I'm getting it now.

Jitter has a finely-tuned *people have hurt you and I want to love you* meter.

I study Grey, making sure he's not gripping anything for support or getting that distant look in his eyes like he did Sunday night when I thought he was going to pass out in his doorway.

He seems fine though.

As fine as I assume he can be in this position, anyway.

"You don't think you can find a compromise for your boss," he says.

"I think it hurts to watch your life's purpose go up in smoke through no fault of your own."

He looks away. "That is its own particular brand of torture."

I know he knows. He told me as much Sunday night.

We both know he's doing the same to me that his partner did to him, except *I still get it.*

"What did Chandler do to you?" I ask.

He doesn't answer.

I wonder if Emma knows.

As if it matters. I won't bring her into this. I can barely bring myself to ask Theo what would hurt Chandler the most for fear he'd ask her, no matter how much I tell him not to.

I hunch forward and cradle my coffee in my hands, which are getting colder by the minute, even inside my gloves.

"Are you staying here in the Tooth?" I ask. "Is that the long-term plan?"

"I don't know."

"People won't come to a kombucha bar for breakfast," I say. "They won't drop in for a five-minute chat while they're waiting for their morning fermented tea the way they drop in for a quick visit while they're waiting for their latte. And the locals won't abandon the tavern and the other restaurants they go to for dinner for something new in town."

"If that's the case, that'll eventually be someone else's problem."

Exactly the answer I was afraid of. "Please don't make me fight dirty. I genuinely like you too much as a person to want to fight dirty."

His eyes flare and then go dark as he shifts to look at me straight-on. "Define *dirty.*"

The fact that he's turned on and not wary shouldn't be a relief.

Nor should it make my breasts tighten and my clit tingle.

I straighten and face him, ignoring the distinct lack of space between us. "I will save my café by any means necessary."

"You think you'll find my skeletons."

He shouldn't be leaning into me with his gaze dropping to my lips.

And I shouldn't like it nearly as much as I do. "I don't want you to have skeletons."

"You wouldn't use them against me."

"You have no idea what I'd do."

"Okay, Duchess."

Fuck.

The bastard just called me a good person.

"If I kiss you, I'm pretending you're still Duke," I breathe as our lips inch closer and closer together.

"If I kiss you, I know I'm kissing Sabrina."

"That's a horrible thing to say to me."

His lips tip up, but the smile doesn't diminish the smoky desire in his eyes. "You're a good person."

"You just don't want me to play dirty."

"On the contrary. I'm intrigued at the idea of you playing dirty. I want to know what you define as *dirty*."

I want him to do dirty things to me. I want him to pull me into the storage closet at the café and tease my clit with that long thumb. I want him to kiss me until I can't breathe. I want him to rip my shirt off and shove me against a wall and thrust into me while I ride him. I want to suck his cock and I want to ride his face and I want to have our night in Hawaii again.

"We need to leave here before we both turn into icicles," I breathe.

"I'm not cold at all right now."

His lips brush mine. I grip his coat, pull him into me, and I let myself go.

I pretend we're in Hawaii. That the night never ended. That we're kissing, our tongues dancing as we claw each other's clothes off. That he's pinching my nipples and growling out that uninhibited noise of sheer pleasure while I shove his pants down off his hips and tackle the buttons on his Hawaiian shirt. That I can hear the surf rolling in through the open door of his balcony.

So hot when you do good deeds, he said while he nipped at my earlobe.

I want to do good deeds to you all night long, I'd replied.

I crawl into his lap, straddling him, ignoring Jitter making a disgusted grunt and the sound of my coffee tumbler bouncing on the snowy ground.

He fists my hair and kisses me deeper.

Why can't this be simple?

Because men aren't good for the women of your family, I remind myself.

It's okay, I add. *This is just for the sex.*

As if I can actually believe that now.

Despite our differences, Grey feels like a friend. And *that* is something I've *never* felt in the same way for any of my other flings.

"Why—so good?" he says while he pulls me closer and rocks, rubbing my clit against the thick erection hiding in his pants.

"Bad—always—good."

He growls.

246

Growls.

And it's so fucking hot to have a man growling over me that I almost come on the spot.

He growls again, lower and thicker, but at the same time, he freezes. "Jitter?"

"No jitters," I gasp, rocking against him.

He shifts me to the side and lunges for something. "No, *Jitter.*"

Jitter.

My dog.

I forgot my dog's name, but Grey's scrambling to untangle himself from me while holding my dog's collar.

And *Jitter* is growling.

At—*oh fuck.*

He's growling *at a porcupine.*

"Oh no no no," I whisper.

"Do. Not. Move," Grey breathes. "Jitter. Down. *Now.*"

Jitter whine-growls.

"Jitter, get *down,*" I hiss.

Quietly.

And gently.

So as not to terrify the two-foot-long rodent currently staring at us with dark, scared eyes and its quills on edge sitting on a rocky ledge just beyond the gazebo.

Grey has a grip on Jitter's collar and is tugging him back closer to us.

The primitive sex beast in my vagina wants to know if his muscles are bulging under his coat.

The rest of me is smart enough to tell her to shut up if we want to survive this without a quill to my dog or to any of our faces.

The porcupine isn't moving at all.

"Good boy," Grey says to Jitter. "Good puppers. Back. Back we go."

Jitter eases back onto Grey's legs and whines.

Grey gets a grip around his body like he can hold back my hundred-pound dog if Jitter decides to charge.

I'm panting.

Grey grabs one of my hands and squeezes through our gloves, still clutching Jitter. "Gonna be okay."

"I'm supposed to be the experienced mountain woman telling your beach bum ass that," I whisper back.

"Quit being funny."

We sit in silence for what feels like an eternity, Grey squeezing my hand and holding my dog until the porcupine eventually decides we're not a threat and lumbers around the gazebo to climb under it.

"Time to go," Grey says.

"*So* time to go," I agree. "Thank you. For—just thank you."

He drops my hand and grabs my coffee tumbler, which has leaked all over the ground. I untie Jitter's leash from the picnic table leg and hold him tight while we scurry back to our cars.

Grey insists on seeing me into mine first, but he holds my door open after both Jitter and I are in the car.

"I don't want to hurt you," he says.

I hold his gaze. "Likewise."

"You're playing dirty now?"

"Change might be inevitable, and I might have the utmost respect for you wanting to find peace and closure, but Bean & Nugget serves a vital purpose in our community. I won't let it go without a fight."

What he does next startles the crap out of me.

He leans into my car, pecks my cheeks, murmurs, "I hope you find what we need, but even if you don't, looking forward to every minute of the next twelve days," and then shuts me inside my car.

My breath whooshes out of me.

It's game on.

And I don't know if that's good or bad.

For either of us.

19

Grey

SABRINA SULLIVAN HAS INVADED every one of my thoughts at every moment of every day, and it doesn't matter what I do to try to shake her, she manages to cement herself in there even more firmly.

Worse?

From the moment the words *find it* left my mouth, hope has taken hold.

Hope that she comes through with an alternate plan to destroy Chandler in a way that I haven't been able to puzzle out myself.

I've been working on it too, but I don't have the connections or the background knowledge of this town and how he fits in it to have any fresh ideas myself.

Since yesterday morning, the dude-bro's taking up a lot of space in my head. That five-minute exchange cemented my need to make him pay, not just for what he's done to me, but to *everyone* he's hurt.

Even his wedding getting canceled and him starring as the villain in the world's most viral video hasn't changed him.

Since yesterday evening, though, all I can think about is playing dirty with Sabrina.

Kissing the ever-loving hell out of her.

Stripping her out of her clothes.

Licking every square inch of her body.

Making her scream my name in utter ecstasy.

My *real* name.

And this is a problem.

Because I'm walking around prepared to go *Super Vengeance Man* while constantly suppressing a hard-on, which makes it hard to think.

You don't see Thor distracted from saving the world because he's battling boners.

I've sunk to new lows, and I'm now demanding Zen find out every morsel of gossip they can about Sabrina.

I close my eyes, I think about her.

I open my eyes, I think about her.

I go to Bean & Nugget, I think about her.

I get home, I think about her.

I avoid her, I think about her.

I see her, I think about her.

I comp someone's meal because I heard them compliment another customer, I think about her.

I hold a door for someone, I think about her.

I call the number on the collar of a stray dog sitting outside the café, I think about her.

A less chilly breeze blows, and you guessed it, *I think about her*.

Fine.

Fine.

I'm destroying Chandler Sullivan because he made Sabrina cry.

Fuck everyone else in town.

He's going down because he made Sabrina cry.

That's the bare, simple truth of it.

"You didn't get *anything* out of her old gymnastics teacher?" I ask Zen on our way into Bean & Nugget early Tuesday morning.

"I learned I can still do a cartwheel," Zen reports.

"I meant anything *helpful*."

"If you ever need to torture me, you should hold me upside down, because while I can cartwheel like a nine-year-old—that's all momentum—I can't handstand to save my life."

I stop at the back door, hands freezing, toes going numb, and give my nibling a *you know that's not what I mean* look.

As usual, Zen is immune, but they smile as they finally give me the information I'm waiting for. "Sabrina Sullivan was mouthy but mostly walked the line of not being *too* mouthy while being friendly and helpful when she took gymnastics as a kid. She would've gone a lot further if she hadn't twisted her knee in second grade, which her teacher suspected was a fake injury, but could never prove. And she also said if a kid didn't want to be in gymnastics, then it's better for them to find what they wanted to do. And considering Sabrina was, in fact, born in the kitchen

253

right next to the sink and basically grew up there, there's no question Bean & Nugget is where she belongs."

"It took you five hours last night to find that out?"

"No, I stuck around and did an adult gymnastics class."

"You did an adult gymnastics class," I repeat.

"It was fun."

"You *participated*."

"In corduroy pants and a button-down shirt."

Now *I'm* the one stopping us from entering the back door when the cold is generally something I'll avoid at all costs. "And?"

"Does the name Austin George ring a bell?"

I frown. "Is that one of the neighbors who dropped off food?"

They laugh. "*Uncle Grey*. He's a gold-medal gymnast from like twenty years ago?"

"*Oh.*"

"He and his husband run the gym in town now. Bought it like eight years ago. So *after* Sabrina's brief rule as the terror of Tooth Gymnastics."

I bite back the question about how Sabrina's now a *terror*. "That doesn't mean they get the instant Zen seal of approval."

"Yes, it does."

"It does?"

"When one of your childhood idols offers to help you do a cartwheel, you do the fucking cartwheel, and then you stay and gossip with all of the fabulous ladies who were there for class before heading to the salon where Sabrina's mother works for an apparently *super* late night rendezvous that might've been hosted by a local Wiccan who's *Wiccan cool*. Heh."

I refuse to admit how much my entire body perks up at the mention of Sabrina's name again and how much I don't really care about the rest of that sentence. "*And*?"

"And I don't remember any of their real names, so take this with a grain of salt, but Myrtle has a grandson who just switched college majors for the fourth time, Viola's Subaru is at that age where she knows it'll last another ten years, but also, if she sells *now*, she'll get a better deal than if she lets it get any older on a trade-in, and Sue Ellen's daughter seriously needs a divorce, in Sue Ellen's opinion, but if you ask me, Sue Ellen is a judgmental hag who sees what she wants to see and has no idea what her daughter's marriage is really all about."

"You're fired."

Zen is grinning broader than I've seen them grin in ages when talking about anyone other than me or my sister's gastrointestinal issues. "Myrtle also said Sabrina saved her from going on a date with a guy who turned out to be some kind of scam artist in the obscure profession of toy train collecting. Something about passing off replicas as vintage. Viola reports Sabrina's the reason the old mayor lost his reelection bid six years ago, and the new mayor's the reason tourists keep coming to the train station and the old mine even in winter now. Oh, and the Valentine's Day heart walk on Main Street next week was apparently Sabrina's idea too, and if we back out of hosting the speed dating station, the general single population of the Tooth will be what runs us out of business and also makes sure that the kombucha bar fails. Sue Ellen thinks Sabrina knows things about her and is saving them for a rainy day, but I couldn't get out of her what gossip she thinks Sabrina knows, so she's probably either in debt or secretly has a crush on some crusty old dude."

"You're rehired, but on probation."

"Uncle Grey, you know all the right things to say to make a person's dreams come true. P. S., freaking *ask Sabrina out already*. She is *so* not on Team Cheese Turd. Plus she can make or break this place after you renovate it. Also, you'd be doing me a favor if you got laid again." Zen throws the back door open, and we step inside to a disaster of a kitchen.

Disaster may be something of an overstatement. But there shouldn't be dishes in the sink at five in the morning. The grill shouldn't be on. I shouldn't smell coffee this strongly. And the dining room light *definitely* shouldn't be glowing, nor should voices be coming from there.

Zen doesn't seem to connect the *something's wrong* dots.

I look behind me.

Why are there six cars in my usually empty lot?

What the hell's going on?

"Yes, yes, do the dishes," they say perkily. "Look at me. Who am I? *Oh, I'm so excited! I have piles and piles of dishes! I'm going to sing my heart out at the top of my lungs like I'm Cinderella to see if it'll annoy my new boss so he quits looking at me like he wants to strip me out of my clothes!*"

"You're fired again."

"You'll have to do the dishes."

Is it possible to have a permanent cramp in your eyelid?

All I wanted was to hear everything they could tell me about Sabrina, and then they did it, and now I don't know which way is up and if they just insulted me or not.

"Who's here this early?" I ask Zen, as if they'll have any more of an idea than I do.

"My powers of deduction tell me someone who's messy," they reply.

"Your powers of deduction are so acute this time of day."

They grin and head for the dining room.

I hang up my coat, which is beginning to smell exactly like the café, peek inside Jitter's doghouse and come up disappointed that he's not there, and then I follow my nibling.

"Zen!" an unfamiliar woman's voice says. "You made it. Good. We were getting worried."

"Morning, Iris," Zen replies cheerfully.

"Come sit by me," someone else says. "Look. I got the special Guatemalan coffee beans from my friend for you to try. Here. Have a cup."

"You are a goddess."

What on *earth*?

I stop in the doorway and survey the Bean & Nugget dining room, which is housing roughly a dozen people at five in the morning, all of them drinking coffee and enjoying pastries.

There's Devi who owns the art gallery and her grandmother who runs House of Curry, which makes delicious food when you're not wearing it. Shirlene, the health department inspector. Marley, our neighbor with the little girl who knocks on Sabrina's door regularly looking for Jitter. Bitsy, who dropped by a mouth-watering casserole the other day that was just as good as her English Sunday dinner, which is a sentence I never expected to come out of my mouth, but is still true. A few other people look familiar, but I can't immediately place their names or where I've seen them.

And then there's a woman who's so startlingly similar to Sabrina, but with a few more crow's lines at her eyes, that it must be her mother.

Her mother.

That'll make a guy nervous this early in the morning.

I take an extra breath, tell my dick to stay *down*, and let myself look at Sabrina too.

Naturally, she's here.

Naturally, she's gorgeous. Sipping coffee and laughing at something Devi said. Completely in her element. Her hair's slightly damp, like she didn't have time to dry it all the way after her shower, and now I'm remembering her request to see what I could do in the bathtub.

I shoot a glance at her mother again, and that helps get my cock back under control.

Then I notice Jitter. He's sprawled on his back by the fire with his fur and fluff and jowls so askew that he looks more like furry, mis-assembled IKEA furniture than he does like a hundred-pound not-still-a-puppy, but not-yet-a-dog dog.

"Oh, Grey, good, you're here." Bitsy smiles and waves me into the room. "We need some male input on the speed dating event next weekend."

"The...what?"

"Speed dating," Sabrina's mom supplies. "Bean & Nugget hosts it every Valentine's Day."

"Are you participating this year?" someone asks me.

Zen chokes on their coffee.

I almost choke on my own spit.

"You should," someone else says. "You've been single for, what, two years now?"

Half the people in the room are shooting sly glances at Sabrina. The other half are watching me.

Including Sabrina.

The weight of her gaze is even heavier than the weight of her dog when he presses his waggling body against me, which I wouldn't mind him doing right now for a distraction.

But Jitter's snoozing like this is too early for him today.

"Uncle Grey is totes single," Zen says.

I am.

But I'm *not*.

As in, I'm not too keen on getting back in the dating game.

Probably.

Unless it involves some kind of friends-with-benefits arrangement with the woman whose café I've sworn to destroy.

How, exactly, did I get myself into this again?

One of the older ladies claps. "Oh, good. I'll tell my daughter you'll be there."

"I don't—" I start.

"Back up just a second," an even older lady says. "My granddaughter's coming in from Denver for this. *And* she already knows him."

"Are you sure it's wise for Addison to be in Snaggle-tooth Creek right now?" Sabrina's mother says. "I hear it wasn't the most pleasant for her when she came up last week."

A hush falls on half the group.

Three ladies share *so it's gonna be a throwdown* glances.

Wish I didn't know what that looked like.

Wish I wasn't the reason it's being tossed about.

"Can we all please remember that *Chandler* is the biggest problem in the Tooth?" Sabrina says. "Marley, have you talked to Gail Kingston yet about those custom tissue packs?"

"No, I talked to Laney instead when I dropped off dinner for her yesterday. She is *so smart*. She said we should use the printing space to say *he's not worth these tears. Dry them up and know you're worthy*."

"What will the men get?" someone asks.

"Laney asked the same thing! I told her to surprise me." She turns to me. "Don't you worry about a thing, Grey. Laney's a total professional, *and* she's been one of Sabrina's best friends for as long as I can remember. She won't do anything that embarrasses Bean & Nugget."

"But we have other questions for you," someone else says. "Would it be okay if we brought in three extra tables? It's such a popular event, we don't want to have to turn anyone away."

"So many singles, but they're all so *picky*," someone else mutters.

"They—" I start.

"The extra tables are fine," Zen says.

"Oh, *thank you*, Zen. Here. Have you tried Iris's lavender muffins?"

Lavender muffins.

I feel my eyes flare and I shoot a look at Sabrina.

She's smiling, but shaking her eyes *no* at Zen.

Iris.

Iris is Mrs. Pineapple. Sabrina told me about these muffins in Hawaii.

I start to clear my throat, but it's too late.

Zen's taking a massive bite.

Sabrina stifles a noise. We make eye contact, and she goes pink in the cheeks.

I start to grin.

Until Zen makes a noise of their own.

"Aren't they delicious?" Sabrina's mom says.

"So much," Zen lies.

They turn a subtle but desperate look my way.

Sabrina squeaks again.

Everyone looks at her.

"*Jitter*. You silly thing. What kind of a noise was that?"

The dog snorts, flips one way, hits the fireplace hearth and gets stuck before flopping back the other way. He spots me, barks once in utter jubilance, scrambles to his feet and charges, knocking over the tray of muffins on the way.

"*Oh my god*," Zen whispers.

I pass them my tea.

They gulp.

Iris squints at them.

"Swallowed a dog hair too," they force out. "God, Sabrina, bring a dust mop when you bring Jitter."

"Grey, can we still use this space next year for speed dating?" Bitsy asks. "You'll still have tables, won't you? There's nothing like the fairy lights on the lake at night, and you just can't see them as well anywhere else."

"We could do speed dating *on* the lake," Iris says. "Bet we'd have *way* more success stories that way."

"But it *has* to be here," Bitsy replies. "John and I met at speed dating here. It wouldn't be the same if it was somewhere else."

"Zen, are you okay?" Sabrina's mom asks. "You poor thing."

"Still stuck in there," Zen says hoarsely.

"Maybe it's actually residual cheese dust."

There's another round of everyone sucking in a breath while they dart glances between me and Sabrina and her mom sits there sipping her own coffee like she's completely innocent and didn't remind everyone of the cheese dust on purpose.

"Oh, god, I didn't mean you should do speed dating," one of the women says. "Right. Right. You and Sabrina—"

"Are not dating," Sabrina says lightly. "I don't date."

"That's what your mom said before she got pregnant with you," the oldest woman in the room whispers.

And I'm out.

Out out.

Retreating to the kitchen because I know when I'm in over my head, and it doesn't matter what Sabrina's mom says to that.

I have to leave.

The voices continue in the dining room.

There's laughter. Conversation. Excitement. The clink of coffee cups on the tables.

And Zen's in the middle of it.

Like they belong.

I have *never* seen Zen adjust to a place like this. Even when we were in San Diego after I kicked Felicia out, when it was just the two of us, they didn't like accompanying me for anything to do with work.

Your researcher friends treat me like a specimen, they told me once. *Maybe it's in my head, but I don't like it.*

Here?

Here, they're joining in like they belong. Finding a *gymnastics class*, for fuck's sake. If I tell them I could've warned them about *Mrs. Pineapple's lavender muffins*, they'll laugh their ass off and then some, and probably serve me iced coffee in my chai mug tomorrow for revenge, and we'll be even.

It makes me want to bail right now. Put the café up for sale. Just give it to Sabrina.

Get them out of here.

Before they get hurt.

I angle a glance inside the room and catch Sabrina watching the kitchen door.

She looks away immediately, reaching for her mug as she says something to the woman beside her.

I flush hot, then cold, then hot again, and then I go lightheaded.

Dammit.

I *don't* want to leave.

Even knowing this infatuation has to eventually come to an end, that I have to trust the people in this community to accept Zen and me for who we are, that I'll eventually crave research again in a way that won't be satisfied by running a kombucha bar with a bee theme and live beehives, I don't want to leave.

And that's scarier than hell.

20

Sabrina

THERE ARE some lines that I've sworn to myself I'll never cross.

But I've never been backed into a corner like this before, and I've never felt like a task was as impossible as figuring out what Chandler loves.

My mom doesn't have a clue.

Grandpa doesn't know.

Laney gaped at me when I asked her.

The triplets fell all over themselves stuttering *golf* and *cars* and *hating Theo*, none of which can give us an actual plan of revenge for Grey. Even if Chandler's favorite golf course would let us paint *Chandler is an asshole* on the side of a golf cart, that's probably not sufficient.

I won't bother Emma with this. Absolutely not.

I'm five days into Grey's challenge to me to find

anything else he can use against Chandler, and I have *nothing*.

"What did Chandler do to him?" I whisper to Zen while we're watching the local fridge repair person finally tackle the leak while our local drywall guy fixes the dent in the wall behind the fridge where it nearly rolled into the bathroom during the cheese incident.

Which is the only thing I can bring myself to call it.

"Not my story to tell," they reply.

"But you'll share anyway," I say confidently. "It's in his best interest. I can't be fully effective at my job if I don't know all of the circumstances that led to this assignment."

"Uncle Grey loves puzzles. He's given you all the clues you get to solve this one. By the way, *warn a person next time they're about to eat chewy soap.*"

"I tried. You weren't looking at me."

"Try harder."

"Is there any chance he'll give up this dream of being *Super Vengeance Man* and just let us keep running Bean & Nugget as it is?"

They sigh and make a pucker face. "You know he's rich as fuck, right?"

If I could gag with my eyeballs at how much I don't care about the size of his bank account, I would.

They actually grin back, but sober quickly. "Very, very worst case for Uncle Grey financially is that this place turns into a big ol' tax break. You can't buy it off of him. If I can't talk him out of it, there's zero chance that you can talk him out of it. And if you don't give him something real, he will slap a bee the size of a freaking school bus on the side of this building without a moment's hesitation."

"He can do that and still let us keep the café."

"I heard Emma was the rose-colored glasses one of your group."

I wince.

They make the pucker face again. "Sorry, Sabrina. Can't help you. And I say that as someone who's *also* listening to all of the gossip to see if I can find another way, and as someone who's done all of the market research that supports the idea that a kombucha bar would be more popular here than you think it would. Tell me the ski tourists who stay here because it's cheaper than the resorts twenty minutes away wouldn't pack the place every night."

They have a point, and I have definitely picked up on the vibe that this renovation is more than petty justice. That Zen's smart and Grey's usually smart but hurt, and they could make something fabulous out of their kombucha bar.

So knowing that Grey has a beef against Chandler that won't be satisfied by anything less than destroying something of Chandler's, that they have a solid plan for making this place a success later, and that sex won't convince Grey to let me keep my café, it's time for the last idea I have.

I can either cross a line that I never would've considered crossing since the day I was born, or I can watch the café that's been my entire life's purpose wither away and die.

So line-crossing it is.

He said he wanted to see me play dirty.

This is as dirty as I can go and still live with myself.

I do it at Laney's house while Jitter waits for me outside so that my neighbors won't have any chance of overhearing me through the walls. Laney and Theo are elsewhere, so I have the house to myself aside from their litter of kittens.

Then Jitter and I head home, where I fix myself an afternoon pour-over coffee, turn on the Razzle Dazzle channel for comforting background noise—it's showing a movie that Laney, Emma, and I have seen so much, I can recite it by heart—and I text her.

It's done.

LANEY
HUGS, my friend. Go well?

Better than expected.

LANEY
Good!

Maybe?

LANEY
You think he'll find out?

Definitely. The question is HOW SOON he'll find out. If the café isn't shut down with a massive SABRINA SULLIVAN IS THE BIGGEST LINE-CROSSING ASSHOLE IN THE UNIVERSE sign spray-painted in the windows by the end of the week, we'll have half our answer.

LANEY
When did you hang up?

Twenty minutes ago.

LANEY

You're not fired yet?

Nope.

LANEY

Then I'm trusting your instincts that this was the right step. What's next?

Waiting to hear. I'll keep you updated.

LANEY

You okay?

No.

LANEY

Does it help if I remind you that your complicated feelings and hesitation in doing this mean you're a good person without a lot of other options to protect something you love that serves a massive purpose in our community?

You are entirely too loyal.

LANEY

Nope. Just completely correct in my convictions.

Have you seen Emma this week?

LANEY

frowny emoji No, and Theo thinks she might be sleeping at her office.

He's seen her?

LANEY

Briefly.

This is bad.

LANEY

He's been taking her breakfast to make sure she eats, and she keeps telling him she has a lot of work to catch up on.

I'll take her a pretzel from Sir Pretzelot tomorrow afternoon.

LANEY

Good idea. She's definitely working tomorrow. I had chicken wings delivered to her for dinner, and Theo told me her dad and uncle are checking in on her regularly too. And I know at least three of her clients have brought her giant food baskets.

I...didn't hear that. OH MY GOD. No one's talking to me about Emma AT ALL except for you. Are they tiptoeing around me? Do they think I'm awful?

LANEY

NO. No. Stop. Deep breath. No one thinks you're awful. They think you have enough on your plate right now.

No one has ever kept me in the dark like this. I haven't heard a single WHISPER about Emma in the café. Not about anything since the wedding and the video. They only ask me how she is. They don't tell me how she's doing.

LANEY

I'm coming over.

I'll go see my mom.

LANEY

I'll meet you at her place.

I'm trying really hard to tell you not to worry about me and I can't make myself say it. I don't fall apart, Laney. Why am I falling apart?

LANEY

Because shit's fucking tough right now.

I love sweary Laney, in case you didn't know. Sweary Laney is a bright spot in my day.

LANEY

Apparently I've had a few special words bottled up for a while now. Feels good to let them out.

And I'm sure Theo rewards your efforts appropriately.

LANEY

I wasn't going to rub it in. Are you staying home or going to your mom's?

I'm going to Mom's.

LANEY

Meet you there.

I'll pick you up. Theo's bad side is the last place I can afford to be right now.

LANEY

I won't let him be mad at you.

I sincerely don't know what I did to deserve you.

LANEY

YOU ARE A GOOD PERSON, SABRINA SULLIVAN. That's what you did. Don't let having to fight hard for what should've been yours in the first place make you doubt that.

You spelled "dirty" wrong.

LANEY

You're not fighting dirty. You're fighting hard. And you're not alone, no matter what you have to do. HE could solve this by finding a different way to get revenge on Chandler, and we don't even know what Chandler did to him. This is not your fault and you're doing what you need to do.

Stop. You're making my eyeballs leak. Sit tight. I'm coming to get you and then Mom and I'm treating you both to dinner. No arguments. I have to balance out my karma in the universe.

LANEY

Your karma's already balanced, but if this is what you need, I'm here for you.

21

Grey

Who's a creeper who heard the neighbor's front door shut and is now peering out between the blinds of his living room to watch Sabrina stride across the parking area with longer steps than should be possible given her height, her dog trotting happily beside her, as they head for her car?

Me.

That's who.

I'm the creeper.

Worse?

Watching her is distracting me from the one phone call from a family member that I was willing to return when I finally looked at my voicemails from the past two days.

"Grey?" Mimi says on the other end of the phone.

I make myself step away from the window as Sabrina bends and hugs Jitter before opening the back car door for him. They look so *right*. And I want to be out there with them.

"Yes," I say too strongly. "Yes, I think Miami this time of year would be perfect for you."

"I don't know," she says slowly, which is how she does everything these days.

Slowly.

It's been horrible to watch. Ever since her sister passed away a year ago, she's gotten slower and quieter, like she's retreating from life. She visited me a time or two in California—I actively hate being anywhere near the rest of my family and she's always loved to travel, so I usually pay for her to come see me instead of going to her—but I was always so focused on chasing the next big data point with my bees at work that I didn't do much good for her.

"Seems like there might be too many old people there," she finally says.

"Plenty of young people too though. Almost spring break."

"Oh, that's *too* wild."

"What about the Outer Banks? The Carolinas? Warm. Younger old people. Older young people. Bet you could get your shuffleboard on."

She laughs a little, and the tightness in my chest eases.

I worry about Mimi.

She and Zen are the only two family members I have who appreciate me for me, and I do my damned best to return the favor. My father is the only child she had, much to my grandfather's disappointment. The old bastard made sure everyone knew nothing was enough for him.

One kid? He should've had six, and they would've all been his property. Three houses? His acquaintance had four, *all* with pools and gardens. Mimi went gray before his friends' wives and needed to dye her hair. His lawyer's kid went to boarding school, so his son and his grandchildren needed to go to a better boarding school. Those Vanderbilts had that mansion down in North Carolina, so the Cartwrights needed a mansion on their original apple fields in upstate New York, which is eventually what drained the family trust fund.

But that wasn't my grandfather's fault.

It was lazy contractors doing shitty work and asking for too much pay.

Mimi did her best, but my old man turned out just like his old man.

I used to ask her regularly, when I was younger, why she married him.

Because life isn't always what you hoped it would be was the only response she'd ever give me. *But you, young man, have a pure heart, quick brains, and a good soul. Don't settle for anything less than what you deserve.*

I realized after Felicia that she didn't say I had *good judgment when it comes to women.*

"I'll figure out where to go," Mimi says. "Enough about this old lady. Tell me about you."

I turn the corner from the living room into the kitchen and nearly jump out of my skin.

Zen's leaning in the doorway to the mudroom, watching me with the kind of suspicion in their eyes that you'd expect of someone who probably saw me spying on the neighbor and decided to hang out quietly to scare the shit out of me instead of calling me on my stalker behavior.

They're probably hoping—again—that I pull my head

out of my ass, give up on this plan to change the café, and ask Sabrina out.

We can find another building to have a kombucha bar, they've said more than once.

And I've replied every time with *why would any smart businessman give up the best real estate in town?*

"I'm alive and well," I report to my grandmother.

She makes a noise like she doesn't believe me.

So does Zen.

"How's work?" Mimi asks.

Heat creeps up my neck. "Fine."

"Zen told me you haven't even started thinking about building another lab or looking for loopholes to get you back to working with bees."

"That's why it's fine."

She laughs for real this time. "And what, exactly, are you up to with all of this time suddenly on your hands?"

Guilt claws on top of the heat.

I don't like lying to Mimi, but *I'm failing spectacularly at vengeance against an old bully since I'm done being shit on by the people who are supposed to love me or at least not hate me* isn't something I'll be telling her. And as much as we've researched and believe in the idea of the kombucha bar, we wouldn't be on this path, in this place, without the initial vengeance part.

"I'm going to a different beach," I report.

I was technically on a different beach about two weeks ago.

Zen glares harder at me.

"You're at the beach now?" There's a tinge of excitement in her voice that I haven't heard in ages, and it makes me feel even more like slime. "Which beach? I'd consider a beach even if the people were too old or young if you were there."

"I'm not there yet."

If Zen's glare gets any hotter, they'll melt the windows.

I clear my throat. "Just finishing up a few things, and then I'll be on my way."

"Which beach?" Mimi repeats.

"Haven't decided yet."

"When will you decide?"

"Soon."

It's about forty-ish degrees outside.

Ever since I landed myself in that ambulance right after Vince told me he'd made us a lot of money by selling my research, my fingers and toes have gone numb at any temperature under sixty degrees.

But right now, I'm sweating.

I'm sweating, and I can't shed layers fast enough.

The only other time I've been this warm in a cold place was when Sabrina was straddling me at the gazebo the other night.

"Well, you let me know when you decide," Mimi says. "And then you let me know if you have room for an old lady to tag along."

"You know I always do."

"Is Zen with you?"

"Would they be anywhere else?"

"Good. I like knowing you have each other."

"Want to say hi?"

"Oh, no, I spoke with them earlier today. But do give them another hug from me."

I make direct eye contact with my nibling.

They are displeased.

They are *very* displeased.

Jaw working. Mulish glare. Hands curling into fists and then releasing.

They've added two rings to their right hand since we got here. One turquoise, one a fidget ring.

There's little doubt who's to blame for the necessity of a fidget ring.

That would be me.

And this unhappy Zen?

This unhappy Zen will *not* be satisfied by me asking a woman out on a date.

Is this because I'm lying to Mimi?

Or did I do something else?

"Always happy to pass on hugs," I report to Mimi.

"And that's why you're my favorite grandson."

"How's your new chef working out?" Distract. Distract. Distract.

"I fired him."

"*Mimi.*"

"He kept cutting my steak like I'm an invalid."

"Did you ask him to stop?"

"Repeatedly with telekinesis. When he didn't pick up on the vibes I was throwing down, I changed the locks."

My brows shoot up.

If Mimi's back on sarcasm, she must be feeling at least a little better. "Good for you for knowing what you want in a personal chef."

"And how are *you* eating?" Mimi asks.

"Very well." That, at least, is the full truth. The neighbors and various townspeople have made sure my fridge is stocked. I'm even putting some of the weight back on that I dropped right after Vince's bombshell. Feeling like exercising again too.

"Good," Mimi says. "You keep taking good care of yourself, and if you don't mind an old lady tagging along, let me know when you head to the beach."

"You're always welcome, Mimi. Good to hear you excited about traveling again."

"Now put Zen on. I just remembered I need to ask them something about this band they're obsessed with."

"Love you, Mimi."

"Love you too, my best boy."

I hold my phone out to Zen.

"Don't even *try* to hug me right now," they mutter darkly.

Fair.

They know I'm lying to Mimi, which is the sin of all sins.

But they're all sunshine and happiness when they put my phone to their ear. "Hey, Mimi! Don't tell me you forgot to mention that a hottie was hitting on you at shuffleboard."

They march to the living room and then upstairs, voice fading but still clear enough for me to hear the full conversation.

And it's definitely about a band.

Zen's door shuts. I fully expect they're either planning on giving me the silent treatment for the rest of the day for lying to Mimi, or they're planning to chew me out for making them an unwilling accomplice.

The right thing to do is to warm up something from the fridge—there's leftover chicken noodle soup and it's calling my name, and our kombucha is basically perfect—

and go spend a few hours locked in my own room doing the sixth wooden puzzle I've started since we got here.

This one's a bright phoenix with particularly intricate puzzle pieces.

Instead, I'm heading back to the living room window and peeking outside.

She hasn't left yet.

Looks like she got a phone call.

Who's she talking to? What's it about? Should I go out there right now and apologize?

I need to rip off that bandage. Just do it. Get it over with.

"You know you have zero chance with her if you destroy her café, right?" Zen says from the landing above me.

I jump. "I don't date."

"Everyone else at that speed dating meeting thought you left because you don't people well," they say. "But you can't fool me. And you're in over your head with this *Super Villain Man* bullshit. No shame in changing course, Uncle Grey. No matter what changing course looks like."

I know this.

They know I know this.

And they know I won't strike back for their brutal honesty.

"Has Sabrina found anything yet?" I ask.

"If she had, don't you think she would've told you?"

Fair enough.

Fuck.

22

Sabrina

WORK IS as uncomfortable as it's ever been Saturday morning.

Grey's being nice to me.

Nice might not be the right word.

He's actually been mostly pleasant in the nearly two weeks since he got here. Or he's been the irresistible hottie who keeps doing all the right things to make me want to kiss him again.

Since the gazebo, I feel like we've been playing this game of *who will break first, and how much will we both enjoy it?*

Like it's inevitable that we'll try to work this out between the sheets, even though it won't give either of us what we want outside of a bedroom.

But the bigger problem?

He's acting like he doesn't know what I did yesterday.

Which either means he's *that* good, or he actually doesn't know.

Not like I had a lot of options.

I *cannot* find a damn thing on Chandler.

And I'm not bothering Emma with that question when I've been pussyfooting around debating with myself if I want to talk to her.

Midmorning, when I drop off a fresh tea at his seat—which I would do for any regular, for the record—he stops me. "Hold on a second."

"Don't like chai anymore?"

"Hmm? Oh, no. Chai is perfect. Thank you. I just got the bill for last week's food delivery."

I brace myself.

"Thank you for managing that."

Decker's hanging out at a window table, noise-canceling headphones over his ears, but I don't miss the look he slides me.

It's one hundred percent *is the dude playing mind games with you?*

Yes, I handled the food like I always do, but I added in a few extra treats for the crew, and I know it's pushing the bottom line.

And I know he's enough of a numbers guy to notice, and he probably knows I'm a good enough manager that I'll make up the difference in the next two weeks.

If I care to.

"It's what I do," I say.

"I know. Thank you." Grey sips his tea, closes his eyes briefly, and sighs, a slight smile tipping his lips, and then nods to me once more. "Also, let the staff know I'm changing the time off structure. You all work too hard and deserve more vacation time."

I catch my jaw before it hits the floor.

"Does this mean you're letting Bean & Nugget stay as it is?"

Blue eyes lift to mine.

My heart stops beating.

Just flails to a stop, like a fish that's finally quit trying to get back in the stream.

We have an audience.

It's not just Decker.

Three ladies from a local knitting group who come here every Thursday morning are watching. So is one of my mom's closest friends.

"No, but good effort," Grey says.

Motherfucker. "*No* for now. If you convert this building, I'll quit."

His brows slowly lift. "If you quit, you wouldn't be my employee anymore."

And there goes my belly dropping at the implication that we could explore this unwelcome attraction between us without the complication of Bean & Nugget as a massive boulder in the way. "I hold grudges."

"Zen already paid my penance by eating that pineapple...cookie."

I almost laugh.

Swear I almost do, despite the danger that my café is in, which is growing by the day.

Instead, though, I pinch my lips together, nod once, and then I swing my hips on my way back to the kitchen.

Decker texts that Grey was watching my ass the whole time.

I get zero crap from Grey for taking an unscheduled twenty-minute break to sit with a friend who's nearly hyperventilating over a relationship problem and wants my advice.

When Marley drops in and asks where Jitter is, Grey tells her that the dog will be back tomorrow if he has anything to say about it.

Every day, he's becoming so much more like the man I met in Hawaii that I corner Zen as the lunch rush is easing. "Did he find something on Chandler and he's just waiting for me to figure it out?" I whisper.

They roll their eyes. "No."

"I'm an expert in people, and I don't think he's acting normal for someone who's here for vengeance and isn't getting all of the information he wants."

"Maybe he *does* have the information he wants."

"You just said he doesn't."

"I said he doesn't have what he wants on *Chandler*. I didn't say he didn't have what he wants on *you*."

My stomach drops to my toes. "What does that mean?"

"It means I'm the only person who can tell you if he knows what I know you did yesterday."

All the blood drains from my face and pools in my stomach—yes, the stomach down in my toes—where it churns like sour milk. "I...worked and then hung out with my mom and my friend Laney?"

They arch a pierced brow.

Now is not the time to remember I have to pee when I get nervous.

Been too long since I've been this level of nervous.

"If you didn't want anyone to know what you did,"

they murmur, "you wouldn't have given my great-grand-mother your real name."

They have an excellent point. "Your great-grand-mother? Did I see her yesterday and not know it?"

"You are *so* lucky I think you're fabulous and your dog is even better, and that I think Uncle Grey's making a huge mistake with how he's approaching what he's trying to do here. Although in all honesty, I support the Cheese Turd getting what's coming to him for every shit thing he's ever done to anyone in his entire life. Also, I'm unbelievably excited at the idea of running a kombucha bar. And those are the only reasons I'm not ratting you out. You'd be so fired and this place would get shut down."

"Is this where you try to blackmail me for a very unclear something that you think I did?"

I absolutely did it.

I called Grey's grandmother because I know—*I know*—he has a good relationship with her and *I have to stop him*.

No matter how much I like him, I *cannot* bear the thought of Bean & Nugget no longer being Bean & Nugget.

But I can tell by the way Zen's eyes are darting around my face, studying me, that they suddenly have doubts if it was me, or if it was someone pretending to be me.

They finally snort softly. "I am officially Switzerland in this whole debacle. That's all I'm saying."

They turn to head back up front, but just as quickly spin back to me. "No, actually, that's not all I'm saying. *This* is the last thing I'll say about it—if you call *anyone* else who shares DNA with either of us, I'll personally light this building on fire."

"I—" I squeak, but they're gone.

This is when I'd normally text Laney and Emma and ask them to please remind me that desperate times call for desperate measures, and I wouldn't have called his grandmother if I hadn't trusted they had a good relationship.

And that I knew there was no way I was getting out of Zen what I wanted to know about Grey's purchase of the café.

This is also when I'd normally high-five myself for getting another hint that all is not roses and fairy kisses in the Cartwright family, which is another path to follow if I have to play dirty.

Instead, I feel like an absolute heel.

I like Zen, even if they're not telling me all the secrets.

And now they don't trust me.

Getting off work half an hour later doesn't help, because getting off work means I need to do something else that twists my stomach in knots.

Just before I clock out for the day, I whip up a special salted caramel hot chocolate in a to-go mug and pay for it and three chocolate croissants. Then it's off to pick up Jitter and drop into Sir Pretzelot.

If I'm doing this, I'm bringing everyone's favorite buffer.

Emma's office is in a complex up the mountain from the historic district of the Tooth where my dentist and eye doctor also have space. When Jitter and I arrive at her building, we make our way to her second-floor unit. Despite it being Saturday, the door opens easily when I turn the knob.

Theo's right. She's burying herself in work.

"Hello?" I call softly.

Em's a one-woman show, so she doesn't have a receptionist, though her accounting practice has grown enough that she should probably consider it soon. I hear the wheels on her desk chair squeak before she appears through the half-closed inner office door.

She's in a black cardigan with her blonde hair tucked up in a pencil bun, and her brown eyes are lacking their normal bright cheer. Instead, she's sporting bags beneath her lower eyelids, and her cheeks look even thinner than usual.

My heart twists.

She's struggled to keep weight on her entire life, and this isn't helping.

"Hey." I lift both bakery bags and the largest reusable to-go mug that Bean & Nugget sells. "Just dropping off tax season treats."

She eyes the food, then forces a smile. "Thanks. I'm a little tied up. Do you mind leaving it on the desk out there?"

"Only if you promise you'll eat some of it." Jitter strains on his leash, but I hold him tight, and no, I'm not entirely sure how I'm balancing everything. "Sit, Jitter."

"I'll eat something," Emma says. "Thank you."

She scoots her chair back to her desk and out of view.

My throat burns. "I'm really sorry, Em," I say quietly. "I'm here if you need anything."

"I know," comes back just as softly. "Thank you."

She doesn't say anything else, and I don't know what else to say either, so I leave the hot chocolate and the pastries on the desk in her entryway, then pull Jitter back outside to the parking lot packed with snow.

I don't want to go home—it's too close to Grey and all of my complicated feelings about him, even if he's not *there* right now—so instead, I take Jitter to a local park. I strap on the snowshoes and leg gaiters that I keep in my trunk this time of year, and my puppers and I head out into the wilderness, following my favorite trail.

I'm not a hundred yards from the parking lot, though, before I hear a noise behind me that will *always* make me turn around.

It's the distinctive *urp!* of someone slipping on the path.

"Are you okay?" comes out of my mouth before I fully process what I'm seeing.

Grey is picking himself up out of a snowbank beside the snow-packed trail.

Jitter lunges with a happy bark, his back end wagging ferociously, and he almost pulls me over despite the extra traction provided by my snowshoes. "*Slow*, Jitter."

He listens as well as a mountain lion chasing an elk would to the same command.

"I meant to do that," Grey says as he makes it all the way to his feet.

He slips on the packed-snow path but catches himself this time.

I squeeze my eyes shut and count to five.

When I open them again, he's still standing there.

Watching me.

Shit shit shit.

Does he know I called his grandmother and he's pretending like he doesn't? Did he tell Zen to lie?

Is he here so that he can shove me off a cliff and pretend it was an accident?

He doesn't really strike me as the type, but then, I never thought I'd be the type to call a man's grandmother to tattle on him for buying my family's café either.

Not that that was my *only* purpose in calling.

But it was a major part.

"What are you doing?" I ask.

"Wow. Is that your suspicious face?"

It's the smirk that does me in.

How he pulls off a self-deprecating smirk that also says *I like your suspicious face* is beyond me, but I get a little warm glow in my chest all because of that smirk. "This is my concerned face. A beach bum who's constantly wrapped in seventeen layers to stay warm, who has dizzy spells, and who isn't wearing spikes on a snow trail is always concern for us locals."

"A *beach bum*? You keep calling me that."

"You've lived on the California coast for the past eight years. Ergo, beach bum. Do you need help back to your car?"

He smiles.

Full-on *smiles* with his whole, entire face.

Just like he did in Hawaii. I gesture to his whole head, encompassing every part of the grin. "Put that away. I'm playing dirty and I am now immune."

He ignores me. "You ever seen a beach bum this pasty?" He points to the very small area of his face where I can actually see his skin. It's basically just his upper cheeks and his nose.

The rest of him is covered in beard, hat, scarf, coat, gloves, jeans, and boots.

He looks like a J.Crew catalog model.

But taller.

And no, I don't know how tall J.Crew models usually

are. I just know this man is toweringly tall, with massive hands and feet and other parts that I am actively *not* thinking about.

"Maybe you have an excellent skin care routine," I say.

"No, you're confusing me with Zen again."

Other than both of them being taller than me, that's not possible, and I almost give in and laugh.

But only *almost*.

I do *not* have the emotional bandwidth for attraction to this man when I know he's going to hate me very, very soon.

I don't know if I even have the emotional bandwidth to be his friend.

Jitter finally succeeds in pulling me all the way next to his new favorite person, where he pushes his body against Grey firmly enough that Grey slips again.

"You need to go home," I tell him.

"Wanted some fresh air."

"Here?"

"Yes."

"How often have you been to this trail?"

"Haven't. Yet. Why I'm here now."

"So you followed me."

"I saw you pulling over here and wanted to do a good deed and make sure you weren't wading into a property war between Mr. Avocado and Mrs. Marshmallow Fluff."

He's doing it again.

He's being *Duke*, and it's both my favorite thing ever and also what puts me on guard. I sigh softly and shove my hair back out of my face as the wind rustles it. "I can't find anything else on Chandler and *I am now playing dirty.* Go away."

"Can a guy not simply want to go hiking on treacherous ice and snow with a captivating woman?"

"No." Because I don't trust myself to not throw myself at him and confess what I've done, which will ruin the entire impact. "Jitter. C'mon, boy. We're going for a hike, and Grey's going to learn the hard way that tourists are a mountain lion's favorite snack."

Jitter harrumphs at me, then lies down on the path right at Grey's feet.

Grey shrugs. "Hate to tell you, but if Jitter wants me, there's nothing I can do to stop him."

He knows.

He absolutely knows I called his grandmother, and he is going to torture me with pretending he doesn't until I cave and tell him that *Ms. Hot Mess on the Beach called his grandmother*.

I stare at him.

He stares back like he knows this is the start of a staring contest, and he knows I'll win, but he also won't make it easy on me.

And he doesn't.

My eyes are burning and freezing at the same time before he breaks, though he doesn't so much break as he speaks while also holding me captive with his bright blue eyes. "May I please join you so as to not offend your dog?"

"You hate the cold," I remind him.

"Says who?"

"Says my powers of observation."

He shrugs, palms up and everything. "You're not wrong. But your dog wants me to come, so I have to suck it up. I don't make the rules. Jitter does."

I pull in a massive breath through my nose, then blow

it out slowly, feeling myself giving in to what I want when I know just how dangerous it is.

And I'm not talking about him walking on this path in those boots, which he truly cannot do.

Too much ice.

And his jeans will get soaked, and I'll have to carry him back when he passes out from the cold.

"Is stress the only reason you get lightheaded?" I ask.

"That's what my doctor suspects at this point."

"Are you drinking enough water?"

"Have you met Zen? Tall, slender, blond hair, pain in the ass? My self-appointed personal assistant who would leap in front of a speeding train to stop it if they thought it might veer offtrack and possibly scuff one of my finger-nails wrong? You think they'll let me get away with not drinking enough water?"

"We're going to dig into that later."

"That'll be a fun conversation."

He's back.

The man I met in Hawaii is fully back, without me inviting him back this time, and every cell in my body is reacting to the flirtation.

This feels almost the same as if Emma would forgive me.

Like everything is right in the world with one of my best friends.

I shouldn't feel that way, but I can't help it. *I like him.*

"Are you more in danger at high elevations?" I ask.

"Not that I'm aware of."

"So what's not fine?"

He pauses.

Jitter whines and tries to roll over Grey's feet, making

him take another half step back and nearly tumble again. "Stress," he finally says. "Standing up too fast. Not eating enough. Not hydrating enough."

"Porcupines and powdered cheese?"

He actually laughs.

I am in so much trouble.

"Is it permanent?" I ask.

"This is trail conversation."

"Have you *ever* been on a snowy trail?"

"I'm a beach bum, remember?"

Yep.

I'm doing it.

I'm giving in to the charm he's laying down, and I'll regret it, but this?

This is fun.

I want fun. I miss fun.

And orgasms.

Which are *not* on the table here.

"Stay. Both of you. And *do not move*. Don't even shift your weight. Understand?" I shove Jitter's leash at him without waiting for an answer, then march back to my SUV in my snowshoes.

Lucky and Decker both regularly join me on hikes, and they both regularly forget their own snowshoes, so I keep spare spikes in my car. No extra gaiters to keep Grey's jeans dry, but I have a backup set of hiking poles, so I grab those and a spare water bottle and return to the trailhead.

"Put these on," I order the man.

He lifts his brows, then looks at me as he takes the strap-on cleats that'll give him traction on the trail. "On...?"

"*Your feet.*"

"Don't know if you've noticed, but my feet are a little larger than yours."

"They're my boyfriend's."

His eyes flare while he jerks his head to look at me.

Say what you will about Greyson Cartwright, the man is *not* always the smoothest.

Grumpy? Sometimes. Annoying? Also sometimes. Adorably charming when he wants to be?

Unfortunately.

But if he were cast in a Razzle Dazzle film, he'd be the awkward librarian who can't quite hide all of his feelings. And while I love Jonas Rutherford, the channel's biggest star, and while it absolutely pains me to admit this, I'd watch Grey in that role in a heartbeat.

Even after all the heartburn he's given me these past few weeks.

"You have a boyfriend," he repeats.

"Long-distance. It's brand new. Military. He's stationed in Korea right now. We have phone sex every night before I go to bed."

"That's your *toothbrush*," he stutters.

I suck in a breath.

He goes red as all the hearts that have started going up around town before Valentine's Day.

"Are you sure?" I ask.

He snags the cleats, hands me Jitter's leash, and squats quickly, bending over his feet while he figures out how to strap on the spikes.

"I didn't realize you'd taken the bedroom that shares a wall with mine," I say. "*Very* good to know."

"You don't have another boyfriend."

Another? "Are you sure?"

"You don't date."

"Maybe I found my soulmate and changed my mind."

"Yesterday?" He's still staring at the ground, working a lot harder than he should have to in order to get the spikes on.

And when he straightens, he's managed to go straight-faced again, though he's still pink in the cheeks.

I'll be kind and assume it's the cold getting to him.

But more, I can't answer his question.

I don't want to play games.

I don't want to lie.

All I want to do is take a hike with him.

"Which way?" he asks, pointing at where the trail forks just ahead.

And I pick a direction.

I'm heading up my favorite path with a man that I should not be attracted to and my dog who loves him.

Gossip help me if he wants to be alone here because he knows I called his grandmother.

23

Grey

SABRINA SHOVES HIKING poles at me and then nudges Jitter toward the fork on the left without waiting to see if I'll keep up. I step cautiously, but the tools she gave me for my boots have good traction.

"Wow. Makes a big difference. Thank you," I say to her.

"Welcome to physics."

"I know physics."

She slides me a look. "Do you know it as well as you know, say, how to run a restaurant?"

That wasn't sly at all. "I know physics better."

"Believable."

"But I'm a fast learner."

"Also believable. Speaking of learning, I heard Zen say your villain era doesn't really suit you."

Zing. She lines up, takes her shot, and she scores.

"Midlife crisis."

"You're thirty-three."

"You've done your homework."

"You'd expect nothing less."

She's not wrong.

And even knowing it's dangerous, I like knowing that she's thinking about me as much as I'm thinking about her.

Also?

Not a single soul has asked me if I'm okay after my dizzy spell the other day. Nor has anyone other than Sabrina asked what Chandler did to me or how I feel about my former research lab partner *actually* being in his villain era.

They've only hinted that they suspect Sabrina and I are hooking up.

She's not posting secret videos of my confessions all over the internet.

Not like someone posted a video of the House of Curry food fight my first week here.

Sabrina seems to take her gossip seriously. She's upfront that she knows everything and will disclose it when she thinks it's necessary. I've seen it in action. And not just with the woman who posted the wedding video, though that was definitely the most direct.

We hike in silence for a few minutes save for the sound of Jitter's happy panting and the crunch of our shoes and poles on the trail. It's fascinating to me that the path is covered in packed snow, like this trail is hiked often, even in the winter, though we seem to be the only people here now. The sky's a clear blue peeking through the pine trees, and there's something unexpectedly peaceful and almost enjoyable about being out here.

My fingers are cold. My toes are cold.

But not unbearably so.

"Is what your lab partner did to you the only reason you're in your villain era now?" Sabrina asks.

And honestly?

I like that about her.

No hiding. No games. No small talk. She's straight to the point.

I shake my head. "Just the final straw."

"And the rest of the straws?"

"A lifetime of being manipulated."

She slides a look my way. Does she know it was my family? Does she suspect it?

Or am I reading more into that look than is actually there because I *want* to tell her?

Some older lady came in yesterday and was grilling Zen about their personal history and our relationship, which sent Zen into a retreat.

I know Sabrina noticed.

Not because she said anything.

But because she *did* something. She popped out from the kitchen, where she still insists she belongs at every opportunity, and asked the woman something about an old friend, which distracted the lady from grilling Zen and put her instead on a tangent about a cheating husband.

"I didn't put together that *manipulation* was the right word for it until Zen used it for the first time after they moved in with me," I add.

"Your ex?" she asks.

"Yes, but she wasn't the first."

I get another side glance.

"My parents and siblings," I clarify.

"You're younger than the rest."

She has done *all* of her homework. "The inconvenient one who was blamed for arriving ten years later than the previous youngest child, stealing the *baby* spot in the family, and needing things they'd all grown out of. Yes."

Her nose wrinkles. "You didn't have nannies?"

"When my mother could see the writing on the wall about the direction the family trust fund was headed? The nannies were only for when other people were watching."

She glances at me again, and I wish I had the power to read faces the way she seems to.

It matters to me not just that I'm honest with her, but that she knows I'm being honest.

That she knows I'm putting my secrets on the line and trusting her with them.

That she knows I'm not tearing apart her café because I enjoy punishing *her*.

It's Chandler. I need a win over an asshole.

"Jitter, slow down," she says.

He grins back at us with his larger-than-life doggie grin, then forges ahead, not at all bothered by slippery or uneven spots on the snow-packed path.

Or willing to take directions on how fast or where to go.

"My mom never wanted kids," she says quietly after we've taken two more turns on the path between towering pine trees. "She didn't want to get married. Her dream was to be free as the wind to go wherever she wanted in the world with nothing tying her down. Work just enough to make ends meet and fund her travels. But when she found out she was pregnant after a short-term fling with a guy who was passing through, she decided to keep me.

And she's never once made me feel like I kept her from the life she would've had otherwise even though she hasn't traveled much since I was born."

"I always wondered what it would've been like to know I was wanted."

"And not grow up to want to be *Super Vengeance Man*? I'm sorry, but clearly, your suffering was necessary for the good of the world." She grins at me, and I nearly go lightheaded.

In the good way.

She hasn't sparkled at me since Hawaii, and Sabrina Sullivan with teasing mischief twinkling in her bright green eyes takes my breath away.

My steps slow.

Her smile falters. "I didn't mean that."

"I know."

"Everyone should feel wanted."

"I have people in my life who fulfill my emotional needs."

"Drink your water."

"I'm fine."

"If you pass out on the trail, I'm going back to my car without you and leaving you to the mountain lions."

"That jives with who you were in Hawaii."

She stops fully and turns to face me. "*I don't date.*"

That muscle in my chest squeezes and dips like I'm on a runaway train.

I don't want another long-term relationship. I don't want to date either.

Except I can't get this woman out of my head, and the more I see her here, where she belongs, doing what she was born to do, the more I want to know everything there is to know about her.

She's my new research project.

Fuck.

Fuck.

I need to get back to a lab. Give my brain something else to obsess over.

But the thought still hurts too much, whereas the idea of making something *right* doesn't hurt.

Or it wouldn't, if it wouldn't hurt her too.

"I don't either," I assure her with a confidence I don't feel. "We can be friends who not-date together. Maybe naked sometimes."

Her pupils dilate, and she sucks in a quick breath.

My dick goes half-mast.

I would absolutely not-date this woman nonstop for the next week if we could do it naked.

And there's the rest of my hard-on.

Go hike with Sabrina, my brain said.

So we can ask her to get naked, my other brain said.

She bites her lower lip.

I take a half step toward her, wanting to bite that lower lip myself, but she ducks her head and spins back to the trail. "C'mon, Jitter. Sun's setting too soon."

I subtly adjust myself, then follow along while Jitter happily leads again, clearly knowing where he's going.

"This a private trail?" I ask Sabrina.

"Nope. Just not very busy close to dusk."

"You walk alone out here often?"

She slides me a glance, and I can't tell if she's still suppressing a desire to pull me off the trail and do what comes naturally out here in nature, or if that's just me and my teenage fantasies.

"I'm not alone," she says. "I have my dog."

"So you and Jitter have done this a lot by yourselves?"

"Laney and Emma used to come with us a lot."

"Mm."

"Laney has a broken leg."

"I noticed."

"Emma's back."

"I heard."

"If you see her and say a single dick thing to her, I will haunt you for the rest of your life."

"You'll be dead?"

"I'm an overachiever. I can haunt you while I'm still alive."

"Probably easier that way."

She cuts another glance at me. "You know I don't actually believe you'd be a dick to Emma."

That makes me smile. "Only because we have a common enemy."

"Why *is* Chandler your enemy?"

"Wow, really nice hike until you said the Cheese Turd word."

She coughs, and I'm certain she's covering a laugh, though I'm not certain if it's a happy laugh or a desperate laugh, and now I feel like an ass.

I don't want to hurt her. But I don't know how to change course without feeling like I've let someone else get the better of me again.

"Are you drinking the water I gave you?" Sabrina asks.

"Just had a big gulp."

She draws to a stop and turns to face me again as the trees open up around us. "Take another one."

Felicia had no qualms about ordering me around. Neither did my siblings for most of my life.

But I *like* it when Sabrina does it.

Sit down. Drink your tea. Wear safety tools on your feet. Have you eaten?

It's vastly different from *buy me this. Go here with me. Smile bigger for the picture. Can you pretend you're happy to be here? Make Zen get a real job and not be so dependent on you.*

I loop the hiking poles over one wrist and obediently drink from the water bottle.

But as I lift it, I catch sight of something unexpected on the horizon, and it's not until I feel the chill of water dribbling down the side of my mouth that I remember I'm drinking and jerk the bottle away to stare.

The pine-shrouded valley gives way to snowcapped mountains touching the majestic orange glow lighting the wispy clouds in the sky. There's a hazy softness to the peaks, and the sky has melted from the deep blue I noticed this morning to a soft baby blue hugging the glowing clouds.

So this is why people tolerate the cold.

To not just stare at the landscape from behind glass, but to be part of it. Breathing in the clear air, chilly but *alive*. Nothing between me and the sky but a few green pine branches. Snow and rock beneath my feet.

The oddest sense washes over me, and it takes me longer than it should to recognize it.

Belonging.

Belonging in my very existence. One with nature. Here with purpose. Accepted into the surroundings because nature made me too. No judgment. No manipulation.

Simply being as a tiny dot here in this vast array of beauty.

There's a pull deep in my chest. *This is where you'll make a difference.*

It's vastly different from *this is where justice will give you peace.*

I suck in a deep breath, the extra burst of chilly air pulling me back to myself. Sabrina and Jitter have stepped over to stand on a rocky outcropping. She's holding her phone up and snapping a picture.

"You've lived here your whole life and you still take pictures." I don't want to disturb the peace, but I can't not comment on it.

She doesn't look back at me. "It's still beautiful."

Jitter plops down into the snow and pants happily, and once again, there's that pull.

I miss my dog. I miss laughing. I miss believing in the good in people.

And I've never stopped wanting to feel like there could be a place in this world that I belong. Where I could trust more than a small handful of people.

I look back at the mountain peaks, shadowed by the glowing orange clouds, and wonder how long it'll stay.

Then I steal another look at Sabrina.

She's squatting next to Jitter, pouring water into a small collapsible dish for him as he laps it up before she's done. She finishes pouring, snaps the bottle shut, tucks it back into a side pocket in her backpack, and then rubs his neck. "Who's such a good boy?"

He grins at her, then goes back to drinking.

While lying in the snow.

He's so fucking adorable.

"Good boy," she says again, then she rises and looks back at the sunset over the mountains. "We need to go soon though."

"You have somewhere to be?"

"I always have somewhere to be."

"You don't sit still well."

"I don't do *alone* well."

"But you don't date." *Shut up, idiot. Quit pushing it.*

"Okay, Mr. Travels with His Nibling Personal Assistant."

She bends over Jitter again, rubs his ears, and kisses the top of his head before gathering his water bowl, wiping it out, popping it flat, and tucking it back into her bag. "C'mon, Jitter. Time to go home."

He straightens and stretches, looking bigger than Sabrina herself.

She smiles at him and scratches his back. "Such a good puppy."

I want her to smile at me like that. Smile at me. Touch me. Kiss me. Right here. In the chilly evening that's getting chillier by the minute with the sun dropping lower but still illuminating the low-hanging clouds over the mountains in that brilliant fire-orange glow.

She swings her backpack over one shoulder, and as she's shifting the leash to her other hand, Jitter straightens and sniffs the air.

I straighten.

Sabrina gets her other arm through the strap, and Jitter tenses.

I open my mouth. "Jitter, don't—" I start, recognizing that look after the porcupine incident, but it's too late.

He lunges, barking and pulling Sabrina with him. I

spot a red fox tearing across the path to disappear up another hill into the trees.

"*Ahhhh!*" Sabrina shrieks as her snowshoes get twisted beneath her and she goes down, face-first into the snow, still clenching the leash.

I dash after the dog. "Jitter, *stop*," I order.

"Jitter, *halt*," Sabrina yells.

He whines and slows and pauses, looking back at both of us.

Then he whines again.

I grab the leash. "Got it. You can let go."

"He doesn't usually do this." She grunts while she tries to untangle her legs, but her snowshoes keep getting tied up together.

"I've noticed."

Jitter whines again and sinks back to the ground, puppy dog eyes out in full effect while he army-crawls closer to Sabrina.

"You're a good boy," she tells him. "But we don't chase wildlife. Especially while we're on a leash. Okay?"

He whimpers.

"Can you please pet my dog and tell him I'm okay?" She keeps trying to disentangle her feet and legs, and it seems to be a struggle.

"She's okay, Jitter." I scratch his back the same way she did, and instantly regret it.

I want my dog back.

I want friends I can say that to.

And I want to lift Sabrina out of the snow and carry her down off this trail.

"*There.*" She gets her legs untangled, reaches for one of

her hiking poles as I'm turning to assist her, and in seconds, she's back on her feet. "Oh, *fuck*."

I lift a brow.

She growls to herself and bends over. Mutters some more, which prompts Jitter to whine more.

"You okay?" I ask her while I squat next to the dog and stroke his thick fur.

"Broken strap," she mutters. She pulls off one of her snowshoes and holds it up for me to see. "It'll slide right off my foot."

This is a problem.

And I see an easy solution that I suspect I'm far happier about than she is. "Huh."

She squeezes her eyes shut and sucks in a massive breath.

"Okay," I say. "I'll give you a piggyback ride."

The suspicious look is back. "You will *not*."

"I will. It's getting dark. I need to get out of the cold. You probably do too. Fastest way down the path when you have a broken snowshoe. Not like we're trading footwear so you can give me a piggyback ride."

Those bright green eyes probe my face.

It's like she's asking if this is a trick. If I planted the fox so Jitter would run so I'd have to offer to carry her. If I'm planning to drop her. If I'll enjoy having her arms and legs wrapped around me.

Only the last one is a resounding *yes*.

"Who'll hold Jitter's leash?"

"I can handle you both."

She flashes a cocky grin like she can't help herself. "Big talk, boss-man."

"I'd rather you call me *Super Vengeance Man*."

"I'll consider it if you get me safely back to my car."

Yes. "Climb on up, Duchess."

"You wish," she murmurs.

"Hawaii was fun."

I get another eyeball of *don't push this*, but after she's pulled off her second snowshoe and hung them both on her backpack, I squat in front of her and she climbs onto me, wrapping her arms around my neck and her legs around my hips and holding on as if she thinks I'll drop her.

"The only reason you're not rolling in the snow being pelted with snowballs right now is because I want to get home," she says as I stand.

"This the last snowfall of the year?"

"Not even close. Tell me if you get lightheaded."

"Doing fine." Better than fine.

And possibly terrible at the same time.

I want her to kiss me again.

And I know if she does, I'll probably break and agree to not change her café, and then I'll realize I don't actually need to be here, and all of this will come to a screeching halt.

If I don't belong in a lab, and I'm actually terrible at being *Super Vengeance Man*, and I don't want to go back to Connecticut even if it would put me closer to Mimi, then who am I and where do I fit in this world?

It's a heavy question.

And I still want to kiss Sabrina again. Peel back every layer of her clothes until she's completely bare. Study her skin. Her curves. Her breasts and her pussy.

And *pretend* I belong.

"I had a dog," I tell her while I follow Jitter down the

path, Sabrina's body pressed tightly to my back. "My ex took him in the divorce."

"I know."

"You know?"

"Someone showed me your old Insta."

I should be alarmed, but instead, all I feel is warm. "What else do you know?"

"That I would do terrible things to anyone who took Jitter from me. And I'm sorry. That must've hurt."

"I didn't cheat on her."

"I wouldn't have thought you did."

"She gave me an ultimatum. Kick Zen out, or she was gone."

"That was dumb of her."

I actually laugh.

"How long have they been your personal assistant?" she asks.

I hesitate, but only briefly. I would've told Duchess in Hawaii. I can tell Sabrina now.

Worst case is she betrays me and I destroy her café.

That was supposed to be funny, but even in my head, it's falling short.

"Zen showed up on my doorstep shortly after they turned sixteen. Said I was the last blood relative they were giving a chance to let them be who they were before they disappeared completely."

"Oh, shit."

"I barely remembered them from when I lived back east. Didn't spend a lot of time with family once I left for high school—"

"*Left* for high school?"

"Boarding school."

"That's a real thing?"

"That is indeed a real thing."

"Ew."

I readjust my grip on her legs. "So Zen asked if I wanted housekeeping and cooking services in exchange for room and board while they finished high school, and it turns out it's really hard to say no to a kid who looks like they fit in with the rest of the family about as well as I always thought I did."

"They cook?"

"No. They're awful."

She laughs.

"Repeat that and *you'll* disappear."

"Do they clean?"

"Yes. Very well."

She doesn't ask anything else.

Doesn't mean I don't want to tell her though. "When I told Zen I'd send them to college, they informed me the only way they'd take my money was if they were allowed to pay me back."

"By being your personal assistant?"

"Works out well for both of us. I forget to eat and shower when I'm in the middle of something, and they have an inherent distrust of the world at large. I give them a safe place. Honestly, they do the same for me."

She falls silent, but she rests her head on my shoulder.

And I could walk like this for days.

Which is another reason I need to abandon my plans and leave.

Zen says they've never really fit in anywhere.

I'm not sure I have either.

It would be too easy to fall into the trap of thinking we could fit here.

I don't know how far we've gone when Jitter stops and angles around a bush on the trail.

"Not today, Jitter," Sabrina says.

Jitter whines and gives her the most pitiful look I've ever seen. Between the floppy jowls and the utter despair in his big brown eyes, there's no question what we're doing.

We're letting Jitter lead.

"*Hey,*" Sabrina says while I turn off the path.

"Have to check it out," I reply. "Someone could be hurt. Maybe Timmy fell down the well."

"Timmy? Who's Timmy?"

"You never watched *Lassie* reruns as a kid? Even I watched *Lassie* reruns as a kid."

"What's *Lassie*? Hey. *Wait*. Don't—"

"Sorry, but when a dog tells me to go somewhere, and it looks urgent, I listen."

I'm not sorry.

I'm delaying putting her down.

And Jitter *is* very insistent that we follow this skinny, snowy path through the pine trees and around larger boulders.

"There's not a problem," Sabrina says. "He just wants to go see something that we don't need to see today. It's getting dark. Seriously, we need to get back to the parking lot."

"What does he want to see?"

"*Jitter*. Back on the trail."

I tug the leash and retreat. "C'mon, Jitter. Before we both end up in the doghouse."

He snorts, but he listens and heads back to the main trail.

"I feel you, buddy. I'll bet it was something good."

Sabrina sighs. "It's just my grandparents' old house and yard. You can kinda see it through the trees."

I squint into the growing dimness and spot a single light twinkling beyond the trees. "They still live there?"

"No, the family put renters into it after Grandma died and Grandpa moved into a retirement community."

"Must still love it if you and Jitter go visit often enough that he knows the way."

"I—yes."

There's more to that story.

You can hear it in the hitch in her voice.

Wonder if it had to do with Chandler.

After a minute, she takes a big breath and lays her head against my shoulder again. "Laney, Emma, and I used to walk through this part of the park after school as often as we could once we discovered an old treehouse right on the edge of Grandma and Grandpa's property."

I start to smile. "You had a clubhouse."

"We had a *club*. We were the ugly heiress society."

I clamp my mouth shut so fast, my jaw audibly pops.

"It was Theo," she says. "Emma's brother."

"The porn guy."

"*Naked inspirational knitter*, but yes. Laney and I met him in kindergarten, and when we were all in third grade, Emma leveled up and joined us. She's a year younger but super smart. She'd get straight A's—or whatever it was they gave us in third grade—and he'd get parent-teacher conferences. He and Laney *hated* each other, and I know it rubbed him wrong that his baby sister was outshining him at school, and we were all kind of *heiresses*. Me to Bean & Nugget, Laney to Kingston Photo Gifts, and Emma to their dad's taxidermy business, not that she wanted it. Anyway, that's what he called us. And it made Laney so mad that she told us we were going to own it and make him rue the day he made us tighter."

"She actually said *rue the day* in third grade?"

"You haven't had a chance to talk to her much yet, have you?"

"I have not."

"She's mellowed since third grade."

"Haven't we all."

She sighs and tightens her grip on me. "I miss those days," she adds quietly.

I can't imagine missing being younger.

But I would've if I'd grown up the way she did.

"You talk to Emma yet since she got home?" I ask.

"Oh, good, the parking lot." She squirms. "I think you can let me down now. The path should be solid enough for Jitter and me to get to the car. Thank you for the lift."

We can barely see where the cars are parked from here, but I squat and let her down anyway.

I know when I've pushed too far.

Maybe.

"You have dinner plans?" I ask. "Zen and I have this fridge full of every kind of food you can imagine."

"I do. But if you're looking for someone to share with, the senior center would probably take you up on the offer. Hope you didn't get too cold. See you at work tomorrow."

"Sabrina—"

"You are entirely too attractive for my own good. Thank you for the help. Thank you for being kind to my dog. Thank you for considering leaving Bean & Nugget as it is. But I have to go before I do something stupid."

"Maybe it's not—"

"Oh, yes, it is. Just trust me. It *very* much is."

24

Sabrina

I SPEND Sunday working at the senior center with Mom and Jitter, who probably does more work than I do for all of the joy he brings the residents. Seeing Grandpa and hearing stories from the old days from everyone at the center is usually all it takes to cheer me up, but it doesn't work.

Mom spends all day telling me to go see Emma.

I keep insisting Emma will come to me when she's ready. That she's behind at work. That she's processing things and needs space.

Even though I know I'm hitting a breaking point.

And going home, knowing I'm sleeping mere feet from Grey? That he's on the other side of the wall? Hearing him moving around, occasionally clearing his throat or running water in the bathroom?

It's torture.

Absolute torture.

I sleep like crap. When I doze, I dream Emma's feeding me to a pot-bellied giraffe that her dad's stuffing for his taxidermy business, and that she keeps saying *gossip is for assholes* while Laney and Theo ride mating hippopotamuses.

I am not okay, and I finally break.

I call in sick, and then I go huddle in my kitchen at the farthest point from the wall I share with Grey and Zen, and I call Laney. "Are you working today?"

"Let's see… It's a Monday, so in theory, I would be doing the things I usually do on a workday, except I'm exploring this whole *be more fun* side of my personality, but the last time I skipped work, I broke my leg, so—"

"You did *not* break your leg because you skipped work," Theo says in the background on her end of the phone.

I slide to the floor in front of my fridge and rub Jitter's belly when he flops to the ground and rolls over like he's trying to get into my lap. "It's remarkable how much I agree with him these days."

"If I hadn't skipped work that day—" she starts, but she cuts herself off with a shriek of laughter. "Okay! Okay! I would've just broken my leg in the breakroom instead!"

"Is he tickling you?" I am not jealous of my friend. I do not want a man in my life. I am not contemplating knocking on my neighbor's door and asking if we can get naked in the name of stress relief when I'd be secretly thinking it was something so much more than that, much like I suspect he'd think it was more than that after everything that's happened between us since he got to town.

Dammit.

"No, he's piling kittens all over me and they're climbing on my head," Laney says. "And I'm working from home today. Are you working today?"

"Called in sick."

"Are you sick?"

"Physically? No."

"Are you avoiding your boss?"

"Some."

"You want to go talk to Emma," she says.

This is what Laney and Emma and I have always had. We've known each other for so long that we can practically read each other's minds.

"I saw her Saturday and she's just not *her* and I *hate* that," I tell Laney.

"And she'll know what Chandler loves."

"*No*. No." My hand curls into Jitter's fur. "I will *not* drag her into this."

"I can," Theo calls.

"Go feed your cats or scoop some litter," I retort. "Do *not* bother her with my problems. I refuse to pump her for information. I want—"

"Things to be normal again," Laney finishes for me.

"*Yes*. They'll never be the same. But we've always found normal again. And we can't find normal if we're not talking."

We've been through so much together. Emma's mom passing away when we were in middle school. Hard teachers. The heartbreak of break ups with first boyfriends. Whispered tales of when we each lost our virginity. Stressing over which colleges we could afford or which we hoped to get scholarships for.

My mouth getting me in trouble.

PIPPA GRANT

Laney stressing entirely too much about perfection.

Emma daydreaming about buying my grandparents' house to live in with her perfect dream Ken doll man and having a million babies and dogs and cats, and watching deer and elk and fox and bears wander through the yard while she washed dishes.

She daydreamed about *washing dishes*.

And it was so perfectly Emma that neither Laney nor I questioned it. I still wouldn't.

"Come get me," Laney says. "I can reschedule my meetings. I'll go with you."

An hour later, I pull up to the old single-wide trailer that Theo lived in at the edge of their dad's land before he bought his cabin further up the mountain in a more secluded area on a much, much larger lot.

I thought I was a gossip.

I have *nothing* on Theo Monroe when he wants to know something, and he's apparently been tracking Emma's movements very closely. I would've started at her office, but Theo was *very* firm in his orders to go to his old trailer. *She worked late last night then went to Dad's place. Should be up soon.*

The lights aren't on. Will she be mad if we wake her up? Or should we sit here and wait? Will she appreciate the items in the back of my car that I'm bringing as a peace offering? Will they even work on snow?

"It'll work," Laney says from the passenger seat.

"I didn't say anything."

"Your face did. *It'll work.*"

I back up my SUV into the closest spot I can fit where Laney will have the shortest path to the front door. We haven't had fresh snow in a few days, so I can't tell if the tracks around Emma's current hideout are old or new. There's no visible movement inside the trailer.

"Should I have texted first?" I ask Laney. "Should we have waited until after work today? Do you think she's still asleep?"

"No to all of that."

"You're sure?"

"Hand me my crutches."

Okay. She's sure.

I climb out and walk around to her side, retrieve her crutches from the back seat, and open her door for her.

She swings down like she was born on crutches and heads to the front door.

I pop my trunk.

And five minutes later, when Emma finally answers Laney's knock, I have one full human-size hamster ball blown up.

"Um, hi." Em glances between us like she's having regrets about opening the door. "What's going on?"

"I love you and I miss you and I'm sorry, so I'm blowing up your hamster balls so we can fight it out," I blurt.

She blinks at me, then at Laney, and then at the hamster balls.

"Are those the present Theo gave me for my wedding?" She says it so softly, I almost can't hear her.

But I do.

And I nod. "I'm so sorry, Em. If it'll make you feel better to pop them and throw them in my face, I don't care. If you want to just shove me down the hill while I'm in this one, I don't care. Whatever it takes. *I miss you.* And

I'm worried about you. And I want to make it up to you, and I—"

"I'm not *mad*," Em says, and her voice cracks. "I don't want to—Sabrina. I'm *mortified*. The *entire world* saw that I'm an *idiot* who let myself be gaslit by a man who only loved me because it meant *he won*. And you would've warned me, but you knew I wouldn't listen because I was an idiot. I don't deserve you. I don't deserve either of you. How can *anyone* love someone as stupid as I am?"

"Em—" Laney starts while Emma crumples to the ground.

"Oh, god, Em." I abandon the hamster balls and charge up the rickety steps to the trailer. The generator is barely pumping out enough heat to keep this place warm, which tracks.

Theo hates the heat as much as Grey apparently hates the cold.

He wouldn't have minded the temperature.

Emma, meanwhile, is practically turning blue under her massive quilt.

"Get back in the car," I tell Laney. "Em, get shoes. We're going to—to—"

I look at Laney. Her house? Busy neighborhood.

My house? Busy neighborhood.

"Theo's house," Laney confirms.

"I don't understand why he doesn't hate me," Emma sobs. "I almost married a guy who made him go to jail."

"Because he knows people make mistakes, sweetie." I pull my friend into a hug. She's at least half a foot taller than me when she's standing up, but here on the ground, we're on level hugging height. "And we love you and we're worried about you and we want to be here for you and *you are not stupid*. You lead with your heart and that's my favorite thing about you."

"My heart—h-hurt you," she gasps. "It p-picked wrong."

"Your heart went where it thought it could do the most good," Laney says.

Em sobs harder.

I stifle all of the frustration in my entire body that I can't make this better for her and hug her even tighter. "Fuck those people who make assumptions about you because of that fucking video, Em. Fuck Addison for posting it. Fuck everyone who's hurt you. Fuck them all. Let me fix it. Let us fix it. *Please*."

"I put everyone else second when all they wanted was for me to see that I deserved better," she sobs. "All you wanted was for me to wake up and realize I couldn't fix him. I don't deserve you."

"*Emma*." Laney thumps her crutches until she's close enough to drop them and balance right to squat and wrap us both in a hug too. "Enough. You deserve both of us and so much more. Sabrina's right. We're getting you out of here and out of your head. First Theo's house, and tonight, we're going *out*."

"Laney, no, I absolutely cannot—"

"Hide from all of the people in this town who adore you and are worried sick about you for one more day," Laney interrupts.

"And if a single one of them says the word *viral video*, I'm spilling every secret I'm desperately trying to forget I know about them," I tell her. "And then I'll quit gossiping. Soon. I swear. I—"

"No, don't change," Emma says. "Too much has

changed. Don't you change too."

"*I've missed you.*" And I'm about to cry too. I hate crying. *Hate* it. "I'm so sorry, Em."

"No, I'm sorry." Her tears are dripping in my hair, and I don't care. "I'm sorry I pushed you away. I've been so embarrassed, and I'm faking everything being fine, and *nothing is fine.*"

"It will be," Laney says.

"We'll make it fine," I agree.

"We'll make it fine *right now.*"

"As soon as we get you warm."

"You don't hate me?" Emma whispers.

"*Never,*" Laney answers for both of us.

"I thought you hated me," I tell her, and *dammit*, my voice cracks.

That does it.

Em starts sobbing all over again.

Because I'm an idiot.

But I'm an idiot who can fix this. "You really can shove me down the hill in a hamster ball if it would make you feel better, even if you're not mad at me," I say.

Em laughs through her tears. "Stop. I'm not pushing you down the hill in that hamster ball."

"Theo would probably buy you a house if he got to watch," Laney says.

Emma stops crying.

I look up at Laney.

She cracks a grin.

And then all three of us bust up laughing hysterically.

It's not *normal.*

Not yet.

But it's a solid start.

25

Grey

SABRINA ISN'T at work today. She called in *sick*. But she's not sick.

Not according to Shirlene, who stopped in for a cup of coffee and mentioned she'd seen Sabrina leaving House of Curry with a to-go bag big enough to feed six linebackers around lunchtime. Or according to Myrtle, who came in hoping for a lemon scone near the end of the day and was apparently offended enough that Sabrina hadn't made them before calling in sick that she was willing to lean in and say *she's not sick, I heard she's headed to Silver Horn tonight with Emma and Laney*. Or according to Fiona, who came in for a sandwich, looked me up and down, and said *no wonder she picked today for the mental health day she's needed for months*.

Like Sabrina doesn't want to be near me after the

number of times I've crashed her private times the past week.

Like I'm a damn stalker.

"You have *such* a problem," Zen mutters to me multiple times throughout the day.

"Yeah, I can't find a company to make my fiberglass bee," I reply once.

Or another time, "My SCOBY went moldy. Definitely a problem." Can't make kombucha with moldy SCOBY. Must not have sanitized the jar properly.

Zen doesn't believe that's my problem.

I don't believe that's my problem.

But they don't call me on it.

Out loud.

They are clearly telegraphing all day long that I know the solutions to my problems and it's my own fault if I don't implement the solutions.

I sleep like crap, and when I realize at three a.m. that the massive snow dump that people have been murmuring about all week has started, I pull myself out of bed.

Can't sleep. Can't sit still. Can't hear Sabrina breathing through the wall.

I know she's home.

I heard her toothbrush again.

I got a boner over it again.

Debated again with myself if I wanted to switch rooms with Zen, then decided I like torturing myself.

But now, I'm up. If we get as much snow as predicted, Zen says they've heard it's likely that half of downtown will be closed. It's the responsible business owner thing to do to get into the café and plan on managing coffee and basic food for the few customers we'll have in case the rest of the crew can't make it through the blizzard later.

I leave Zen the car and a note, strap on the spikes that I bought myself at the sports gear shop downtown yesterday, and hike downtown.

Where I realize I can make a pot of tea, but I'm basically useless when it comes to running a cappuccino machine. Good thing I know how to YouTube.

Bad thing though?

There's something about teaching myself how to use a cappuccino machine that sparks a desire to test a few things.

Like I'm back in a lab.

Not with bees—I miss my bees—but any chance to engage the *what would happen if* part of my brain has always made me happy.

I've finally gotten the hang of the cappuccino machine when everything inside me goes on high alert.

Not like *there's a bear that just walked into the kitchen* alert.

More like *I feel like Sabrina's on the other side of my bedroom wall* alert.

I almost dismiss it—when I'm in the middle of a puzzle, I lose track of time, space, my own name, where I am—but hope ultimately takes me to the back door.

And when I fling it open and take in the falling snow swirling around two dark figures rapidly approaching who come to a quick halt just close enough that I can confirm dog and owner, I can't suppress a smile. "Sabrina. You're early."

She freezes like she's been caught with her hand in the honey jar. "Good morning."

"Feeling better today?"

There's zero guilt in the look she aims my way. Wariness, yes. Guilt, no. "Yes."

"Good."

"Did you sleep here?" she asks.

"No."

Jitter lunges, straining the leash and pulling her along until he can lick my hand. It's second nature to lean the short distance required to scratch his back.

He's a good dog.

"Did you stay awake here all night?" she presses.

Am I smiling bigger at her concern? Yes. Yes, I am. "No. I thought I'd get in before the snow and cover inside."

She blinks.

Blinks again like it's unnatural for me to actually *work*.

My cheeks warm despite the frigid temperatures blasting into the kitchen. "Even *Super Vengeance Man* needs to learn to pour drinks. Come in. I taught myself to use the cappuccino machine, but I don't like coffee, so I can't make a positive determination about the outcome of my efforts."

Once more, she doesn't have a quick answer. It's not lack of coffee. She's carrying her coffee tumbler in her free hand.

And maybe it's a trick of the light, but I think she's softening.

Like maybe she thinks I'm cute when I call myself *Super Vengeance Man*.

I think she's cute when she's standing in swirling snow, watching me over her coffee tumbler. I also think she's cute when she's competently holding onto her massive dog despite the pull it looks like he's putting on the leash to lean against me and pant up at me.

"Do you actually think it's wise to accept a drink made by someone who calls himself *Super Vengeance Man*?"

"I'm not trying to get vengeance on *you*."

She grimaces. "*Yet*."

"I'm a fair person. You didn't do anything wrong."

"*Yet*."

Right.

Her deadline.

It's on the tip of my tongue to tell her I can wait longer, that I can get my vengeance on Vince instead, that it doesn't matter anymore.

But it *does* still matter.

I'm so fucking tired of people doing shitty things and getting away with it.

If I don't hold firm now, when will I?

And I have faith in her.

I know she can find something, even if I can't.

"C'mon." I hold the door wider and beckon them inside. "It's cold out here. Jitter, want a treat? Got a whole bag inside."

Jitter barks and lunges.

"*Cheating*," Sabrina says while she stumbles along behind him.

I grin at the dog. "Good boy. Sit."

Jitter sits.

I grab the pack of treats out of the top drawer in the desk and look at Sabrina. Probably need to make sure she's okay with this.

Her eyes narrow. "You can't *not* give it to him *now*."

Yes. "It's the same kind you give him."

"How do you know?"

"I asked your mom."

"When did you see my mom?"

"I needed a haircut."

She looks so taken aback by the news that I wonder if there was some kind of invisible line I wasn't supposed to cross there.

Or is it that she hadn't heard?

I give Jitter the treat and get a reward of him once again leaning against my legs and gazing at me with so much adoration, you'd think the treat was an entire steak dinner.

"Go kennel," Sabrina tells Jitter.

He looks at me.

Sabrina folds her arms and looks at her dog.

He flops to the ground, then rolls onto his back, pushing me back three steps.

"Kennel," she repeats.

He whines.

"He gets lonely," I say.

"So get in there with him."

Jitter barks, flops back to his stomach, rises, and trots to his doggy house.

He looks back at both of us like he understood exactly what we said, and he's waiting for me to follow.

"I have to watch your mom try the coffee I made," I tell him with a shrug.

Jitter snorts, but he finishes walking into his house and flops to the ground again, where he puts his nose between his paws, his jowls flopping over his legs, and gives us the most heart-wrenching puppy dog eyes.

"Did you train him to do that, or did he come with those guilt-makers?" I ask.

"Those are the reason he's mine."

"It's sweet that your mom adores him but worries he'll crush you in your sleep."

"Did you have pets before Duke?"

Weirdly, the question doesn't feel like it came out of nowhere. And it doesn't sting as much as I'd expect. I shake my head and gesture for her to follow me up front. "No."

"So what made you decide to get a dog?"

"He moved in to my trash can and Zen adopted him."

"I almost got my first pet that way, but my mom refused to keep a raccoon as a house pet."

That's absolutely adorable. I can picture her baby-talking a raccoon, feeding it food scraps, making a bed for it on the floor next to hers, and it makes me smile.

Again.

I don't know that I smiled this much when I was dating Felicia. And that thought isn't as terrifying as it should be.

I gesture her to go around and sit at one of the stools on the other side of the counter.

"Here." I set a large café mug in front of her once she's settled. "How's this taste?"

I think it tastes like crap, but then, I think all coffee tastes like crap. Zen says it's a genetic deficiency on my part.

Sabrina lifts the mug to her nose and sniffs. My cock goes half-hard.

When she closes her eyes, sniffs again, and then sips, I have to adjust myself.

There's something about watching her taste a drink I made that has me utterly enthralled.

I can brew a pot of tea.

I can clean.

I can cook.

But I don't do it often because it's just me and Zen and they insist on earning their keep, and also, they prefer takeout.

Watching Sabrina drink something I made—no, wait—*shit*.

She's not *drinking*.

She's nearly choking into the mug.

"Mmm," she says without making eye contact. "Delicious."

It is *not*. "Delicious?" I repeat back.

"So...unique. And daring. Very bold."

"It's bad."

"No, no, it's— Okay, yes. It's bad. It is objectively bad. Did you make it with dirty dishwater?"

"No."

She sniffs it again, her nose wrinkling. "Did you ferment the coffee beans in a field of decaying lemons?"

That shouldn't be funny, but I can't suppress a snort of laughter. "Closer."

"No offense, but I think *Super Coffee Murderer* would be a more appropriate nickname for you. *The Bean Meanie. The Latte Villain.* Is that—did you brew this with pine needles?" She coughs an exaggerated hacking noise and pounds a fist to her chest, making her breasts bounce, which in turn makes my dick strain toward her. "I think there's pine tar stuck in my throat."

"It's a pour-over with heated kombucha and then

steamed with the cappuccino thing," I tell her. And yes, I'm very proud of learning the word *pour-over*.

"That...is not something I would've thought to try."

"Don't know if it works if you don't try it."

"This was incredibly imaginative of you, but it does not work." Her brows furrow. "Why do you smile bigger the more I insult you?"

"You're not insulting me." I push a second cup in front of her. "Failure is half the process when it comes to learning and experimentation. Here. Try this one too."

"Did you make it with kombucha?"

"No. For this one, I put my dirty socks on top of the beans."

She snorts, a smile teasing her lips, that sparkle back in her eyes as she lifts the second cup. "I smell cinnamon."

"Your nose gets a gold star."

"I don't smell coffee."

"It's magic hidden coffee."

She sips.

And she chokes. "Oh my god, you weren't kidding about the socks. Are you sure there's nothing poisonous in here?"

"I'm a scientist at heart. You can trust me."

"What *is* that?"

"Warm cinnamon kombucha, actually."

"No."

"Yep."

"I *knew* it wasn't coffee."

"Gold star again."

"I can't believe you like this stuff but you don't like coffee."

"People are weird. Here. Last one."

She eyes the final mug, this one blue with foam that's probably too high.

"It's actually coffee. With milk." I push it closer to her.

She picks it up and sniffs.

Then sniffs deeper.

I lean closer. The snow has melted out of her curls and her cheeks are still pink, likely from the cold. Whatever shampoo she used is mingling with the scents of coffee and chai, and I want to kiss her.

Again.

That's all I want to do. Kiss her. Touch her. Strip her. Bury my hands in her curls and inhale the scent of her. Lick her. Eat her. Take her.

Her eyes drift closed while she sniffs the coffee once more, and I want to be the mug when she puts it to her lips.

She sips, and then a soft *mmm* floats through the air.

If I wasn't already hard, that *mmm* would've done me in.

Check that.

I'm now over-hard and it hurts.

Still wouldn't trade this pain.

"Wow." She licks the foam off her upper lip. "That's actually good."

"Thank you."

Her gaze snaps to mine.

Don't think it's the ego in the *thank you* either.

I think it was the huskiness in my voice.

I'm leaning so far over the counter that it wouldn't be a stretch to kiss her lips.

Snow's swirling outside. No cars going by. No one in the surrounding shops.

I could do it.

I could kiss her and no one would know. No one but the two of us.

"You made this yourself?" she asks.

"Me, that cappuccino machine, and YouTube. I had faith in YouTube and myself. It was the machine that was the wild card."

She doesn't smile at my joke.

"Sabrina—"

"You don't want to do this," she says quietly.

"Do what?"

"Flirt with me."

"Flirting with you has been the highlight of my year."

"And it's going nowhere."

"Why?"

"Are you serious right now? *Why*? Because there's this big elephant called *my café* standing between us. Because I'm a gossip. Because you can't trust me. *I am playing dirty.* Before the end of this weekend, you're going to hate me."

"It's oddly reassuring to hear someone say *you can't trust me* out loud."

"That is not a normal thing to say."

"Villains always say *you can trust me*. The fact that you doubt yourself speaks highly to the likelihood that you're not a serial killer or a narcissist. Want me to pull up a few research articles? Bet you another sip of the bad coffee that I can find six in under a minute that'll prove me right."

She stares at me over the good coffee. "It is such a good thing that we're never going to come to an agreement on Bean & Nugget."

My gut twists.

It's not something I can control. It's not something I *want*. But it's something I feel to the very pit of my being.

I don't want to hurt Sabrina, but I *cannot* tolerate the thought that one more person has manipulated me and won.

She's watching me like she knows everything I'm feeling.

Maybe she does.

Maybe that's part of why she's such a good gossip. She knows what will hurt the most.

"What did Chandler do to you?"

Maybe I'm feeling extra mellow today, or maybe it's the false security that comes with thinking we're snowed in here together, but answering the question is easier than I thought it would be. "My junior year of college, he arrived on campus and made friends with my apartment mate. Would've been fine, but he also decided his favorite new hobby was tormenting me."

She cringes. "That is unfortunately believable."

"I could handle it—wasn't any worse than I dealt with in high school or sometimes from my siblings—but he ultimately set my research on fire and tried to pin it on me."

"He set your bees on fire?"

Shouldn't be a surprise that she's done her research. It's Sabrina. Of course she has. "Six beehives wiped out. Ten years' worth of genetic bee work for one of the professors. Chandler used my passcode to get into the lab, so it looked bad. I was able to convince them I hadn't done it, but the trust was broken, and they wouldn't let me back into the lab unsupervised. I had to switch schools."

"We didn't hear about that back here."

"Shocking."

"And I'm sorry he did that to you."

Her apology makes me tense in a way that her questions didn't. "Wasn't your fault."

"We used to excuse his behavior as part of his *big personality*. We shouldn't have done that."

"Did you learn something from it?"

She grimaces. "Just a little bit."

"Good. Remember it."

She sips the coffee again, a small smile coming to her lips as she licks the foam away again. "This is good. You should consider running a café."

"I make an even better kombucha latte."

Her entire expression twists in disgust and makes me laugh.

Laughing with her makes me want to kiss her again.

"I like you, and I don't like people," I hear myself say.

"I like you, and I don't do relationships."

"Why?"

"Because I come from a long line of women who didn't sleep with the men everyone thought they did and it's given me trust issues."

My lips part. "You don't trust your mom?"

"My grandmother was an amazing woman. My mom is an amazing woman. I trust them implicitly. But both got completely and totally screwed by the men who got them pregnant. I don't trust *men* to do the right thing."

Of all the things I expected her to say, this was not it.

"My grandfather isn't my grandfather." She's watching me while she talks, like she'll find out more about herself based on however I react. "Not biologically. I'm not actually a Sullivan. I'm not supposed to know that—very, very few people know it, actually—but I do, and it's one of the reasons I will adore my grandfather until the end of time. He stepped up and married my grandma and took care of her and raised my mom as his own, making both of their lives more comfortable than they would've been otherwise, even if it wasn't a grand love story. More like a mutual respect story. Everyone thinks my big genetic secret is who my father is. Not who my grandfather is."

"Do you know your father?"

"I know who he is. That's more than enough."

"So...you're not telling me we're secretly related?"

Her eyes flare wide, and then she tips her head back and laughs. "If you're this funny come next Monday, I might actually agree to go on a date with you."

"If I'm this funny next Monday, I might have better options."

She snorts so hard she has to wipe her nose. "Oh god. Tell me you didn't see that."

"You're human. Horrors. Good thing I'll have better options on Monday."

Her peal of laughter lights up my entire soul.

I don't just *want* to kiss her.

I *have* to kiss her.

"Sabrina—"

"*Aroof!*"

"*Aaaahhh-CCCHHHHHOOOOOOOOO!*"

The dog's bark is fine.

But the sneeze startles me enough that I jump.

Because that wasn't Sabrina.

That came from the kitchen.

She's already shifting off her stool. "Are you kidding me?" she yells. "It's four in the freaking morning."

"Four-thirty," comes a male voice I don't recognize

from someone who definitely shouldn't be in the kitchen. "Em's up and wants a cinnamon latte but won't ask for it. Laney says to surprise her. I want a lemon scone."

I follow Sabrina into the kitchen and find a man with shaggy brown hair and tattoos all down his arms squatting at Jitter's doggy house, rubbing his shoulders and taking doggy kisses all over the face.

Jealousy rears up and I'm barking, "Who the hell are you?" before I realize what's going on.

The guy flips a look over his shoulder and grins at me, and *fuck*.

It's the naked knitting guy.

"Predawn entertainment," he says dryly. "You must be Grey."

"You're Theo."

"And he usually uses the front door." Sabrina hands him the package of treats I got for Jitter.

"You weren't open yet," Theo says.

"Scones take an hour."

"I can wait."

My eyelid is twitching.

She is *not* making scones just because he asked her to when she hasn't made them for me in too many days.

"Simmer down," Sabrina says to me as she reaches for her apron. "He has the recipe himself at home if he wants them that badly."

"And she'll charge me double just for being cheeky," Theo agrees.

"*Cheeky*?" She grins at him. "Where'd you pull that word from?"

"Laney's making me read the dictionary."

"You're already to C?"

339

"I got bored and flipped to random pages."

"I'm sure she'll be shocked to hear that."

"Completely flabbergasted."

"You really have been jumping around."

My jaw clenches.

Logically, I know this is old friends giving each other shit for fun.

Emotionally, I want to tear him limb from limb every time she smiles at him.

And he's smirking at me like he knows it.

"You ever had kombucha?" Sabrina asks him.

"Better question is if I've ever had kombucha when I knew what I was drinking."

And now he's the fun one too.

Petting Sabrina's dog.

Making her laugh and roll her eyes.

They belong here.

They *fit* here.

And the only thing I came here for is revenge.

Belonging?

That's not for me.

26

Sabrina

FOR THE SECOND night in a row, Jitter and I join Emma, Laney, and Theo at Silver Horn.

The snow's still falling. The roads are awful. But so few people are out that this place is practically empty. And since Alina and Jerry, the owners, live upstairs, it didn't take much to convince them to open for us.

It's a great chance for Emma to get out of hiding again.

And for me to spend time with friends in a place that Grey can't reach.

"Is he awful?" Emma asks me as we're diving into a charcuterie board.

"Who?"

"Your new boss."

"Not when he's making googly eyes at her," Theo says.

And yes, Jitter's sitting on Theo's lap again despite my orders to both of them to get the dog on the floor.

"He's complicated," Laney supplies.

The two of them are far less lovey-dovey tonight than they've been any other time I've seen them since we got back, and I'm positive it's for Emma's sake.

I'm also positive she knows it.

"Complicated how?" Em asks.

Laney looks at Theo.

Theo looks at me.

My brain does a quick sort of *what's the least painful thing to tell her*, and she frowns.

"Don't sugarcoat it," she says. "Please don't sugarcoat it. I'm sad, not weak."

"He's a very nice person who wants to convert the building into a kombucha bar."

"*No*. Sabrina. Oh, no. Are you okay?"

"I'm working on finding an alternate solution for him so that we can all get what we want. No luck so far, but I did a thing that arrives tomorrow that might change his mind. I hope. Or he'll fire me on the spot. Time will tell."

"Has he ever been here before? To town?"

I shake my head and grab a bite of cheese.

"Tiara Falls would probably go crazy for a kombucha bar. Why not use that Bean & Nugget location?"

I squeeze my eyes shut. "Do I have to answer that?"

"Chandler fucked him over," Theo says. "This is revenge."

"He's commissioning a giant fiberglass bee to hang on the side of the building," Laney adds quietly.

I peek one eye open to watch Emma's reaction.

And it's not good.

Quick blinks. Looking down at her ginger ale. A heavy sigh. "I'll talk to him."

"You are *not* talking to Chandler," Theo growls.

She sets her jaw, which isn't like Emma at all, but it's not *wrong*. "I'll do whatever I damn well need to get over what he did and move on." She slides a look at me. "I meant I'll talk to your new boss. He might listen to someone *else* who's been screwed by the same guy." She winces, and her slender shoulders droop. "Or he might think I'm just as much a part of the problem."

"You don't have to—" I start, only to get cut off by my dog woofing and leaping to his feet.

Yes, while he's still in Theo's lap.

Theo's eyes go wide, and he curls into himself, covering the family jewels.

Laney gasps in horror.

Emma does too.

I squeak, unable to make any other noise.

"Missed," Theo chokes out.

"Are you sure?" Laney's voice is high-pitched.

So is Theo's. "Panicked. That was close. But sure."

"*Jitter*," I finally force out. "*Down*. No barking. You know better."

He whines and looks at the door, peering over the couch. Not hard for a dog of his size even if he were on the floor, but he has his back paws on the cushion and his front paws on the back of the couch. He's taller than I am that way.

But my dog's size is not a problem.

Not like what he's staring at.

"Oh, fuck me," I mutter.

Theo turns around.

Laney tries and mostly just *oomph*s around her cast.

Emma makes a strangled noise and leans closer to me. "Is that him? Is that your new boss?"

"Who gave him the password?" I hiss.

"I heard he dropped a five-hundred-dollar tip for Blossom at the pub the other night," Laney whispers, making my shoulders bunch higher. *Why didn't I hear this before?* "I think she caved."

"It's me," Zen says, peeking out from behind Grey to make eye contact with me like they know exactly what I'm whispering over here. "Nobody can resist this face. I talked the password out of your mom when she gave me a haircut this afternoon."

They're in suit pants, a black-and-white button-down, and a trench coat, and it's so *Zen* I nearly forgive them for bringing Grey just because they look so fabulous.

Grey, on the other hand, is in dark jeans and a plain blue button-down. His dark beard is getting thick, and without the beanie he usually wears everywhere, I can tell Mom did a fabulous job with his haircut too.

Also, she and I are having a serious talk about *telling me when she sees my biggest problem.*

Zen's smile drops as their gaze shifts to Emma.

Emma tenses.

Zen's chin wobbles. They blink quickly, then poke Grey and mutter something I can't hear. He frowns at them.

Not a disapproving frown.

A worried frown.

Zen pokes him again and glares, and he lifts his hands in surrender, then heads to the bar.

Jitter leaps over the couch to join him.

And in the time it takes Laney to whisper, "What was

that? What was *all* of that?", Zen has beelined the short distance from the door to our lounging area.

They squat in front of Emma. "I want to hug you so bad. I know what it's like to spend years trying to make people love you when they're physically incapable of it."

Em sucks in a breath.

And Zen scoots back. "Sorry. I just—you got fucked. I hate when people with good hearts get fucked so big, and I don't know you, but everyone here loves you, and I like them, so you must be a good person. I'll quit being a weirdo. Your drinks are on us. My uncle, I mean. He knows what it's like to get fucked too."

"Emma, this is Zen," I say softly. "They're my new boss's keeper, and they do a fabulous job despite the hardships of the job."

Em holds out a hand. "It's lovely to meet you, Zen."

"I went viral on my campus in college when someone recorded me singing in the shower," Zen blurts while they shake Emma's hand.

Grey's head whips around like he hasn't heard this story and he's ready to put on his *Super Vengeance Man* suit and go take care of whoever hurt Zen in college too.

"Simmer down," Zen says over their shoulder, clearly knowing what's going on behind them. "I took care of it."

"How?" Grey asks. He pockets his wallet and approaches our group with far more wariness than Zen had.

"That's filed under *you don't need to know*," they reply.

"Sit," Emma says. "Please. Join us. Are you hungry? We have plenty of food."

Grey eyes Theo.

Theo eyes him right back.

Neither man says a word to the other as Zen slides onto the curved couch on Emma's other side, leaving only the chair beside my end of the couch open for Grey.

Laney makes a face at me, and I do my best to telegraph *they had a pissing contest over who got to have more of my attention this morning.*

Pretty sure she gets the message, as she pinches her lips together in a classic Laney *I will not laugh out loud at the ridiculousness of that* face.

The minute Grey's seated, Jitter lunges into his lap.

"Jitter, get down," I order.

Jitter whines.

Grey pulls a treat out of his pocket, tells my dog to sit, which he does *in Grey's lap*, and then gives him the treat.

Then he shrugs at me. "He's a good boy."

Emma slides her brown eyes in his direction, then back at me.

Why is your dog in love with the guy who wants to take over your café? is the clear question here.

And wouldn't I like an answer to that as well.

Zen suddenly seems to realize there are more people here than just Emma. "You're Theo. Oh my god. Is it weird to say I loved your channel? If it's weird, I won't say it. But like, you got me through a really rough patch in college when all of my friends graduated before me and I was in a bad low spot of not really loving myself."

"Aww, I told you that you were doing superhero work." Laney smiles at Theo.

Grey's jaw flexes so hard his whole beard moves. "Why didn't I hear about these problems in college?"

Zen waves a dismissive hand. "You were in lust with Felicia, and I didn't want to interfere with your happiness." They look back at Theo. "I won't mention that again either. But since people get judgmental about porn stars, I just wanted you to know you were doing good in the world."

"Naked inspirational knitter," he says.

"If you ever do it again, knit with your feet. Just trust me."

Emma cracks up.

Actually cracks up with real laughter.

My eyes get hot, and it takes everything in me not to launch myself around Emma to hug Zen.

It's *so* good to hear Em laugh.

"If he does that, it wasn't my suggestion," Zen tells Emma. "Sorry. Forgot you two were related. Speaking of related, Sabrina, I saw your cousins. They asked if I had any magical sway to convince you to take a DNA test. What's that all about?"

On the surface, I know it's about the triplets using peer pressure to convince Laney to take a DNA test too.

But below the surface—if Grey told Zen what I told him this morning about my grandfather, I deserve this.

That's why I told him.

So that when his grandmother gets here tomorrow, he can choose to respond by telling the entire town my own biggest secret. My mom's biggest secret. My grandma's biggest secret.

I'm playing with fire.

It's only fair to give him a weapon too.

"What's going on here?" I gesture to them, making a vague circling motion around their body. "You took a week to warm up to me enough to say hi, and you're out here spilling deep dark secrets and being all *you* the first time you meet Theo, Laney, and Emma. What's this about?"

They jerk their head toward Theo. "I trust his taste. I didn't know you were friends before. You're officially cleared now because you have the friend endorsement of a man I've seen naked. Ah, sorry, Laney."

Emma snort-giggles.

Laney shrugs. "You've seen it, but only I get to touch it."

Emma snort-giggles harder.

"So. Sabrina." Zen looks at me again. "I sniff a story. Why do your cousins want you to take a DNA test?"

"They fell down the social media rabbit hole about DNA surprises and they're looking for drama in our little town," Laney says.

Zen squints at her. "You need DNA tests for that when you have Sabrina?"

"*Hey,*" I say.

Zen grins at me. "That was all love. I want your superpowers."

"Did you give them caffeine?" I ask Grey. "This is truly more words than I've ever heard out of them."

"They're a big fan," he mutters back.

"I'm merely in a good mood because good things are coming," Zen announces.

And that one lands.

They know I'm toast tomorrow. And I think they're genuinely excited to see their great-grandma, who should be landing in Denver in the next few hours.

Our blizzard isn't affecting the city. It's isolated up here in the mountains.

"All right," Grey says. "*Now* I'm concerned."

As he should be.

Alina brings us another charcuterie board and refills all of our drinks. Laney engages Grey with questions about bees. Zen peppers Emma and Theo with questions about taxidermy animals and which of the stories they've heard about Theo's antics when he was younger are true.

They all are, naturally.

And honestly?

It's fun watching my friends adopt new friends.

Especially new friends that I like entirely more than I should.

I know this is an optical illusion. That Grey petting my dog, Zen laughing with Theo and Emma, things feeling normal, all of it is temporary.

A *just for tonight* thing.

Just like Hawaii was temporary.

I'm thinking I should take Jitter and go home when Emma slides a look at Grey during a lull in everyone's conversations.

"Chandler hurt you too," she says. "I'm sorry. I wish I could do more, but *I'm sorry* is all I have right now."

Grey's blue eyes flicker toward me, his shoulders hunching slightly. The change is enough for Jitter to quit panting happily and look at him with a soft whine.

I didn't tell her.

I want to tell him I didn't tell her anything he told me about why he has a beef with Chandler.

But would he believe me?

He shifts his attention back to Emma. "Not your fault."

"He told me about you shortly after Thanksgiving. He said you were looking for investors in a business opportunity, though, not that he was selling the café to you."

Grey flinches.

"Why did everyone believe his lying ass?" Zen asks.

"Because it's hard to face that someone you've known and trusted forever is capable of hurting and manipulating and gaslighting you," Laney says.

"Even when you should know it's not normal or okay," Emma whispers.

"Knock it off." Theo leans across the low table between us to squeeze her knee. "Not your fault I didn't tell you."

"Yes, it is."

He growls.

"You've never let someone in your life that you believed you could change if you just worked hard enough?" I ask Zen to try to answer their question. "You've never seen someone's potential and wanted to help them achieve it?"

They wrinkle their nose. "Calling me out about Uncle Grey when he's sitting right there isn't very polite of you."

Grey tosses a napkin at Zen, who flashes him a grin. "Okay, okay, you can be taught. You dress so much better these days than you did when I first found you. It's a start."

"How did you find him?" Laney asks.

"Caught him digging in my trash—no, wait, that was his dog."

"You're *this close* to walking home," Grey says.

Zen grins. "I'll catch a ride with Sabrina. So, there was this family reunion one time, and Uncle Grey shows up for the first time in *years*, and I was like, 'Who's that weirdo doing experiments on the potato salad?' and when I heard he sometimes forgot to shower or do his laundry, I decided to adopt him."

I'm one hundred percent certain no one believes them, but none of my friends question their version either.

The rest of the evening is weirdly enjoyable.

Weirdly only because I know this feeling of friendship won't last.

And eventually, it's over.

We all pack up to head home.

And I wonder just how quickly everything will change once Grey's grandmother arrives in town tomorrow.

27

Grey

"QUIT BEING A STALKER," Zen says, making me snap away from peeking out of my living room blinds.

It's not quite five in the morning. I was waiting for them to finish getting ready so that we can head to Bean & Nugget.

And while I was waiting, I was listening.

And while I was listening, I heard Sabrina moving around next door.

And when I heard her open her front door, I peeked out to watch her and Jitter leave for their morning walk.

"I was checking to see if it snowed more overnight," I tell Zen.

"It hasn't snowed since before we hit the speakeasy last night, and you know there's no more snow in the forecast for at least a week." They stride to the front door, fling it open, and lean out.

"Morning, Sabrina," they call as they step outside without a coat.

"Morning, Zen," comes back.

"Hungover today?"

"Not at all. You?"

"I'm fabulous. Who's a good puppy? Yes, who's the bestest puppy?"

My front door shuts, and I can hear nothing else going on outside.

I can hear what goes on *inside* the unit next to me—including that toothbrush that still makes stars dance in my vision in the good way when I let myself imagine it's Sabrina pleasuring herself with a vibrator—but I can't hear what's going on outside.

So I do what any sane man who's obsessed with a woman he can't have would do.

I pull on my coat, hat, and gloves and join them.

Under the guise of it being time to leave, naturally.

Both of them go silent when I open the door.

Sabrina's in leggings under a thick, puffy jacket, showing off every one of her curves. Her eyes sparkle under the porch light. Her hair seems extra curly, and I want to wrap it around my fingers while I bend down and—

I clear my throat and lecture myself about respecting people's boundaries *again*. "Morning, Sabrina."

"Good morning, boss-man," she replies cheerfully while her dog lunges for me and rubs his fur all over my pants and coat.

Annoying, that.

Not the dog.

Being called *boss-man*, I mean.

It's annoying because it reminds me that the deadline I gave her to find me another way to ruin her cousin is almost here, and as much as I'm madly in obsession with her, I can't bring myself to say the words *talk to me about how you can buy this building back from me, even if it's a nickel at a time*.

"Ready, Zen?" I ask.

"Um, no. I haven't had breakfast, and I'm still in my pajamas."

"Guess you're walking to work."

"I'll give you a lift," Sabrina tells them.

"Perfect. See you at work, Uncle Grey."

I don't want to go to the café.

I don't even *need* to go to the café.

For the first time in years, I want to linger closer to a woman that I still don't fully trust, but that I *want* to trust.

Not her fault.

She hasn't done a damn thing wrong.

I just don't trust easily.

I head to the café rather than standing there looking like a stalker, then decide this is the last place I should be today.

Willa was in early this morning, and she's decorated the café for Valentine's Day.

There are hearts hung on strings in the windows overlooking the lake. Pink and red streamers twisted from the fireplace in the center of the room to the exterior walls. Red candleholders with heart-shaped candles floating inside each of them.

"Are you participating?" she asks me as I'm taking it all in.

"No."

355

She slides me a look that I interpret to mean *because you're secretly dating Sabrina, or because you have another reason?* "I heard you were at Silver Horn with Sabrina and her friends last night."

"Coincidence."

"But her dog sat on you."

"Her dog has awful taste in humans."

"Nonsense. Theo's his favorite human after Sabrina, and Theo is good people. Also, please leave the cappuccino machine alone until we've fully trained you."

Between the décor and the very clear *you are causing issues here* vibes, I decide it's better to check out and run over to Tiara Falls for the morning. There's an issue with the Bean & Nugget building that I'm selling there, and I'm happy to let that issue take my entire morning.

When I'm done, I take myself out to lunch in Tiara Falls. And since Sabrina's shift should be over when I've finished, I head back to Snaggletooth Creek and the café there.

And I find it an absolute zoo. The parking lot is packed, and I have to park down the street and walk back.

Odd for midafternoon. This is the time of day when things usually slow way down.

When I step in the back door, the kitchen is empty.

But there's a swell of voices louder than anything I've heard coming from the dining room.

I follow the voices into the front, then I go lightheaded at the sight before me and have to grip the doorframe.

It's not that half the townspeople of Snaggletooth Creek seem to be here. It's not that there's no one at the register, where we have a small line of customers waiting to order. It's not even that Sabrina's still here and sitting in my favorite chair in front of the gas fireplace, with her dog on the floor gazing at the person in the matching chair with utter adoration.

It's that *Mimi is here.*

"Boarding school!" Sabrina's saying while everyone else crowds around. "That explains so much. Was it a specialized boarding school, or a general boarding school?"

"Don't answer that," I say to my grandmother as my vision clears, belatedly remembering that I told Sabrina myself that I went to boarding school.

My grandmother.

She is *not supposed to be here.*

But she's smiling in a way I haven't seen her smile in *months.* Possibly longer.

Her straight silver hair is cropped close to her head, definitely newly cut, and for a split second, the thought crosses my mind that Sabrina's mom might have trimmed it for her.

Ridiculous.

Of course she didn't.

Mimi's in pink lipstick and wearing bright-red dangly teardrop earrings that are making her ears droop more than the normal effects of gravity. Her wrinkled cheeks wrinkle deeper as she flashes me the brightest smile I've seen on her face since her sister died almost a year ago, sending her into a grief so much heavier than anything I witnessed when my grandfather died.

Considering just how much of a bastard he was, that makes sense.

But it's been awful watching her retreat into being a

shell of the person she was while living under the cloud of missing her best friend in the entire world.

"Grey!" she says. "You're back. Sabrina was just telling me how kind you were to save their family from massive debts by buying this quaint little café from them. Without telling me."

"What are you doing here?" I ask.

Her eyes twinkle. They *twinkle*. She hasn't twinkled in so long. "Making friends."

"Sabrina's the biggest gossip in this town," I blurt before I can remind myself that I like being on her good side. "Don't tell her *anything* you don't want anyone else to know."

Everyone in the room cracks up.

Everyone.

Including Zen. And Mimi.

"Sweetheart, when you're my age, you won't care who says what about you either, including people who have seen you naked."

And now I'm picturing Sabrina naked.

Beneath me.

On top of me.

Sideways and upside down and in a bedroom and on the beach and against a tree.

Fuck.

"But don't worry," she adds. "I'm not telling anyone anything about my favorite grandson that they can't find out with a simple internet search."

Sabrina props her cheek on her fist, one-handing a steaming mug of coffee. "Your favorite, hmm?"

"Such a sweet boy. He was a surprise ten years after his next-closest sibling, and the poor thing got the short end of every stick. Tired parents, the family trust fund running low—"

"How did you get here?" I interrupt. Zen's been with me practically nonstop. They didn't go get her. They couldn't have. They didn't have the car.

And they didn't say Mimi was coming.

They would've told me that Mimi was coming.

"I walked," Mimi says dryly. She sips coffee, then closes her eyes and sighs with deep satisfaction. "That is *delicious*. Where did you say these beans are from?"

"Honduras," Sabrina answers. "We don't serve them here, which isn't *my* choice, but when you said you loved coffee, I broke into my home stash for the best stuff."

I look at Zen, but they seem to be actively avoiding making eye contact with me.

"Zen—" I start, but Mimi interrupts me.

"Grey, you need to serve these beans here." She sips and sighs again, and it doesn't matter how wrong this is or who told whom what.

She looks *happy*.

For the first time in over a year, Mimi doesn't have a cloud of sadness and gloom hovering around her.

"Whatever you want, Mimi," I force out around an unexpected lump in my throat. "When did you get here?"

"Last night. I stayed at that hotel at the airport, and Sabrina's friend Theo drove all the way over to pick me up this morning. You know. The naked knitting one. Isn't that sweet of them to make arrangements for me?"

Sabrina's friend Theo picked me up.

They made arrangements for me.

All while we were *sitting and having fucking drinks together last night.*

I look at Zen again.

They look back at me this time, a slight guilt bringing a blush to their cheeks, but a belligerent *I am not on your side on this one* in their steady gaze.

"You got in a car with a complete stranger?" I can barely keep my voice controlled.

"Of course not. Even if I didn't know exactly who everyone here was after that video, I'm still sharp enough to hire the family's private investigator before trusting a minor character in a viral video and her porn star friend when they invite me to town."

Sabrina chokes on her coffee and comes up laughing, though there's some strain in her expression if you know how to watch for it.

And I do.

I know how to watch for it.

"Oh my god, what did he find on us?" Sabrina asks.

"*She*," Mimi says pertly.

"Did she find anything good?"

"Not on you. You're remarkably boring for someone with so much personality and who knows everything there is to know about everyone else."

Sabrina visibly lightens.

No one else seems to notice. And I don't think I'm making it up just because I know some of her secrets.

Mimi smiles. "But *Theo*. My goodness, I can't believe I'm saying this, but he was actually disappointing in person after everything she dug up on him."

Sabrina laughs again. "Miss Madeleine, you are the best."

"The feeling is mutual." She turns to me. "Now. Greyson. You didn't tell me you *bought a coffee shop* in the

Arctic Circle. I had to hear it from a stranger calling to express concern about your overall well-being."

A stranger calling to express concern.

Sabrina's cheeks go pink too.

And not a *cute* pink.

A *guilty* pink.

Way guiltier than Zen's pink.

My blood pressure hits the roof, which is a bad place for it to be.

How long has she been planning this? Is *this* why she's been keeping her distance?

Because she knows I'm going to murder her for this?

"Sabrina." I jerk my thumb toward the kitchen. "A word."

She holds my gaze while she takes a long sip off her own mug, despite the redness getting redder in her white cheeks, and then says, quite simply, "No, thank you."

Like bringing Mimi here gives her the upper hand.

"We need popcorn," Zen murmurs to Mimi.

"So it seems," Mimi replies.

Sabrina rises. "You should visit with your grand-mother. That's far more important than threatening to fire me. Jitter. Come. Who's a good boy who wants to go on a hike now that Mommy's shift is over? Who's a good boy?"

"*A word,*" I repeat. *There are lines.*

This is one of them.

And she knows it.

How many times did she tell me she was playing dirty?

And how furious am I that I'm still worried that *her* secrets might come out since Mimi hired a *private investigator*, even if that was all Sabrina's own fault?

"Now," I say.

She ignores me.

Zen and Mimi look nothing alike, but they're sporting matching amused pursed lips.

And I have to grab a fucking chair because I'm seeing dots in my vision and feeling that familiar pressure behind my eyes that says a dizzy spell is imminent.

And not a light dizzy spell like the one I had a minute ago.

A *hard* dizzy spell.

"Oh, no," Sabrina says distantly while people shift around me.

The dog whines nearby, and something heavy settles on my feet and against my legs while my vision goes nearly black.

A chair scrapes against the brick floor, and someone grabs my arm. "Sit, Uncle Grey," Zen orders.

They sound like they're in an echo chamber.

So does the dog's whine.

I follow directions and sit, and nearly fall forward, but Zen and the dog don't let me.

The pressure fades, and my vision starts to clear.

So do my ears.

And that's when I realize what's missing.

All of the noise of a room full of people.

Everyone's staring.

Half the town just saw me nearly pass out.

Look weak.

Damaged.

Broken.

"Willa, we have customers waiting," Sabrina says. "Iris, did you see the Valentine's Day decorations? Willa

362

did such a great job with them, didn't she? Portia, did I hear your brother's coming to the speed dating event tonight? Isn't he living in South Dakota now? Is he coming home for good, or is he just looking for a good time?"

Voices slowly pick up again.

"That was a bad one," Zen says beside me.

"You think?" I mutter while I stare at the floor, pressing my fingers to my temples.

No, not the floor.

Jitter, who's staring up at me like I have officially scared the shit out of him, and he'd like it if I didn't do that again.

Nothing is right.

Nothing is okay.

Except Mimi's here, her cane making its distinctive thump on the floor as she carries her slender frame across the café to sit next to me. "Too much stress, Grey," she says quietly. She squeezes my hand. "Maybe give an old lady fewer reasons to worry about you, hmm?"

"Working on it."

"Not very well, by the looks of things."

The scent of chai hits my nose a split second before a mug clinks to the table beside me.

And that's not Zen's hand holding the mug.

Those are definitely Sabrina's short fingers and clean nails.

She doesn't say a word.

Not to me, anyway.

"Good boy," she whispers to the dog while she scratches him between the ears. "You stay. I'll be back."

I don't want her to leave.

I want her to sit here and scratch *me* behind *my* ears.

I want to thank her for effortlessly steering everyone back to focusing on something *other* than the fact that I almost passed out in the middle of the café.

Fuck, I want to thank her for bringing Mimi here, even if I'm feeling completely naked at the idea that she's been talking to my grandmother behind my back about what I'm doing here.

And I want none of the people here to know that I have any weaknesses.

Weakness makes you vulnerable.

Vulnerable lets them take advantage.

And now the whole town knows there's something wrong with me.

28

Sabrina

THE CHECK-IN LINE for speed dating is endless.

And every last one of the women asks the same thing. "Is Grey Cartwright joining us tonight?"

Half of them add *the question*, "And is he okay? I heard he almost passed out here this morning."

"Hadn't eaten," is my cheeky answer. "You know men."

I have zero doubt the meal patrol will have a sign-up to take him breakfasts and lunches in addition to his dinners before the night's over. Or at least to have someone else helping Zen make sure he's eating those meals here.

The things we gossips do to make sure newcomers feel welcome in a community.

And to psychologically and food-logically sway them to reconsider what they're doing to the community.

The worst part of all of the questions about Grey though?

I don't want them to like him.

Because he's mine.

Dammit.

Even when I know he's pissed at me, and rightfully so, *I want him to be mine.*

I want him to be the friend that *Duke* was in Hawaii.

It just felt so right. So *easy*. And even with our differences, I feel like I can trust him.

He's trusted me with some hard things about himself. He thinks *I'm* worth it.

Or he did.

Until this morning.

"Are you participating, Sabrina?" Kayla asks.

The question takes me by surprise—she's the first to ask all night—but worse?

Worse, it makes me want to turn around and see if he's watching me.

He's been pissed at me for four solid hours now.

And I've been successfully avoiding him for those four solid hours, despite spending half of them here at Bean & Nugget, getting the café set up for speed dating.

Jitter is like a paperweight, but for people. He was a Grey-weight today.

That helped keep Grey from hunting me down.

"I know you usually do," Kayla adds in a whisper, "but I heard you have a boyfriend you're not talking about, so I didn't know…"

I have a *what?*

I absolutely do not have—*oh my god.*

I burst out laughing, then clamp a hand over my own mouth.

Grey gossiped about me.

She leans closer. "Who did you tell you had a boyfriend and why? You *never* have a boyfriend. *Ever*. But Yolanda swore Fiona claimed her source was impeccable, even if she couldn't say who it was."

Grey's watching me.

I can see his reflection in the window, thanks to the darkness outside, and he is definitely watching me. A shiver slinks down my spine.

"People change," I tell her. "But that particular relationship didn't work out."

"You had a boyfriend?"

"I was in a very short-term relationship." With myself. I'd still be in it, but I'm taking a short break from myself while I deal with the fact that I don't like that I'm attracted to a man whom I need to not be attracted to.

"Your favorite kind, right?"

She laughs.

I laugh.

It's true.

"Next, please," I say, waving her inside with a smile.

Which promptly dies a horrific death involving all the worst things you can think of when I see who's standing in line behind her.

"We're full, go fuck yourself," I tell Chandler.

"Sabrina," my grandfather chides.

He's standing just behind Chandler, his stooped, white-haired form easily hidden by Chandler's bulkier figure.

And it doesn't surprise me in the least that Grandpa

367

would've forgiven him, no matter how much I know it hurt him to see the café leave the family.

Grandpa forgives a lot.

He truly is the best man in the entire universe.

"Sorry, Grandpa." I smile at him, but put that smile away when I turn back to Chandler. Just *looking* at him makes my blood pressure rise. "We would have a spot open for you, but it's a rule that if you've tried to get married within the past month, you have to sit out speed dating."

Grandpa eyes me, clearly knowing I'm making up that rule on the spot and clearly thinking I should practice forgiveness too.

I shrug at him. "One *could* say I'm trying to spare someone's ego when no one here wants to talk to him, but fine. Hundred dollars for a ticket, please."

Chandler chokes. "A *hundred dollars*?"

"Oh, you spent everything off the sale of the café already? Pity."

"The sign says *twenty-five*."

"It's a hundred," Devi says as she comes up beside me. "Twenty-five is the senior rate."

"Better come with a blow job," Chandler mutters.

"I hear there are machines for that," I reply perkily.

I expect another look from Grandpa, possibly accompanied with a soft but chiding *Sabrina*, but it doesn't come.

Why?

Because he's squinting at something across the café.

You didn't think the *only* reason I called Grey's grandmother was because he bought my café and was threatening to ruin it, did you?

Please.

"Who's that?" Grandpa asks.

"Who?" I ask back.

"The woman who's staring at me. She seems—she's not from here. But I feel like I know her."

I look behind me. "Madeleine Cartwright? That's Grey's grandmother. Have you met Grey yet? He owns the café now. I think you'd like him."

"Could you shut up?" Chandler mutters while he shoves four twenties at me.

"No, she can't," Devi answers for me. "And you're short two twenties."

"This is extortion."

He's right. He's only short one twenty for the already inflated price we quoted him, but I'll take Devi's side over Chandler's any day.

I would take a poisonous toad's side over Chandler's any day.

"You could try to find a new girlfriend without speed dating," Devi says. "Maybe somewhere like Florida. Or in Europe. Or Siberia. Basically, anywhere thousands of miles from here."

I gesture her into my seat. "Here. You finish. Grandpa, come on. I'll introduce you."

When I rise and turn, though, Zen is helping Mimi slip into the kitchen and six people are blocking our way.

And yes, she's absolutely *Mimi* to me now.

She insisted.

First impressions from this afternoon? I adore her just as much in person as I have on the phone.

An excited murmur goes up as Iris calls for all of the ladies to take a seat. She's running things this year.

"Is Grey participating?" one more woman asks me.
"That poor man. His divorce was awful."

And that's all it takes to set off the whisper chain.

"I saw a picture on Insta, and it looks like his sister's
still really close friends with his ex-wife. Like, *they went on
vacation together*."

"I heard she took his dog."

"I saw an article that said he had to pay her a hundred-
million-dollar settlement because of a loophole in their
prenup."

"*Oh my god*."

"Ladies," Iris calls again. "Seats! Gentlemen, let the
ladies through. They'll be seated while you move from
table to table."

Grandpa stills, looking at the kitchen.

"Madeleine Cartwright?" he says to me.

"That's what she told me her name was. But do you
know, I heard she went to Carnegie Mellon too. About
the same time you did. I wonder if you knew each
other."

He eyes me with bright blue eyes that are getting
watery at the edges. "You're trouble."

"You used the wrong word for *the best*," I squeeze his
arm. "Want me to get you a seat by the window so you can
watch everyone be totally goofy as we all try to put our
best feet forward?"

His gaze wavers. He's staring at the kitchen, but he
looks to the table at the edge of the front window, where
he used to tuck himself in to work on payroll and inventory or share a cup of coffee while chatting with artists
who wanted us to display their creations and fellow business owners along Main Street.

He's never participated in speed dating, but he's always come to watch. Grandma used to come too.

"I'll sit," he says. "You go get a table. Find a nice man who makes you happy."

Not likely.

Someone grabs me by the arm and pushes me into the nearest seat. "Numbers are uneven."

"We could kick Chandler out," Kayla whispers.

"We are not assholes," they reply. "Besides, how much more fun is it to watch him strike out tonight?"

"You ready for this?" Frannie says from the next table. "It's so weird that Laney's not joining us, isn't it?"

"Laney hasn't been here in three years anyway."

"I know, but I thought she'd have her year after her bad breakup and then be back. Instead, we get you. This is fun."

"Gentlemen, line up," Iris calls. "And, go!"

Three-quarters of the men swarm the room, looking for an open table.

Decker slides into the seat across from me.

"We're cousins," I remind him with a smile.

He winks. "Not by blood, apparently. That makes you fair game to the powers of my irresistible charms."

I crack up, despite the sentiment making me throw up in my mouth a little.

If I were watching this from the outside, that would be hilarious. And so, I'm happy to let every other woman in this place think that my cousin is a catch.

I'm not the only person in the family with zero intentions of settling down.

He lounges back in his seat with a broad grin, threading his fingers together as he rests his hands over his *Don't piss off the writer or he might kill you in a book* long-sleeve T-shirt. "Jack and Lucky are gonna be so jealous that I got a crack at you first."

The fact that I'm not laughing right now speaks volumes to how worried I am about whatever Grey will have to say when he finally corners me. "You are ridiculous."

"And you're stressed."

"Never." I am so stressed.

"Where's Jitter?"

"Mom came and got him. Too many people tonight."

"First timer has started," Iris calls. "You have three minutes."

I glance around the room and spot my other two cousins.

Jack was apparently a slowpoke. He has a look of *these three minutes might kill me* on his face as he leans back and Addison Hunter leans forward, drawing something on the table with her finger.

Probably explaining to him that since she's in finance and he's an engineer, they'd make smart, competent, beautiful children.

"Ew," Decker mutters.

Lucky, on the other hand, is on the opposite side of the room, actively engaged in an animated conversation with Viola Hammerbach. She's twenty-five years older than he is.

And she was his kindergarten teacher.

"Are they catching up, or is he flirting with her?" I ask Decker.

"I asked him yesterday who his favorite teacher of all time was, and he named her, so it's anyone's guess. Shame about her husband. Good for her for getting back out there though."

I look back to where Grandpa was headed to sit along the wall.

Not there.

Grey's noticed too.

He's two tables down, apparently pulled in to make numbers even, which I'm attempting to actively ignore. And speaking of ignoring, he's completely ignoring whatever Kayla is saying to him at their table.

"So who is she?" Decker asks.

"Oh my god, did you sit with me because you want to hit on an old lady and think I'll just give up the scoop? I'm off gossip, remember."

He cracks up.

Fair.

I was totally giving him shit. "I hear she's Mr. Cartwright's grandmother," I murmur.

"You hear?"

"Mm-hmm."

"With what degree of certainty?"

"Given what we all know about genetics…"

"*She was in his life as his grandmother*, correct?" Decker clarifies.

"Correct."

"And you're sure?"

"Yes."

"As in, she was the woman in that picture in Grandpa's yearbook that I found?"

"Mm. I assume so."

"Why's she here?"

PIPPA GRANT

"She got on a plane and flew here from wherever she's from?"

"*Sabrina.*"

"Time!" Iris calls. "Everyone move. No, this way. *Lucky.* Other way. There you go. Mrs. Hammerbach has you all flustered, doesn't she? Talk as soon as you sit. We're not giving time for moving tables from here on out."

"Did you do that?" Decker asks while he rises.

"Introduce Lucky to his kindergarten teacher? No. Also no to setting the rules for tonight."

"We're talking later about why Grandpa disappeared after making *I'm seeing a ghost* eyes at the new old hottie in town and *why you didn't tell me you called her*. Don't deny it. I know you did."

"Get moving, Decker, or people will think you're asking for my phone number."

He makes a face and dives for the table in the next row, settling in across from Devi.

Walter Blunderman, whom I've known since he used to yell at Laney, Emma, and me anytime we got too loud in our treehouse, since his property bumped up against Grandma and Grandpa's yard, eases his way into the seat Decker's just abandoned.

Grey is taking the seat at the table beside me.

Dammit. I was hoping they'd move the other way.

"Hi, Mr. Blunderman," I say with fake cheer. "Bad arthritis night?"

"Getting better. That herbal tea Fiona whipped up for me made it a lot worse, so I'm doing better since I'm off it. You still know too much about everybody and their brother?"

"Nope. I'm off gossip."

374

"That's not what I heard."

I fake gasp. "*Mr. Blunderman.* Are *you* taking up my previous occupation? I love it. Tell me what else you've heard."

"Nope. You're off gossip. Bones might be creaky, but my ears still work."

I miss half of what he says.

Not because I don't want to listen to him, but because every time Grey says something to Isabella next to me, his voice rumbles in my ears over everything else.

Get a grip, Sabrina.

You don't do this.

Men are dicks. They don't make 'em like Grandpa Harry anymore. Look at what Laney's father did. Look what your own father did. Look at what Chandler did. Even Theo's a dick, but at least he's a known dick, and he knows I'll cut off his dick if he pulls a dick move on Laney now.

I'm not a man-hater.

I'm just so fucking wary after everything I've seen over the years. The couples who make it, who truly adore and respect and accept each other every day of their lives? They're so rare.

I'd rather be alone with my dog and tight with my besties.

And when they have kids, I'll be the best damn Aunt Sabrina to ever exist.

They *are* my family.

And three minutes goes by entirely too fast while I'm desperately trying to convince myself that I'm still anti-relationship and that I don't want anything to do with this wounded, vulnerable, sometimes dorky, always hot man at the next table.

My stomach tightens. My pulse flutters. My fingers tense. And all too soon, I'm wishing Mr. Blunderman a great time tonight while he pushes out of his chair and heads to the next row.

Grey drops into the seat and hits me with a glare that tells me every last second of the next three minutes will feel like an eternity.

It's time to face the music.

29

Grey

Sabrina Sullivan has fucking *audacity*.

She has the nerve to *smile* at me as I take the seat across from her at this horrific singles mixer, which is the last place on earth I want to be right now. But Zen and Mimi conspired against me, and now here I am.

And with fucking *Chandler Sullivan* sitting just a few tables down too, thinking he has the upper hand *again* because I didn't fight against his pricktastic attitude last week.

"Grey! Long time no see." Sabrina flips a plastic cup off the stack in front of her, fills it with water from the carafe that's been placed on every table, and pushes it to me. "Drink. You look dehydrated. How's your grandmother liking town?"

"You fucking called my grandmother," I hiss.

She lifts both brows, copper like her hair, which is

curlier tonight. A single strand has fallen out and lays across her breast, a wave catching the light every time she moves and making me want to go complete caveman, shoving across this table and kissing her until she apologizes.

"I know everyone's grandmother in town," she says. "Or I did, if they're not still with us. I just wanted her to know how much the community appreciates that you saved my family from having all of our credit ruined for overdue taxes, no matter what you do next with the building."

I don't know what makes me more furious.

That she did it, or that she's pretending she did it for any reason other than to *tattle on a grown fucking man to his grandmother*.

When she said she was playing dirty, I didn't expect her to go *this* dirty.

Add in that it feels so damn good to have Mimi here that I want to kiss her again to thank her, and I'm a mess.

A complete disaster of complicated feelings.

"Leave. My grandmother. Out of this," I manage to force out.

She holds up both hands. "Sure. I won't talk to her anymore. But I make zero promises if she asks me a direct question. Manners and all that."

I start to feel the lightheadedness take hold, and I remind myself to breathe.

My vision blurs in the corners, but I can still see her taking a sip of her water while she watches me like she knows what she's doing to my blood pressure.

Breathe.

Breathe.

Water.

Fucking dammit. She was right about the water.

I sip. I breathe. My vision clears.

Are people watching?

Is fucking *Chandler* watching?

Christ. *Fuck.* He probably heard. He probably heard what everyone else heard.

Grey Cartwright was so overcome at the sight of his grandmother that he fainted dead away.

Motherfucking fucker, this is *not* how any of this is supposed to go.

"Leave my grandmother alone," I repeat to Sabrina, calmer.

Gotta stay calm.

She holds my gaze without blinking, which is the most fucking annoying thing about her. That woman can silently dare you to a staring contest and then win it without getting the slightest twitch in her eyelids.

Is it because she drinks so much coffee?

Or does she have staring contests with herself in the mirror? Is that her third-favorite pastime after drinking coffee and using her toothbrush?

"I know I should regret what I did, but I—" she starts, only to be interrupted by the moderator calling time.

I look at the dude to my right, who seems to think he's taking my seat. "This one's mine. Go around."

"Yeah, *Sabrina*," the dude says. He holds out a hand for a fist bump. "We knew it wouldn't end with a one-night stand."

"Jesus effing Darwin on a honeycomb," I mutter.

She stifles a giggle while she waves the fist bump away.

"Oh my god, that was adorable. And quite the mental image."

I suck in another deep breath and down the rest of my water.

She refills the glass before I can move.

Fuck.

I am not in control here.

"I didn't call her to talk about you," she says as everyone else settles around us. "I mean, yes, you came up. Possibly I should say I didn't call her *only* to talk about you. You're the reason I went down the rabbit hole in the first place, but ultimately, it had very little to do with you."

"Very little to do with me."

"Correct."

"She said you told her I almost passed out in my entry-way." I'm keeping my voice as low as I can. I swear there's not as much noise in here as there was five minutes ago.

Are they watching?

Are they listening?

"She asked how you were doing, I said you were doing great, she asked if you'd had any more of your dizzy spells, and since you're the only person I tell lies to, I told her the truth."

"That's a lot of words for *I called your grandmother to guilt you into not doing what you want to do here.*"

She refills my water again.

Shit.

Didn't even realize I'd drank it.

I lean even closer. *God*, she's gorgeous. The green eyes. The cute nose. The slightest hint of freckles on her nose. The hair. That hair on her black sweater that I want to pick off and don't dare in public.

Or private.

Or anywhere.

There are a lot of *worst things* about this situation.

At the moment, my *worst thing* is that I trust her with Mimi.

I clear my throat. "Mimi thinks I'm a fucking savior here because everyone in this damn town told her I saved the café and not a single one told her I'm planning to gut it from the inside out."

"You still can be the savior here. There are other buildings that I could get put up for sale for you. Give Emma time to heal, and we can find something appropriate to make sure *someone* knows his time of playing the charming guy in public while being an asshole behind everyone's back is over."

"I'm no one's savior." *But I fucking want to be.*

"When you look at all the ways a person can let you down, the bar to be a savior is exceptionally low these days. I don't think you're a savior. I think you're a complicated man who deserves some closure."

"Time!" rings out again.

Sabrina rolls her eyes and waves the next guy past. "We both know how this would end, right, Jeremy?"

"I'm not opposed to another fun night," he replies.

I look up.

The dude's lanky. Wearing glasses. Big nose. One eyebrow hair is twisted up onto his forehead wrong.

"Appreciate the offer, but you'll do better in about three tables," Sabrina replies.

"Change your mind, you let me know." He winks.

I almost come out of my chair to slug him.

"You *slept with him*?" I hiss at Sabrina while the guy heads to the next row.

"Small town. Slim pickings. I've slept with a lot of these guys."

I remind myself she's trying to get my blood pressure to do its thing and take another long drink of water.

She leans over to grab the water carafe from the table next to us, then gestures something to someone behind me.

"I called your grandmother because I found a picture of her with my grandpa in his college yearbook," she says without ceremony.

My jaw comes unhinged. I snap it back shut.

"I can show you too, if you want. They looked friendly. And my grandpa's been lonely since my grandma died, so since you were here, and everything I could find online suggested your grandmother was a widow, I called her to see if she remembered him and if she wanted to come see both of you."

"You...called my grandmother...to set her up...with your grandfather."

She frowns. Squints up at the ceiling. Taps her finger to her chin while she wiggles her head back and forth like she's debating if she wants to tell me that's exactly what she did, or if she wants to stretch her story closer to whatever it is if I'm wrong.

And then she shrugs. "Sure. Close enough. In the interest of honesty, yes, I also called her to see if she can talk you out of converting my café into a kombucha bar. But a big part of it is that I hate seeing people lonely. I don't care if they become friends or if they do something romantic, I just thought it would be nice to connect two old people who I thought might like to see each other again in a time when they've each lost someone important to them. I'm sorry about your great-aunt, by the way. She sounded like a lovely person."

"*You looked up my aunt too?*"

"No. Zen was telling me about her. Anyone Zen adores has to be a good person."

"Time!" rings out while someone replaces the water carafe at our table.

Sabrina refills my water before I can move to do it myself.

I don't push back from my chair.

She doesn't wave me on.

"You gonna finally move, you old bastard?" Chandler Sullivan says entirely too close to my head.

Before I can react, Sabrina's out of her seat and in his face. "*Leave.*"

"Make me," he replies.

"The quiet way or the loud way?"

I shove out of my seat too.

I am *not* letting someone else fight this battle for me, and I am *not* letting him get away with any more shit like he pulled last week either.

And that little voice in the back of my head telling me that this isn't fake hatred that Sabrina has for the man who bullied my scrawny ass in college can shut up.

Not the time.

Chandler turns to me.

Takes a step back.

Looks up.

Up.

The asshole is looking *up* at me.

PIPPA GRANT

Didn't used to be like that.

"Fuck, dude, you got tall," he says. "Couldn't see that when you were sitting down. You wanna tell this bitch—"

I have him lifted to eye level before he can finish that sentence. The prick's not light, but I have rage operating on my side. "You will walk out this fucking door, then walk out of this fucking town, and never fucking come back if you don't want every single person in this room to find out every single way you've ever been a complete and total shit in your entire life. Go fucking bully someone else. Better yet, go fucking bully yourself and leave the rest of the world in peace."

I drop him.

He teeters on his feet and doesn't fall, but to my utter satisfaction, he's gone whiter than a ghost.

"Do I need to repeat myself?" My vision is getting foggy again. My head is getting light.

But I fucking did it.

I stood up to him.

"So you sleep with a woman—" he starts, but he doesn't finish.

"You've already used that line, you twatopotamus," Sabrina says. "Say one more syllable and everyone finds out what you did the night your wedding didn't happen."

"What did he do, Sabrina?" one of the triplets calls from one corner.

"You haven't told us yet," another of the triplets calls from the opposite corner.

Iris bustles over to us. "Chandler Sullivan, you are *booted*. Get out. *Get out*, before I get your grandfather. And your parents. And *Emma*."

Sabrina sucks in a breath.

384

So do half the people in the room.

Chandler blinks.

Then blinks again.

"Where's Emma?" he asks.

"None of your goddamn business," I growl through the dots in my vision.

"He slept with a reality TV star that he found on the beach an hour after the wedding didn't happen," Sabrina tells the entire room. "Leave, or I'm going back to what you did to Bean & Nugget when Grandma died."

He glowers at her.

"I'd do what the lady says," I say, not liking the way I need to grip the chair to hold myself up, but I'm doing it. I'm holding myself up and I'm pretty sure I'm glaring directly at him.

"Fucker, I thought we were friends."

"Friends don't destroy their friends' lives and then let everyone else take the blame for it."

"Maybe you can find some new friends at McDonald's," Sabrina says.

McDonald's? There's not a McDonald's here.

That's random.

That's *too* random.

That's—*holy shit*.

Aunt Applebee and Uncle Five Guys are secretly having an open marriage because they can't stand each other or their dear child Little McDonald.

"His parents' marriage—" I start, and then the most beautiful thing in the world happens.

Chandler Sullivan squeaks in actual fear.

He squeaks. And he shrinks. And he goes red in the

face. "Shut your—" he starts, but I take a menacing step toward him and he shrinks even further.

"Leave, or we will completely and unequivocally destroy *everything* you've ever loved," I growl. "And for the record, I'm starting *right here*. There'll be bees. So many bees. Bees *everywhere*."

"I'm fucking leaving, you douchebags," he snarls. "There's nobody here worth knowing. Your numbers are uneven, and fuck you all."

True to his word, he storms to the front door, flipping off the entire room of people.

"Somebody take Addison's phone," the third triplet yells.

"I'll sit out," Sabrina tells Iris. "Grey, just drink out of the carafe. Hey, you all remember that year the fairy lights short-circuited on our statue of Ol' Snaggletooth and we thought his head was going to burn?"

A few people titter nervously.

Someone gasps.

I assume that's Addison being tackled in the corner and having her phone taken away from her.

"Well, can't say this won't be the most memorable speed dating event the Tooth has ever seen," Sabrina says. "Who wants to be the person talking about this at their wedding? Somebody's falling in *love* in here tonight, aren't they? Hey, Bitsy, wanna hit the timer? Iris, call it for us, yeah? Let's go!"

Voices pick up again around the room.

"Go go go," Iris calls while she pulls the door shut behind Chandler.

"Have fun tonight," Sabrina says softly to me. "Good luck."

"Wait—" I start, but she doesn't.

Instead, a perky blonde leaps between us.

"Hi," she says. "I'm Oakleigh. We haven't met. You were supposed to be at my table, but I thought I'd just come to you."

I try to smile at her, but I can't.

Not while I'm watching Sabrina head through the kitchen, knowing she'll be slipping out the back door and off to god only knows where in this town.

"Sorry," I murmur. "I have to go."

And I do.

I stood up to Chandler.

I did what I came here to do.

But I think there's something more that's my real purpose here.

Something bigger.

Something terrifying.

But I'm about done with being afraid. It's time to put *Super Vengeance Man* to bed, and start being *Super Grey* instead.

Just me.

All by myself.

Doing my best and taking a leap of faith.

30

Sabrina

I SMILE through telling Zen that I have to go because my mom says Jitter has diarrhea, which I know they know is a lie. Then I sneak out the back door without a word to Grandpa or Mimi, who are sitting at chairs at the desk in the kitchen, leaning in to each other and talking faster than I've heard Grandpa talk in ages.

It's not *fast*—Grandpa doesn't do anything fast, and I don't think Mimi Cartwright does these days either—but it's *faster*.

I catch phrases like *three kids* and *favorite grandson* and *so hard to lose my sister*.

Like they don't want to waste a minute and they're jumbling up every bit of catching up after nearly seventy years apart in half an hour.

Pretty sure they don't even notice that I'm leaving.

I slip and almost wipe out on the icy asphalt, but I

finally reach my car at the very, very, *very* back of the lot. Just as I'm sliding into the driver's seat, though, the passenger's side door opens, and Grey lets himself in.

My heart thumps in utter panic. My fight-or-flight instincts decide freeze is the way to go.

And then something even worse happens.

Two tears slide down my cheeks. "Go away."

"You told me about your mom and your grandma so we'd be even when Mimi got here. So I could use it against you."

"You're very dumb for a mathematician." He's damn brilliant, and he doesn't belong here.

Not because we don't have smarty-pants residents, but because he's not built to run a café or a kombucha bar. He's built to solve puzzles and manage beehives and use that brain to fix the world's problems.

Sometimes I feel like I barely know him, but other times I watch him staring down puzzles at one of the tables, or poring over blueprints, or just getting lost in thought, and I know—*I know* that he needs something bigger in life.

That he's hurt right now. That the people who shouldn't have let him down in his home life, in his work life, in his school life have all failed him.

He was in his *mid-twenties* when he invented a better cereal bag.

There is *so* much more that this man can do with his life. So many more contributions to the greater good of the entire world.

If only people would stop hurting him.

I want to be that person.

I want to be that person who shows him that there are people who want the best for him.

And for the first time in my life, I understand why people fall in love. Why they take the chance. Why it's worth the risk.

I've spent my life mastering gossip to make the world a better place.

What if *loving* someone makes the world a better place?

"Sabrina."

"Please go. I don't want you to see me like this." *I don't want you to be nice because that will be the final straw to make me believe in things that still terrify me.*

He takes one of my hands in his, his long fingers wrapping around the back of my hand, his thumb brushing my skin, and I realize he's not wearing a coat.

No coat. No gloves. No hat.

He didn't stop to grab any of it before following me out here.

But his hand is warm, and his grip is firm in the best way, and just holding his hand is making my panic recede and my heart race for other reasons.

My nipples go erect.

My vagina finally pushes herself out of the steel box I've locked her in the past few weeks.

"He ultimately won't care what you do to it," I whisper. "Even if he loved parts of the café, this won't hurt him the way you want it to."

"He hurt you," he says.

"He hurt Emma. He didn't hurt me. He pissed me off."

"He hurt you."

"I'd have to care about him and his opinions for him to hurt me."

"*Sabrina*."

I want to look at him, but I'm terrified of what I'll see.

Kindness.

Empathy.

Understanding.

Grey, *Super Vengeance Man*, determined to tear my cousin limb from limb for putting my family's café in danger.

Super Vengeance Man showing up to avenge my injury would be the worst.

The *absolute* worst.

"Please just tell me you hate me for calling your grandmother and that I'm fired and that you're buying all of downtown so that if I never want to see you again, I'll have to move."

"Why do you want me to hate you?"

"Because I like you too much and that's a bigger kind of scary than the size of my anger at Chandler."

He doesn't answer.

Not with words. But with his hands, he brushes his thumb over the skin on the back of my hand. His other hand oh-so-gently pushes my hair back over my shoulder, and then his fingers twist in my curls.

My breath catches. It feels like fairies are dancing across my scalp, little bits of pleasure radiating over my skin.

He lifts my hand to his mouth and presses his lips to my palm, and my stomach drops to sit on my thighs.

"I was ready to hire a private detective to track you down after Hawaii." His voice is husky, deeper, his words slower, like the confession weighs more than his vocal cords can handle. "Even after you disappeared. Even with

392

the awkward flashing of the maid and the brush-off note. You were magic. You were this magical, sparkling, determined angel of a woman and I wanted to find what was wrong and fix it. And now I'm what's wrong."

"You are *not* what's wrong."

"I am. Now *I'm* hurting you."

"Your idea—what you want to do—it's fun. It's exciting. It's *new*. The people here will love it in their own way."

"You won't."

"I will. I'll adapt. I'll find a new purpose. It's not about Bean & Nugget. It's about Snaggletooth Creek. It's about my community. I can—I can find it still. I just need to remember that."

"Sabrina." He kisses my palm again, his hot lips against my skin making my vagina ache.

"Please go back inside."

"That's what you want?"

"No." *Dammit.*

I open my mouth to correct myself, to say what I should say, even if it's a lie, but before a single sound can escape my lips, he's brushing his against them.

And *god*, they feel good.

Like they were made for kissing me.

I squeeze his hand and hook my other hand behind his neck, pulling him in for a deeper kiss.

This isn't what I should do, but it's what I *want*.

I want this funny, intense, vulnerable man. I want him to kiss me and come home with me. I want him in my bed. I want to laugh with him over coffee and tea in the morning. I want him to walk my dog with me. I want to show him my home, my town, *all* of it, and watch him fall in love with *all* of it the same way he fell in love with the view on our hike.

I want him to stare at me like he stared at the sunset.

I want to shield him from the people who hurt him and I want him to be the solid shield between me and the people who hurt me.

I deepen the kiss, leaning over the center console and into his space. A low, eager rumble in the back of his throat with his hands roaming lower down my back makes my vagina clench.

We're in the far back of the lot.

Everyone else is inside.

No one will see us.

And that's the thought process that has me climbing over the console and into his lap, where I'm squished between him and the dash.

He fumbles for the seat controls.

"Hands on me." I lick his neck under his beard and reach for the switch. "Got this."

"No interruptions." *God*, that husky need in his voice.

It's making my panties wet.

The seat whines and slowly, slowly, *slowly* slides back to give us more room.

He snort-giggles, and *oh my café au lait*, is it adorable.

How is he this sexy and irresistible despite *everything*?

"Don't do that," I order.

"Do what?"

"Laugh."

"You like it when I laugh."

I shush him with my lips sealed over his, thrusting my tongue into his mouth until he makes that desperate rumble in his throat again. I shift in his lap so I'm straddling him and reaching down to recline the passenger seat at the same time.

We angle back slllllloooooooowwwwwwwlllllly.

And now it's me.

Now I'm kissing him and pawing at the buttons on his shirt with my free hand, and I'm the one snickering.

He snort-giggles again.

The seat millimeters back. It's not even inching. It's millimetering.

But then he slides his hand up under my skirt, and I'm not laughing anymore.

My breath catches.

The seat stops because I've lost control of my fingers.

All I can do is part my thighs wider while his hand explores my ass, teasing it lightly and then kneading it and then sneaking beneath my panties to touch my clit with his knuckle.

"Wait," I make myself say.

He freezes.

I gulp in air and drop my head to his chest. We're half-reclined and he has his hand inside my underwear and I don't *want* him to stop.

But I *need* him to.

Just for a minute. "I don't want the café."

"Sabrina—"

I shift again, my eyes crossing as I brush my clit against his still hand, and I make myself look him straight in the eye. "No. *No*. Listen to me. I can sleep with you, or I can fight you for Bean & Nugget, but I *cannot* do both and still live with myself. I want you. I want *you*. Home isn't a building. Home isn't the past. Home is wherever you're loved. That—*this*—it matters more. To me."

He still has my pussy in his hand, still frozen.

"I *will not* hurt one more person in my life the way I hurt Emma," I whisper, and my voice cracks.

I mean it.

The café is his. I'll stand by his side and help him turn it into whatever he wants. He's trying to break free of all of the things in his past that hurt him, while I'm trying to cling to everything in my own past that brought me joy without challenging myself to reach deeper beyond what's always come easy.

"I believe you."

"*Why?*"

"Because I've watched you. I've studied you. I've tried to *not* like you, to *not* want you, but no matter what you do, no matter what you've done from the very first moment we met, I can't help but have the utmost respect for you."

"You're supposed to tell me I'm an asshole and you know I'm using sex to try to get my café."

"It'll take more than sex to convince me to give you back your café."

"*I don't want it.*"

He smiles.

The grumpy jerk *smiles*. "May I please move my hand now?"

"To do good or bad things with it?"

"Both?"

My vagina clenches again. "Can you do the good first?"

He crooks a finger between my thighs, sliding it from my clit to my vagina, and my eyes cross.

I whimper when he slips his finger inside me, rocking against his hand.

"This kind of good?" he murmurs while he fists my hair in his other hand and pulls me closer to lick my earlobe.

"More," is all I can say.

"Like this?" He adds a second long finger, circling and spreading them inside me while I rock against him.

"Yes," I pant. "Don't—deserve—*oh fuck right there.*"

This isn't right.

I shouldn't be the only one feeling good right now. I should be undoing his pants. Stroking his magnificent cock. Licking his magnificent cock. Sucking on— "*Oh yes yes yes god yes please please aaaaaaaahhhhhhhh!*"

Stars explode behind my eyes as I tumble over the edge and into the depths of a deliciously heady orgasm. My thighs clamp around his hand while sensations I haven't felt since Hawaii rock me to my core.

"So damn beautiful," he breathes, still teasing my climax higher.

"So good," I pant through the absolute heaven that is Grey Cartwright's fingers inside me.

And it's not enough.

I lean forward and kiss him as the tremors leave my body, sucking on his lower lip, remembering I have two working hands and putting them to use on his pants. "Take my panties," I order between kisses.

"Another pair?"

"*Oh my god*, stop being more adorably funny."

"Only if you quit being so damn sexy."

This.

This is the man who crept under my skin in Hawaii. The man who made me feel like I'd be okay when I was sure I'd never be good for anyone again. The man who has been so hurt by so many people but is still willing to trust me.

I pop the button on his pants, reach inside to free his cock, then slide into the wheel well of my car so I have a better angle to lick that beautiful, thick, straining erection.

"Sabrina—"

I swirl my tongue around his head, and he cuts himself off with a strangled moan.

It's cramped down here. I bang my elbow on the door when I grip the base of his penis and my other elbow on the gear shifter when I push myself up just far enough to suck his head into my mouth. There's barely room for my hips and my back is pressed to the dash, and he's making the most incredible noises while I suck him deeper.

"*Sabrina*," he gasps.

I roll my tongue up the underside of his cock, swirl it around his head again, and then take him to the back of my throat.

He gurgles something incoherent and fists my hair in his hands. I cup his balls and roll them together while his hips vibrate under my arm like he's trying to hold back from thrusting into my mouth.

I suck.

I tease.

I *love it*.

Making him lose control, pleasuring *him*, treating *him* is making me ache to have him inside me again. I want him to play with my breasts and my pussy and kiss me until I can't breathe.

I want him to fall asleep in my bed and wake me up by

pinching my nipples and then take me from behind. I want to sit in his lap and feed him scones for breakfast and then I want him to carry me back to bed.

I want to walk Jitter with him.

I want to have snowball fights with him.

I want to take him to Marmot Cliff and show him the stars on a moonless night.

I just *want. Him.* I want him in a way that I know is so dangerous, but also so *right*.

His grip tightens in my hair. "Can't—hold—Sabrina —I'm—"

I tease his balls and rub my tongue along the underside of his cock once more, and it suddenly spasms as he comes down my throat with a moan of utter pleasure.

So. Much. This.

The two of us. Laughing. Arguing. Making up.

I am so head over heels for this man.

"Sabrina," he pants as his body sags.

I let his softening cock go, pressing a kiss to the tip before attempting to climb out of the wheel well. "So, you wanna come sleep on my side of the wall tonight?" I ask.

"No."

Everything inside me goes still with fear. "N-no?"

"I want to stay awake on your side of the wall all night."

Tears hit the backside of my eyelids. "You are such a goof."

"You like that."

"I do."

He's falling asleep in my passenger seat. So much so, in fact, that he merely murmurs a soft *mm* when I tuck him back into his boxer shorts.

It's impossible to suppress a smile at the sight of him so relaxed.

Almost as impossible as climbing back out of the wheel well.

And *that* task proves so very difficult that I ultimately end up tumbling out of the side of the car when Grey finally stirs enough to realize what's wrong and help me out.

Worth it, though.

Especially once we get back to my house.

31

Grey

SABRINA HAS a bathtub the size of a normal person's walk-in closet, and I have to remind myself I can afford to build my own house with a bathtub this size before I do something insane like propose to her just to get access to this tub all the time.

"Are you sure you want me to join you?" Sabrina asks.

"Mm." My eyes are half-closed, but I can still see her approaching, completely naked, in the candlelight.

I didn't *mean* to get in the bathtub first, but the floor was cold and the steam was rising off the water coming out of the faucet, and she *did* swear she was just running downstairs to get water for both of us and would be *right back*, so I thought it was legit to climb in and wait for her.

And now I'm in heaven.

Absolute heaven.

"Water warm enough?" she asks.

"Love the warm."

"I've noticed." Bubbles and bath water slosh around my chest as she settles into the tub too, straddling me once again. "Am I warm enough?"

I loop my arms around her, low enough that they're still under water. "Mm-hm."

She presses her lips to my neck and slides her hands up my sides, making my cock lift with interest.

It's two o'clock in the morning.

We've been at it like rabbits since she obliterated the last of any lies I could tell myself about wanting her just for fun with that blowjob in the passenger seat of her car.

I like this woman.

I like her more than I thought I would ever like another woman.

When she told me she's giving up on convincing me not to change Bean & Nugget, I believed her.

Maybe I'm a fool. Maybe I'm a sucker.

But I'd rather make another colossal mistake and know my heart was in the right place than keep playing the role of *Super Vengeance Man*.

"What does your tattoo mean?" Sabrina murmurs as she paints a trail with her lips along my collarbone, her fingertips lingering on my ribs.

"Deeds, not words."

"Latin?"

"Yes."

"When did you get it?"

"When I switched universities." I nuzzle my nose into her hair. "If I got another, I'd find the Latin for *stop being a dumbass and quit repeating history*."

"You're safe here."

My heart swells.

Again, I believe her.

I know I should be wary, but fuck it. This *thing* that's lingering at the edges of my soul?

I think it's peace.

That other thing lingering between us?

That's my hard-on.

She rubs her pussy against it, making me even harder.

You'd think we haven't already done this twice since we tumbled in the back door.

"You're safe with me too," I tell her.

"That's what your mouth says, but this little guy between us says I won't be able to walk tomorrow."

"*Little*?"

She giggles, the sound vibrating through my chest as she lays her head on my shoulder, teasing my nipple with one hand right at the bubble level of the bath and casually drawing figures on my back with the other. "He's little compared to the length of your leg."

"He's majestic."

She lifts her hips, still snuggling me, and slides onto my dick.

"*Fuck*," I breathe as she squeezes her inner walls around me.

"Agreed," she whispers. "He's majestic. I like him."

I haven't had sex without a condom in years. Felicia didn't want kids and insisted on double protection every time. There wasn't anyone after her until Sabrina in Hawaii.

But I've figured out her tell when she's lying, and she wasn't lying when she looked me in the eye, told me she's on birth control, and I'm the only person she's been with

403

since her annual check-up in December, when she got a clean bill of health.

I'm setting aside *Super Vengeance Man* and being *Super Brave Man*.

Sounds dorky.

Small risks, small rewards.

Big risks, big rewards.

Get burned enough, you don't want to take the big risks anymore.

But Sabrina—the heart she shows to her community without even knowing it, her code of ethics about gossip, her straightforward insistence that she'd play dirty to save her café—she's reminding me that I still have a lot of life to live.

I still have so much to learn. To discover.

To fight for.

She lifts her hips and slides back down my erection, slow and steady while she stays curled against me, peppering my skin with gentle kisses wherever she can without moving her head.

This is sleepy sex in a warm bubble bath and I adore it.

I adore her.

So, *so* much.

She's still flexing her hips, lifting off me and settling back down, slow and steady, the squeeze of her pussy dragging out the exquisite pleasure of a building orgasm.

"I should be passed out cold but I think I'm addicted to you," she murmurs. "I can't stop."

"You can sleep tomorrow."

"If my boss doesn't fire me for calling in again."

"I'll talk to him."

She laughs, tightening her vagina around my cock, and

a leisurely stroll through a bubble bath to climax land turns into an urgent desire to thrust into her.

I flex my hips, and she tenses in my arms. "Oooh, I like that."

"Do you?"

"Good little man between us."

She pumps her hips again, and I tilt my pelvis and thrust into her.

"More." She lifts her head, rises until I almost slip out of her, and then holds my face with her bubbled hands, kissing me while I thrust up and she sinks down.

We're not slow, but we're not frantic. Her lips are swollen and cherry red, and she has a hickey forming on her shoulder that was definitely my doing.

Mine whispers through my head while the pressure builds in my balls, warning me I'm close.

Mine whispers louder as her eyes slide shut and she tips her head back, all of that glorious curly red hair falling into the bubbles while the spasms of her orgasm squeeze me tighter.

Mine comes as a shout as she gasps my name and grips my ears, pushing me over the edge into my own orgasm, buried deep inside her in this safe cocoon where nothing else exists and nothing else matters.

Mine.

Just *mine.*

That flush on her cheeks. Her eyes unfocused but somehow still holding mine. The way she rubs her breast like she's feeling her release in her chest and it's too much.

Like she feels it too.

We could be so much more than what we are.

If one of us is brave.

PIPPA GRANT

If one of us will say it.

If one of us will leap.

Her shoulders drop and she slumps back against my chest. "*How*?" she murmurs.

"My other title is *Super Orgasm Man*," I murmur in her hair, my cock still spasming deep inside her.

She laughs.

I suck in a breath. *Super Sensitive Cock Man* might be more appropriate in this exact moment.

"Do you really have a comic book collection?" Sabrina asks.

I tense.

It's reflexive.

"I used to read Jack's anytime I had to stay with the triplets while my mom had a night out," she murmurs. "And I always hated that I felt like I wasn't getting all of the good parts of the story. Like I'd missed so much for there being several issues that came and were lost under his bed since the last time I was there."

"The nuance," I murmur. "Of course you'd love the nuance."

"And the details."

"The gossip."

"Damn right."

"I divorced Felicia when I found out she was running a podcast about living with difficult men." Fuck me. Where did *that* come from? "S-since we were—it's gossip. I mean, some people think—never mind. I didn't say any of that."

"Behind your back?" Sabrina asks.

When I hesitate, she wraps her arms tighter around me.

"Yes," I finally confirm.

"How'd you find out?"

"Vince—my old business partner—he knew. He listened to it. I walked into the lab one day, heard him laughing his ass off, went to see what was so funny, and I heard her. At first, I thought she was on the phone. When I realized what it was—between that and all of her shit about Zen—I was done. My family said I couldn't take a joke, but—"

"But your spouse is the one person who should respect you the most," she finishes.

"Yes."

"Grey?"

"Yeah?"

"I mean it. You're safe here. Not just *here*, in my bathtub here, but all of the Tooth. You're safe here."

I close my eyes and drop my nose into her hair again and hold her tight.

I believe her.

I might be a fool, but I believe her.

And when I hear a soft snore coming from her face on my chest, and the water cools beyond comfortable, I get us both out of the tub, dry her off, and carry her to her bed, where I hold her for the rest of the night.

32

Grey

LEAVING Sabrina while she's still sleeping mid-morning feels like opening an old wound.

Like the next time I look at her townhouse, it will have disappeared. Like I'll never see her again at the café or anywhere else in Snaggletooth Creek. Like I'm leaving myself exposed for her to disappear again.

But I have a breakfast date with Mimi, and I want to know how her evening was.

Up to a point.

I don't need details if hers ended like mine did.

I do, however, need her advice.

"That's the same face you had when you were puzzling out how to combine plastic and beeswax, except I think you're dwelling on something much heavier right now," Mimi says when I join her and Zen in the sunroom of the bed and breakfast Sabrina arranged for her. While there are six four-person tables in here, we're currently the only occupants.

A wall of windows overlooks a snowy yard and pine-covered mountain peaks in the distance, and a colorful painting of a bear holding a coffee and tea service over the buffet on the opposite wall. Winter weekdays must not be popular for the bed and breakfast crowd. Or else we're eating late. "And you've been wearing it off and on since I got here yesterday," she adds.

"You ever contemplate justice, Mimi?" I ask while I put my napkin in my lap. My tea is steeping and for the first time in months, I feel a sense of peace.

Optimism, anyway.

Though it's short-lived thanks to Zen, who makes a noise over their coffee cup that could mean anything from *finally, we're getting somewhere* to *Uncle Grey is a moron*.

"A time or two," Mimi answers me. "I *was* married to your grandfather for too many decades."

"Why'd you marry him?" Zen asks.

"I was sent to college to find a husband. When my first choice fell through, I went with the backup plan. And it was a poor backup plan."

"Why'd you stay?"

"Murder is illegal, and he could afford better divorce attorneys."

They're both laughing when the hostess comes in carrying three plates of a gorgeous eggs benedict with a side of yogurt parfait and orange slices.

Zen has no memories of my grandfather, which is something I'll forever be grateful for.

He was a scary old bastard. Passed it down to my

father, despite Mimi's best efforts, and that explains everything anyone ever needs to know about my family.

Mimi waits until our hostess has departed, fork poised over her food while she watches me finish fixing my tea. "What justice are you contemplating?"

That's a much more complicated answer now that I know why Mimi's here.

She confirmed Sabrina's story yesterday afternoon, ending with *I used to sometimes think about how I could've been living in the mountains running a little bakery with the man of my dreams, but what good are wishes that can't come true?*

"Grey?" Mimi prompts.

I shake my head. "There's someone here who...hurt me. And I thought—"

I cut myself off with a sigh.

Liking it here was never part of the plan.

But I do.

I like it entirely more than I feel like I deserve.

"You thought destroying something of his the same way he destroyed something of yours would be justice?" Zen prompts. "But then you found out you'd be hurting a lot of other innocent people along the way?"

I meet their gaze. My college years aren't something we've ever discussed. All I said about buying Chandler's café was *I'm looking forward to seeing how it feels when the shoe's on the other foot.*

But I get the feeling they know more of the story, if not *most* of the story.

"Knowledge is power," they say quietly. "Sometimes it's all the power you have."

"Am I understanding this right?" Mimi says. "You

bought a café and saved a man from financial ruin to…get revenge?"

"I paid him less than what it's worth," I mutter.

"Face it, Uncle Grey." Zen pops a bite of eggs benedict into their mouth. "You're not built for being a bloodthirsty man of vengeance."

I'm not.

Especially when following through with my plan will hurt Sabrina.

She says she'll adapt, that she wanted me last night more than she wanted her café, but it doesn't feel right.

Not because I think she lied.

I think she was being completely honest.

It's more that Bean & Nugget isn't broken.

It's beautiful.

It's beautiful because *she* runs it.

She belongs to Snaggletooth Creek, and Snaggletooth Creek belongs to her.

Same for Bean & Nugget.

"It's never too late to turn something ugly into something beautiful," Mimi says.

I cut a glance at her too, knowing she's right, and starting to finally understand what I need to do to find the peace I came here for. "You've been cagey about what you and Harry Sullivan talked about last night."

"Bah. I'm not cagey. I just can't remember."

"She doesn't want to tell you that they're getting married," Zen pipes up.

"*Zenbow.*"

"Full-name me all you want. I know that's where this thing is going."

"I am *too old* to get married."

"So take him for a test drive and see if you want to invite him out to your retirement compound."

"Stop talking," I order Zen.

"Please. She's been lonely, not dead. But use a condom, Mimi. Just because you can't get pregnant doesn't mean you can't get an infection. Do you know how many articles I've read about the rampant spread of STIs in retirement communities?"

"Did I not just tell them to stop talking?" I say to Mimi.

Also, my face better not be turning red.

"Like you don't want to be still getting it on with the ladies when you're in your nineties," Zen says.

"Mimi, how would you like to have all of your dreams come true and run a café in the mountains while we all decide if this guy you have your eye on is worth your time?" I say.

And then I hear myself.

And all of the pieces of this puzzle click.

That's what I'll do.

I'll give the café to Mimi on the condition that she pass it to Sabrina when she's done with it.

"Oh, now that sounds like a lovely plan," she says. "Do I have to do anything?"

"Just sit in the corner and talk to all the old people about the weather," Zen says. "Sabrina and I have everything else under control."

"What if I want to talk to the young people about their lives?"

"You can do that too," Zen says, "but you should know there's a very dedicated contingent of old people here who demand that the café's owner acknowledge the weather with them at least once a day. Also, if you're the new owner, you can put a halt to all of the construction plans."

"Construction plans?"

"Uncle Grey's sitting on a contract to completely gut the inside of the café and turn it into a kombucha bar—I'm sorry, a *kombrewchery* called *The Hive* where he'll brew his own kombucha and convince the county to give him a liquor license so he can serve and sell mead too. And he's putting a gigantic bee on the outside of the building so that Chippy Choochoo Sullivan will freak out every time he looks at the café he used to own. Sorry, Mimi, most of Harry's grandkids are great, but the Cheese Turd is *not*."

"Take the café, Mimi," I say.

She laughs.

"I'm not joking," I say slowly. "Take the café. For a day. For a week. For however long you want it."

She laughs again over her breakfast.

"Was Harry Sullivan your first choice?" I push. "Was he the man you wanted to marry instead of Grandpa?"

Her laughter stops, and she eyes me like she doesn't want me putting the pieces of *this* puzzle together.

"Was he?" I press.

"That was seventy years ago, young man."

"Why did you break up?"

She sighs. "That's not my story to tell."

Fucking *gossip*. "Did you know Elsie Sullivan?"

Zen stops eating and looks between us. "What's going on? What do you know?"

"Did you?" I press Mimi.

Everything Sabrina said last night about the other reason she called Mimi is tumbling through my head and clicking like a key in a lock.

Mimi holds my gaze. She's not sad. Not slow. Not weak. "Very briefly."

I lift my brows.

"She was Harry's best friend's little sister."

"Best friend from here, or from school?"

"Both. They grew up here together, then both went to Carnegie Tech before it became Carnegie Mellon."

"And Elsie?"

"Came to visit on occasion."

I swallow.

I can't ask the next question.

I can't ask and not betray the trust I want Sabrina to have in me.

"They got married when she got pregnant," Mimi says. "Harry thought it was important to do right by his best friend's little sister."

I stare at Mimi.

Zen's staring at me. I can feel it.

But I will *not* ask what I still want to ask.

Was Harry really the father of Elsie's baby?

"He broke my heart, but for the very best reason," Mimi says.

And then she goes back to her breakfast like she didn't just say *I forgive him for dumping me to marry a woman who was pregnant with another man's baby.*

"How did I end up buying a café to get revenge on the grandson of the man who broke your heart in college?" I ask Mimi.

The man that Sabrina says isn't her real grandfather.

The man that Sabrina also says is the gold standard against whom she judges all other men.

Mimi laughs. "The world works in mysterious ways.

Now eat. I have a date with Harry in an hour, and I'm not sitting here with you while you don't eat your breakfast when I could be doing my hair and makeup instead."

I dive into my breakfast.

It's good to eat. Definitely worked up an appetite last night.

"I mean it," I tell Mimi. "If you want to run a café in the mountains, it's yours. Five years or five minutes. I don't care. Spend some time living a dream."

"Greyson, that is a ridiculous way to spend your money."

Zen snorts in utter amusement. "Take the café, Mimi. By my calculations, he could buy and ruin a café every month and still reach billionaire status in another seven years."

"Do you want to keep working as my personal assistant or not?" I interrupt.

They grin and don't answer me.

Directly, anyway.

"When you told me we were coming to Colorado so you could get vengeance against a random dude who owned a café, I had no idea I'd like it as much as I do. Maybe I don't want to be your assistant anymore. Maybe I want to stay and work for Mimi at *her* café and hang out with her and her boyfriend instead of you."

"Oh, honey, Harry is *not* my boyfriend," Mimi says. "And I do *not* need a café."

Zen rolls their eyes. "You're in your nineties, Mimi. You don't have time to waste debating if you want to be boyfriend and girlfriend or live out some old dreams. Forgive, forget, pick back up where you left off, save Uncle Grey from his horrible plans of thinking he can actually be

Super Vengeance Man, and grab life by whatever balls it has left for you."

"That's...more like the romantic you I expect," I tell them.

"I aim to be very direct and tolerate zero bullshit from the people in my life."

Mimi's eyes are twinkling.

They're actually *twinkling*. "So you think I should take this café?"

"Please, Mimi. Save me from my horrible boss and give me a new direction in my life."

She laughs. "I'll think about it. In the meantime, Greyson, please go run my café for me today. And give Harry's granddaughter a raise. She works hard. She's earned it."

She does work hard.

She's the reason the café runs as smoothly as it does.

And she's right.

It won't hurt Chandler at all for me to destroy it.

Super Vengeance Man was a bad idea.

But coming here wasn't.

Coming here showed me what I actually want. What I need for closure from all of the people who've stabbed me in the back. And how I want to spend the rest of my life.

"Can you run the café today?" I ask Zen.

They blink at me.

Blink again, then look at their phone. Their eyebrows shoot up.

And then they grin at me. "About time, Uncle Grey, but give a person some warning when you know the manager's going to be out for the day since she didn't sleep at all last night."

Now I am *definitely* going ruddy in the cheeks. "I want the café back when you're done with it," I tell Mimi.

"For your kombrewchery?" she asks.

I shake my head. "For something better. Excuse me. I have some research I need to do." I kiss them both on the tops of their heads, and then I take off.

I do.

I know *exactly* what I need to do.

And it's perfect and just and right.

Finally.

33

Sabrina

WEARING a flashing neon sign that says *I had sex with Grey last night* would probably have been less inconspicuous than fielding the number of knowing looks I get when I stumble into Bean & Nugget four hours late for my shift.

With coffee from home that Grey didn't brew for me, but did set up to minimize brain power this morning.

My favorite tumbler. My coffee grinder. My beans. My pour-over filter. My teapot full of water.

All right there on my counter along with a note.

Thank you for one of the best nights of my life. -G

What does that even mean?

And what does it mean that I haven't seen Grey all day?

And that *Mimi* is apparently my new boss?

And that I want to cry with the absolute sweetness that is Zen telling everyone that Grey bought the café to give

419

Mimi a chance to live out the dreams she had as a young woman?

I think I love him.

I think I'm a goner.

And I'm *so* much more okay with this than I ever thought I could've been.

He's seen me at my worst. And he's still here.

Or he was.

Last night.

This could work, the very, very most skeptical part of my gossip-loving brain whispers. *He is your one.*

"Go home," Zen says to me an hour after my shift ends.

"I'm making up my time."

"*Sabrina. Go home.*"

"I got her, Zen," Decker says. He's been hanging out under all of the leftover decorations from last night's speed dating event too.

"Where's Grey?" I ask Zen.

They roll their eyes. "He got a look this morning that could mean anything from *we're hightailing it out of this joint and moving back to San Diego where it's warm* to *I figured out that butterflies are the secret ingredient to clean energy and have to go lose track of time and space in the name of research.*"

My lips part, and it takes a hot second for my brain to catch up. "Who's feeding him?"

"Um, the entire community if he's at the townhouse. If he's not, I have a tracker on his phone. I'll find him before he starves to death."

"C'mon, Sabrina." Decker hooks a finger into the back of my shirt. "Nappy-poo time for you. I'm sure you'll see your sweetie-weetie soon enough."

"Can you be a little more immature?"

He grins.

The triplets are a couple years younger than me, and they don't normally act like it, but they have their days.

I let Decker push me into my car and follow me to my house to make sure I get there safely. As soon as he leaves the parking lot, I dash outside and knock on Grey's door.

No answer.

I knock again.

Still no answer.

Then I remember *my mom still has my dog*, and I load up and head back downtown.

Jitter's the toast of the salon, and Mom tells me I can't have him back.

She also tells me if Mimi hurts Grandpa, I'll be in trouble.

"Zen says Grey gave Mimi the café," I tell Mom.

"And how do you feel about that?"

My eyes flood. I try to blink it all back, and I can't. "Really good," I whisper.

It feels like his way of saying he's gotten what he needs to feel even with Chandler.

I don't understand it, but I *feel* it.

I don't see him the rest of the day.

Saturday, Grandpa hangs out with Mimi all day while she fusses over the menu, samples coffees, and asks if she can bake oatmeal cranberry cookies to put in the display case.

"Your café, Mimi," Zen says.

Grey's not in.

Zen goes flat-faced whenever anyone asks about him.

Including me.

It's Valentine's Day.

And I haven't heard from him since yesterday morning.

Before yesterday, I wouldn't have thought a thing about not hearing from him.

But now?

Now, this is weird. And worrying.

I know things happen. I know stuff comes up. I know this might not be about me at all.

But I still corner Zen when my shift is over. "Did I do something wrong?"

They pull a face, and then the unthinkable happens.

Zen hugs me.

Not a little hug either.

A *tight* hug.

"Can you chaperone Mimi and Harry tonight and make sure they don't break anything?"

"What did I do?"

"You called Mimi and set them up, so them wanting to go skating at midnight on a frozen lake under questionable lighting is *your* responsibility."

"*To Grey.*"

They hug me even tighter. "He told me to start the paperwork to give the café to you once Mimi's done with it."

I suck in a breath. "*I don't want the café.*"

"Okay, Queen Gossip of the Tooth."

"*I don't.* I told him that *and I meant it.*"

"All I got out of him before he left was that he needed to find closure."

"*He left?*"

Zen lets me go and rolls their eyes. "And this is why I didn't want to tell you anything."

"Is he coming back?"

They wince.

My heart thuds to the floor and makes a bigger mess than the mashed potato fight mixed with the powdered cheese incident.

"Can you give him my phone number?" I whisper. "I never did."

"Are you—of course you're not kidding me. *Of course.* You two are ridiculous."

The Valentine's Day skate sucks.

Everyone else has fun, but Emma and I work the hot cocoa booth with Devi for the small business owners' association, both of us staring glumly at everyone on the midnight ice, the lake lit up with fairy lights. The only bright spots for us are Laney and Theo—Laney on the ice in a wheelchair that Theo's pushing—and Mimi and Grandpa Harry.

"I figured out a better revenge than ruining Bean & Nugget," Em tells me as things are shutting down. "But now Grey's gone and we don't know why and I can't help anymore."

"Would it make *you* feel better to do it?" I ask her.

She grins.

It's an honest *Emma* grin that makes me feel a decade younger.

An then she shakes her head. "Not as much as it would help him, but I'll consider it solo if he doesn't come back."

"You think he'll come back?"

"I think I hope he does, since I've never seen you hung up on a man like this before."

"We had a fling in Hawaii my last night there," I whisper.

She gasps. "*Oh my god*, and you're *just now* telling me this? Details, Sabrina. I need *all* of the details."

It feels awkward at first—*So, Em, I felt like an absolute heel after your wedding and needed to do some good deeds*—but as her face lights up more and more as I tell her everything I remember from the time I met him to the time I ghosted him, I feel something breaking free inside of me.

The guilt.

The guilt is going away now that we can talk about it.

"He...was there to cause trouble at your wedding," I tell her.

"Do you know what Chandler did to him?"

"I do."

"Did Chandler deserve it?"

"*You* did not."

She squeezes my hand. "I think my life will be a lot better in this new direction I'm heading."

"If you want me to forget Grey because of what he was willing to do to you on your wedding day—"

"No. *No.* Guys who abandon grand revenge plans to give their grandmothers cafés and support their grandmothers dating old flames from seventy years ago are the good guys. And if he'd been the reason my wedding had broken up, but I still found out everything I know now, I'd still be grateful. The universe saved me. That's the important thing."

I fling my arms around my friend, my head barely hitting her boobs because she's so much taller than me. "I love you, Em."

"I love you more, Sabrina."

"I'm glad you're my Valentine."

"Can I buy you a hot chocolate spiked with espresso?"

"You seriously know the way to a girl's heart."

Sunday morning, I wake up to a cryptic text from an unknown number. *The right kind of justice isn't easy. Back soon.*

What does that mean? I text back, hope blossoming in my heart once more, but I don't get a response.

"He's probably forgetting to charge his phone," Zen tells me when I charge into Bean & Nugget on my day off.

"Where. The fuck. Is he?"

"I could tell you, but Mimi just decided she's done owning a café. The paperwork will get rolling in the morning to turn it over to you, so you're going to be very busy very soon here."

"For. The very. Last. Time. I. Do not. Want. The café. I want. To know. *Where. The. Fuck. Is. Grey?*"

"He's staging a coup and buying out the company that bought out his research," Mimi pipes up. "That's my brilliant boy."

I gape at her. "He's moving back to San Diego?"

"It's lovely this time of year," she says. "Actually, it's lovely every time of year."

Fuck this.

Absolutely *fuck this*.

All of it.

From here to eternity.

I am fucking *done* with Super Vengeance Man.

34

Grey

It's a beautiful day to get back what's mine.

Even more beautiful day to watch the looks on the faces of the four men whose lives are about to get very uncomfortable.

I snap my folder shut and lean back in my seat. "Final offer, gentlemen."

Vince clamps his unhinged jaw shut while his white skin goes a mottled purple. "Are you fucking for real? This is the most asinine, childish shit you've ever pulled."

"Ah, yes. I'm *asinine*. That's so much worse than being manipulative and attempting to put a man in a corner if he wants to continue his work in peace. What was your finder's fee on this deal, by the way? Hope it was enough to pay for the lawyers you'll need when their original backers find out this was an inside job."

The three other men at the table stiffen.

"They're out, by the way." I peer at them over my glass of kombucha. Raspberry mint. Rather delicious. "We had a fascinating brunch yesterday morning. Them. Me. My attorney. Their attorneys. I can honestly say I never knew civil litigation had so many complex layers to it."

We're on the deck of one of my favorite San Diego steakhouses, overlooking the marina while I lay out the terms of their surrender to me.

And yes, I mean *surrender*.

The cost of them replacing me after I left the research world will far outweigh the cost of them selling their company to me at a loss. Especially now that the venture capitalists funding the start-up that Vince was supposedly a silent partner for have decided they no longer have interest in working with people who would fuck over their only researcher.

And once I own the company, I own my research again.

Once I own the research again, I can finish it.

While I'm building a new lab where I won't have a business partner but will have a life.

I haven't slept since I left Snaggletooth Creek. I've eaten, but only when I've gotten lightheaded and realized what was wrong. I've asked questions. I've gossiped. I've dug and dug and dug for what I needed, and I found it.

Proof that owning my research but not owning *me* if I refuse to do more research puts this company in a pickle.

"Offer expires at midnight," I tell them. "I'd take this one if I were you. The next one will have at least one less zero attached. Enjoy dinner. It's on me."

I start to rise as a commotion breaks out behind me. "Ex*cuse* me, do you know who I am?" a startlingly familiar voice says.

I whip my head around.

"No, madam, I have no idea who you are," the maître d' replies.

Sabrina Sullivan, the goddess who has haunted my every ten-minute nap in the past three days, lifts her nose high while her massive dog gives a joyful bark. "Good. That means you won't be able to tell them who just brought her dog in here. I love being a nobody."

"*Ma'am*," the maître d' snaps as Sabrina strolls past him.

Am I hallucinating?

Is this what not sleeping and getting proper justice will do to a man?

Or is Sabrina marching past the maître d' stand, spotting me and turning into an avenging angel of gossip and destruction while her eyes narrow and flames shoot out of her ears?

Is she wearing an *Avengers* suit?

I blink.

No, that was definitely a fantasy-based hallucination. But the sundress and the strappy high-heeled sandals and the way her curly red hair is blowing in the wind is sending me straight to my happy place.

She's *here*.

"Ma'am, you need to stop," the maître d' repeats.

But I've been spotted by a very large brown-and-white Saint Bernard, who woofs joyfully and lunges toward me.

People at the few occupied other tables turn. One woman scoots out of the way.

"*Ma'am*. I am calling the police if you don't—"

I finally find my voice. "She's with me."

"Oooh, you *wish* I was with you," Sabrina retorts as

429

Jitter reaches me. "What in the *hell* do you think you're—stop recording this right now, because if you think I won't toss that phone over that balcony and then dig up every secret every person on this earth has ever known about you and use it against you to haunt you for the rest of your days, you are dead wrong. I've done the viral thing once and *I am not doing it again.*"

She scans the deck.

Every single person at the seven occupied tables puts their phones away.

I smile.

Can't help it.

"And you can put *that* away too," she orders, pointing to my face. "If you think *smiling* is getting you out of trouble, you, too, have a long life of regrets ahead of you."

I need to stop smiling.

I do.

She *should* be mad at me. I didn't call her.

I didn't have her number, but I didn't ask Zen for it either until they sent it to me, and I think I got so tied up in what I was looking for that I might have forgotten to check if she texted me back.

"I'm sorry," I say while Jitter pushes against me, tail wagging so hard he nearly knocks over a chair at the closest table.

He's such a good boy. My favorite good boy.

"You don't *look* sorry," Sabrina says.

Yep. I'm still smiling. "You're here."

"What are you doing here?"

I jerk a thumb over my shoulder. "Destroying their lives."

"Oh my god, Grey." She sucks in a deep breath.

I know that breath.

It's the breath of *java give me patience*.

"That's Vince," I tell her. "My former friend and partner. And the fucklebuckets he sold my research to."

She leans around me and peers at them. "Oh, sweetheart, do *not* test me," she says. "Give. Me. The. Phone."

Swear I *hear* Vince gulp.

She twitches her fingers.

He tries to put the phone away.

"Jitter, fetch the phone," she says.

"Very funny, Ms. Nobody," Vince says.

"Give her the phone before he rescinds the offer, you idiot," one of his companions in dastardly deeds says.

"He can't—"

"Jitter, *fetch*," Sabrina repeats, pointing at Vince.

Jitter woofs.

The maître d' gives me the glare of all glares.

I grin at him too.

"Definitely feel that offer dropping," I muse with a pointed look at Vince. "Give her the phone. Unlocked. So she can delete the video."

"Grey—" he starts.

"I know about your child support issue," Sabrina says to him.

Fuck, I love her.

My heart swells and my eyes prickle with the sudden realization, but it's true.

I do.

I don't need to go back to Snaggletooth Creek and *see if this goes anywhere*.

It's already gone somewhere for me.

I love this woman.

431

I love her confidence.

I love her heart.

I love the code that she lives and gossips by.

I love that Vince is visibly trembling as he hands his phone to her so she can delete the video he was taking of us.

She makes quick work of what she needs to do while Jitter pushes against me, panting happily and wagging his tail with enough force to classify it as a weapon of restaurant destruction while I happily rub his thick fur all over his wiggly overgrown puppy body.

"If I were the type of person to throw electronics in the ocean, this would be gone right now. You're lucky I'm not stabbing it with a steak knife. *Respect people's privacy, asshole.*" Sabrina points to the table and circles her finger around it. "I don't know what else was going on here, but whatever he apparently just offered you, *take it.* Trust me on this."

"Sir," the maître d' says to me, "I need the dog to leave."

"Duchess?" I murmur.

Like hell they're getting her real name.

"Don't *even* try to get on my good side with that smile right now," she replies pertly. She nods to the maître d'. "Thank you for your understanding. Jitter, come. Grey, you too. *Now.*"

I'm smiling again while I follow her out of the restaurant and onto the street. "You're here."

"*You left me.*"

"I was coming back."

"*You didn't tell me that.*"

"I got tied up in research and straightening my cape."

Am I stepping as close to her as Jitter will let me, settling my hands on her hips and still smiling like I've forgotten how to frown?

Yes. Yes, I am.

But then she blinks and her eyes take on a sheen that suggests tears, and I can't smile anymore. "Sabrina, I'm not laughing at you. I'm so damn glad to see you, and I can't—"

She clutches my arms. "I kept telling myself you didn't ghost me to get back at me for Hawaii, that I knew better, but *I just didn't know*. And I *miss* you and I'm not supposed to miss you. I have a heart of iron when it comes to men but *you gave Mimi the café*. That's what my grandpa did for my grandma when they got married. He built the café for my grandma because she was so sad that the man she loved had knocked her up and dumped her and she knew Grandpa didn't love her. She kept telling him she knew she was a burden. But even with his own heart breaking, he didn't want her to think she was a burden, ever. So he did the only thing he could to make her happy. Do you have any idea how impossible it is to not think you're every bit the man that my grandpa was when you do the same things he did? When you build something to make someone else happy no matter the cost to you?"

I clear my throat and blink a few times. "I didn't build it."

"But you saved it and you gave it to her and then you *fucking ignored me* and I have a damn *title to the building* in *my name* now, and *how fucking dare you*? Do you know what I have to do now? I have to change it. I have to change it and call it *Bee & Nugget* and install your beehives in the windows and put your massive, gaudy fiberglass

433

PIPPA GRANT

bee on the outside of the building and sell kombucha so that it can be *ours* instead of *mine* or *yours*."

She sniffles.

Jitter whines and sways between pushing against my legs and pushing against her legs.

"If you'll come home," she adds in a whisper. "If you'll please come home and do this with me."

Home.

I lean down to wrap my arms around her, squishing Jitter between us so he doesn't have to choose, and bury my face in those glorious curls, breathing in all of her. The subtle coffee scent. The light, clean shampoo. The lemons. "I want to be home with you. But I wanted to be *whole*. Not living for revenge. Not doubting my worth."

"I missed you so much more than I'm supposed to ever miss anyone."

"I was coming home for Tuesday."

"Tuesday?"

"Random Acts of Kindness Day. It seemed a better holiday than that fake heart holiday to spend with my Duchess."

"Stop making me cry," she whispers.

"I'll kiss all the tears until I make you laugh again."

"I'm not supposed to love you but I can't seem to help myself."

My heart swells so hard and fast that I should be going lightheaded.

But instead, all I feel is warmth.

Warmth and peace and acceptance and belonging and *love*.

"I *am* supposed to love you," I whisper back. "That's

what life's been trying to teach me. And I'm ready now. I'm ready to spend the rest of my life loving you."

"And *answering my phone calls*," she says on a laugh and a sniffle.

I kiss her ear. Her cheek. Her nose. "I will always answer your phone calls."

"No, you won't, and that's okay." Her sparkle is back. "But most of the time. Most of the time, when you're not hip deep in concentrating on something amazing, you'll answer my calls."

"Highly likely." I brush the tears off her cheeks with my thumb. "I'm so glad you're here."

"I'm so glad you're coming home."

Home.

I am.

I'm going home. With the woman I love and her dog and her community, to my grandma and my nibling-slash-best friend and the place where it's so easy to feel like I belong.

"Bee & Nugget?" I say.

"Zen's already ordering the sign. *Do not test me.*"

I smile and pull her in for a kiss, well aware that there are people watching us again, probably recording us for posting somewhere on the giant web of the internet, knowing that it won't go viral because who cares about two people kissing?

Nothing scandalous here.

"I love you, Sabrina Sullivan. You'll always be the duchess of my heart."

"I love you more, Grey Cartwright. And I can't wait to get you a superhero cape for your next era."

EPILOGUE

Sabrina

"I'M GOING TO MARRY HIM," I tell Laney, Emma, and Zen over drinks in Emma's garage in the house she was planning to share with Chandler three weeks after Grey and I get home from an epic road trip of doing random acts of kindness from California to Colorado.

Laney squeals and bounces on her toes, finally free from her cast and now in a boot instead.

Zen grins. "I'm making you sign a prenup."

"Make sure he gets the café in the event we get divorced," I instruct them. "And I don't want a dime of his money. Put that in there too."

"He proposed?" Emma asks.

"No, but when he does in five years, I'm absolutely saying yes."

All three of them crack up.

The men bent over what was supposed to be Emma's

wedding gift to Chandler—a '57 Cadillac convertible that he had apparently been telling her he wanted for years and also apparently knew was supposed to be his wedding gift—all pause and look up at us. So does Jitter, who's in his happy place in the corner by the garage door.

And Duke.

Yes, Duke. Grey's dog.

He paid off the bills for his ex-wife's birthday party in exchange for getting his dog back, and now I'm living with the very best man in the entire world and our dogs, who made fast friends.

"Should we be suspicious?" Theo asks us.

He and Grey have mostly been giggling nonstop since Emma unveiled the car and explained why she invited us over. The triplets got called in for their various levels of expertise with refurbishing and refinishing classic cars. And honestly, they're giggling too.

"Carry on." Zen makes a shooing motion. "You don't need in on the girl gossip yet. Also, I vote for the doors being wings instead of attaching wings. Have you ever seen a bee wing up close? That'll be epic on the doors when you open them."

Grey giggles again.

Not even kidding, he's *giggling*, and I'm so here for it.

"I'll give you the door-wings, but there's not a fucking chance I'm compromising on the antenna," Theo says.

"*Antennae*," Zen corrects. "Two. One on each side of the windshield."

"But we have to make sure the top will close right," Jack says.

"I have faith in you," Lucky says.

438

Decker's bent at the back of the car. "If you don't put the stinger on, I'm tossing you off Marmot Cliff."

Emma smiles over her ginger ale.

"Is this bringing *you* closure?" Laney asks her.

She nods. "There's a lot of good that came out of my destination wedding. You and Theo. The kittens. Sabrina and Grey. The changes at Bean & Nugget. Zen moving here. Mimi moving here. You taking that DNA test."

I swing around to gawk at Laney. "*You took it?*"

"Yesterday," she confirms.

"How do you feel?"

"Relieved, actually. I know it could be hard on my mom if it comes back and says my dad's their father, but the triplets deserve to know the truth. So no matter what it says, no regrets. It's not lose-lose, you know? Mr. *Super Vengeance Man* over there would probably say the truth is always win-win."

She's right. Grey likes the truth. "It's *Super Bee Man* now, please. I have the cape on order."

"Oh, I have a mock-up," Laney says. "Forgot to tell you. Remind me when we go inside to grab my phone."

"Fantastic."

"Do your parents know you're doing the test?" Emma asks Laney.

Laney shakes her head. "Telling them is a decision for another day. The triplets don't want their dad to know either right now. They'll decide what they want to do if we find out they're right."

Their dad being my uncle, the man who raised them.

"No matter what, you'll all handle it great," Zen says. "It's the Tooth. That's what you do."

They're not wrong.

439

Grey's siblings descended on the town not long after we got back from California, claiming to be worried about Mimi's mental and physical health if Grey was moving her to such a cold and nasty place and finding her a boyfriend, and the Tooth totally *Toothed* them.

And because they're all a touch horrible, they were so uncomfortable with the kindness that they left within thirty-six hours after barely seeing Grey, Zen, or Mimi at all.

He has a new number now.

And he owns the company that bought out his lab.

And he bought an empty lot not far from Theo's place where he intends to build a better lab for research on bees at elevation.

And the cherry on top—I didn't have to threaten Theo or any of the triplets to convince them to be friends with Grey. He just *fits* here. Especially now that he's found the best way to get peace with what Chandler did to him in college.

"What's good for *you*?" I ask Emma.

"This, definitely." She gestures with her glass to the car and the men still giggling over their plans to fix it up and paint it like a bee. Emma offered it flat-out to Grey—*I know he hurt you and I hope this can give you some peace on that front*—and Grey's insisting it'll be a communal car for all of us to share and use whenever we want.

So that the bee-mobile is driven around town more often.

Increasing the chances that Chandler will see it.

"Five strapping men in your garage?" Zen asks. "Emma. I had no idea you wanted to star in a *why choose* romance novel."

She laughs. "No, you goober. Watching *them* be happy. That's good for me."

"And the revenge part?" Laney asks.

"Let's call it *closure*." Em sips her ginger ale again. "Chandler and I hadn't slept together since like October. He said the wedding was stressing him out, but the truth is, he didn't want to marry me. He just wanted everyone else to think he was awesome. It's been hard to face, but also good, you know?"

"You think you'll ever date again?" Zen asks.

I poke them. "Seriously?"

"Maybe we ease into that kind of inquisition?" Laney says.

"No, no, it's okay," Emma says. "Everyone knows I always wanted the husband and the kids and the picket fence, right? Legitimate question."

I wrap an arm around her and squeeze.

Laney does too on the other side.

"At least I'm getting part of it," Em says softly.

Zen nods. "That's a kick-ass white picket fence outside. Or it will be. Once we build it."

"No," Em says even more softly. "*Another* part."

I freeze.

Laney makes a strangled noise.

Zen squints at Em.

"Something happened on my runaway-moon." Em's whispering so quietly now that we're all leaning in to listen. "Some*one*, more accurately. Someone good."

"*Emma*," Laney gasps. "*Spill. Now.*"

The men all turn to stare.

"It's over," she says quickly. "It was one of those *we're both going through hell after super rough break-ups* kind of

441

things. Mutual support, you know? But I...brought home...an unexpected souvenir."

I cannot actually speak.

Laney's mouth is a perfect *O*.

Zen gasps and grabs my shoulder like they'll fall over if they don't.

Em fans her shiny eyeballs. "This is a good thing. It's a really good thing. I think—I think this is how I'm supposed to have my own happily ever after. Just me and a baby."

"You don't know who he is?" Laney whispers.

"I do. I'll let him know. But I don't think—I don't think he'll want to be involved. It's...complicated. And honestly, it's probably better this way."

"Oh my god, Emma," I breathe.

The men are still staring.

My eyes are getting hot.

"And this is a good thing? You're sure?" Laney asks.

Emma smiles through tears. "Honestly? This is *the very best thing*. If I can't have everything I wanted, this is what I wanted the most."

"Your kid is going to have the best aunts and uncles *ever*," Zen says reverently. "Can I be an honorary auncle? Please? *Please*?"

"Of course," Emma says.

"Who. The fuck. Do I need to kill?" Theo asks.

Em laughs. "Sit down and shush."

"Not kidding, Em. I have a get out of jail free card with the sheriff. I will absolutely use it for murder."

"I can research how to make a body disappear," Grey says.

"Already done," Decker offers.

Grey blinks at him.

"I'm a *novelist*, dude. You don't even want to know what my search history looks like."

Lucky and Jack both drop to a knee, then get into a shoving match.

"I was going to make an honest woman of her."

"Asshole, shut up. *I'm* making an honest woman of her."

"Get up, both of you," Theo orders. "What do you think this is, the 1950's? Em, tell me which house in town you want me to buy you, and it's done."

Emma sniffles again. "I love you guys. All of you."

"We're here for whatever you need," Laney tells her.

"Including disposing of these yahoos so you can do motherhood your way," I agree.

Theo's still glaring, but we all know he'll come around.

The triplets will show up for anything she asks. As will Grey and Zen. And the entire town.

It's what we do.

Always.

"You're sure the father won't want to be involved?" Laney asks Em.

She nods, but not without hesitation. "I'm positive. It's for the best. It truly, truly is."

"But you'll tell him?"

This time, there's no hesitation in the nod.

"You're having a *baby*," I whisper.

"I'm having a baby," she whispers back.

We all burst into tears.

Tears of absolute joy.

She's right.

Her wedding was a disaster, but it led to so many

happily ever afters. And as all of the men surround us for a giant group hug, I know the next part of our stories will only get better.

No matter what complications and unexpected wrenches come our way.

PIPPA GRANT BOOK LIST

The Girl Band Series (Complete)

Mister McHottie

Stud in the Stacks

Rockaway Bride

The Hero and the Hacktivist

The Thrusters Hockey Series

The Pilot and the Puck-Up

Royally Pucked

Beauty and the Beefcake

Charming as Puck

I Pucking Love You

The Bro Code Series

Flirting with the Frenemy

America's Geekheart

Liar, Liar, Hearts on Fire

The Hot Mess and the Heartthrob

Copper Valley Fireballs Series (Complete)

Jock Blocked

Real Fake Love

The Grumpy Player Next Door

Irresistible Trouble

Three BFFs and a Wedding Series

The Worst Wedding Date

The Gossip and the Grump

The Tickled Pink Series

The One Who Loves You

Rich In Your Love

Standalones

The Last Eligible Billionaire

Not My Kind of Hero

Dirty Talking Rival *(Bro Code Spin-Off)*

A Royally Inconvenient Marriage *(Royally Pucked Spin-Off)*

Exes and Ho Ho Hos

The Bluewater Billionaires Series (Complete)

The Price of Scandal by Lucy Score

The Mogul and the Muscle by Claire Kingsley

Wild Open Hearts by Kathryn Nolan

Crazy for Loving You by Pippa Grant

Co-Written with Lili Valente

Hosed

Hammered

Hitched

Humbugged

Pippa Grant writing as Jamie Farrell:

The Misfit Brides Series (Complete)

Blissed

Matched

Smittened

Sugared

Married

Spiced

Unhitched

The Officers' Ex-Wives Club Series (Complete)

Her Rebel Heart

Southern Fried Blues

ABOUT THE AUTHOR

Pippa Grant wanted to write books, so she did.

Before she became a USA Today and #1 Amazon best-selling romantic comedy author, she was a young military spouse who got into writing as self-therapy. That happened around the time she discovered reading romance novels, and the two eventually merged into a career. Today, she has more than 30 knee-slapping Pippa Grant titles and nine published under the name Jamie Farrell.

When she's not writing romantic comedies, she's fumbling through being a mom, wife, and mountain woman, and sometimes tries to find hobbies. Her crowning achievement? Having impeccable timing for telling stories that will make people snort beverages out of their noses. Consider yourself warned.

Find Pippa at…
www.pippagrant.com
pippa@pippagrant.com

Made in the USA
Middletown, DE
28 October 2023